# CIERRA SOLANGE

# Let Me Be Seen

*For every girl who whispers,*
*"Does anyone see me?"*
*He does, and He always.*

She gave this name to the Lord who spoke to her: "You are the God who sees me, for she said," I have now seen the One who sees me."

–Genesis 16:13

# Contents

# Prologue

*Six years earlier*

Rain tapped against the tiny barred window, soft at first, then steadier, like the sky was breathing with them. The room was dim and cold, two girls pressed close on the floor, knees brushing, fear tightening every breath.

One of them cried quietly, rubbing her palms against her jeans as if she could scrub the guilt off. "I'm so sorry," she whispered.

"I never meant for this to happen. I thought he was going to protect us. I thought he meant it when he said he'd keep us safe. I never would've asked Mommy to sign anything if I knew... if I knew this was what he really was."

The other shook her head, voice thin.

"Please. Stop. It's not your fault."

A tremor ran through her, sharp and unexpected, and she pressed a hand to her stomach. The first girl reached for her immediately.

"Are you hurting?"

She didn't answer at first. Her eyes lifted toward the window where rain streaked the glass in long, trembling lines.

"Look," she whispered.

"It's raining."

Her voice wavered.

"That means God's painting again."

The other girl let out a small, disbelieving scoff. "You don't even believe in God."

"I know," the girl murmured.

"But... we need something to hold on to. Even if it's pretend. Just, hold on with me."

Their foreheads touched for a single fragile second. Two shaky breaths. Two sisters trying to stay whole.

Bootsteps echoed down the hallway.

They froze.

The lock turned. The metal door slammed open.

A man filled the doorway, two others behind him, shadows stretching long across the floor.

"Get up," he commanded.

Neither girl moved.

His jaw tightened. Then he pointed to one of them.

"You."

"No, wait," the other cried, reaching out, but hands were already dragging the chosen girl across the ground. Her fingers scraped hard against the concrete as she tried to hold on, slipping farther away with every pull.

The door slammed.

Silence thickened, until the man stepped back inside.

He moved slowly this time, deliberate, cruel. His shadow swallowed the floor as he crouched in front of the remaining girl, lifting her chin with two fingers.

"I told you what happens when you don't obey, he murmured, voice low and venom-slick. "So now I'm taking the one thing you love."

A yelp cracked through the hallway, sharp, strangled, cut short. The kind of sound that breaks something inside you forever.

Her breath hitched.

"No, no, no, please," she cried, trying to leap forward, but the man shoved her back with one hand, smirking.

He laughed, a short, mocking sound, and tapped his phone.

"Go ahead," he said, holding it out like a prize.

A voice crackled through the speaker.

"It's done."

Her knees buckled. A sob ripped through her, raw and desperate. She fell forward, hands trembling against the concrete as she cried, her whole body shaking, grief swallowing her like a wave she couldn't outrun.

She lifted her head, tears streaking her face, fury breaking through the devastation.

"You won't get away with this," she choked out.

His smile widened, cruel and confident.

"I already have," he said, and walked out, leaving her screaming into the dark.

# 1

# Chapter 1

**Franklin**

I wasn't looking for another assignment. Especially not one like this.

The last case still clung to me like smoke; seeping into my clothes, my thoughts, the way I moved through a room. I hadn't even filed the final report when Claire showed up at my door. No call. No warning. Just her and a folder.

She didn't say much, just held it out, eyes sharper than usual, jaw tight.

"I need you on this," she said.

That was all.

I took the file. Sat with it. Opened it.

Redacted statements. Emergency relocation protocols. Trauma markers flagged in every report. The kind of case that doesn't just sit on your desk, it sits on your chest.

And scribbled near the bottom of a sealed document, barely legible in the margin:

Ricky.

My stomach twisted. The last time his name crossed my desk, a girl ended up dead. This time, I wouldn't be too late. I read the file twice. Walked straight into Clay's office and dropped it on his desk with more force than I intended.

He didn't flinch. Just glanced at the folder like it was another unpaid invoice, muttered, "Here we go again. Another broken girl."

My jaw tightened.

"What do you mean by that?"

Clay leaned back in his chair, arms crossed, like he was already tired of the conversation. "They talk, they vanish, they fall apart. You get invested, I get blamed, and someone winds up dead. Or did you forget about our last case, Vanessa?"

His tone was dry, clinical. Like he was reciting a statistic, not talking about a human life.

And maybe he wasn't wrong. We'd buried witnesses before. Watched justice slip through the cracks while monsters like Ricky smiled for cameras. Vanessa's face hit me; bright, determined, and gone before I could save her. Clay had been there too, and I still hated the way he said her name like she was just another casualty. I carried her, and every other name, like weights in my chest.

But this... this felt different.

"Don't look at her," I said, voice low.

"Look at the case. It's him."

He didn't argue with that. Just leaned back, then pushed the file across the desk with a sigh.

"Fine. But you owe me."

"For what?"

"If I need a couple nights off... you'll cover for me, right?"

I nodded.

"Yeah. I got you."

He gave a short nod, but didn't look at me.

"You planning to disappear, Clay?"

He gave a short laugh. "Just saying, if I need a few nights off, you'll cover."

"I don't mind," I said.

I did, but not because of the extra hours. It was the way he said it, like he was already halfway gone, like he knew something I didn't. And I wasn't running. I couldn't. Every instinct in me, natural and spiritual, told me this case was different, that God had His hand on it, that He was calling me to stand in the gap no matter what it cost. Maybe it was desperation, maybe it was divine. Either way, if protecting her was the key to bringing Ricky down, I would walk straight through fire to do it.

"I'll go talk to the boss," I said, already heading for the door, heart pounding harder than I wanted to admit.

Claire was pacing the hallway like she'd been holding her breath.

"We're taking the case," I told her.

Her shoulders dropped with a visible exhale, and a flicker of something warm passed over her face.

"Thank you, Detective Franklin. This really means a lot. I think... I think we can finally get him."

She meant it. Not just the words, her whole posture shifted. Steady brown eyes behind rimless glasses, shoulders squared the way I'd seen a hundred times in courtrooms and briefing rooms. Claire Mitchell wasn't just my supervisor; she was the first Black woman to ever head this division, a title she carried like armor. Dark skin, natural coils swept into a neat twist at the crown, everything about her radiated steadiness and authority. She didn't play politics. She fought for survivors with everything she had. That was why I trusted her, why I'd even considered saying yes.

For too long, Ricky had slipped through cracks most people didn't even know existed. Every time we got close, something collapsed. A witness turned up dead. A lead went cold. Files mysteriously disappeared. We all knew what that meant, he had help. Power. Protection.

But now... now we had someone different.

Someone alive. Someone who could name names.

And maybe, just maybe, someone who could survive what came next.

If she was the one who could end it, then I'd be the one who kept her breathing long enough to testify. If I had to stand between her and hell itself, I would. That's what I believed God called us to do: stand in the gap. Protect. Cover. Especially when no one else would.

"We're finally going to get him," I said, then paused.

"But be real with me. You think this setup will actually work?"

Claire cracked a smile. "Yes. Clay'll rotate in while you're out, it'll be full-time."

Then, more tentative, "What'd he say when you told him?"

I shook my head. "Didn't say much. But the look on his face said enough."

Claire's smile faded just slightly, the weight of it settling between us. We both knew Clay could carry a grudge like a badge.

"Thanks," I said.

Claire stepped in closer, her voice lowering.

"Go home. Handle what you need to with your father. Make

the arrangements. This isn't a week-long op, Franklin. It's a year. And I know you've still got things to settle before you go off the grid."

I swallowed. Nodded once.

"Thank you... When does this start?"

"Tomorrow."

"All right."

As I headed home to make arrangements with my father, I couldn't shake the weight of how much had changed these past few years. Time had crept up on him, slow at first, like fog rolling in, then all at once. He'd been living with me for the last three years and lately, it felt like I was watching a strong man slowly unravel, thread by thread. His body had started betraying him, and I'd finally stopped pretending I could manage it alone.

That's when I hired Jennifer.

She was steady. The kind of woman who didn't flinch at hard things. God-fearing, sharp-tongued when necessary, and blessed with the kind of patience I never had.

When I stepped through the door, her voice met me before I even saw her.

"Hey, Mr. Detective," Jennifer called out from the hallway, voice thick with that familiar mix of sarcasm and patience.

I followed the sound and found her shaking her head.

"He's at it again," she said.

"Refuses to take his meds; claims they make his mouth taste like chalk and regret."

She rolled her eyes, but there was affection in it. Same as always.

I let out a low breath, half amusement, half exhaustion.

"All right. I'll take it from here."

"You sure?" she asked, tilting her head slightly.

"Yeah... Actually, there's something I need to talk to you about."

Her smile dimmed, just a little, as she stepped closer.

"What's going on?"

I told her as gently as I could that the new assignment was long-term nearly a year and while I'd still call and check in, I wouldn't be here, not like before.

She didn't flinch. Didn't blink. Just nodded and smiled like someone who already knew. "You don't need to worry about us, Frankie. We're good over here. We might fuss and fight, but I got you."

I felt it, the quiet kind of faith that doesn't need explaining.

"Thank you," I said quietly.

"For everything."

We hugged, and when she pulled back, her eyes held that soft authority I only ever saw in people who walked closely with God.

"Good luck, Frankie. And remember Psalm 91. Say it every night. Say, 'The Lord is my refuge, ' and mean it."

I nodded, the words already forming on instinct.

"No harm will overtake you, no disaster will come near your tent..."

She didn't miss a beat.

"For he will command his angels concerning you to guard you in all your ways."

Her southern drawl wrapped the verse like a hymn, and for a moment, the fear I'd been holding shrank in her warmth.

"I will," I said.

"I promise."

She gave me one last nod, then slipped out the door with the same quiet grace she'd walked in with.

"Wi-Fi's messed up again," my father called from the living room, voice gruff and familiar.

"Keeps cuttin' out like it's mad at me."

I stepped in and smiled.

"Hey, Dad."

He looked up from the couch, eyebrows raised.

"Thank God. Jennifer was about two seconds from catchin' these hands the way she been actin' today."

I couldn't help but laugh.

"I hear you've been giving her a hard time about the medicine."

"I'm not takin' that mess on an empty stomach. Now she got me on this diet. No meat. Just leaves and sadness."

"Well," I said, easing down beside him, she's trying to keep you around."

"I ain't tryin' to be around that long unless steak's involved."

I chuckled.

"Would that help?"

He gave me a slow side-eye.

"Yes... Wait, hold on. You offerin' steak? What's goin' on?"

"Why does something always have to be going on?"

He squinted.

"'Cause you only bring steak news when it's about a case."

I shook my head.

"You just know everything, huh?"

"So what is it?"

I let out a slow breath.

"Looks like we've got a real shot at catching Ricky. But I've been assigned to protect a witness until the trial."

He leaned back, quiet for a moment.

"Finally. I know he's the one you've been after for years."

"You know it. Me and Clay,"

He scoffed. Loud.

"What now?"

"I just don't like that Clay guy. Never have. Something about him rubs me the wrong way."

"It's probably 'cause you're blunt and he's blunt."

"No," he said, shaking his head. "You can be blunt and still be decent. He's blunt and ruins it."

I burst out laughing. "And you're not?"

He smirked. "Not like him."

I told him I'd be gone starting tomorrow. He nodded slowly, letting it settle.

"So I'm stuck with Jennifer full time?"

"She'll have backup," I said. "I'll come when I can. Call every day."

He grunted, which I took as reluctant agreement.

Later that night, I started packing.

The apartment was thick with that kind of stillness that makes you hear everything, the slow zip of a duffel, the soft rustle of fabric, the creak of a drawer that never used to make noise. I laid out what I needed: suits, plainclothes gear, my journal, my Bible. Tried to imagine living out of bags, stepping into a year that wouldn't belong to me. A new rhythm, a new war. I paused at the edge of the bed, suitcase still half-open, and bowed my head.

The silence pressed in tight.

"Lord," I whispered

"I surrender this assignment to You. I don't know what's waiting behind that door tomorrow, but You do. You've seen what Ricky's done. You've heard cries I never got to. You said vengeance is Yours... so I'm laying it down. If justice comes, let it come by Your hand. Not mine."

I opened my journal and let the pen move.

At first, it was lists. Loose ends. Case notes.

But then came the image. David. Not on the battlefield, but in the cave.

That moment when Saul was right there, sleeping. Exposed. And David could've ended it. Could've justified it. But he didn't. He held back, not because Saul deserved mercy, but because David feared God more than he craved blood.

And suddenly, I knew why the memory hit.

I'd seen Ricky. Tracked him. Had him in my crosshairs more than once. But there was never a warrant. Never a legal thread strong enough to pull. I could've taken him out. God knows I wanted to. But every time I raised my hand, something stopped me. Because doing it my way wouldn't be justice, it'd be vengeance and God doesn't play by those rules.

So I waited, holding on to the thought that maybe, just maybe, this was the moment God would hand him over the right way. The hope was enough to let me sleep.

Morning came fast. Light sliced through the blinds like a promise, sharp and unavoidable. I said goodbye to my dad with no frills, just the squeeze of his hand and a long, steady look. He didn't need to say anything, and neither did I.

The safe house sat on the edge of the city as if it didn't want to be found, concrete bones dressed in brick, smothered in trees. No welcome mat, no signs of life, only a lock and a silence too heavy for daylight.

I stood outside the door, tension curled in my gut, and prayed one last time.

"God... give me patience. Give me strength. Let her see You in me. Even if she doesn't know what she's looking at."

Then I stepped inside.

Chaos hit first.

A slap. Screaming. Furniture shifting.

"Don't touch me!" a woman cried out.

"Don't touch me! I gotta get out of here, he's gonna kill me! He's gonna kill me!"

I rushed in.

Clay stood near the couch with his arms half-raised, useless and unsure, his eyes wide, not with fear, but with the kind of exasperation that made it clear he was more annoyed than alarmed. She was backed against the wall like a cornered animal, wild-eyed and barefoot, fists clenched, trust nowhere in sight.

"She's losing it," Clay snapped. "I told you, she's unstable!"

"Back off," I said sharply. "I've got it."

He didn't move right away, so I stepped between them and that's when it happened.

Her hand cracked across my face with a sound that echoed.

Heat bloomed across my cheekbone, but I didn't flinch or step back, I just reached for her wrist, slow and steady, and held it with a gentleness that told her I wasn't going anywhere.

"You're not there anymore." I said.

Her eyes locked with mine; wide, panicked, searching for a trap I wasn't setting. She didn't see a protector. Not yet. Just another man in a locked house.

"No," she whispered, her voice breaking.

"No... he's gonna kill me. You don't understand. I don't wanna do this anymore..."

I kept my tone even, soft but anchored. "You're safe here. I promise you that."

She stared at me, like the word promise had been stolen from her vocabulary a long time ago.

But slowly barely her breathing began to shift. Shallower. Quieter. Her fists loosened.

"What's your name?" I asked.

She blinked. Once. Then again.

"...Alana."

**Alana**

My hand cracked across his face before I even realized I'd moved. The sound echoed, sharp, final. My palm burned, heart slamming against my ribs as I shoved myself into the corner. Breath came in gasps, lungs straining like the air had thickened. I didn't think; I just moved.

"Breathe," Franklin said, voice low.

"Don't tell me what to do," I snapped, the words trembling out before I could stop them.

The walls pressed in. My fists clenched, ready for the hit that never came. I flinched anyway, arms halfway raised to cover my head.

"Don't touch me!"

But nothing happened. He just stood there. Calm. Steady. Unmoving.

That stillness broke me more than rage ever could. It wasn't right. It wasn't safe. Safe wasn't real.

I lashed out again, shoving at his chest. "I said stay away!"

Behind him, the other man scoffed. That sound cut deeper than any fist.

A flash hit me.

*My sister's laugh, quick and bright.*

*The two of us spinning in the kitchen, socks sliding across the tile.*

Then just as fast, dark tile, Ricky's shadow, his hand on the back of my neck, pressing me down until my cheek scraped the floor.

I jolted back to the room, knees pulled tight to my chest, rocking hard.

"Why did I even agree to this?" The words tore out raw, shaky. My chest seized, vision blurring. Every creak in the house sounded like Ricky's boots in the hallway, every breath like the hotel bathroom where he'd locked me for two days, laughing while my body shook.

Franklin's voice cut in, steady, almost gentle. "You're safe now."

Safe. The word ripped through me like glass. Safe was what Ricky used to whisper right before the door locked, before his smile turned sharp.

I snapped, slapping at Franklin again, wild, more fear than fury. "Don't say that! You don't get it, you don't know what he does!"

He didn't raise his voice. Didn't move. Just crouched lower, careful, as if sudden movements might shatter me.

"Hey," he said softly. "You told me your name. I'm Franklin. I'm here for you. That's it."

The sound of his voice anchored me for a heartbeat, but I couldn't trust it. Couldn't trust him. Couldn't trust anyone.

My sister's eyes, brown, wide, filled with light, flashed again, and it knocked the air out of me. I curled tighter into the corner, words slipping before I could stop them. "This is for her."

15

Franklin's brow furrowed. "For who?"

"None of your business," I snapped, the words sharp and hot. Then it broke out of me anyway, ragged and raw. "For my sister. He killed her. Ricky killed her."

Clay let out a scoff and pushed off the wall. "I can't deal with this." He stalked toward the door.

"Good," I spat, voice shaking. "Then leave."

That's what Ricky's people always did. The moment I showed fear, the second I stopped being useful, they left. Walked out like my trauma was exhausting. Like my pain didn't matter unless it could be hidden.

But Franklin didn't leave. He crouched closer, still keeping space. "Can I get you something? Water? Food?"

My hands trembled so hard I had to press them against my arms. "I don't know what I need. I just... I need to breathe."

He nodded, patient. "Okay. Do you want to go outside?"

I nodded fast, desperate.

He helped me to my feet, gentle but firm, and led me toward the door. The second air hit my skin, my lungs remembered how to work. The world tilted slightly back into place. He guided me to a chair on the porch and stayed near, not crowding me, just there.

"In and out," he said quietly. "That's it. Just breathe in... and out."

I locked onto the rhythm. The breeze grazing my cheek. Sunlight glinting off the porch railing. Trees swaying, steady. For the first time since I walked into that house, I didn't feel like I was suffocating.

I glanced at him. Flinched when I found him watching me.

"I'm fine," I snapped, voice shaking.

He let out a soft laugh, not mocking. "You're not. But I'll

get you some tea."

Then he went inside.

I stayed, eyes on the trees. They stood tall, stretching toward the sky like they had nothing to apologize for. Sunlight filtered through their branches, shadows shifting across the ground. Something about them rooted me, reminded me to breathe, reminded me I was still here.

And then the smell hit, a faint trace of cologne and old wood drifting from the open door. My stomach turned before my mind caught up. For a heartbeat the porch blurred into another room: a narrow bed, cheap curtains, Ricky's shadow in the doorway. My fingers dug into the armrest until the splintering wood bit my skin.

Franklin came back with the tea, holding it like it mattered. I took it with shaking hands, the warmth grounding me as I wrapped my fingers around the cup.

"You don't have to pretend I'm worth saving," I whispered.

He didn't rush in with answers or promises. Just sat beside me, quiet and steady. "I'm not pretending."

His eyes stayed forward, voice calm. "You have no idea how long I've wanted justice, real justice, for Ricky. I'll do whatever it takes. Even if that means helping you."

He turned then, no pity in his face. "And I don't mean that in some savior kind of way. I mean it because I see you as someone."

A bitter laugh tore from me, sharp and broken. "Someone? Who could I possibly be? I'm just a nobody. Worth nothing. I don't even know why I'm still here. They say they want to protect me, but for what? There's nothing left to protect."

He turned, and there was no pity in his face. "You remind me of Esther."

I blinked. "Esther? Like... the queen? In the Bible?"

He nodded. "Yeah."

A laugh scraped out, all edge. "I'm not that. The only reason I know her name is because Ricky made us read the parts about women who were handed over. He said the Bible proved obedience was holy. Said queens were given, not asked. When he gave me to men, he called it God's plan."

A muscle jumped in Franklin's jaw, but his voice stayed calm. "Have you actually read her story?"

"No." I stared past him, heat crawling up my neck. "I only know what he shoved down my throat."

"Then maybe now's the time to read the real thing," he said quietly.

I rolled my eyes, the sarcasm automatic. "Sure. Since I'm suddenly free to study."

"I'll be here if you have questions," he said.

I took a sip of the tea. It was warm, simple, asking nothing of me. Suspicious, almost. I looked back at the trees, tried not to think about his words, but they lingered anyway.

Safe. That's what he called me. Safe.

And for one shaky breath, I almost believed it. Almost let something open inside me.

Hope.

But I knew better. Ricky used to call me special, used to talk about purpose like I was a prize. Every word was a setup.

So no. I wasn't falling for that again. Not now. Not when I'd finally learned to stop reaching for things that were never real.

# 2

# Chapter 2

**Franklin**

It had been a couple of days since I brought her to the safe house, and the dust was only just starting to settle. Enough to give Claire her update.

"Yes, she's fine," I said, keeping my voice steady as I stepped away from the porch and paced near the driveway. "We just had to deal with a little scuffle."

Claire's tone was firm but edged with concern.

"Are you sure that you and Detective Clay can handle this? We need this case to happen."

I took a breath, grounding myself.

"I'm sure. I know what this case means, and what it might cost. We're fine. She's fine. I was able to get her grounded again."

"Good," she said, though her voice didn't soften. "If there's even a hint of trouble, please tell me. I can have backup arranged immediately."

"I appreciate that. Thank you."

She hesitated. "And Clay? How's he handling the assign-ment?"

His name made my jaw tighten, the image flashing back, him walking away like her trauma was something messy he didn't have time for. He'd done it before, more times than I could count. But now wasn't the time to unravel all that. Not yet.

"Detective Franklin?" she asked again.

"Yeah," I answered quickly. "Sorry. Clay just pulled in. He's fine. We're good. We've got it under control."

"Okay," she said after a pause. "I trust you. I'll check in during debrief."

"Alright bye," I said, ending the call and slipping the phone back into my pocket.

I turned back toward the house just as Clay pulled up, stepping out with two coffees and a bounce in his step that hadn't been there yesterday. That was always the sign, coffee meant he and his wife had made up. A peace offering and a victory lap, all in one.

He handed me a cup like yesterday hadn't happened.

"Good morning," he said, that cocky grin already in place.

"How's the wild card holding up?"

I paused, the phrase landing wrong.

"She's not a wild card, Clay."

He raised a brow.

"Relax, man. Just a figure of speech. You know how we talk when things get tense."

"Not this time," I said. "Not with her."

He rolled his shoulders like he wanted to brush it off, but didn't.

"We don't know what's ahead. And she doesn't need to

feel like some unstable charity case. She needs to know she matters. So let's call her by her name. It's Alana."

Clay's expression changed. He wasn't proud, but he wasn't defensive either.

"You're right," he said. "I hear you. I'm not about to undo the work we've done. I know what Ricky means to you. I'll back off."

That was one thing I could count on with Clay. We clashed often, but when something mattered, we knew it. We had a code, an understanding that didn't need explaining.

And this; this mattered.

He knew what Ricky had taken from me, the sleepless nights, the endless dead ends, the wreckage he left behind. And Alana... she was the thread that could finally unravel it all.

We took our coffee and walked the perimeter of the property slowly, eyes scanning for anything out of place, any disruption that didn't belong. The motion sensors were still intact, the security cameras held their angles, and there were no tire tracks along the gravel that hadn't already been accounted for. No footprints in the dirt. No branches broken near the fence line. Still, I didn't let myself exhale. Not with Ricky still out there. Not with everything she knew.

Clay moved along the edges of the fence while I checked the alarm panel again, going through every checkpoint like we were prepping for an ambush instead of standing in a government-approved safe house. We double-checked the locks, marked the blind spots, made quiet mental notes about rotating shifts more frequently once the sun went down.

One thing caught me, Clay walked right past a motion sensor and brushed it off like it was nothing. I stopped short.

"You see that?" I asked.

He didn't even break stride. "It's fine."

"Fine?" I pressed, keeping my voice even. "Since when do you walk past tech without checking it?"

Clay gave a shrug, eyes fixed ahead. "Battery must be low. Happens all the time. Nothing to worry about."

But that wasn't like him. He didn't miss things. Not small details, not ever. And it stuck with me. Everything else checked out, clean, secure, textbook, but I've seen secure fall apart before. I wasn't about to make the mistake of trusting it twice.

Once we finished the sweep, I stepped back inside and made my way toward the one thing I'd been avoiding since day one: the file. The real one. The unredacted report sitting on the kitchen counter with her name stamped across the top in bold print, like it wasn't tied to the living, breathing person behind the next door.

Alana.

That name had already started to mean something more than just logistics and testimony. And when I flipped the folder open and began reading through the pages, I could feel that meaning dig deeper into my chest with every line.

She'd been Ricky's "top girl" since sixteen. Still in school. Still a child.

The report said they first met him in a grocery store. Their mother was alive, but emotionally checked out. Ricky started showing up in small ways; buying cereal, offering help, and slowly ingratiating himself into their lives. He didn't pose as a pastor. He didn't have to. All he needed to be was kind. Present. Helpful. That was enough to earn their trust.

I kept reading, *slowly, deliberately*, because something in me knew that to rush through her story would be just another kind of betrayal, another way of silencing a voice that had already been quieted too many times. Her photos shifted with each passing year, faces changing, hair growing longer or shorter, smiles forced or absent, but her eyes never changed. In some, they were hollow; in others, they burned. But in all of them, they carried the same weight, like she was screaming without sound, like survival itself had carved a new language into her that only the broken could begin to understand.

And she had learned it fluently.

The deeper I went, the harder it became to sit still. I felt it in my spine, in my chest, in that sharp tug behind my ribs that always showed up when a case stopped being professional and started being personal.

This wasn't just another lead. It wasn't a string of data or a timeline with gaps. This was a girl who'd been used, erased, discarded and somehow, she was still here. Still standing. Still trying to do the right thing when she had every reason to disappear.

And now she was under my protection.

I closed the file slowly, letting the edges rest beneath my palms as the pressure returned, not just because of what she'd lived through, but because of what it would cost to keep her safe.

Because if I failed... she wouldn't get another chance.

Not this time.

Not on my watch.

After a while, I got up to get some water, but the file still lingered in the back of my mind, every detail etched behind my eyes like it had been branded there. I reached for a glass, then paused, remembering how she had calmed when we sat outside earlier. She'd said almost nothing, but the tea had helped. It was a small thing, but sometimes small things were the only tools we had left.

I poured another cup and walked quietly to her room, knocking once before I opened the door.

The second I stepped inside, I saw her body tense. Her shoulders rose, her spine went stiff, and I recognized it instantly, not fear of me specifically, but fear of what came after footsteps and doorknobs and uninvited voices. Her trauma was doing the talking before either of us said a word.

I kept my voice low. "Hey... I brought some tea."

She looked at me with suspicion, narrowing her eyes slightly like she was trying to figure out my angle. "You know you don't have to bring me tea every day."

"I know," I said. "I just poured myself some and thought you might want a cup too."

She stood, slower than before, and took the mug from my hand with fingers that barely brushed mine.

"Thanks," she muttered, like it cost her something to say it out loud.

Our eyes met, but not in the way people like to write about, not soft, not charged with curiosity or electricity, not anything that hinted at romance or revelation. It was quieter than that. More guarded. Heavy in a way that didn't beg to be explained, just understood. Like we both recognized that something too big was sitting between us, and neither of us had the language or the strength, to move it.

I tried to hold a neutral expression, but something in me moved, just slightly. I wasn't trying to pity her. I wasn't even trying to connect. I just wanted her to know she wasn't invisible.

She must have read too much in my silence, because her

eyes turned sharp again suspicious, then bitter, like the look someone gives when they've been disappointed too many times to trust kindness.

"You gave me the tea," she said flatly. "You can go now."

I nodded, backing up a step. "Right. Just let me know if you need anything."

She didn't answer. Just turned away and closed the door behind me.

I stood there for a second, still holding the doorknob, the heat from the mug fading in my hand.

I told myself it didn't matter. That what she needed now was structure, not sympathy. That I could keep this professional if I stayed sharp. If I didn't let the weight of her story sit too long in my chest.

But the truth was, I didn't know if I believed that anymore.

Later that evening, I stepped outside. I needed a second to breathe. To put some distance between me and everything I'd read in that file.

I pulled out my phone and called my dad. Sometimes hearing his voice was enough to steady the ground beneath me.

"Hey, Dad," I said as he picked up.

"What's up?" he answered, easy and familiar, like he'd been waiting on the call.

"How's these past couple of days going with the assignment?"

I rubbed the back of my neck, watching the sky shift behind the trees.

"It's going."

He didn't miss a beat. "All right now, kid. I know that tone. What's going on?"

I exhaled. The words had already been waiting in my throat. "It's just... heavy. Reading her file was bad enough, but seeing her today? It's different. It hit harder than I expected. The things Ricky did to her, what she's been through it's not just disturbing. It's evil."

He let that sit for a moment before answering, his voice slower, more deliberate.

"You said this was your purpose. That God called you to this kind of work. And I know it doesn't feel like it right now, but maybe that's the confirmation you needed. Just because she wasn't protected before doesn't mean she's unprotected now."

He paused.

"God sent you to cover her, Franklin. Don't miss that. When He sends someone to protect, it's never one-sided. He's not just doing something for her. He's trying to show you something too. Let this stretch you. Let it teach you what it needs to."

His words landed heavier than anything in that file.

"Thanks, Dad," I said, quiet.

In the background, I heard Jennifer call out, a little too loud. "Tell your daddy it's dinner time!"

I smiled, the tension in my shoulders easing just a little. "You're not giving her grief, are you?"

He chuckled. "I'm old, not boring. What's the point of living if you can't cause a little trouble?"

I laughed softly. "All right, Dad. Talk to you soon."

Dinner was quiet. Too quiet. Clay kept his distance, answering only when he had to, his words clipped, practiced. Alana stayed tense, her eyes darting to corners, fork barely moving.

I cleared my throat, trying to break the silence. "We'll rotate shifts on the feed tonight. Clay, you want first?"

He gave a short laugh, no humor in it. "Why ask me? You're the lead on this case. Claire made that clear. Whatever you say goes."

Alana's brow furrowed. "What does that mean?"

"Nothing," he said quickly, though the edge in his voice stayed. "Just that the boss always hands him the reins. He's the one calling the shots. I just follow orders."

I set my fork down, my tone low. "Clay, this isn't the time. You don't bring that up in front of her. If you've got a problem, you bring it to me."

He leaned back in his chair, a smirk tugging at his mouth. "Relax, man. I'm just messing around."

But the way his eyes lingered told me it wasn't a joke. Not entirely.

The rest of the meal fell back into silence, the weight thicker than before.

Later that night, sleep still wouldn't come. The house was still, but my mind wasn't. Images kept looping , her voice shaking, her hand at the door, the quiet plea in her silence when she didn't say goodbye.

I got up, poured a glass of water, and opened the security feed , not out of habit, but because I needed something steady to keep me from unraveling. The footage cycled frame by frame: hallway, porch, kitchen, repeat.

One angle caught me and held.

She was sitting outside. The mug of tea still in her hands, cold now, forgotten. The porch light washed her face in soft streaks of gold, catching the curve of her cheek, the way her lashes shadowed skin that hadn't felt peace in a long time. And for the first time since she stepped into this house, she wasn't flinching. She wasn't curling in on herself, wasn't bracing for the next invisible blow.

She was still. Fragile, borrowed stillness, but enough. Enough to remind me why I said yes. Enough to ground me in the reason I kept showing up, even when walking away might've been easier.

No matter what this case demanded of me, no matter what it broke along the way, I'd carry it to the end because she was still fighting.

And if she was still fighting... then maybe, just maybe, she'd survive this.

**Alana**

"Help me! Help me!"

My sister's voice ripped through the dark, high and desperate. I ran toward it but my legs felt trapped in mud, heavy, useless. Ricky's hand clamped around her wrist, yanking her backward. She clawed at the floor, her nails leaving bloody streaks as he dragged her away.

I woke up gasping, heart pounding so hard it drowned out everything else. Sweat clung to my back like the nightmare had followed me here. My eyes swept the room , unfamiliar walls, too-quiet corners, shadows that didn't belong to me. For a moment I couldn't tell if I was still trapped in the dream or if the dream had simply changed locations.

It took too long to remember where I was. *Just a dream*, I told myself, gripping the sheet. *Just a dream.* My body didn't believe it. Ricky's voice still echoed in my ears, my sister's screams still ringing raw inside my chest.

I pressed one hand to my chest, the other to my stomach,

trying to anchor myself.

Inhale. Exhale. In and out. Controlled. Slow. Like maybe if I could control my breath, I could control the fear too.

"You're safe," I whispered once. Then again, softer. I didn't believe it, but I said it anyway.

My shoulders dropped a fraction, panic still humming under my skin. Beige walls. Unfamiliar switch. A door that didn't close all the way. My eyes fixed on the crack at the base of the frame and I swore it moved.

I slid out of bed and pressed the door shut until the soft click came, fingers lingering on the knob like that sound alone could hold the past out. The fear stayed anyway, quiet, heavy, familiar, a weight I knew how to carry.

I wasn't safe. Not really. Not until Ricky was gone for good. And even then, maybe never. Survival wasn't healing. Justice didn't guarantee peace.

Prison would be a reward for him. Meals. Structure. A bed. And I'd still be here checking locks at midnight, waiting for footsteps.

Franklin had said the same words. "You're safe." Like they became true just because he said them low and gentle. But Ricky used to say that too, smiled when he lied, promised new life, promised I mattered.

So no, I'm not believing a man just because he sounds nice and brings tea. At least with Clay, I know what I'm getting. He doesn't soften his voice or pretend my fear is sacred. He looks at me like I'm a problem, and maybe that's easier than whatever Franklin's trying to be.

Men like Clay don't surprise you. They tell you exactly what they think. I've seen that look in his eyes before, in hotel rooms, stairwells, in the silence when money hit the dresser.

The look that says, *You're used up. You're done.*

Even if Franklin doesn't look at me that way, that's not enough to make me believe he won't. Not yet.

I lay back down but sleep doesn't come. My eyes drift to the window, the shadow under the door, the vent in the ceiling. Every creak sounds like footsteps, every hum like a lock clicking.

By dawn my throat is dry, mouth coated with the bitter taste of fear. All I can think about is tea, something warm to steady my hands.

I pull on my hoodie and slip down the hallway, steps soft on the cold floor. The kitchen light is already on.

Detective Franklin stands at the counter with two mugs, one steaming coffee, the other tea. Of course it's tea.

He glances up like it's nothing, like we're just roommates in a quiet house with matching mugs. For a second that almost makes me laugh. *What kind of man notices things like that? Brings tea without asking?*

I take the cup without a word and head for the back door, needing distance. I don't look back, but I hear his footsteps. Of course I do.

Because I'm not free. I'm not just some woman on a porch; I'm a witness, a case file, and he's the one keeping me alive long enough to testify.

Still, I say nothing.

I sit down and sip the tea, pretending his presence doesn't affect me.

And then, he speaks.

"Can I sit?"

I shrug, not looking at him. "It's a free country, right?"

He chuckles, and something about the sound doesn't feel

forced. "I'm not sure about that anymore, "he says, and for whatever reason, we both laugh.

Real laughter.

Small. Short-lived. But real.

And for a second, just one small second, my guard starts to lower only slightly, only halfway, but enough that it surprises me.

Then he asks," Did you sleep in?"

I stop laughing. My voice comes flat, almost cold.

"I can't sleep in. Not until Ricky's out of my life for good."

He nods, the smile fading from his face. "Yeah. I hear that."

I watch him for a moment. There's something in his tone, the way he stares out at the trees, that makes me wonder what this man is carrying. So I ask, not because I want to bond but because I want to know what makes a man like him keep showing up.

"What's your beef with him anyway?"

He doesn't answer right away. He leans back, eyes still focused on the trees like they're telling him something I can't hear.

"It's a long story," he says quietly. "But I've been chasing him for a long time."

And something in his voice tells me it's not just about justice.

We sat for a while, sipping from our mugs, watching the breeze move through the branches. For a heartbeat, it almost felt normal.

"You've been quiet," Franklin said, not looking at me. "I get it. Sometimes silence is easier."

I kept my eyes on the trees. "You're used to women like me being quiet?"

"No." He shook his head, a faint smile without humor. "I'm

used to witnesses shutting down because no one ever told them the truth. I try not to be that guy."

I risked a glance at him. "Then why are you here? Really."

He hesitated, thumb tracing the edge of his mug. "Because the first time I lost a witness, it didn't just cost the case. It cost a person. I swore I wouldn't let that happen again."

The name landed between us. I didn't know what to do with it, so I just held my cup tighter.

He cleared his throat. "This isn't friendship. I know that. But it isn't just a case to me either."

My fingers curled harder around the mug. "It is to me." The words slipped out sharp, before I could stop them.

"I know," he said quietly. "You don't have to trust me. Not yet."

The silence that followed was heavier but different , less like a wall, more like a space we didn't know how to cross.

I stood slowly, gathering the cups. For a moment it felt like something normal, something small I could control. A simple act that steadied me, made me feel almost human again in a house that still didn't feel like mine.

But as I turned, my hands started to shake from the inside out, tension spilling through my fingers. The tea cup slipped before I could catch it. When it hit the floor, it didn't just break , it shattered, sharp and sudden, cutting through the air and slicing something open inside of me.

The sound was louder than it should've been. Not just porcelain on wood, but a memory cracking wide open.

And suddenly I wasn't here anymore.

I was back in that hallway, back in that dim, stale room with the door that never quite closed right, back in the silence that came before the shouting, the silence that made me hold my breath because I knew what was coming. Ricky's voice crawled up through the memory like a hand around my throat, thick with blame and cruelty.

"You stupid, stupid girl. You can never do anything right."

I dropped to my knees, the floor hard beneath me, hands bracing like I was preparing for a hit. My breath caught shallow and sharp. The edges of the world blurred. I curled in tight, just trying to disappear.

"I'm so sorry," I whispered, over and over, the words tumbling out like instinct. "I'm so sorry. I'm so sorry."

The panic moved fast, clamping down on my lungs, choking off the air. My heart pounded in strange places, wrists, neck, ears, pressure blurring what was real and what was memory.

Then... a voice.

Not Ricky's.

Franklin's.

Soft. Measured. Not too close.

"You don't have to apologize," he said, steady but not sharp. "It's okay. Things break."

The words cut deeper than I expected. Ricky used to say the same thing, but with venom, like *I* was the broken thing. Franklin didn't sound like that. He didn't move toward me. Didn't touch me. He just let the silence sit, calm and level, like I didn't scare him.

And that unsettled me more than anything.

Because when someone doesn't punish you for falling apart, it doesn't feel safe. It feels like the breath right before it all goes wrong.

I stood up fast, muttered another "sorry," and slipped down the hall. Hands clenched, lungs burning. I closed my door behind me and pressed my back to it like that could keep the world out.

I didn't cry. I didn't scream. I just whispered into the dark, "You're fine. You're fine. You're fine." Over and over until the words dissolved.

But memories didn't listen.

*Her laugh in the kitchen, spinning me in circles until we both fell. Her voice off-key, singing with her eyes closed. Her scream the night he dragged her away.*

I curled tight beneath the blanket, clinging to those flashes until exhaustion finally pulled me under.

When I woke again, the room felt too quiet. Safer than voices, but not safe enough. My eyes drifted until they caught on the nightstand. A Bible. Worn edges, corners curled. A sticky note marking a page.

I stared at it, unsure if I wanted to touch it or throw it. My fingers moved anyway, flipping it open. The first verse I saw was underlined: *"For I know the plans I have for you..."*

A bitter laugh slipped out as I shut it hard. Plans. Hope. A future. Try surviving Ricky and then tell me what that verse feels like.

Curiosity pulled me back. I opened it again, slower this time. The sticky note landed me in Esther. Of course. My mouth twisted. "Nice try, Detective Franklin," I muttered under my breath.

I set the Bible down, more tired than angry, and sat on the edge of the bed. If he thought a highlighted verse and a bookmark were enough to undo what I'd lived, he didn't know who he was dealing with.

Later, I slipped outside for air. Anything to escape the smell of sweat and old dreams.

And there he was.

Detective Franklin, sitting in a chair, Bible in his hands. Calm. Still. Not performing. Not trying to be impressive. Just... steady.

I froze in the doorway, watching. He wasn't preaching or pretending. He wasn't fixing me. He was just a man, quiet, surrounded by trees, holding something sacred like it belonged to him.

It unsettled me more than rage ever could. Because how can you sit that still? How can you believe after everything you've seen?

The questions burned hot, sharp:

*Where was God when I said no and he didn't stop?*

*Where was God when I bled through the sheets and no one came?*

*Where was God when my sister screamed and he smiled?*

*Where was God when the lock clicked and the light went out?*

*Where was God when I forgot what my own voice sounded like?*

*Where was God when I begged Him to kill me, just to make it stop?*

*Where was God when I stopped hoping He'd answer?*

No answers came. Just silence.

Still, underneath the anger, something small stirred. Not faith. Not hope. Just confusion. Because for all the years I'd been surviving, I had never seen anyone carry pain like that , with peace. Not the kind you fake to make others comfortable, but the kind that settles deep, earned through fire.

I didn't go to him. I didn't speak. I just watched from the porch for a long time, hidden in shadows, trying to make sense of what kind of man sits that still, that quietly, in the middle of a mess like this.

He didn't move like Ricky. Didn't look like him either. And

that alone left me on edge.

Because I didn't know what to do with someone who wasn't trying to own me, control me, or dismiss me. Someone who just sat steady, like he had nothing to prove.

That kind of calm feels dangerous when you've only ever known chaos. Part of me wanted to test it, to see how far it would crack. But the other part , the part that hadn't completely died yet , just wanted to believe there might be something real in his quiet.

3

# Chapter 3

**Franklin**

A month into the assignment and she still stayed with me , in my head, in my prayers, in the space between work and sleep. I'd expected the risk. I hadn't expected how hard it would be to keep her out of my chest.

She was still guarded, still carried that weight in her shoulders, but the walls weren't as high anymore. Some mornings she even let me sit outside with her. No words. Just tea and quiet. In those moments, when the noise died down, I caught glimpses of someone Ricky had almost erased: a flash of humor, a raised brow sharp enough to be a full conversation.

But the trauma was still there too. In the way she flinched at a door closing too hard. In how she automatically placed her back to a wall. Muscle memory. Survival.

I told myself I was protecting her. Some nights, lying awake, I wondered if I was trying to fix something in me instead.

This wasn't just another protection detail anymore. The line between my job and what I was carrying blurred a little more each day, settling into my chest like a weight I knew I wouldn't walk away from clean.

And lately the quiet had changed. Not eyes exactly, but intention. The calm around us felt borrowed, like someone was holding their breath just outside the edges of safe. It made me question whether I was thinking with my badge or with my heart.

As I walked the perimeter that morning, I ran through protocol like I always did; motion sensors, camera placements, window locks, but the pressure wasn't just about routine anymore. It was about timing. Things were shifting faster than we planned. There was a rumor floating through the task force that someone had tipped Ricky off. And if that was true, then the clock wasn't just ticking, it was spiraling. We didn't know how long we had before he made his next move, but I could feel it tightening.

Ricky knew we were coming. That much I could feel. And if he couldn't reach Alana physically, he'd try something else. He always did.

I found Clay near the kitchen, already scrolling through the latest case notes on his tablet like this was just another day, like none of this was pressing in on him the way it was pressing in on me. He looked up when I walked in, and for a second, I could see it, the flicker of detachment, that same distance in his eyes that made me question whether he was still all-in, or if he was just going through the motions, waiting for this to all blow over.

"You hear back from Ramirez yet?" I asked, heading straight for the coffee pot.

He shook his head. "No answer. He was supposed to check in last night, something about a warehouse lead in Arlington.

Could've been nothing, but…"

He shrugged. "It's not like him to go dark."

I paused, mug half-raised. "You try again this morning?"

"Twice."

That didn't sit right. Ramirez was reliable. Steady. And if he was onto something, he wouldn't just vanish, not without warning.

Clay didn't seem fazed. Just went back to his tablet like missing agents weren't a big deal. Either he wasn't worried or he was pretending not to be.

"I'll give it an hour," I said, glancing at the empty hallway. "Then I'm calling it in."

Clay didn't look up from his tablet.

"Got a memo this morning," Clay added, flipping the screen toward me for half a second.

"One of Ricky's old charges got dismissed. Technicality."

I narrowed my eyes. "What kind of technicality?"

He shrugged. "Botched chain of evidence. File went missing."

A cold prickle moved across my shoulders. That wasn't just sloppy. That was inside help.

"They're cleaning up," I said slowly. "Covering their tracks."

"Or someone's just bad at paperwork," Clay offered with a smirk.

But I didn't buy it. Not today. The air felt off, like the calm wasn't natural. Like we were being watched without knowing it.

I turned toward the window. The trees outside swayed gently, the sun bleeding through in fractured patches. Too quiet. Too clean. And that's what put me on edge.

Because in this line of work, silence didn't mean safety.

It meant the next move was already in motion.

After Clay disappeared into his room, I stepped outside, letting the screen door ease shut behind me as I moved into the quiet dusk. I was headed to Bible study, my one standing commitment outside of this assignment, I almost didn't go. But something about the stillness in that house felt more dangerous than whatever I might face on the road.

But the second my feet hit the steps, I felt it.

The air outside was unnervingly still, the kind of quiet that makes your gut hum before your mind catches up, like the street itself was holding its breath. I lifted my phone, pretending to check for signal, but my eyes had already locked on the edge of the block.

A car sat just beyond the streetlight, parked too neatly to feel casual. The engine was off, the windows black, the tires angled perfectly straight. It hadn't moved since I stepped outside, and something about its patience tightened the coil in my chest.

I snapped a photo , plate, timestamp, angle , and logged it the way I always did when something refused to sit right. Over the years I'd learned it isn't always movement that gives people away; sometimes it's the complete absence of it. And this car didn't shift, didn't hum, didn't breathe. It just waited.

I let out a slow breath. "Lord, give me clarity," I prayed under my breath. Not strength, not justice. Just clarity. And the answer came sharp, as clear as the silence itself: stay.

Bible study could wait. Tonight, my place was here.

Back inside, I found Clay at the table with his tablet. "There's a car parked past the streetlight," I said. "Been sitting there too long. Could be nothing, but it doesn't feel right."

Clay leaned back, eyebrows raised. "Plate?"

I showed him the photo. He studied it for a second too long before giving a casual shrug. "Might be a neighbor's friend. Or somebody waiting on a drop."

"Maybe," I said, though the knot in my chest didn't loosen. "Either way, I want eyes on it. If it's still there in the morning, we run it."

He tapped something into his tablet. "I'll flag it."

It was the right response, but there was a flicker in his face , a subtle shift I almost dismissed. Like he'd already filed it under *minor* instead of *urgent.*

"Appreciate it," I said, heading for my room.

"Don't lose sleep over one parked car," Clay called after me, his tone too easy, too casual. "We've got bigger things to worry about."

Maybe he was right. But instinct told me otherwise.

Later on that night the house was quiet, lights dimmed, but I heard the faint buzz of the TV before I saw her. Alana sat curled up on the couch, hood pulled over her head, legs tucked in tight like armor. The glow of the screen lit her face, softening the lines I'd come to recognize , tension, vigilance, fear she tried to mask with indifference.

She didn't notice me at first. Her shoulders were loose, and for a split second, I caught something I hadn't seen before. A laugh. Small, quick, gone almost as soon as it slipped out.

When the floor creaked under my step, she stiffened, pulling the hood lower like a curtain. "What are you doing up?" she asked, her tone clipped, defensive.

"Couldn't sleep," I said, staying by the doorway. "Mind if I sit?"

She didn't look at me. "It's a free country."

I eased onto the other end of the couch, careful to leave space between us. The movie played on, some Adam Sandler comedy I hadn't seen in years. She kept her eyes on the screen, like if she ignored me long enough I might disappear.

We watched in silence for a while. Then a ridiculous gag landed, and despite herself, a laugh burst out of her again. She bit it back quickly, shoulders tensing as if she'd given too much away.

I didn't say anything. Just let the sound hang in the air before turning back to the screen. A few minutes later, another joke slipped through, and this time my own laugh followed. Quiet. Not at her, just at the absurdity on the screen.

Her eyes flicked toward me, suspicious, like she was testing whether I was laughing at her or with her. I kept my gaze forward, the corners of my mouth tugging just slightly.

For the rest of the movie, we sat that way. Separate. Guarded. But the silence wasn't sharp anymore. Not quite peace, not quite trust, just the small, unspoken acknowledgment that for a little while, in the middle of all the chaos, we could sit in the same room and breathe.

When the credits rolled, she pulled the hood tighter and stood. "Don't get used to it," she muttered, heading for her room.

I nodded, more to myself than to her. "Goodnight, Alana."

The door clicked shut down the hall, and I stayed on the couch a little longer, letting the echo of her laugh linger in my chest. Not hope exactly. But something close.

**Alana**

I didn't want to think about last night.

The sound of him walking in, quiet but present. The way he asked if he could sit, and how I tossed back, *It's a free country*, just to remind him not to get comfortable.

He sat anyway. Not too close, not too far. Just there. Watching the same stupid comedy I'd put on to drown out the silence.

And I hated how, for a second, it almost worked.

Because somewhere between the dumb jokes and the glow of the screen, I laughed. Not big, not loud, just enough for it to slip out before I could stop it. And when I did, I felt him notice. Not in a mocking way. Just... notice.

That's what pissed me off the most.

I didn't need him noticing things about me. Didn't need him sitting there like silence was enough, like he could just *be* without trying to take something. I wanted to be mad about it, to hold onto that edge, but instead I fell asleep harder than I had in weeks.

Six full hours. No nightmares. No sweating through the sheets. No jolting awake to Ricky's voice clawing down my spine.

And I hated it.

Because I wasn't supposed to feel that kind of rest. Not here. Not while Ricky was still breathing. My body betrayed me, relaxing in a house I still didn't trust, near a man I still couldn't believe.

The anger simmered under my skin when I got up, pulling on the hoodie I'd been wearing like armor since day one. I walked into the kitchen needing distraction.

Clay was already there, slouched in a chair like the morning owed him something, eyes glazed and jaw tight like his bad

43

attitude had arrived before sunrise.

I didn't want to talk. But I said "Good morning" anyway out of habit, out of politeness, out of some leftover instinct that still hadn't learned how to stay quiet.

He didn't respond. Just muttered something that barely passed as a word and didn't bother to look at me.

So I said it. Not loud, just clear enough.

"Must suck waking up next to that attitude every day."

His head snapped up. Chair screeched across the floor as he stood, all muscle and tension and empty rage. Two steps and he was right in front of me. Too close. Too familiar.

My body didn't move, but my insides did, that same cold lockup I used to feel whenever Ricky walked in the room just a little too quiet.

"Listen here," Clay hissed, breath hot against my cheek. "You think just because Franklin's babysitting you, you can run your mouth like you matter? You're nothing but a file they dumped here. A charity case."

I didn't shrink. Didn't flinch. I stepped forward instead. Into the heat. Into the danger. Into the part of me that needed someone to act ugly enough to remind me what I was made of.

"Go ahead," I said, voice shaking but eyes steady. "Hit me."

I needed him to snap. To make this feeling real. To remind me I was still made of fire, not just fear.

He blinked. Not because he was shocked, but because I meant it.

"I bet you've been dying for a reason," I said. "So take it."

Then the door opened.

"What's going on in here?" Detective Franklin's voice cut through like cold air through fire.

Detective Franklin stepped in with purpose not rushed, not

frantic, just firm. His gaze flicked from me to Clay, and I saw the shift in him. Not panic. Not confusion. Just control.

Clay backed off. Too quickly.

"Just a friendly conversation," he muttered, brushing it off with a smirk that didn't reach his eyes.

But Franklin didn't even look at him.

He came straight to me, his presence steady, his voice low. "Come with me."

He didn't touch me like I was fragile. Just stood beside me close enough to offer cover, far enough to give space.

The second that door closed behind us, I breathed.

Franklin turned to face me. His voice wasn't soft, but it wasn't sharp either. Just layered.

"What are you doing, Alana?"

I didn't answer.

He tried again, firmer now. "You were trying to get hit. Why?"

"Why do you care what I want?" I snapped before I thought about it.

"Because I'm trying to understand you," he said. "I'm trying to help. But you can't let yourself feel safe, can you?"

My chest tightened.

"It's not that I want chaos," I muttered. "It's just all I know."

He was quiet for a moment. Then I said what I hadn't told anyone else.

"Clay reminds me of Ricky. His eyes. His silence. That waiting-to-explode feeling. It's all the same."

Franklin sighed, dragging a hand over his face. "I know Clay's a lot. I don't always like how he moves either. But he's not Ricky. And whether you believe it or not, he's here to protect you."

I laughed, bitter and sharp.

"I need you both to stop acting like enemies," he continued. "We're here until Ricky's behind bars. That's the mission. I'm not letting this implode before we get justice."

His voice had risen just slightly enough for my body to react. I flinched. Just a twitch, a shift of the shoulders. But he saw it.

Immediately, his tone dropped. Regret flashed across his face. I didn't owe him anything. But maybe I owed Detective Franklin my effort.

"I'm sorry," he said. "I didn't mean to raise my voice."

He paused, breathing deep, eyes holding mine.

"You're not just a witness, Alana. You're the wall between him and every girl he still thinks he can hurt."

I couldn't hold his gaze after that. Couldn't stand in the heat of that truth. So I just shrugged, turned, and walked back inside.

Because being seen *"really seen"* isn't always safe.

I stayed in my room just long enough for the shaking to stop not because I was sorry, but because Detective Franklin had asked me to apologize. And maybe, deep down, I knew I'd let my anger speak louder than it needed to. So I stepped back into the kitchen where Clay was still sitting, slouched in his chair like the whole house was beneath him, eyes fixed on the counter like I wasn't even worth glancing at. I stood a few feet away, not out of fear, but because the air between us still felt thick, and I didn't want to breathe him in.

"I'm sorry," I said, the words dry but real, my voice steady enough to carry weight even without warmth.

He let out a short laugh, like it was a joke. "Yeah, right."

Before I could respond, Detective Franklin appeared from

the hallway, his footsteps quiet but full of intent, and the shift in energy was immediate. His tone wasn't loud, it didn't have to be.

"She just said she's sorry," he said evenly. "Now it's your turn."

"I'm not saying sorry to her." Clay leaned back in his chair, arms crossed tighter, scoffing like the idea of apologizing was beneath him.

Franklin's eyes didn't waver. He stepped forward just slightly, his voice still level, but with an edge that cut through the tension like a blade.

"What did I tell you about that? She's not a case file or a problem. She's a person. And you're not going to treat her like she's anything less."

He looked between us his eyes firm, his presence commanding and I saw it then. He wasn't just frustrated. He was disappointed. In both of us.

"This little power struggle ends here. We're not going to let something this petty sabotage the entire case. We're too close to let pride get in the way."

Clay didn't respond. He moved again, looked away like he was done listening.

Franklin didn't push it. He just turned and walked out, calm and collected, but I could feel the heat under his restraint. For a second, I thought he was gone for good, tired of being the one holding everything together. But then, a few minutes later, the front door opened again, and he stepped back inside, slower this time, more composed.

He walked over to me, not rushing, not crowding me, just showing up in that steady, deliberate way he always did. He didn't say much at first just looked at me like he was deciding how honest to be.

"I'm not walking away from you," he said finally, voice low. "I just needed to breathe."

Something in my chest eased, and before I could look away, he added, softer this time, "You don't have to carry everything in fight mode, Alana. I see you."

He said it without drama. Without expectation. Just a fact. And somehow, that made it harder to ignore.

I didn't say anything. I couldn't. I just nodded, barely, and turned back toward my room, the door clicking shut behind me as I crossed the threshold and sank onto the edge of the bed, legs heavy, heart heavier.

And since all of this began, I let the quiet sit with me not as punishment, not as isolation, but as something else. Something that sounded a little like the word I still don't trust.

Hope.

Later, after the silence in the room stopped pressing against my skin like judgment, I finally lay down. I didn't cry. I didn't speak. I just stared at the ceiling with Franklin's words echoing in my chest, still unsure how something so gentle could feel so loud.

*"You don't have to carry everything in fight mode."*

He didn't say it like an order. Just truth. And that scared me.

I pulled the blanket tighter, letting the weight of the day settle into my limbs, and for once, I didn't feel the need to brace myself. I didn't need the armor. I didn't need the sharpness. I just needed stillness. Not because I trusted him yet. Not because I believed in what he believed in. But because, somehow, even with all the pain between us, I knew he wasn't going to walk away.

That kind of presence? It was unfamiliar. Dangerous, even.

Because when someone stays long enough, you start to wonder if maybe you're worth staying for. And I've never been good at wondering without wanting.

So I let the quiet hold me. I let the flicker of safety settle low in my chest where the fear used to sit. And though I didn't know what came next, though the war wasn't over, and Ricky still roamed free, I breathed deeper.

Not because I was healed.

But because I wasn't breathing alone.

# 4

# Chapter 4

**Franklin**

It's been a few days since the fight between Alana and Clay, and even though things on the surface have settled, I can feel the shift in the air around her, quieter, heavier. She isn't cold or angry, just withdrawn, like she's retreating into a version of silence that keeps her safe. And it's not like the early days, when silence came with sharp edges and fear. This silence is different. It's thoughtful. Guarded. Something broke open that night in the kitchen, but instead of letting it bleed, she sealed it shut and buried it deeper. She still takes the tea. Still drifts past me in the morning. But it's quieter now; like she's trying to disappear without fully vanishing.

I keep replaying it in my head; what changed, what she saw in him that made her push so hard. The way she looked at him. The way she stood there like she was daring him. That wasn't defiance. That was pain. That was history.

We were starting to find our rhythm again.

Laughing.

Drinking tea.

These small, weightless moments where she didn't flinch when I walked in the room. And then it all slipped, like trying to hold water in your hands. One second it felt like progress. The next, it was gone. Even knowing I can't fix her, every inch she pulls away feels like I failed to keep her anchored.

So this morning, I make the call.

"Good morning, Boss," I say as Claire picks up.

"Morning, Franklin," she replies, chipper but careful. "How's it going over there?"

"It's good," I say automatically, then pause. "Actually... I think it might be time we bring in a trauma counselor."

The line goes quiet for half a second; too quiet. Then her voice comes back, lower.

"Did something happen?"

She doesn't usually pause like that. Not unless something political is brewing behind the scenes.

"No," I say slowly. "Not exactly. But she's holding everything in, like she's afraid of what might spill if she speaks."

Claire hums thoughtfully. "Alright. We'll reach out to someone in the network. But talk to her first. Let her know it's her choice. If she's not ready, we wait. But if she is, don't miss the window."

"You're right," I say. I'm already thinking about how hard it'll be to reach her in this state.

Claire softens. "You okay?"

"Yeah," I answer quickly. "I just... I hate seeing her like this."

She doesn't respond at first, just lets the silence hold.

Then I ask, "Any updates on Ricky?"

She exhales. "Lead went cold again. It's like he's always

one shadow ahead, like he's listening through the walls."

I grip the phone tighter, feeling the frustration coil in my chest.

"But," she adds, "we've still got the one thing he doesn't know about. The weapon he won't see coming. When the time's right, she's going to bury him."

"I just need her to stay willing," I say. "And safe."

"You keep her safe, Franklin. Keep her close. When it's time, we'll move. Just don't let her close off before we get there."

"I won't," I say, meaning it.

But right before we hang up, there's a faint click, too quick, too deliberate. My gut tightens. A split-second static shift in the line. I freeze.

Not a dropped signal. Not static. Just... something. A tick in the line that didn't belong. A thought flickers, if the line was tapped, was it Claire they were listening to, or me?

"You still there?" Claire asks.

"Yeah," I say, glancing toward the front window, every instinct going quiet.

"Talk soon."

"Talk soon." The line goes dead.

I stay still for a beat, staring at the wall but not really seeing it. That sound, it could've been nothing. Could've been a glitch in reception. Could've been.

I check the signal on the phone. Strong. No interference. No reason.

I hang up, then slowly move toward the window and scan the tree line again. Calm. Still. Empty.

But something in me is stirring. I don't ignore it.

Because with Ricky, danger never knocks. It listens first. It waits until you exhale. And lately, it's been listening too well.

After checking the perimeter, I walk the length of the porch twice, scanning everything with quiet focus, the tree line, the phone box, the fence.

I pause at the far end, eyes narrowing.

There's a faint scuff in the dirt just outside the patched section, could be from the wind, could be from an animal. But it wasn't there yesterday. The boards still hold. The wire looks untouched. But I don't like almost.

Nothing else seems out of place. No reason to sound an alarm. But with Ricky, it's never the obvious signs. It's what shifts quietly. I finish the sweep and head inside, starting the kettle for our morning tea.

It's the one thing she still accepts. We don't sit outside together anymore not since the fight, but she still takes the cup. It's not a ritual now. Not conversation. Just a small, silent exchange. But it means something. As the steam rises, I glance out the kitchen window, and for a second I picture her sitting there again, the way she used to, before the silence settled between us. A familiar ache twists in my chest. Not quite grief. Not quite longing. Just the ache of what could've been.

So I pray.

No bowing. No theatrics. Just a whisper under my breath as I lean over the counter, watching the water rise.

"God, help me see her the way You do, not as the broken thing the world labeled her, but as the one You're rebuilding. Not the case file. Not the fear. Show me what's underneath. Teach me how to be gentle with what's still healing. Help me notice what's too quiet to say out loud. Help me see her without needing to fix her."

When I turn around, I don't expect her to be there, but she

is.

Standing just inside the kitchen, hoodie pulled over her head, socks on, arms wrapped around herself like she's still figuring out if she belongs in the warmth.

Her eyes meet mine; tired, but not wary.

"I came to get the tea," she says quietly, like she's stepping into something sacred without meaning to.

I step aside. "Morning."

A soft curl touches her lips. "Morning."

She reaches for the cup, holds it close to her chest like it's armor, then starts to turn away.

But pauses. Looks back.

"Do you do that every morning?" she asks, voice low, like she's afraid the question might change something between us.

I nod. "Yeah."

She tilts her head. "You always pray about me?"

There's no sarcasm. No edge. Just curiosity, raw and open.

"Yeah," I say gently. "I do."

"Why?"

"Because I want to understand you," I say. "And I figured the Jesus would know better than I do."

She lets out a breath that almost becomes a laugh quiet, caught somewhere between disbelief and agreement.

"Yeah," she murmurs, turning down the hallway. "He knows all."

She disappears down the hall, and the quiet she leaves behind hums through the house. I stand there longer than I should, tea cooling in my hand, the echo of her question still hanging in the air. *Do you always pray about me?*

By afternoon, the stillness feels heavier. I sit across from

Clay at the kitchen table, the glow from the security screens washing the room in pale blue. We're combing through storm-night footage again, routine, but necessary. The wind had knocked out the power for nearly twenty minutes that night, and even though everything rebooted clean, I need to see for myself.

Clay breaks the silence first. "Everything good out there this morning?"

I glance up. "Yeah. Why?"

He leans back, studying me. "Saw you by the fence line before sunrise. Looked like you found something."

My pulse tightens. "Just checking the patch. Nothing new."

"Hmm." He turns back to the monitor, but there's a flicker in his expression, something halfway between curiosity and challenge. "That section's always been a weak spot. You think someone's been near it?"

"Not sure," I say. "Could be wind. Could be nothing."

Clay nods slowly, eyes still on the footage. "Or it could be him."

The word *him* lands like static. Ricky. The ghost that never stops listening.

I don't respond right away. The footage scrolls by in slow, colorless frames, empty yard, still trees, no movement. But my mind isn't on the screens anymore. It's on her question from this morning, on that click in the phone line, on the way Clay knew exactly where I'd been standing.

When the last clip ends, I move to the window. The yard looks calm, the kind of calm that doesn't belong to peace but to warning.

"We need to tighten things," I say quietly.

Clay looks up. "Meaning?"

"Drills. Silent ones. If he's watching, I want to know how fast we disappear."

He nods once, and the conversation dies there. But even after he walks off, I stay by the glass, eyes tracing the tree line, heart beating in that slow, measured rhythm that only comes before a storm.

I fill the kettle again, pour two cups, one for her, one for me. It's a small ritual, steady in a world that keeps shifting under our feet. No conversation, no questions. Just the quiet passing of warmth between our hands. For now, that's the only kind of protection I can give.

I knocked gently on her door.

"Alana? Can you come out for a sec?"

She opened it a few seconds later, hair up, hoodie on, eyes tired but clear. No hesitation. Just quiet curiosity.

"Okay," she said.

I walked to the table and waited for her to sit, then slid the tea across. She took it without question, both hands wrapped around the cup.

"There's something I want to talk to you about," I said.

Her posture changed immediately. "What happened?"

"Nothing," I said quickly, reaching out before I could stop myself, but the moment my fingers brushed her arm, she flinched. Her reaction was immediate, shoulders locking, eyes searching for a threat that wasn't there. I froze, then stepped back, giving her the space she needed.

"Sorry. Nothing happened. I just think... we need to start running silent drills."

She didn't answer right away, just stared like she was scanning my face for cracks. Then her shoulders repositioned.

"So I passed the first round of your weird little trust test, huh?"

I smirked. "Something like that."

"Well, I'm only doing it if I get to pick the code word."

I raised an eyebrow. "Deal. But nothing ridiculous. If it's 'unicorn panic, ' I'm vetoing."

She let out a real laugh; sharp, sudden, honest. That wall she kept between us didn't crumble, but it cracked just enough to let something good through.

I leaned in slightly. "There's something else."

Her eyes met mine again, no walls this time. Just a flicker of caution.

"What's up?"

"I wanted to ask if you'd be open to talking to someone, no pressure, no agenda. Just space to breathe."

She went quiet. Then slowly shook her head. "Not yet."

"I get it," I said.

She looked down at her tea. "Thanks for asking, though. It's not that I don't want to. It's just... I just started trusting,"

She stopped.

Froze like the words slipped before she could catch them.

My chest tightened.

She didn't finish the sentence, but I heard what she couldn't say. And it landed heavier than any confession.

And I carried it like a gift.

"I understand," I said quietly. "When you're ready."

She nodded. "Is that everything?"

"Yeah," I said.

The door clicked shut, and I exhaled into the emptiness. Every conversation with her feels like standing on sacred ground, beautiful, fragile, one wrong move from collapse.

Later that night, after dinner and dishes were done, after

Clay had gone quiet and Alana had slipped into her room, I sat in the corner with my journal open, the lamp casting soft gold across the page. The air felt too still. Like the house was holding its breath.

My pen moved slow. My heart slower.

God, I wrote, *"be close to her."*
I paused.
*"Be close to me.*
*Be close to Clay.*
*Let this house be filled with You.*
*Let even the distance between us be holy ground."*
She's softening. Still guarded. Still unsure. But I see it, the light she keeps trying to hide. The strength You buried beneath the pain. The kind that survives.

My hand hovered. Then I wrote one final line.
*"You said You're close to the brokenhearted. Psalm 34:18. So be close, Lord. Be near. Be near to her. And don't let her slip away."*
I've learned that prayer isn't always an act of faith. Sometimes it's a form of surrender when control no longer works.

## Alana

The next night, the house was quiet, almost normal.

When I stepped out of my room, the smell of something warm and buttery drifted down the hallway. Franklin looked up from the stove when he heard my door creak open, that small half-smile already waiting like he'd been expecting me.

"Caught you right on time," he said. "Dinner's not burned. I'm calling it a win."

I blinked at the sight of him in an apron, sleeves rolled,

stirring a pot like he'd been doing it his whole life. "You cook now?"

He shrugged, reaching for a towel. "Miracles happen. Don't tell Clay, it'll ruin my reputation."

The joke tugged a laugh out of me before I could stop it. It felt strange in my chest, light, unfamiliar, the kind that made the walls feel a little less like they were closing in.

Then I saw Clay. He was leaning against the counter, arms crossed, watching us with that half-smirk that never reached his eyes.

"Didn't know we were playing house," he said. His tone was even, but something underneath it scraped.

"Just dinner," I murmured, forcing a polite smile.

He didn't answer. His gaze moved over me once, slow and deliberate, and my skin reacted before my mind could. A shiver ran down my arms, goosebumps rising beneath the sleeves. The air felt heavier, too close. My body knew the threat even when logic tried to argue it away.

Franklin caught the change in me. His voice stayed calm, steady. "Clay, grab the plates."

Clay hesitated, jaw tightening, but did it. The noise of ceramic hitting the counter was sharper than it needed to be.

When I looked back, Franklin was already at the table, serving the food. His eyes met mine, steady and sure, and the tension in my chest loosened. He offered a small, knowing smile, one of those quiet gestures that said *you're okay* without using words. I found myself smiling back before I even realized it.

The air lightened. My heartbeat slowed. It wasn't peace exactly, but it was close enough to remember what it felt like.

I slid into the chair across from him. The plate in front of me steamed softly between us, smelling like garlic and something safe.

"How's the pasta?" he asked, voice easy, almost teasing.

I blinked. The bite of linguine on my fork had been spinning for minutes. I hadn't even noticed.

His voice hadn't startled me. I just hadn't realized I'd drifted.

"This just made me think about my sister," I said before I could stop myself.

His fork paused mid-air, but he didn't speak. Just watched; steady, open.

"Pasta was our thing," I murmured, eyes on the plate. "We'd pull up YouTube videos and try to cook everything from scratch. Sauce, noodles, the works."

A breath of laughter slipped through. "Every single time, it tasted awful. Like... impressively bad."

The memory came back warm and real, the music, the garlic, the flour dusting the counters. My sister's laughter filled the kitchen, bright and reckless, like nothing in the world could touch us.

"We didn't care," I said. "It wasn't about the food. It was the dancing. The kitchen turning into our world for a few hours."

A beat.

"Even when Ricky was around... sometimes he'd blast music and let us take over the living room. Just watched us be silly like it didn't cost him anything."

The smile faded before I even noticed it was there. A cold knot settled behind my ribs. That familiar ache in the wake of something soft.

"I think we felt free in those moments," I whispered. "Even if we weren't."

The story spilled out of me before I could stop it, flour in the air, garlic burning at the edges, my sister's laughter cutting through it all like sunlight through smoke. For a moment, it didn't feel like a story. It felt like it was happening again.

When the memory finally loosened its hold, I blinked back into the room and realized how quiet it had gotten. Franklin hadn't said a word. He was closer than before, his chair turned slightly toward me, one arm resting across the back of mine. His hand wasn't gripping, just there, steady, anchoring, the kind of touch that didn't demand anything.

I hadn't even felt him move.

The warmth of his hand settled through me like calm water finding a cracked shore. My breath stuttered, caught somewhere between comfort and panic. No one had ever touched me like that, without control in it. Just care.

When I finally looked up, his eyes were already on me. Not studying. Seeing. And for a second, that look unraveled something I'd spent years stitching tight.

Before I could figure out what to do with the feeling, Clay's voice broke through.

"Well, this got real deep for a pasta night."

His tone carried that slick amusement that always scraped my nerves raw. The sound of it was enough to pull me back into myself. My shoulders tensed. The air that had felt safe a moment ago turned thin again.

I pushed the chair back too fast, the legs screeching across the tile. "I should,"

My voice caught. "I should go."

Franklin leaned forward, quiet but steady. "You're okay.

61

You don't have to run off."

The words were soft, not a command but an offering. He rose halfway, instinct pulling him closer before his hand found my arm. The touch was gentle, anchoring, but my body didn't know the difference between safety and danger yet. The same warmth that calmed me also burned.

I froze. "I don't know," I whispered, the words trembling out before I could stop them. "I don't know."

His brow furrowed, guilt flickering across his face as he drew his hand back. "It's alright," he said quietly. "Take your time."

The air between us tightened. Everything in me wanted to stay, to sit back down, to breathe, but survival has a louder voice than comfort. I stood, pulse wild, breath uneven.

"Thank you," I managed. My throat ached. "For dinner."

He didn't answer right away. His eyes softened, searching mine like he wanted to say more but knew better. "You're welcome," he said finally, and the quiet in his voice felt like a prayer.

I turned, taking a few uneven steps toward the hallway. The warmth of his hand still lingered on my skin, and I hated how much I missed it the second it was gone.

Behind me, his voice came low and careful. "Alana."

I stopped.

"Thank you," he said. "For letting me see her."

My chest tightened. He meant my sister, but it felt bigger than that. Like he was thanking me for letting him see *me*.

The air in the room changed again, too full, too real.

I didn't look back. If I did, I wouldn't have left.

The door shut behind me, and everything cracked.

The air went heavy, pressing against my skin until it burned.

My chest squeezed tight, and before I could stop it, the sob came out, quiet, broken, angry.

"No," I whispered. "No, no, no."

I started pacing, barefoot against the cold floor. Every breath came wrong, sharp around the edges. The memory of his hand on mine, steady, kind, made something inside me twist. I wasn't supposed to feel that. Not yet. Not when Ricky was still out there. Not when my sister was gone.

A tear slipped down before I could catch it. Then another.

I reached for my journal, flipping it open to a blank page. The pen trembled in my grip. I pressed it down hard, trying to write, but the words blurred before they formed. The ink bled and spread, messy and dark, like my thoughts refused to stay caged.

"I can't feel free," I whispered. "Not until he's in a cage. Not until she can rest."

My voice broke on the last word. Guilt climbed up my throat. "I shouldn't have laughed," I choked out. "She's dead, and I laughed."

The page tore before I even realized I was ripping it. Then another. And another. The sound filled the room, sharp, steady, grounding. By the time I stopped, little white scraps covered the floor like snow.

My breathing slowed. I grabbed a clean page and started to draw instead, lines, corners, doors. The house. The gate. The hall that creaks. Each line came cleaner, calmer, more deliberate. Not panic, preparation.

When I finished, I folded the paper tight and slid it under the mattress. Then I moved to the closet and pulled out the duffel bag.

Clothes first. Then the journal. My hands shook, but they

didn't stop.

The soft zip of the bag cut through the quiet.

And then, just as I reached for the last thing on the dresser, his voice slipped through the memory, low and steady,

*Thank you. For letting me see her.*

The words hit harder now. And I hated that some small, fragile part of me almost wanted to stay.

# 5

# Chapter 5

**Franklin**

I woke up feeling like I hadn't really slept. My body had rested, but my mind hadn't stopped turning over the night before, the way she'd shut down, the look on her face when she left the table. I kept asking myself if I'd pushed too far, if the story about her sister had cut deeper than I realized. The question followed me into the morning, settling heavy in my chest.

I sat at the edge of the bed, rubbed my palms down my face, tried to shake it off. The unease didn't fade; it just changed shape, quieter, heavier. I got up anyway, moving through the hallway on instinct, each step careful, like I didn't want to wake the house, or the guilt sitting in my ribs.

When I reached Alana's door, the air pivoted again. The door was cracked, not wide, just enough to make me pause. She never left it like that. Even when she slept, she kept the world closed out. I hesitated, the smallest knot tightening in my chest, and knocked gently, fingertips brushing the wood.

"Alana?"

My voice was soft but steady. I eased the door open a little wider and saw the bed, made, perfectly made. The blanket was smooth, not a single wrinkle, the kind of order that didn't belong to a restless night.

Something in my chest dropped. Not panic. Not yet. Just that quiet pull deep in the gut, the kind that tells you something's off before your mind can catch up.

The air in the room felt different, too still, like it was holding its breath. I stepped inside, scanned the corners, waiting to hear the rustle of sheets or a sigh from the hallway. Nothing.

A slow heat crawled up the back of my neck. My heartbeat started to thrum hard and uneven, and I found myself rubbing a hand down my face, like I could wipe the unease off.

I checked the kitchen next, hoping for a mug on the counter, a damp teabag in the sink, anything. But there was nothing. No sound. No trace of her. The silence pressed against me, thick and close, until I could feel the weight of it behind my ribs.

I moved to the back window, trying to shake off the chill working its way through my spine. Maybe she was outside. Maybe she'd needed air. Maybe.

But when I looked out, the yard was empty, empty except for Clay, leaning against the porch railing, phone pressed to his ear, laughing like it was any other morning.

I stepped out onto the porch. The air hit sharp and cold. My pulse hadn't slowed.

"Clay," I called, sharp enough to cut through his laugh.

He turned, phone still at his ear. "What now?"

"Have you seen Alana?"

He frowned, confused. "No. Why?"

"She's not in her room."

He shrugged. "Maybe she's in the bathroom."

"She's not."

He sighed like I was being dramatic. "Man, she's probably sitting somewhere trying to cool off. You know how she gets."

My jaw tightened. "How she gets?"

Clay glanced away. "I'm just saying,"

"Don't." My voice came out quiet but hard enough to stop him. "When did you last see her?"

He hesitated. "I don't know. I've been out here."

"Doing what?"

He lifted the phone a little. "Talking. You want a transcript or something?"

I ignored the jab. My eyes drifted past him, scanning the yard , not because I wanted to, but because the stillness out here felt wrong. Too neat. Too quiet.

And then I saw it.

The far corner of the fence , the same section I'd patched after the storm , looked off again. A board near the bottom had splintered outward, rough at the edge like someone forced their weight through.

My heart sank. The same kind of drop you feel when instinct turns into proof.

"Clay," I said slowly, pointing toward the fence. "Tell me you checked that section this morning."

He followed my gaze, brow furrowed. "What section?"

"That one." My tone sharpened. "The corner by the trees."

He squinted, shrugged. "Looks fine to me."

"It's not fine." My voice dropped lower. "It's broken."

The words hung between us for a second before they landed. Clay's face went pale.

"You told me you secured it," I said.

"I did!" he shot back, his voice cracking. "I swear I did,"

"Then how the hell did she get through?"

"I don't know, man! Maybe she panicked. Maybe she,"

"Stop." I took a step closer, the anger steady now. "You were supposed to be watching."

His expression twisted. "And you were supposed to keep her from running."

That last line hit harder than he probably meant it to. I stared at him until he looked away.

The words *"broken girl"* were still hanging in the air when I turned away from Clay.

My eyes caught on the fence again, the far corner I'd meant to reinforce and never did. The boards were split outward, the ground torn just enough to show the path she'd taken. A single thread from her hoodie clung to a nail.

The sight hit hard.

I moved toward it before my mind could catch up, boots cutting through wet grass. My pulse hammered against my ribs, heat rushing up my neck. I crouched, fingers brushing the splintered edge.

It wasn't just fear that came. It was guilt, old, familiar, and sharp.

Because I'd been here before.

For a moment the world shifted, the smell of gunpowder, the sound of sirens, Vanessa's hand slipping from mine before the light left her eyes. I blinked it back, but the image stayed, heavy as the morning air.

"Franklin." Clay's voice cracked through the haze, smaller now.

"Go inside," I said quietly.

He hesitated. "Look, I didn't,"

"Go."

He did.

I stayed there another beat, the fence staring back like a mirror I didn't want. My chest felt hollow. My throat burned. I pressed my palms together, breathing through the tremor until my hands steadied. Then I went inside and opened the surveillance feed.

There she was, Alana, moving with intent, calm and quiet, a duffel over her shoulder. The same look I'd seen on survivors right before they disappear for good.

And Clay, in the frame behind her, laughing into his phone. Never once looked back.

I didn't call him this time. I just stared until the time stamp blurred, then picked up my phone.

Claire answered on the second ring. "Franklin?"

"She's gone," I said. "Fence gave way. She slipped out before sunrise."

Silence. Then, steady: "Can you find her?"

"I will."

"I trust you," she said. "Don't sound alarms yet. If she's running, she's scared. She needs to be found, not chased."

"I understand."

"Franklin..." Her voice softened. "This isn't your fault."

But it felt like it was.

When the call ended, I stepped outside again. The yard looked the same, but nothing in me was. The trees stood still, the air thick and unmoving.

I closed my eyes.

*Lord, I don't know where she is. But You do. You saw her before I did. Loved her before she believed she could be loved. Lead me. Guide me. Keep her unseen until I find her. Keep her safe until I can.*

The words came out low, not rehearsed, just breath, just truth.

I opened my eyes and looked back at the broken fence.

She wasn't too far gone to come back.

But I couldn't lose another one. Not again.

**Alana**

The moment I saw the split in the fence, my body moved before I even decided to. It wasn't fear this time, it was release, a quiet knowing that whatever waited beyond that opening couldn't be worse than staying where I was. For a second, it felt like something holy had parted just enough for me to slip through, like freedom had been waiting on the other side the whole time.

I didn't grab a jacket. I didn't think twice. I just ran, and the air met me with a cold so sharp it made me gasp. But it wasn't a bad kind of cold, it was clean, alive, full of promise. The kind that wakes you up from the inside out.

The forest stretched wide around me, branches brushing my shoulders as the ground shifted beneath my feet, and for once the sound of my heartbeat didn't scare me. It matched the rhythm of the earth, steady and certain, like I was supposed to be here. The deeper I went, the lighter I felt. Every breath came easier, every step unchained something in me I didn't know was still locked.

I wasn't thinking about who might notice or who might care. I wasn't looking back for anyone to follow. The quiet didn't feel like danger anymore, it felt like peace.

A laugh slipped out of me, soft at first, then full, spilling into the open air before I could stop it. It surprised me, the sound of it, how foreign it felt. I couldn't remember the last time I'd laughed without waiting for something to go wrong.

For the first time in years, my body didn't belong to fear. The trees didn't feel like walls, and the wind didn't sound like warning. I was just moving, blood warm, lungs burning, free in the only way I'd ever understood it.

And for that brief stretch of morning, before the world remembered my name, freedom didn't hurt. It felt like home.

They thought they were watching me, keeping me safe, reading every twitch like they understood the way I moved, but I was watching them too. I memorized the rhythm of their days: the scrape of Franklin's chair at midnight, the soft hum of the kettle before dawn, the porch boards groaning when Clay paced with his phone pressed to his ear.

He always made the same slow loop, talking low into the receiver like the night itself was listening. I'd lie there counting the seconds between his steps, tracing them in my mind until they matched the sound of his laugh. That was my cue.

Franklin fought sleep like it was sin, promising himself he'd stay awake until his eyes betrayed him. The moment his head dipped, the house moved into silence. That was my window.

I'd rehearsed it a hundred times, unlatch the window in my room so the air moved just enough to keep the hinges quiet, slide the back latch without rattling the frame, cross the hall slow in case the camera light blinked. Every move had its place. Every sound had to belong.

The only part I didn't plan was Franklin himself.

When I passed his room, I meant to keep going, but I stopped. He was asleep, fully asleep, face softened, shoul-

71

ders unguarded, the constant vigilance gone. The lamplight brushed over him, catching the Bible on the nightstand, its spine cracked and pages frayed from use. One verse glowed beneath the light: *The Lord is close to the brokenhearted.*

Something in me twisted. Not pain exactly, but recognition.

I should've kept walking. I told myself I would. But I lingered one heartbeat too long, watching the rise and fall of his chest, realizing how human he looked when he wasn't carrying everyone else's weight.

If he woke up, he'd stop me, not to control, but to care. And that was worse. Care makes you hesitate. Care makes you stay.

Then Clay's laugh floated from outside, low, careless, the sound of someone who never worried about being followed. That was my sign.

I moved. Quiet, certain, down the hallway and out the side door. The boards sighed under my feet, but his voice covered the noise.

The night air wrapped around me, cool and clean. I crouched low at the corner of the porch, watching Clay's outline against the light. When he leaned back to stretch, I slipped past, each step landing in rhythm with the wind.

The fence waited in the distance, that rough corner where the wood had splintered after the storm, the same spot Franklin said he'd fix. Moonlight caught the edges, silvering the path like an invitation.

I slid through, the scrape of wood against my sleeve barely a whisper.

And then I was running, arms pumping, lungs burning, the world unfolding wide and open. Not because someone was chasing me, but because for once, no one was.

I wasn't being handled. I wasn't being studied or saved.

I was gone.

At first, the woods felt alive, branches bending with my breath, the ground rising to meet my steps like it wanted me to keep going. The rush of escape carried me forward, heart steady in the rhythm of running. But after a while, the air changed. The adrenaline that had pushed me started to thin, replaced by something heavier, slower, too aware of its own echo.

The trees around me had grown dense and unfriendly, their trunks crowding close, their shadows bleeding into one another until direction stopped meaning anything. My legs burned. My throat ached. The forest floor, once solid beneath my feet, began to feel like water, soft, shifting, without anchor.

I stopped to listen. Nothing. No birds, no wind, no sound of life. Just a silence that pressed against my ears until it felt alive on its own. The kind of silence that hides things.

I turned slowly, scanning the dark in every direction. Everything looked the same, branches hooked like ribs, the faint shimmer of fog curling low to the ground. I tried to retrace steps I hadn't actually planned, but the trail was gone, swallowed whole.

That's when I felt it, a pull deep in my chest, quiet at first, then tightening, steady. Fear doesn't always come loud; sometimes it sneaks in like recognition.

A sound broke it. Small. Close. A footstep sinking into damp soil. Then another.

Not frantic. Not careless. Measured.

I froze, breath locked tight in my lungs. My pulse thundered so loud it felt like it might give me away. Another step. The dry snap of a branch. Something, or someone, moving with the slow certainty of someone who knew the ground beneath them.

I dropped into a crouch, easing behind a thick veil of brush. The dirt was cold against my palms, seeping through the skin. Every muscle screamed to move, to run, but something deeper told me not to. Movement makes noise. Noise makes you seen.

Then came the voice.

"Alana."

Soft. Drawn out. Almost tender. Like it had been practiced.

My name didn't belong here.

The sound slid through the air and settled behind me, low and deliberate, not a shout, not a whisper, but the exact tone someone uses when they already know you can hear them.

It wasn't Franklin. His voice carried steadiness, warmth.

It wasn't Clay. His words always cut sharp, fast.

This voice was different, too calm, too patient. Like a memory wearing someone else's face.

My body reacted before thought could form. I pressed lower into the dirt, arms trembling, heart pounding against the earth. The leaves beneath me crackled, loud enough to make me flinch. I covered my mouth, willing my breath to quiet.

Another step. Closer this time. Then stillness.

The woods were listening.

I had prayed for freedom, begged for a way out, but now that I was here, surrounded by dark that seemed to breathe, it didn't feel like freedom. It felt like something waiting.

The voice came again, quieter, almost kind.

"Alana... you don't have to hide."

And that was when I knew, this wasn't chance.

Someone had been watching.

Someone had been waiting for me to run.

I couldn't breathe.

Not properly. Not fully. My lungs seized like they were being gripped from the inside, every inhale catching halfway, every exhale sounding like a sob I couldn't stop. The ground felt cold beneath my palms, sharp with tiny rocks and twigs digging into my skin, but I didn't move. I couldn't. I curled smaller behind the brush, as if I could disappear into the roots if I just held still long enough.

I wasn't supposed to be out here. I wasn't supposed to feel this exposed. I had asked for escape. I had run for it like it would save me. And now, with the trees watching and the voice echoing in my bones, I realized I had stripped away the only layer of protection I'd been given.

I had left safety behind.

And for what?

Tears hit my hands before I even felt them coming, hot, sharp, and shaking so hard it blurred my vision. My knees buckled, and I dropped into the dirt like the earth itself was the only thing willing to hold me. I pressed my forehead into the cold ground, breath tearing out of me in broken, uneven pulls. If I bowed low enough, maybe the terror would pass over me. Maybe whatever was hunting me wouldn't hear the way my heart was slamming against my ribs like it wanted to escape.

My mouth opened before I even knew I was speaking. The words ripped out of me, raw and desperate, like something buried deep finally clawed its way free.

"Lord... if You're real, if You're actually out here like they keep saying, then please..."

My voice broke. I curled my fingers into the earth until dirt packed beneath my nails, anything to keep me from floating away on the panic crushing my chest.

"They say You're close to the brokenhearted. Well, I'm broken. I'm so broken, and I don't know what I just did. I thought I could do this, but I can't. Not like this. I don't want to die out here. I don't want to go back to what You pulled me from. I just…"

A sob cracked through me, sharp enough to hurt.

"I just want to go home. And I don't even know what 'home' means anymore, but I know I don't want to be alone. So if You meant what You said in that Bible, if that verse by Franklin's bed wasn't just some old underlined promise meant for someone else, then hear me."

I lifted my head, vision trembling, breath stuttering like I couldn't pull enough air.

"Help me find my way back to him."

Silence swallowed the words. My whole body was shaking.

"I need him," I whispered.

I stayed there a long time, folded into the brush, heart pounding so violently it felt like a warning. The woods around me were still, too still. The kind of quiet that makes you wonder if you've gone deaf, or if the world is holding its breath… waiting. Watching. Deciding.

Then… something shifted.

It wasn't loud. It wasn't even clear. Just a small stirring, the faintest sound of leaves shifting though the air was dead still, like a whisper pressed deep inside my chest, telling me to move.

So I did.

I didn't think. I didn't plan.

I just moved.

Not because I was brave. Not because I wasn't still terrified.

But because I couldn't stay crouched in the dirt, praying and pretending I wasn't made to survive. I stood on legs that trembled and swayed, brushing the leaves from my arms, dirt clinging to the backs of my hands. My breath was still shallow, my body still caught in that wild edge between fight and freeze. But something in me had decided, if I got out, I was going to fight my way back.

The woods looked different now, darker somehow, every branch curling as if it wanted to grab me, every crack in the bark feeling like a warning, and still I moved, one foot forward, then the next, listening to everything around me.

I didn't know what direction I was heading in. I didn't know if I was even walking the same path I came from. But I remembered something Franklin had said once, soft and almost offhand while he was watching the trees outside the window: "Sometimes, the body remembers what the heart forgets."

So I let my body lead, moving through the trees with a kind of instinct I didn't know I had, my breath tightening as the forest pressed in around me. The woods felt alive in a way that made every sound feel personal, like the branches were shifting because of me, like the air carried whispers meant for my ears alone, like something unseen was trailing the path I'd just taken.

A rustle above me sent a sharp tremor through my chest, followed by the slow drag of the wind weaving itself through the tall pines, and even though I kept telling myself it was just the forest being a forest, the thought didn't settle. It only sank deeper, reminding me that the danger out here wasn't imagined. It was breathing somewhere behind me, moving with a patience that made the hairs on my arms stand up.

Still, I kept going.

I pushed forward even when the shadows shifted like they were sliding into new shapes, even when the trees felt too close, as if they were guiding me somewhere I didn't want to discover. My steps weren't confident, but each one carried a thread of something I didn't expect to feel. It wasn't courage and it wasn't certainty, but it kept me upright, kept me moving, kept me from dropping to my knees all over again.

Somewhere between the panic tightening my chest and the shaking in my legs, I realized I still didn't know what I believed; the prayer I whispered felt paper-thin against the darkness pressing in on me, and the woods around me moved with a purpose that made every sound feel like a warning. I kept running until a branch caught my sleeve and yanked me off balance, sending me hard into the ground as my arm scraped across the dirt and a sharp sting shot up my side. For a moment I stayed there, breath trembling, the cold earth pressing into my palms and reminding me just how small I was in all this space that didn't want me in it.

Then I heard it, something moving through the trees behind me, slow and deliberate, each step landing with a weight that made my skin tighten. My voice cracked before I could stop it, the words slipping out in a trembling plea as I forced myself upright, my legs shaking beneath me. "Please... please... find me... find me..." And when those footsteps drew closer, steady and certain, fear wrapped around my ribs until I could barely breathe. "Franklin," I whispered into the dark, praying it was him and terrified it wasn't. "Franklin, I need you."

# 6

# Chapter 6

**Franklin**

I stayed on the porch, the phone still in my hand, the silence stretching long and thin around me. The dark pressed against the edge of the trees, thick and unmoving. Somewhere out there, she was already gone.

So I did the only thing I could when I didn't know where else to begin.

I prayed.

Not out loud. Just a whisper buried deep in my chest.

*Lord, I don't know where she is. I don't know what she's thinking. But You do. You always have. You saw her before I did. Loved her before she believed she could be loved. So guide me. Lead my steps. Help me find her before the world does. Before Ricky does. She's not just another witness. She's more than that. Please, don't let her disappear.*

I opened my eyes and scanned the tree line. She had to be close. The wind hadn't picked up yet. Her footprints might still hold. If I moved fast, I could catch her trail before the woods swallowed it. I hadn't heard a car. No alarms tripped. If this was Ricky... he'd either gotten close without breaking a single thread or he'd already been here. Maybe even watching. Maybe Clay hadn't just missed something. Maybe he'd let something in.

I grabbed my jacket and stepped off the porch, crossing the backyard with careful urgency. The gate hung wide open, like a gaping mouth daring me to follow. My boots hit the earth hard as I entered the woods, flashlight angled low. I followed the trampled path of leaves and faint depressions in the dirt, scanning for any sign she'd doubled back or fallen.

She hadn't. She was moving with purpose.

But so was something else.

I should've pushed her harder to take the counselor. I should've caught the way her hands kept shaking the night before. I was so focused on giving her space that I forgot how silence can be a warning too.

The longer I walked, the heavier the silence grew. I slowed at a break in the trees, crouching near a bent patch of brush. She'd come through here, fast, reckless, but something about the pattern was wrong. The branches weren't broken in a clean line; they were crushed inward, trampled from two angles.

Not just one set of movements.

I angled my flashlight lower and saw it, a partial print beside hers, pressed deep into the damp soil. Larger. Wider. Heavy enough to sink.

Not Clay's. Not mine.

I knew that tread. The edge of the heel dragged slightly left, like the man who wore it favored one leg. The same pattern I'd seen in the surveillance footage months ago. The same print outside the shelter where she'd been hiding.

My pulse kicked.

Ricky.

He wasn't guessing anymore. He'd been close enough to find her trail. Close enough to know the exact moment she'd run.

And if she'd run, it meant someone told him she would.

He's not moving blind, I thought. Someone's feeding him information.

The realization hit hard, cold and clear.

This wasn't a random leak or bad intel. Someone had planned this, timed it down to the moment she'd break.

My mind circled back to Clay. He swore he hadn't seen her leave, but he'd been right there on the porch, phone in hand, the gate hanging open. Laughing like a man with nothing to lose.

The image twisted in my chest. He'd been too calm. Too still. Too quiet for someone who'd just let a woman slip past him in the middle of the night.

A branch cracked behind me. I spun toward the sound, flashlight slicing through the dark, nothing there. Just wind, cold and whispering through the trees.

Still, I kept moving.

I wasn't going to let her vanish on my watch. Not again.

The woods pressed closer with every step. Trees rose like sentries. The air felt off, charged in a way I couldn't place. I kept walking, sweeping the flashlight in slow arcs, heart pounding against my ribs in double time.

Claire's voice echoed in the back of my mind

*"She probably got overwhelmed... It doesn't make it your fault."*

But the way she'd said it... the way she hadn't asked a single tactical question... it struck me now as rehearsed. Too polished.

Claire was calm. Too calm. Like she already knew more than she said.

I moved faster.

I remembered the way Alana held the tea yesterday, like it was the only thing she trusted. Like she was trying to believe in something soft again. I should've known that kind of quiet never lasts.

Then I saw it ahead of me, a deeper break in the leaves, a stretch of earth pressed down as if someone had fallen or tried to hide. I moved closer and crouched, running my fingers through the dirt. It was still warm, the heat faint but certain, like the echo of a heartbeat that hadn't fully faded.

She was close. I could feel it.

The air around me thickened, weighted with that uneasy quiet that only comes before something shifts. I rose carefully, sweeping the light in a slow arc across the trees. Everything looked still, but it didn't feel still. Even the shadows seemed to be waiting.

I took one more step forward and heard it, the sharp crack of a branch behind me. Not the light snap of wind or an animal brushing past. This was heavier, deliberate, like someone choosing their moment.

My body went rigid, every muscle braced as I turned toward the sound, the flashlight trembling just slightly in my hand. The dark seemed to move all at once, a blur at the edge of my vision. I barely had time to register the motion before something struck the side of my head.

Pain burst behind my eyes, bright and disorienting, the world tilting hard as my knees hit the ground. The smell of dirt and iron filled the air. My pulse roared in my ears, drowning out everything else as the forest tilted sideways around me.

And then, just like that, the light slipped out. Everything went dark.

**Alana**

Branches whipped against my arms as I pushed through the trees, breath ragged, every step pulled forward by something I didn't understand. Then I saw him, Franklin, crumpled in the dirt, as if the woods had spat him out and left him to die. One arm was twisted beneath him, the other slack across his chest. Blood ran down the side of his head, not a scrape, but a deep, terrible wound, soaking into his hair, darkened by the shadows clinging to us both.

This wasn't how I imagined Him answering.

But maybe it was still an answer.

My knees buckled.

I dropped beside him, hands hovering over his body like I was afraid to touch him. "Franklin," I whispered, and when he didn't move, my voice cracked.

"Franklin, wake up. Please."

I shook him gently, then harder, panic rushing like static beneath my skin.

"Don't do this. Don't do this to me. Please, you have to wake up,"

His eyelids flickered.

A sound, low and rough, pushed past his lips.

"Thank You, God," I choked out, brushing the hair from his forehead with trembling fingers. "You're here. You found me."

He blinked, eyes struggling to focus. "Alana..."

"I'm here. I'm right here."

His mouth moved like he wanted to say more, but his body gave out again. His head slumped, and I caught him just in time.

"No, no, no. Stay with me. I can't do this without you." I pressed my forehead to his. "Please. I need you to wake up."

The sound of footsteps broke through the quiet, fast, uneven, crushing leaves in a rhythm that didn't belong to the woods. My pulse surged as every instinct in me went tight. For a split second, I was sure it was Ricky. The breath locked in my chest, and I pressed my back against the nearest tree, fingers digging into the bark until it bit at my skin.

"Please, God," I whispered, barely able to hear my own voice. "Don't let it be him."

The branches ahead shifted, and a figure pushed through the brush. For a heartbeat, I couldn't move. Then the shape came into focus.

Clay.

Relief hit like air after drowning, sharp and dizzying, but it twisted just as quickly into something else. But his expression didn't match mine. No panic. No confusion. Just that same unreadable calm that made my stomach twist.

"Clay?"

He startled, hand twitching toward his holster until he recognized me.

"Yeah," he said tightly. "I tracked his signal. Is he alive?"

His voice didn't crack. No panic, no shock, just calculation.

I nodded, barely. "He's breathing. But he's not, he's not okay."

Clay knelt beside Franklin, checking his pulse with practiced fingers.

"What happened?"

"I don't know," I said, my voice thinner than I meant it to be.

"I thought I heard your voice... but it was off. Like someone trying to sound like you." I shook my head.

"I found him like this."

Even saying it out loud made the lie taste bitter, like guilt had its own flavor. Clay looked at me a second too long.

"You sure you didn't see who it was?"

"No," I snapped.

He didn't push, but I saw the doubt in his eyes. Just moved to lift Franklin under the arms.

"Help me get him up. We have to move."

I scrambled to the other side, trying to take some of the weight. Franklin groaned but didn't wake. My arms burned as we lifted him together, every step toward the car dragging the guilt deeper, because this was my doing, and now he was paying for it.

This was my doing. And now he was paying for it.

The path back was uneven, slick with mud and pine needles, every step a fight. Clay carried most of Franklin's weight, but I stayed close, one arm wrapped around his waist, the other gripping his jacket like if I let go, he'd disappear. His blood had started to dry near his hairline, but the sweat and heat pouring off him made everything feel worse. Real. Urgent.

By the time we reached the car, my legs were numb and my throat burned with unshed tears. We heaved Franklin into the backseat, his head lolling against the cushion. He muttered something, voice so faint it barely reached me.

"Shh," I whispered, climbing in beside him. "It's okay. You're safe now. Just stay still."

Clay slammed the door, circled to the front, and peeled out onto the road. The engine roared, gravel spitting behind us as the trees became shadows in the mirror.

In the backseat, I cradled Franklin's head in my lap. His skin was clammy, pale beneath the streaks of dirt and dried blood. I ran my fingers through his hair, brushing it gently away from his forehead, whispering broken prayers.

"I'm so sorry," I murmured. "This shouldn't have happened. You shouldn't have come after me."

Claire's voice crackled through Clay's speaker, rapid-fire questions I couldn't answer. I tuned her out, eyes locked on the man bleeding into my hands.

I'd been so sure running was the only way to survive. But now, with Franklin unconscious and covered in blood, I wasn't sure of anything, except the weight of what I'd done.

The tires screeched as Clay pulled into the driveway, and the second the car stopped, we were moving again me and Clay both scrambling to lift Franklin out of the backseat. His body sagged between us, heavy with pain and heat, and every groan he made felt like a punch to the gut.

We got him inside, eased him down onto the couch. His head lolled to the side. His skin was too pale. I hovered close, brushing his hair back again, whispering things I hoped would keep him tethered.

"You're okay," I told him softly. "Help is coming."

His eyes fluttered open, unfocused, dazed. And then...

His lips trembled once, as if searching for a name he'd buried long ago.

"Vanessa," he whispered.

My breath caught.

He wasn't looking at me. He wasn't really seeing me at all.

That name, whoever she was, poured out of him like a wound that had never been closed.

"I'm so sorry," he said again, softer this time.

"So sorry."

I pulled my hands back slowly, like they'd been burned.

*Vanessa.*

The name sat between us like a secret I wasn't supposed to hear, and suddenly everything in me went still.

Was she someone he lost?

Was she someone he loved?

Before I could ask, before I could even breathe; Clay came back into the room.

"Medics are ten minutes out," he said sharply. "Don't open the door for anyone."

I nodded, but I didn't say a word.

Because Franklin had just broken something in me that I hadn't even realized was whole.

The knock came quiet at first. Just a tap. Barely there. But my body locked up like it had been slammed into a wall. I didn't move. Didn't blink. Didn't breathe right. My chest tightened, my fingers curled into fists, and my knees started to tremble. It was like my bones remembered something my mind hadn't caught up to yet. Like I'd slipped into a memory that wasn't mine to relive, but still owned me.

Another knock, louder this time. Rhythmic. Measured. Each one heavier than the last.

I couldn't speak. Couldn't call for Clay. My lips parted but no sound came out. Panic clawed up my throat like smoke in a burning room. I stood frozen, staring at the door, helpless against the fear dragging me under.

Then, his voice. Low. Sharp. Sober.

"Didn't I tell you to come get me if you heard a knock?" Clay yelled.

Like a tether, his voice pulled me back just enough to breathe. He stepped past me, slow and deliberate, hand resting near his weapon as he moved toward the window. A pause. A breath. Then his shoulders eased.

He opened the door.

And there she was.

A Black woman, strong and warm, dark braids framing her face like armor and grace all at once. She didn't hesitate. She didn't ask. She walked straight in like this wasn't the end, like she had come to fight for life and nothing less. Claire.

Behind her, two medics followed, clinical and steady, while I stood in the hallway, half in the past, half in the now, watching them try to save a man I couldn't stop hurting. And something inside me cracked.

Quietly, I turned. Walked down the hall. Shut the door behind me. I slid to the floor, arms wrapped around my knees, and rocked.

Because I didn't know what else to do.

The sirens faded, but their echo stayed in my chest. I could still hear the rush of movement, the scuff of boots across hardwood, Claire's voice directing the medics with calm urgency. I should've stayed. I should've helped. But I couldn't. My body had taken me here like it was trying to protect me from witnessing another goodbye.

I rocked gently against the wall, arms tight around my legs, forehead pressed to my knees. The air felt thick, heavy with everything I hadn't said, and something older started to surface. A memory trying to claw its way back. Guilt, fear, grief, it all sat with me in that small room like ghosts I couldn't evict. My chest ached in a way that wasn't just about what happened tonight. It was about what had happened years ago. About what was still happening inside me.

Because this wasn't just about Franklin. This wasn't just about tonight.

This was about my sister.

The lights. The screaming. The way they took her away on a stretcher and no one ever looked back. That night had lived in me for so long, I'd forgotten what it felt like to let it rise again. But grief has its own memory, and tonight, it brought everything back without warning. I was that girl again; alone, afraid, blaming herself for something she couldn't stop.

And maybe that's why I didn't hear it at first.

The voice.

Faint.

Struggling.

"...Alana?"

My head snapped up. My heart slammed into my ribs. I scrambled to my feet, already reaching for the door.

Because somehow, against everything I feared and prayed, Franklin's voice broke through the silence. He was awake.

# 7

# Chapter 7

**Franklin**

It's been a few days since that night, but the memory still clings to me like smoke, thick, choking, impossible to wash off. Every time I think I've scrubbed it away, it seeps back in through the cracks. I move through the house quietly, checking doors, counting locks, listening for sounds that don't belong.

The silence here isn't peaceful. It's wrong. Heavy. Like the whole place is holding its breath. Even the air feels weighed down, damp and close, brushing against my skin when I pass through the hallway. Last night, a car slowed outside, tires crunching gravel, engine idling just long enough to raise every hair on my neck, before it finally rolled away.

Each morning, before my eyes even open, I reach for the back of my head. The knot's still there. A reminder of how close we came. How close I came to losing her.

They said I wasn't hurt bad enough for a hospital, and that's its own kind of mercy. Hospitals mean questions. Forms.

Names. Too much light. And we can't risk that. Not with Ricky still out there.

So I keep to the edges of this house, where the shadows hold. I pace sometimes, stop at the window, watch the road fade into the trees. The clock ticks. The floor creaks. Every sound feels louder now, like the quiet is punishing me for surviving.

And when I can't stand it anymore, I sit back down and try to piece it all together. What I saw. What I missed. What it cost. But the harder I try, the more it slips through, fragments dissolving like static. Some things just don't come back.

Claire stepped up fast; eyes open, sharp, steady. She's helped Clay keep things tight, made sure no one sees more than they should. But something's shifted between them. Small, subtle things. The way they pause around each other, or avoid too much eye contact. It's not loud, but it's there. Alana sees it too. I can tell by the way she watches them, like she's trying to figure out if she caused it, or if it was always waiting underneath.

But she's here. That's what matters. God got me to her in time. She's not running anymore. Not looking over her shoulder. She's tucked away now, in this fragile hush of shadows and locked doors. And still, there's a tension in her frame that hasn't gone away. A tremble in her hands she pretends not to notice. Sometimes I catch her staring at the front door like she's bracing for it to rattle under a knock.

She's safe.

But she's not free.

Not yet.

We all know we can't stay here much longer. The escape, the noise, the trail we left, it was too loud. Too messy. Every day we linger raises the chance that someone finds us. The only thing holding us here is me.

And I hate it.

Every morning, I lie there, guilt crawling beneath my skin. I keep replaying the moment she ran barefoot, terrified and me, too slow to stop it. I was supposed to protect her. I didn't.

Even when Clay tries to remind me she's safe, or when Claire tells me I did enough, it doesn't touch the part of me that knows better.

I should've done more. I should've been more.

As soon as I'm able to stand, I start making tea. It's become routine. Something I can control. I make two cups. Always two. One for me, one for her. Even though she hasn't touched hers in days. Alana used to sit across from me, hands curled around the mug like it anchored her. I clung to that, something normal, something steady. But now... she barely looks at me. Sometimes she takes the tea and walks right past me. Other times, she doesn't come at all. I know it's not just what happened that night.

It's me.

She's avoiding me and honestly, I get it.

When she came back she was shaken, exhausted, and different; I saw it in her eyes. Something broke between us.

The guilt squeezes around my ribs, sharp and tight. If I hadn't been found in time... if Clay hadn't shown up, she would've been alone. Again. I hate that she had to save me, when it should've been the other way around.

Claire sat me down a few nights ago and told me I'd been saying a name in my sleep.

*Vanessa.*

As soon as she said it, my stomach sank. I didn't have to ask who else might've heard it. Alana's been different since that night; not just distant, but guarded. And if she heard that name... I can't blame her.

And just like that, it all came back.

Vanessa was sixteen. Just a kid. I found her during a sting operation, tucked behind a nightclub, knees pulled to her chest, eyes sharp. Not afraid like most. Just watching. Quiet. Tired.

She gave me her name in a whisper and a thank you. And over time, I saw who she really was. She smiled sometimes; small, fleeting things like she didn't want to be caught. She talked about her mother with this aching kind of hope. Said she used to sit at the window after school, waiting to see her mom's car pull up. Said she prayed every night to find her again.

She didn't want revenge. Just wanted to go home.

And me? Well I wanted to give her that. God knows I did.

I checked in on her more than I should have. Brought her breakfast. Tea at night. Told myself it was part of the job. It wasn't. The truth was, I'd been walking through my own dark stretch back then, one of those seasons where the days blur and the work starts to hollow you out. And somehow, this girl with nothing left still carried light in her. She laughed soft, asked questions that didn't have anything to do with pain. There was an innocence about her, not naïve but pure, like she still believed the world could be good again.

That light... it caught me off guard. It reminded me what it felt like to want to protect something worth keeping alive.

And I needed that.

I swore I'd get her home. Promised her we were almost there.

When I found her mother, someone who'd never stopped

searching; I thought I had the ending she deserved. I wanted it to be perfect. The door opening. Their reunion. The kind of moment that heals something.

I left for less than an hour. Told Vanessa to rest, to lock the door, to keep the lights low until I got back. When we returned, the air inside the apartment was wrong. Too still. Too heavy. The smell hit first, metal and salt. Then the sight. Blood covered the walls in wild, senseless strokes. The mattress was torn open, stuffing spilling like snow across the floor. The curtains hung in ribbons, swaying in the draft from a shattered window.

She was in the corner, crumpled where she'd fallen, her eyes still open as if she'd been waiting for me to come back. Her legs were twisted beneath her, her small frame folded in on itself. And beside her was a single sheet of paper, the handwriting sharp enough to cut through the room:

**Too slow, detective. Try again.**

My body went cold. I couldn't move. Couldn't speak. But her mother did. She dropped to her knees beside her daughter and screamed, an animal sound that split the air and carved itself into me.

"My baby! My baby! I almost had my baby!"

Those words never stopped. They still echo in the quiet parts of my day, in the scrape of a razor, the rhythm of prayer, the breath I can't steady. I told Vanessa I'd protect her. She believed me. And I left her. That's what I see when I close my eyes, the blood, the note, her mother's scream, all of it etched into the part of me that refuses to heal.

I made a promise that day, a vow over Vanessa's body that I would never let Ricky destroy another life. No girl under my watch would ever end like her. But this time, it was too close.

I let my guard down. Trusted the quiet too much. Told myself she was safe, that we had time. I let myself breathe for one moment, and in that breath, she was gone. That's how he moves, quiet, deliberate. He waits for you to exhale, and then he takes everything.

I still see it when I close my eyes. The moment I woke up, felt the cold emptiness in the house, knew before I even reached her room that she was gone. That collapse inside my chest. That guilt that doesn't fade no matter how many times I pray.

Now every morning begins the same way. I make the tea before the sun's even up. I don't think about it anymore; it's muscle memory. One cup for me, one for her. I knock on her door, soft and careful, the way you do with someone whose world has already fallen apart. I tell her it's ready. Then I wait, five minutes, sometimes ten. She never opens the door while I'm there. She waits until my footsteps fade down the hall, until she hears my door close, and only then does she come for the cup.

She moves quietly, almost like a ghost. Doesn't look at me. Doesn't speak. Just takes the tea and disappears back into her room. And I know that feeling too well, the way the air shifts when someone stops trusting you. The distance that grows without a word. I can feel it widening between us, day by day, and I don't know how to stop it.

Claire notices, too. One morning, she sits beside me on the couch, nudging her shoulder lightly against mine. Steam curls from our mugs like smoke from something long extinguished.

Claire nudges my shoulder lightly, the couch sinking between us as steam curls from our mugs. "She'll come around," she says, her tone soft but sure.

I don't look up.

"I don't blame her."

The crack in my voice betrays more than I want it to.

"Franklin," Claire murmurs, letting out a breath.

"It's not your fault."

I let out a humorless laugh, eyes fixed on the cup in my hands.

"Isn't it?"

She turns toward me, voice steady.

"These things happen. She's here now. She's safe. That's what matters."

I nod, but it feels hollow. The words should land. They don't. Something about her calm scratches at me, the way she knows what to say before I ask.

"Where's Clay?" I ask, searching for something else to focus on.

"He had to handle some personal things," she says, taking a sip from her mug.

Too convenient. Too quick. After what happened in the woods, I expected fallout. Instead, he vanished, like someone cleared the board before I could make a move.

"He'll be gone about two weeks," she adds, arching a brow, teasing.

"So it's just you and me. Try not to lose it."

I manage a faint smile.

"No promises."

She laughs quietly, but the sound fades.

"I think it'll be good. Just give her space. Help her rebuild some ground beneath her."

I nod, slower this time.

"You talked to her?"

Claire hesitates, then nods.

"A little. I'm letting her open up when she's ready. Just reminding her that running wasn't wrong, it was survival. She was scared. Anyone would be."

Her words hang in the air. They're right, but they don't sit right. Something in my chest twists. That same old ache, the one that comes from promises I couldn't keep. The ones that left blood on my hands.

The heat rises before I can stop it. My jaw tightens, and I set the mug down too hard. The crack of ceramic against wood cuts through the quiet. "Yeah," I mutter. "I know."

But I don't. Not the way she means. I want to. I want to believe that Alana being here is enough. That what matters is what comes next. But every time I close my eyes, I see Vanessa's face. I hear her mother's scream. I feel the cold weight of that same panic pressing down, reminding me how fast everything can unravel.

If I'd just stayed awake. If I'd seen the signs. If I hadn't trusted the quiet for one second, maybe she wouldn't have had to run. Maybe she'd still trust me. Maybe I wouldn't feel like I'm losing her all over again.

My hands drag through my hair until my scalp burns, trying to pull myself back to the present. It doesn't work. The guilt sits too deep, carved in. So I bow my head, elbows on my knees, and whisper the only thing left in me.

A prayer I'm not sure I still deserve to pray.

**Alana**

This past week, I've felt myself settling into a version of myself I barely recognize. Not healed. Not stable. But present. A little more grounded. A little less like I'm floating just outside my own skin. Maybe it's because Clay hasn't been around. Maybe it's because Claire has. Or maybe it's just that nothing has exploded in the last few days, and my body doesn't know if it can trust that peace long enough to unclench. I'm still waiting for the next hit. Still waiting for the next betrayal. But there's something quieter underneath it all, like a bruise that finally started turning pale.

Still, even with the small steps forward, I can't look at Detective Franklin. Every time I hear him in another room, something in me twists, fear mixed with guilt, a sharp ache that reminds me he's walking around with wounds that wouldn't exist if I hadn't run. I see the way he breathes too carefully. The way he hides the wince when something pulls wrong. The way he tries to pretend nothing hurts. And every bit of it feels like a debt I can't pay back. I can't let myself be the reason someone gets hurt again. I can't see another person bleed because they cared.

So I avoid him. Not because I want to, but because I don't trust myself with the weight of what happened. I wait until he's in his room at night before taking the tea he made. I slip past his door like a shadow, like a ghost. It's the only way I know how to protect both of us. But it doesn't stop the hurt.

Claire notices. She always notices.

Tonight, we're on the back porch. She's sitting on the steps with a mug in her hands, watching me as I pace near the railing. I'm too restless to sit. Too full of something that's been pushing up all day.

"You okay?" she asks softly.

"I said I'm fine," I answer too quickly, too sharply.

She nods once, slow, giving me space. "All right. Just checking."

"I don't need checking."

"I didn't say you did."

Her voice is calm, neutral, not offended or defensive, and somehow that makes my frustration spike. I run a hand through my hair, turning away from her, trying to pull the air into my chest. It feels too thick, too heavy.

"Why do you keep doing that?" I snap.

"Doing what?"

"Looking at me like you're waiting for something. Like you want me to fall apart or confess my whole life or... I don't know." I gesture wildly, frustration bubbling up. "You sit out here every night like we're doing some ritual healing thing, and you ask me questions like I'm supposed to just unravel on command."

Claire quietly rests her mug on the step beside her. "I'm not asking you to unravel."

"It feels like you are."

"Then that's something we can talk about," she says. "But I'm not trying to force you into anything."

"But you don't stop!" My voice rises before I can catch it. "You keep asking if I'm okay. You keep watching me like you're waiting for me to crumble. And I don't know what you want from me, Claire."

"I want to understand you," she says simply. "That's it."

"Well, you don't," I shoot back. "You don't understand me."

She nods gently. "Then tell me what I'm missing."

"I can't," I say, my chest tightening. "I can't tell you everything. I can't sit here and pretend like you can handle all of it."

"I've handled a lot," she says quietly. "You're not going to scare me."

"That's not the point!"

The words burst out of me, sharp, loud.

"I don't want to be understood. I don't want you trying to fix me. I don't want anyone pretending this is something we can talk out over tea like it's some sad story with a moral at the end."

I see the flicker of hurt in her eyes, but Claire stays still. She doesn't rise. She doesn't interrupt.

"You don't know what I've seen," I continue, voice shaking. "You don't know what I've done to survive. You don't know how hard it is to look at someone you care about and know you ruined their life just by existing."

Her brows pull together, but she doesn't speak.

"You want something real?" I say, breath trembling. "Fine. I trusted someone. I thought he loved me. I thought he loved my sister. And because I believed him, because I didn't see the truth until it was too late, she died. And I've been living with that every single day since."

Claire's eyes soften with something like grief. "Alana..."

"No," I say, shaking my head. "Don't say my name like that. Don't look at me like I'm something fragile. I don't want your pity. I don't want your understanding. I just want,"

My voice breaks.

"I just want the noise in my head to stop."

Pearled tears shimmer in Claire's eyes, but she still doesn't touch me. She stays grounded, steady, giving me space to be angry without turning it into something fragile or shameful.

"I'm not here to fix you," Claire says softly. "I'm here because you shouldn't have to sit in this alone. You don't owe me details. You don't owe me your pain. But I'm not walking away from you."

"I don't want you to walk away," I whisper. "I just, I don't know what to do with someone staying."

That's when the trembling starts, small at first, then rippling through my arms, my jaw, the center of my chest. I step back until my spine hits the porch rail, trying to breathe, trying to keep the world steady, but everything feels like it's slipping.

Claire rises slowly, as if approaching an animal too wounded to be touched. "Alana," she says, her voice barely above a whisper, "it's okay to let yourself feel something."

"I don't want to feel this," I choke out. "I don't want to remember anything. I don't want to keep carrying this alone."

"You're not alone," she says. "Not anymore."

The words are so gentle, so sincere, they hit something raw inside me. My legs weaken. My breath stumbles. Claire steps toward me but stops a foot away, giving me a choice. I don't move toward her, but I don't tell her to leave either.

And then my body simply... gives.

The weight I've been holding drops all at once, my knees bending, my hands grabbing at the railing to steady myself, but my arms tremble too much to keep me upright.

The screen door creaks behind us.

Footsteps, slow, careful, familiar.

Detective Franklin moves onto the porch, watching Claire first, then me. Claire looks at him with a quiet understanding, stepping aside not because she wants to leave but because she can see where I'm falling.

My breath breaks.

My shoulders shake.

I can't pull myself upright.

Franklin crosses the space between us with a steadiness I've never seen in anyone. He lowers himself beside me, his presence anchoring the air around us. Claire stays close, hands clasped in front of her, tears sliding silently down her face as she watches, but she doesn't interrupt.

"I can't hold this anymore," I whisper, voice ragged. "I can't."

Franklin doesn't speak. He just reaches out slowly, giving me time to pull back, but I don't. When his hand touches my arm, I break completely, collapsing into him like the weight finally crushed through my ribs. He wraps his arms around me with a strength that doesn't trap, it steadies. And for the first time in longer than I can remember, I stop fighting the fall.

Claire wipes her face quietly, taking one step back to give us space but not disappearing. She stands sentry-like in the doorway, guarding the moment even as she lets me have it.

And in Franklin's arms, with Claire's presence behind me and the night wrapped around us, I let myself unravel. Not into memory. Not into guilt. Just into the truth that I'm tired, so deeply tired of surviving.

For the first time, I let someone hold me.

# 8

## Chapter 8

**Franklin**

She was still in my arms when the world went quiet. Not the hollow kind of quiet that used to suffocate this house, but something softer, weighted only by the sound of her breath shaking against my chest. I kept one hand around her back and the other against the back of her head, fingers buried gently in her hair, holding her like she was something fragile I couldn't risk loosening my grip on. Her face was tucked beneath my jaw, warm and damp, and every time she exhaled, her breath ghosted across the side of my neck, steadying me in ways I didn't expect.

Her body trembled in waves, small but forceful, like each breath cost her something. I tightened my arms around her, slow, careful, pulling her just a little closer when her knees softened beneath her. She didn't try to stand on her own. She didn't try to run. She just leaned into me, letting her weight settle fully against my chest, and for the first time since I met her, I felt her trust me with more than fear. More than survival.

More than necessity.

This was something different. Something deeper.

"Hey," I whispered, bending my head toward her ear, letting my voice fall quiet and steady. "I've got you. You're safe. I'm right here."

Her fingers curled tighter into my shirt at the sound, catching fabric and pulling it in small, trembling fists close to my ribs. The feel of her hands there, grasping, grounding herself, sent a low ache through my chest. Not pain. Not panic. Something like recognition. Like this moment mattered more than either of us understood yet.

Her breath hitched again, a small, broken sound she tried, and failed, to swallow. So I held her closer, pressing my palm to her spine, feeling each sharp inhale beneath my hand. She wasn't sobbing anymore, but grief still rippled through her body, the aftershocks of everything she'd carried alone for far too long.

She shifted, just barely, turning her face into my neck like she needed the closeness, and my own breath stilled. Without thinking, I brushed my nose lightly into her hair, the faint scent of whatever lavender shampoo Claire stocked the bathroom with drifting up warm and soft. I didn't move away. I didn't force space. I let myself take the smallest breath in, subtle, instinctive, because something about having her here, pressed against me like this, felt right in a way I had no business admitting.

Her breathing slowly, gradually began to change. The jagged rhythm eased. Her shoulders loosened under my hands. The tension in her back softened. She sagged into me, not collapsing, but melting, like her body finally believed it didn't have to stay upright by itself.

"Just breathe," I murmured, my lips brushing the crown of her head. "You don't have to carry it alone anymore."

She let out a sound, not a cry, not a word, just a low, tired exhale that shook through both of us. My hands moved in gentle circles across her back, instinct guiding me more than thought. She was warm, trembling, real. And the longer I held her, the more I felt something in myself settle too. A vow forming quietly in my chest, steady and unspoken.

Her breathing synced with mine, matching the slow rise and fall of my chest. It was unintentional, unconscious, but intimate in a way that tightened something behind my ribs. Her fingers loosened their grip on my shirt, sliding slightly until one brushed the back of my hand where it rested at her waist.

Her skin was warm. Soft. Fragile and steady at the same time.

For a moment, our fingers caught, just barely, and something in my breath stuttered. I didn't look down, didn't move, didn't risk breaking whatever delicate thread hung between us. Instead, I gently closed my hand around hers, letting our fingers settle together, not locked but resting. Her pulse fluttered against my own.

This wasn't desire.

This wasn't confusion.

This wasn't anything I had a name for.

It was simply her.

Here.

In my arms.

A soft sound creaked behind us, the slow, cautious swing of the front door.

Claire stepped onto the porch with the kind of quiet that

meant she already sensed the weight of the moment. She didn't speak. She didn't clear her throat. She just paused at the threshold, looking between the two of us with a stillness that said she understood exactly what she was witnessing.

I didn't let go of Alana. Not fully. I only shifted enough so she could lift her head if she wanted to. She didn't, not right away. Her cheek rested against my collarbone a few seconds longer, taking one more breath, maybe two, before she finally eased back.

Her eyes were red and swollen, cheeks streaked with drying tears. But there was something steadier in her expression. Something clearer. Something humbled and human and heartbreakingly strong.

She glanced toward Claire, and her voice came out softer than I'd ever heard it. "I'm sorry," she whispered. "I'm sorry for the fear... for the running... for everything I put you both through."

Claire didn't rush toward her. She didn't hug her or reach for her immediately. She just stepped forward slowly, letting Alana set the pace.

"You don't owe us an apology," Claire said gently. "Fear isn't betrayal."

Alana's throat bobbed as she swallowed, her gaze dropping to

the floorboards.

"I just," She paused, breath shaking.

"I want to move forward. I want to help. I want... justice. For her."

Her sister. The wound she'd kept buried like a grave no one else knew existed.

I watched her closely, every shift in her expression sinking

106

deep. There was no anger in her now. Just something fragile and raw and honest. She turned toward the door, stepping past us both, and as she moved, her fingers brushed mine again, light, accidental, hesitant.

But this time, I felt her linger, not just a brush of skin, not something accidental or fleeting, but the faint, deliberate pause of someone who didn't want to let go too quickly. Her fingers grazed mine softly, like she was testing whether it was allowed, whether the world would break open again if she gave herself one more second of closeness. The contact was barely there, but it held more weight than some embraces I've had in my life. A warmth pressed gently into my skin, traveling up through my hand, settling somewhere deep beneath my ribs. I didn't move. Didn't speak. Didn't dare shift, afraid even the smallest motion might shatter whatever fragile truth lived inside that moment.

Then, with a shaky breath, she withdrew her hand, drawing it closer to her chest as she stepped inside, her shoulders still trembling faintly beneath the hall light. She didn't slam the door or stumble or rush away. She walked slowly, carefully, like someone trying to carry something fragile without dropping it. The screen door clicked shut behind her with a soft, almost hesitant sound, and the porch exhaled around me as if releasing a moment it knew was too new, too delicate, to hold onto.

Claire let out a long breath, the kind people release when they've been watching something unfold in front of them that they can't comment on yet, not because they don't have something to say, but because the truth takes a minute to settle. She stood there with her arms crossed loosely, her expression not sharp or skeptical, but perceptive in a way only someone like Claire could be. She took me in, my stance, the way my chest still rose slightly faster than normal, the imprint of Alana's fingers pressed faintly into the front of my shirt, the lingering closeness still wrapped around me even after she stepped inside.

"So," she said quietly, her voice low and even, "are you planning to pretend that what just happened didn't mean anything?"

Her words weren't accusing or judgmental. They were simply honest, spoken with the kind of clarity that makes denial look small and pointless. I opened my mouth to respond, but nothing made it past my tongue. Every explanation felt too thin, every excuse too hollow, because she saw exactly what I had felt, and what Alana allowed herself to feel.

"Claire," I started, my voice rougher than I intended.

She didn't let me finish. Not out of impatience, but because she didn't need me to. She took a small step closer, her gaze steady.

"I'm not here to tell you what's right or wrong," she said softly. "But I'm here to tell you that I saw something real. Something honest. She broke in your arms tonight, Franklin. And people don't break like that unless they feel safe. Unless something in them believes they won't be dropped."

The porch light cast a pale glow over the railing, catching the faint shimmer of tear stains drying on my shirt. Claire's eyes flicked down to them briefly before returning to my face.

"You held her like she meant something," she continued. "Not like a witness. Not like a case. Like a person you're already protecting with more than duty."

Her words hit deeper than I wanted to admit. I clenched my jaw and looked away toward the yard, where the trees swayed gently in the dark. The shadows felt heavier now, not with threat, but with truth.

"She's been through hell," I murmured. "She needed someone in that moment."

"And she chose you," Claire said, her voice low but unwavering. "You didn't force that. You didn't pull her into you, she walked into your arms. That matters."

I swallowed hard, heat rising in my chest. "I'm trying to do my job."

"I know." Her voice softened more, threading compassion through the sternness. "But don't confuse your job with what your heart is doing. And don't make her into a replacement for your past. She isn't Vanessa. She isn't anyone you've lost. She's her own person. And she's looking at you like someone who finally feels a moment of peace."

I didn't speak. Couldn't. My throat felt tight, and the porch seemed to tilt slightly, like the weight of her words rearranged something in me I wasn't prepared to face.

Claire stepped back toward the door, pausing with one hand on the frame. Her silhouette was outlined by the warm glow inside, and for a moment, she looked less like an instructor and more like someone trying to shield both of us from a mistake, or guide us toward something we weren't ready to name.

"Just be honest with yourself," she said quietly. "And with her. Don't let guilt or fear drive you into something blind. But don't push away something real just because it scares you."

Then she slipped inside, letting the door close behind her with a muted click.

The night pressed in around me, still and heavy, carrying the distant hum of crickets and the faint rustle of branches brushing each other in the dark. I braced my hands on the railing, leaning forward as I took in the yard, the outline of the trees, the faint moonlight catching on the long path leading away from the house, the quiet stretch of space between where she had stood and where I held her only minutes ago.

I lowered my head and shut my eyes, breathing in slowly. The scent of her hair lingered faintly in the collar of my shirt, warm and soft and impossibly grounding. My chest tightened, not painfully, but with a kind of ache I hadn't felt in years, a reminder of what it meant for someone's presence to steady me instead of haunt me.

Her trembling had stopped in my arms. Her breathing had synced with mine. And when she stepped away, she didn't run. She lingered.

That single second, that tiny pause of her fingers against mine, replayed in my mind with a clarity that unsettled me. I pressed my palm lightly over the place where her hand had rested, feeling the echo of its warmth even through the fabric.

Maybe Claire was right.

Maybe something shifted.

Maybe I was just waking up to it.

The porch light flickered once, then settled, casting a soft glow across the front of the house. Through the window, I could see the faintest sliver of light beneath Alana's door, warm, thin, steady. A sign she was awake. A sign she was still here.

I let out a breath, long and quiet, and whispered into the night, not sure if it was a prayer or a vow.

"God... don't let me fail her."

Because the truth was simple, undeniable, and terrifying in its honesty:

Tonight didn't feel like an ending.

It felt like a beginning.

**Alana**

I slipped inside the house and closed the door behind me, letting it latch softly. The moment it clicked, my back pressed against it like my body was trying to remember how to hold itself upright without him. My breath moved in uneven waves, not panicked, just too heavy, too full, like my lungs were still catching up to everything I let out on that porch. The quiet inside felt different tonight, not empty but charged, carrying the ghost of his voice, the steadiness of his hands, the warmth that still clung to my skin.

I lifted a shaky hand to my cheek, feeling the faint dampness that hadn't completely dried. My fingers trembled as I brushed the spot where my face had rested against Franklin's chest, remembering the rise and fall beneath my cheek. I didn't mean to lean into him the way I did. I didn't mean to let myself fold. But when he wrapped his arms around me, something in my body reacted before my mind could catch up. It was instinct, surrender, safety, things I wasn't used to reaching for.

I moved farther into the room, each step feeling strangely weightless, like part of me was still outside in his hold. The lamp on the table cast a warm, honey-colored glow that softened the edges of the space. I sank to the edge of the bed and sat still for a long moment, trying to understand why everything inside me felt rearranged. My hands rested in my lap, fingers unsteady, knuckles still sore from how hard I clenched them while crying. The house was so quiet I could almost hear my heartbeat echoing in my ears, still unsteady, still syncing to the rhythm his chest had kept when I pressed into him.

I drew my knees closer, letting my palms slide down my shins as I exhaled, slow and shaky. My shirt still carried his warmth, faint but undeniable. I could feel exactly where his arms had circled me, one hand spanning my back, the other steady near my shoulder, holding me like I wasn't something broken or dangerous to touch. The memory of that hold wasn't loud or overwhelming; it lived in me like something soft and stubborn, something I wasn't ready to name.

And even though he let go first, I remembered the way I lingered. How my fingers stayed on his skin just a breath longer than they needed to. How it felt like stepping toward the edge of something I didn't know how to navigate. Safety was a foreign language; he made it sound like a sentence I almost recognized.

I lowered my head and let my hair fall forward as the faintest tremor rolled through me, not grief this time, not fear. Just... release. A loosening of something tight and old. I let the quiet settle around me, grounding myself in the room's stillness, letting my breathing even out. And when I finally lifted my head, the lamp's soft light reflected across the walls in a way that made everything feel gentler than it had in years.

But the moment I closed my eyes, memory pulled me backward, not violently, not like a trap, but like a door I'd kept half-shut finally opening with a careful hand. Eva's face came back to me, not in pain, not in terror, just her. My little sister with the half-smile, the stubborn curls, the way she looked at me like I held the whole world steady for her. The porch had taken me back to that place, the place where I still carried the guilt like a second skin, but now, sitting here, it didn't feel like drowning. It felt like remembering because I finally could.

Eva didn't usually come back to me this clearly. Most nights she arrived in flashes, her laugh like a spark, her hair swinging behind her, the warmth of her small hand tucked in mine. But tonight... it was different. Tonight, she came back whole. The memory rose slowly, steady and full, like something I'd been too afraid to let myself open until now.

I drew my knees up to my chest and rested my chin there, letting the quiet settle around me. It wasn't the suffocating silence I'd grown used to. It didn't echo with panic or shame. It felt... still. Like the house was holding its breath with me, giving me space to look at things I always turned away from.

I closed my eyes and saw us standing in that cereal aisle again. The bright colors, the dusty tiles, the hum of the cheap fluorescent lights. Eva was clutching a box of Fruity Pebbles to her chest, grinning like she already knew she'd won our argument. She always won. She had that kind of smile, the kind that softened the world around her. The kind that made me want to be better.

I could hear her voice even now her long, dramatic "please" that always broke my resolve. She had no idea how much power she held even then. No idea how much I needed her laughter in that season, how much I depended on the light she carried without even trying.

Then Ricky stepped into the memory like he always did, sliding into the frame with that easy smile and warm tone. He knew exactly how to talk to us, casual, gentle, never raising suspicion. I remembered the way Eva's eyes softened when he spoke. I remembered the tiny shift in my chest, that unfamiliar mix of admiration and longing. I thought he was good. I thought he saw us. I thought he cared.

And it kills me that I taught her to believe it too.

I inhaled slowly, letting my fingers drag across the blanket in slow, grounding strokes. The guilt settled over me, not choking, not sharp, just present. A weight I knew how to hold now that I wasn't fighting it. I wasn't collapsing under it this time. I was acknowledging it. There's a difference.

I let the memory stretch further, the afternoons he came by with groceries, the nights he sat on the couch talking to Mom like he was doing us a favor, the way he always left the door open just enough for us to mistake it for freedom. I saw it all now with the clarity of someone who's survived enough to tell the truth.

And still, in the middle of all that darkness, there was my sister. My little shadow. My reason for trying to be brave long before I had any right to be. I pressed a hand to my chest, right over the place where her absence still burned. Not in the jagged way it used to, but like a bruise I'd kept hidden under layers of instinct and fear.

I whispered her name so quietly the sound didn't even leave the room. More like a breath, a memory brushing across my lips. It didn't break me. It just settled in the air, soft and honest, like something I didn't have to run from anymore.

When I leaned back into the pillows, exhaustion washed through me, but not the kind that drags you under. It felt earned, like after a storm finally passes and your body remembers what stillness feels like.

And then, without meaning to, my thoughts shifted to Franklin.

I felt it immediately, the warmth creeping up my throat, the flutter of something unfamiliar settling low in my stomach. I pulled the blanket up around me tighter, as if that could hide the truth sitting between my ribs.

I remembered the way he held me, carefully, but with conviction. The way his chest rose against my cheek, steady and sure, guiding my breath back into rhythm. The faint tremor in his hands when I collapsed against him, like he was steadying both of us at once. The quiet strength in his voice when he whispered, "I've got you. You're safe."

And God help me, I believed him.

I wasn't supposed to. I wasn't supposed to let someone's touch feel like protection instead of threat. I wasn't supposed to want to stay there. But I did. My fingers traced the spot on my sleeve where my hand had curled into his shirt, clinging without permission. I could still feel the shape of his body against mine, the way he didn't pull away even when I tangled myself into him like I would fall apart if he let go.

It scared me how natural it felt.

In the hallway, a floorboard creaked softly. I stilled, listening. His steps were slow, careful, like he was trying not to disturb anything, or anyone. When his door closed, a quiet hush followed, wrapping the house in a warmth that made my eyes sting. I wasn't alone in this place. I wasn't abandoned in a storm. For the first time in years, the person on the other side of the wall wasn't a threat.

He was safety.

I let that truth settle without fighting it.

A soft knock interrupted the silence, not loud, just a gentle tap against the door frame from someone who didn't want to intrude. Claire didn't step inside. She didn't press or hover. She just leaned her head slightly into the doorway and offered the softest, most knowing smile.

"Just checking on you," she whispered. "I'm proud of you tonight."

My throat tightened, not with pain, but with the strange mix of gratitude and discomfort that comes when someone sees you more clearly than you want them to.

"Thank you," I murmured, my voice low. "For... everything."

She nodded once, warm and steady. "Get some rest, sweetheart."

Then she slipped away without waiting for anything else, leaving only the faint sound of her footsteps fading down the hall.

I sank deeper under the blanket, exhaustion finally tugging at my limbs. I turned onto my side, facing the sliver of light from the hallway before Claire turned it off. Darkness filled the room in a soft, cocooning way, and as my eyes adjusted, the last thing I whispered into the stillness was small but certain.

"God... if You're really healing me... don't stop."

Sleep came slowly, gently, drawing me under with the echo of Franklin's heartbeat still steadying my own.

# 9

# Chapter 9

**Franklin**

It's been four months since we were moved to this safe house, and what's wild is how much and how little can change in that amount of time. The days blur together here, one quiet moment bleeding into the next. But I see it clearly; especially in her.

Alana.

She talks more now. Not in a way that feels forced or like she's trying to prove anything, but in a way that feels earned like her voice is something she's reclaiming piece by piece. Ever since that night she cracked open in front of us, she's been different. Not perfectly, but lighter. Not joyful or carefree, but her edges aren't as sharp. Her shoulders don't stay drawn in like she's bracing for a blow. There's a softness now. A flickering peace she seems to let herself touch, like she's learning how to live in something beyond survival.

I've seen her smile. Real ones. The kind that slip out when she thinks no one's looking.

And when Claire had to return to the division for a few weeks, and Clay stepped in, I thought it might set her back. The tension between them still lingers, still sours the room like something half-spoiled, but Alana... she doesn't shrink from it anymore. She doesn't flinch when he makes a snide comment or jabs at her soft spots. She just moves through it. Holds her ground without asking for permission. There's a strength to that. A quiet defiance.

Watching her stay steady in the face of what used to unravel her, it does something to me.

She started therapy not long after that night. I don't know how Claire got through to her maybe it was timing, or maybe she finally felt safe enough to want something more, but it stuck. I've seen the difference.

She tells us when she's scared now. When she needs space. She doesn't disappear into silence anymore. She communicates. Not always easily, but openly.

But watching her find her voice again pulled at something I thought I'd locked away for good.

Vanessa's face flashed in my mind not in the way it haunted me in the early years, but in a quieter, heavier way.

Back then, I'd convinced myself I could protect her, too. And when I couldn't... I carried the wreckage for longer than I admitted. Losing her taught me how quickly safety can turn to ashes.

That's the difference now. With Alana, I don't want to wait for regret to teach me the same lesson twice. I want to be ahead of it. I want to be sure.

There are still moments. A sudden crack of thunder, boots overhead, wind slamming the side door too hard and I'll catch her frozen, her eyes unfocused, her body drawn in like she's bracing for something invisible. I've seen her press her back to the wall when the rain pours too loud, trying to vanish into it. It never lasts long. But it still happens.

PTSD doesn't leave quietly.

It lurks. It waits. It resurfaces without warning. And Alana, she's learning how to name it without letting it own her.

The other night, during one of those unexpected thunderstorms, she came and sat by the fireplace without saying a word. Didn't explain. Just wrapped herself in a blanket and stared into the flames. I sat beside her, silent. Eventually, she exhaled, slow and steady, like my presence alone gave her space to breathe.

That's what healing looks like sometimes. Not loud. Not linear. But present.

And she's present now. She's here. Every time she shows up for herself like that, something in me shifts.

This morning, I woke up feeling... steady. No fog. No tightness in my chest. Just breath. Just clarity. The air didn't feel heavy.

I made my way to the kitchen, started the kettle without thinking. Chamomile, just a little honey, lemon on the side. I know how she takes it. I don't ask anymore. I just make it.

When I stepped into the room with her cup, I expected her curled up in her usual corner.

But she was standing there, waiting.

Then she looked at me and said, "Do you... wanna sit outside for a bit?"

No buildup. No fidgeting. Just a gentle ask wrapped in something I couldn't name.

I nodded, handed her the tea, followed her to the porch. The morning was still stretching awake, birds shifting in the trees, fog clinging to the edges of the woods like it didn't want to leave. The quiet had weight, like the world was holding its breath.

We sat side by side on the bench. No rush. No noise. Just stillness. And then she looked at me same look as that night in the hallway. That silent reminder: I'm still here. And so are you.

"I've been sleeping better," she said, voice low. "Not every night. But some. And... I think that counts for something."

"It does," I said, watching her closely.

She cradled the mug between her palms. Steady. Focused.

"I didn't think I'd get to a place where I could just... sit like this. Not flinch at every sound. Not feel like I had to keep looking over my shoulder. But I do now. When I'm near you."

God, I wanted to believe that. That maybe I was part of her peace, not just her rescue plan. Something inside me cracked open at the thought.

The words landed heavy. Or maybe they landed exactly how she meant. Either way, they rooted deep.

She looked down, then back at me with that slow, searching gaze of hers. The kind that peeled layers off me without trying.

"You ever wonder," she asked quietly, "if maybe... the people who were sent to protect us end up being the ones we were supposed to protect too?"

My throat tightened. Not with fear. With something worse. Wanting. Knowing. Every part of me wanted to answer. Every part of me knew I couldn't.

I turned toward her, my shoulder brushing hers. She turned too. And for a second, the whole world paused.

We just stared, holding something fragile and real between us. The silence pulsed with everything unsaid. And I didn't want to run from it. I didn't want to bury it under duty.

I just wanted to say it.

To reach across the space between us.

To speak.

I opened my mouth, heart pounding, the words rising like a tide that had been waiting for permission. I was ready to speak; to ask, to name, to risk whatever fragile thing was forming between us because it finally felt worth naming.

I leaned in slightly, heart thudding. I was going to say it. Not everything, but enough to shift the ground between us. Enough to change what this was becoming. But the sound shattered everything.

My phone rang; loud, sharp, unapologetic. It sliced through the moment with such violence that I saw her body jerk, just slightly, her muscles tensing on instinct before settling again.

I looked down at the screen, my breath still caught in my throat, and there it was an unfamiliar number, no name, no context, just a string of digits humming with unease in my palm.

I didn't answer right away. Some part of me wanted to let it ring out, to ignore it and hold on to the quiet she and I had built. But I knew better. I always know better.

And when I glanced up again, she was still looking at me. No judgment. No pressure. Just an open stillness in her gaze, like she was holding space for something neither of us could explain.

There was no anger in her expression, no fear, just a steady kind of hope lingering beneath the surface.

And maybe, *God help me*, maybe something more.

Something I hadn't earned. Something I didn't know how to protect.

But I wanted to.

I stepped off the porch, letting the door swing gently shut behind me as I lifted the phone to my ear.

"Franklin."

The voice on the other end was clipped and direct, familiar in a way that made my shoulders square before I even realized I was doing it.

"You're not gonna like this," he said, "but I figured you'd rather hear it from me."

I moved to the side of the porch, pressing my back against the wooden paneling, my eyes scanning the tree line even though I knew there wouldn't be anything there.

"Go ahead."

He hesitated for a second not because he didn't know what to say, but because he knew exactly what it meant.

"We've been tracking some chatter. Encrypted. Fragmented. Hard to trace. But a name came up. One I know you've been watching."

My jaw tightened, the tension pressing behind my temples.

"Say it."

"Ricky."

It landed like a gut punch, solid and cold.

"He may have resurfaced. South route. Someone matching his build was seen near a bus terminal off I-85. Still unconfirmed. But that's not what has us worried."

I kept my voice steady. "Then what does?"

The pause was longer this time; too long.

"We think he knows she's still alive."

The words lodged in my chest like splinters.

"We picked up a coded message. Short. But specific. Mentioned a girl who 'used to hide behind books and doesn't anymore.' Ring any bells?"

I didn't respond. I didn't have to.

"Figured as much. Just wanted you to know. If it's him, he's not just watching anymore. He's circling."

"I appreciate it," I said, voice tight. "If anything else surfaces,"

"You'll be the first call."

"Good. I owe you."

"No," he said, his voice cutting clean through any illusion of distance. "Just keep her breathing."

The line went dead.

I stood there for a beat, phone still against my ear even though the line was silent. I didn't want to move. Didn't want to accept what I already knew was happening.

But I turned, forced myself to step back inside.

She was still on the bench, tea in hand, her head tilted toward the trees like the morning still belonged to her.

I didn't interrupt that peace. She looked peaceful. Settled in a way I hadn't seen in weeks. And I couldn't bring myself to steal that from her not yet. I just watched her for a moment longer than I should have and told myself I'd do whatever it took to protect it.

"Hey," I said softly, voice barely carrying. "I'll be back in a few. Clay's gonna stay close."

She didn't ask questions. She didn't push. Just nodded, eyes still on the horizon. "Okay."

I found Clay in the kitchen, leaned against the counter like he had nothing better to do.

"I need you to keep eyes on her," I said. "No distractions. Not for a second."

He shrugged, lazy as ever, but nodded. "Got it."

I didn't bother responding. I went straight to my room, locked the door, pulled out the secure line, and called Claire.

She picked up by the second ring. Too fast.

"Franklin?"

"It's time to move."

Her voice sharpened. "What happened?"

"Ricky may have resurfaced. Worse, he might know she's still alive."

The silence on her end didn't last long.

"Where do you want her?"

"Someplace quiet. Off-grid. Only you and I have the location. No chains, no weak links."

"I'll make the call," she said. "Two hours. I'll text you everything."

I nodded, even though she couldn't see it. "Thank you."

"Just keep her safe."

"I will," I said, and meant it. "Even if I have to burn everything down to do it."

We wrapped up the transfer plan, routes, timing, the new drop spot. Then, just as the conversation shifted back toward silence, her voice dipped.

"And how's she doing?"

I paused. Not because I didn't know what to say, but because there was too much.

"She's different," I said. "Stronger. Calmer. Like she's remembering how to breathe again. Not all the time, but... it's there. In the mornings. In the moments when she forgets to be afraid."

Claire didn't say anything right away. When she finally did, her voice was quieter.

"Just make sure you're not the one seeing too much."

I stiffened. "It's not like that."

I told myself she didn't get it. That she was wrong. But part of me, *deep down*, wondered if she wasn't.

Claire gave a soft, low laugh, but there was no judgment in it; just recognition.

"You don't have to convince me, Franklin. I've seen it before. Trauma creates connections that feel deeper than they are. Urgent. Intense. Like love, but faster. Stronger. It tricks you into thinking it's real because of how much you need it to be. But when the crisis ends, you'll have to be sure what you're feeling wasn't just built on adrenaline and proximity."

I didn't respond. I couldn't untangle truth from what I wanted. She was right. And wrong. And somewhere in the mess of it all, I didn't know which part mattered more.

"You still with me?" she asked.

"Yeah," I said quietly. "I'm here."

"Good. We move tomorrow. I'll send the details when it's safe. Get rest."

Then the line went dead.

I stayed sitting there with the phone still in my hand. I leaned back in the chair, closed my eyes, and let the truth come up slow, steady, undeniable.

*I'm falling for her.*

Not in some fleeting way blurred by adrenaline or proximity. Not because she needed saving. But because of who she was becoming. Because she looked at the world like it might still be worth trusting. Because she listened more than she spoke. Because she didn't fill silence, she settled into it, like someone learning how to live in peace.

I cared about the way her laughter came out soft and unplanned. The way her hands stilled when wrapped around a warm mug. The way she tilted her head slightly when she was deep in thought, not even aware she was doing it. I noticed too much. Felt too much. And I knew exactly what it meant.

I cared about her. Deeply. And it scared me.

Because falling for someone like her, someone still healing, still hunted, still not safe wasn't just risky. It was dangerous. Not just for her, but for both of us.

This wasn't the time. It wasn't the place.

So I sat in the quiet, trying to steady my breath and tell myself what I had to believe, what I needed to believe. You feel it. You name it. Then you get it under control. Whatever this is between us, however real it feels, it can't happen.

Not now.

Not like this.

## Alana

I probably shouldn't have asked, especially when the air between us had just started to soften, not when the quiet was something that felt earned instead of fragile. But I did, I asked. And then he left. It wasn't harsh. It wasn't even abrupt. But the moment I spoke, something in him pulled back. The warmth in his eyes shifted. The safety I'd just started to trust felt like it slipped through my fingers, and then he was gone. Back into the house. Out of reach. And I felt it, like something unfinished had been sealed shut before I could name it. Like I'd held out a piece of truth, and it fell into silence instead of his hands.

I sat there longer than I meant to, the tea cooling between my hands, its heat doing nothing to stop the cold that had crept into my chest. And I won't lie to myself, I was disappointed. Not devastated. Not heartbroken. But disappointed in the kind of way that sits in your throat. Because this time, I hadn't been guarded. I hadn't been defensive. I hadn't tried to keep things distant. I was just curious, about the man who holds silence like it's sacred, who steadies my breathing without saying a word, who whispers prayers into the air like someone might be listening even if no one ever has.

I wanted to know him, not the badge, not the title, not the man who steps between me and danger. I wanted to understand the parts of him that stay quiet when no one's looking. Because something in him doesn't flinch at the storm in me. He just sees it and stays. And maybe that's what scared him. Maybe that's why he left. Because I wasn't hiding anymore. Because I let the truth slip out of my mouth without dressing it in caution.

I glanced back toward the house, half-hoping I'd hear his footsteps returning, half-hating myself for hoping at all. But the porch creaked again and my gut tightened. Not because it was Franklin. Because it wasn't. Because somehow, I already knew Clay only showed up when something needed breaking. When I looked up, there he was, hands shoved deep into his jacket pockets, jaw locked tight like he was chewing on something bitter.

"Did he tell you where he was going?" he asked, eyes scanning the horizon like it owed him something.

I shook my head. "No."

He snorted under his breath, like that confirmed something he already believed. He didn't look at me right away. Just leaned against the railing, watching the woods like he was performing the role of someone alert, someone useful. But the shift in the air was immediate. Where Franklin's presence always brought stillness, Clay's felt like static, itchy, unsettled, wrong.

I didn't speak. I didn't move. Because I was still sitting with the silence Franklin left behind. Still waiting for the answer I never got.

Clay rocked slightly on his heels, the creak of the porch too loud in the stillness. "You two getting close, huh?" His tone tried to play it off like a joke, but there was something sharp under it.

I said nothing.

"Didn't peg you for the 'fall-for-your-bodyguard' type," he added, chuckling like it was harmless, like he expected me to laugh along.

Still, I said nothing.

He looked over at me, waiting. "What? No comeback?"

But his laugh didn't land like a joke. It hit like a dare.

Something in my stomach twisted. I'd heard that tone before, the kind of cruelty that wears humor like a mask. I'd seen it in men who needed to feel bigger, louder, stronger than the women they couldn't understand. His words weren't new. They were recycled from the same empty place.

"Relax," he said, still leaning. "Don't tell me you're catching feelings for the guy."

That's when I turned. Slowly. Calmly. I wasn't angry. I wasn't even surprised. I was done.

"You know," I said, my voice soft but sharp, "for someone who's supposed to be watching out for me, you spend a lot of time turning things into punchlines you clearly don't understand."

He blinked, like he hadn't expected me to speak. Like he hadn't thought I still had teeth.

"I've been through things I wouldn't wish on anyone," I said, steady. "So if watching someone treat me with basic decency makes you uncomfortable, maybe you should ask yourself why."

His mouth opened, ready to defend himself, but I kept going.

"I'm not mad, Clay. I'm not even shocked. I think you've got things you've never dealt with, and somewhere along the way, you decided that taking cheap shots at people like me makes it easier to ignore your own mess."

I stepped away from the railing, slow and deliberate, my shoes scraping softly against the wood. I set my empty mug on the windowsill with more weight than it deserved.

"But here's the thing," I continued, my voice still calm, still level. "What I've been through doesn't make me weak. And it doesn't make me your punchline. My pain isn't your entertainment, and I'm not going to play the role of fragile so you can feel strong."

The air changed. Not because he moved, but because he didn't. He felt it. The line I drew. And I wasn't moving it.

"I've fought for every inch of peace I have," I said. "Through memories that don't come with warning signs. Through silence that made me feel like I was drowning. And now that I can finally breathe, I'm not giving that up so you can feel comfortable in your bitterness."

I glanced at him one last time, unflinching. "If you're not here to protect, don't be here when the storm hits."

He didn't follow me and he didn't speak.

And I walked away not because I was weak, but because I finally understood that I don't have to stay small just to keep someone else from falling apart.

I stepped back into the house with my heart still tight from what I'd just walked away from. Clay's presence still clung to my skin like humidity, but I kept walking, down the hall, past the kitchen, into the quiet stretch of shadowed wood that always seemed to hold its breath. And then I heard it.

"Alana."

His voice was low, too quiet for how deeply it struck me. I turned and saw him coming toward me, eyes already scanning my face like he was searching for something he couldn't name.

"What's wrong?" I asked, even as the truth pressed against my ribs. The room felt different now—charged, tense, like something unsaid was begging to be spoken.

He didn't answer at first. Just reached out gently, his hand resting against my arm, not to stop me, but to steady me. And for once, I didn't pull away.

"We have to move," he said, calm but firm. "There's a chance we've been compromised. I don't know how close it is, but I'm not waiting to find out."

The words hit hard. Not because they shocked me, but because part of me had started to believe I could stop bracing. I had let myself imagine we were safe, or at least safer. And now, all of that was unraveling.

"But... I thought..." I didn't even know what I meant to say. I thought we had more time? I thought this place could hold us a little longer? I thought the ground under my feet was finally something I could trust?

My arms folded across my chest without me realizing it, like I needed something to hold me together.

"Do you think it's him?" I asked.

"Do you think Ricky knows where I am?"

He didn't answer with words. But the look in his eyes told me everything.

That was the moment the fear surged again. The kind that doesn't scream, it whispers. It claws. My legs felt weaker beneath me. My hands started to tremble. I hated it. I hated how quickly the past could slip back inside me without asking.

Franklin moved toward me slowly, the kind of slow that felt intentional—like he wanted me to feel him before I saw him. His hand settled on my arm, warm and sure, his palm fitting there as if it had always known where to go. He didn't speak right away; he didn't have to. His presence did the speaking for him, a soft, wordless promise pressed gently into my skin: *I'm here. I've got you.*

"Hey," he said, voice low, the kind of low that wraps around you instead of piercing through.

"You're okay. We're okay. I'm not going to let anything happen to you. Do you hear me?"

I nodded, even though I didn't feel okay. Even though the shaking hadn't stopped. But my body heard him before my mind could. I looked up at him, and something about the way he looked back at me made everything else fall away.

He wasn't looking at danger. He wasn't looking past me.

There was protection in his eyes. But there was something else too. Something slower. Deeper. Something he'd been trying not to show.

And for a second, I let myself see it. I let myself feel it.

But only for a second.

I stepped back, gently pulling away. Not because I didn't want to, but because I couldn't.

"Okay," I said, voice stronger than I felt. "I'll start packing."

He didn't speak right away. He just stood there, close enough for me to feel the warmth of him, close enough that the moment seemed to gather between us without either of us trying to shape it. His expression held that quiet steadiness he always carried, the kind that never gave away what he was thinking.

I drew in a slow breath.

"Is there anything else you wanted to say?"

The question came out soft, careful, more uncertain than I intended.

He paused—a real pause, not a dramatic one, just long enough for me to feel the shift—then eased a step back, as if distance helped him find his words.

"No," he said. "Nothing else."

His tone was steady, but something about it felt unfinished, like a thought he hadn't allowed to surface. I wasn't sure why the answer made the moment feel heavier instead of cleared.

"Are you sure?"

It slipped out quietly, almost an exhale, not challenging him but trying to make sense of what had changed. My eyes lifted to meet his, and for the first time since we'd stepped inside, he really looked at me—slowly, fully, not rushed or deliberate, just present in a way that made the room feel smaller.

He didn't touch me.

He didn't step closer.

But there was something in the way he held my gaze that made my breath weaken, not with expectation but with confusion at why he suddenly seemed so far away and so near at the same time.

His jaw tightened ever so slightly, his breath coming a little deeper as if he were wrestling with a thought he didn't plan to voice. When he finally spoke, his voice was low, steady, and edged with restraint.

"I can't."

He didn't explain.

He didn't offer anything more.

And even though I didn't understand what he meant, the words settled between us like something he needed to honor, not something I had done wrong.

So I nodded once, quietly, letting his answer stand. I didn't press anymore—not because the moment made sense, but because he looked like someone fighting a battle I couldn't see, and pushing would only make the ground shake harder beneath us both.

I went to the room and I moved toward the bed without knowing why, pacing the floor because my body refused to be still. I couldn't breathe. Couldn't think straight. Franklin's words kept replaying, *We have to move.*

Not again.

Not after I let myself believe I could rest.

I pressed my hands to my face and tried to swallow the panic, but it was already rising, already taking up space. If he said we had to go, that meant Ricky was close. That meant this wasn't just a drill. That meant the walls around this safehouse weren't thick enough anymore.

"Oh God..." I whispered, stumbling back until the edge of the mattress caught my legs. I sat down hard, my hands pressed against my thighs to stop the shaking.

"He found me. He found me."

The words spun in circles, faster and faster. My eyes darted to the corner where my bags still sat, half-unpacked, never fully settled. And suddenly it made sense. I never unpacked because I never truly believed this would last. But I'd hoped. I'd wanted it.

This house wasn't perfect. But it was quiet. Safe. It smelled like cedar and always felt too cold in the mornings, but it had become a place where I made tea because I wanted to, not because I needed to feel normal. A place where I talked about my sister without the grief swallowing me whole. A place where I finally, finally slept with both eyes closed.

And now I had to leave it. Again.

I looked around the room, at the chipped dresser, the soft creak in the floor near the closet, the curtain that never quite stayed still. And it all felt like a life I was being asked to give up again. A piece of peace I wasn't ready to lose.

My breathing was still uneven, my heart pounding like it didn't know how to slow down. What if this time, Ricky doesn't miss? What if this time, I don't get out? What if Franklin gets caught in the middle?

I stood too fast, dizziness pushing against my vision. My eyes landed on the little wooden cross Claire had left on the nightstand the day I arrived. I used to think Claire left it out of habit. But now, I wondered if she knew I'd need something to hold when everything else started slipping. I'd rolled my eyes at it back then. But now, my fingers closed around it like it meant something more.

"Please," I whispered, gripping it tight.

"Please don't let this be the beginning of the end again."

Because I was tired.

Because I had just started to believe.

Because I didn't want to run anymore.

# 10

# Chapter 10

**Franklin**

It's the morning of the move, but everything feels wrong. The light coming through the windows is too sharp, too sterile, making the dust hang heavier in the air like even the walls know we're abandoning them. People move around me, *quiet, efficient*, but it's not enough to shake the silence pressing into every corner. Packing tape rips. Boxes thud. Footsteps echo against bare floors. But no one's really speaking. Not about the things that matter. Not about the way the air feels stretched too thin, or the way every second feels like it's dragging its feet toward something none of us want to name.

I've done relocations before high-risk exits, emergency extractions, last-minute transfers under fire. But this doesn't feel like tactical protocol. It feels like loss. It feels like we missed something. Like we're reacting too late to a threat we should've seen coming.

I freeze mid-pack, one boot laced and the other forgotten. That feeling, that weight in my chest that's been building for days finally lands. I don't move. Don't blink. I just let the realization settle, because I've been avoiding it. That night, *the hit*, I still don't know who did it. I told myself it was random, a one-off, just bad luck. But deep down, I knew better God had been warning me, and I ignored it. No footprints. No strange prints. No sign of entry. Just a brutal strike to the back of my head and silence.

And now I can't stop thinking, what if it wasn't random? What if it wasn't just some prowler or local thug testing a boundary? What if it was Ricky? What if he already knew exactly where we were, and we've been living in the illusion of safety while he circled the perimeter?

But how?

I stand and cross the room, flipping through the files until I find the folder with her name, the only folder I've kept locked tighter than any other. Everything about her has been buried. Sealed records. No digital trace. Public records list her as a disappearance or overdose, just another unsolved statistic. There were only three of us with access to her location. Me. Clay. Claire.

I stare at the log until the lines blur, my fingers tightening around the edge of the paper. The timing. The precision. The lack of evidence. It wasn't random. It wasn't external. Someone got close without being seen. Someone was already inside.

I push out the back door and find Clay near the SUV, running checks on the gear with his usual lazy efficiency.

"Clay," I call, motioning him away from the vehicle. "Let's talk."

He jogs over—easy, casual—but his stance shifts the second he realizes I'm not here for small talk. I don't warm him up. I don't circle anything.

"I've been thinking about the night I got hit," I say. "Something doesn't add up."

He raises a brow, waiting.

"There were no outside prints. No signs of movement. The trail cams were clean. And whoever hit me knew exactly where I'd be in the woods. Knew how to get in, get out, and disappear without leaving anything behind. That's not random. That's precise."

Clay doesn't react much, but his shoulders tighten, the smallest pull under the fabric of his shirt.

"So you think Ricky was here?"

"I think Ricky knew where we were," I reply. "And I think someone told him."

He crosses his arms. His voice stays low.

"You're saying someone on the inside leaked her location."

"There were three of us with clearance," I say. "Me. You. Claire."

He lets that land, then shrugs like he's tossing out a thought that shouldn't mean as much as it does.

"You sure about Claire?"

The pause hits me before I can stop it. I don't hide it well.

"You want to explain that?" I ask.

Clay lifts both brows, not defensive, not heated—just laying something on the table.

"I'm not accusing her. But she's been bouncing between field work and admin for years. She answers to people we don't even meet. Maybe she made a call. Maybe it went sideways. It's possible."

"No," I say, quicker than I intended. "Claire doesn't make mistakes like that."

"Right," Clay says, the corner of his mouth flattening. "Because she's perfect. You ever think maybe you just don't want to see it? Maybe it's easier if she stays clean in your head."

I step closer—not threatening, just enough to let him know where the line is.

"Watch it."

He doesn't move.

"I'm just saying the math out loud," he replies. "If it wasn't you, and it wasn't me, then there's one name left. That's all."

I don't respond.

Not because he's right.

Not because he's wrong.

Just because there's nothing else to say to him.

I turn away and head inside. The house feels empty, most of the gear already packed, rooms quiet in a way that doesn't match the day. I zip the last duffel, check the straps, check them again, then head toward the kitchen with the familiar thought that I'll pour two mugs of tea—one for her, one for me.

But when I walk in, I stop.

She's already there.

Alana's sitting at the table, calm but far away, her fingers curled around her mug like it's the only warm thing left in this house. My mug, *steaming and full*, is already waiting across from her. She doesn't say anything. Just lifts her hand and gestures for me to sit.

I laugh under my breath, caught off guard. "That was my job. I'm the one who's supposed to make the tea."

She smirks, just enough to lift the corner of her mouth. "Well, I figured since everything's about to change... maybe it's time we changed the routine too."

I sit down across from her, wrapping my hands around the cup. "Is that right?"

She nods, still holding that half-smile. "Yeah. Who knows? Maybe I like taking care of you for once."

It catches me off guard. Not the words. The weight behind them. She's teasing, but there's a tenderness tucked inside it, a truth she's not naming yet.

I clear my throat, shifting in my chair.

"That's dangerous talk. You keep making tea like this, I might get used to it."

She laughs, and for a moment, I forget we're leaving. I forget the packed bags and the surveillance and the threat circling us like smoke.

But then her fingers drift along the rim of her mug, and the quiet returns. She stares at the table for a long second before finally saying, "I was starting to like this place."

I don't interrupt.

"I mean... not like I thought it would last forever. But it felt like something close to peace. Like I didn't have to flinch at every sound. Like I could breathe." Her voice gets softer.

"And now we have to move again."

She glances up, forcing a small smile, but I see the ache under it. "It's familiar. Not in a good way. Like when I was with Ricky, never staying anywhere long enough to feel safe."

She pauses, her gaze distant now.

"You know, I always wanted a house. Not a big one. Just something small. Something real. A porch. A stretch of grass. Somewhere that felt like mine."

I couldn't take it, hearing her speak like she'd already buried that dream beside her sister. I had to move. Her voice breaks slightly. She catches it fast, but not fast enough.

"Me and my sister... we never got that. And now I don't think we ever will."

I don't think. I just move.

I get up and kneel in front of her, reaching up slowly, letting my hands rest against her face. Her skin is warm. Her breath shaky. My thumb brushes a tear from her cheek as I tilt her chin just enough to meet my eyes.

"Don't think of this as the end," I say, voice barely above a whisper.

"This isn't erasing your dream. It's protecting it. This move; it's not a loss. It's a seed. It's a chance to get to the place where that house is waiting."

She doesn't look away. Doesn't speak. But something softens. Something holds.

I want to say more. I want to tell her I'll build it myself if I have to.

But the front door opens.

And Claire walks in.

Claire enters mid-step, clipboard in one hand and a forced calm stretched across her face. She pauses only for a second when she sees us me kneeling, Alana crying, the closeness we didn't mean to reveal. The moment she stepped in, the air shifted cooler, sharper, like her presence pressed pause on something sacred. Her eyes scan the room with that practiced detachment she always wears in high-pressure moments, but I catch the flicker. The narrowing of her gaze. The way she clocks our proximity and files it away without saying a word.

I pull back slowly, my hands lowering as I stand. Alana straightens too, brushing a hand over her cheek as if that could undo the emotion that just passed between us. And like that, the moment is gone, still burning, still real, but no longer safe to touch.

Claire walks further into the room, her boots hitting the hardwood like a reminder that we're still on a mission. "Well," she says, drawing out the word with that clipped tone that lives somewhere between knowing and indifferent, "good morning to you two."

I clear my throat and take a small step back. "Claire, what are you doing here?"

She arches an eyebrow, unimpressed. "You really thought I wasn't going to show up for the move? Come on, Franklin. This isn't just a routine switch. We've got one shot to make sure this goes clean. You think I'd leave that to chance?"

She drops her bag and opens a folder like nothing just happened, like she didn't walk in on something we weren't ready to name. But I know Claire. She doesn't miss a detail. She just stores them until the moment's right.

"Extraction timing still good?" she asks, flipping through her notes. "Drivers are in place. Convoy is staggered. No flagged chatter on our feeds. Everything looks clean."

"For now," I reply, but my voice comes out tighter than I intended. "That's what bothers me."

She looks up, expression unreadable. "Go on."

I glance toward Alana, she's pretending not to listen, but I know better so I nod toward the hallway.

"Let me talk to you privately."

Claire follows without hesitation. Once we're clear, I stop and face her, lowering my voice. "I'm not trying to stir the pot, but I can't keep pretending everything's fine. Something's been off ever since that night I got hit. And I can't shake it."

She nods once, giving me space to continue.

"No breach on the house. No prints but ours. I chalked it up to chance, maybe even an ambush. But now with Ricky possibly knowing she's alive; it doesn't add up. Someone had to tell him. Or someone slipped. And they didn't go after her. They went for me."

Claire's arms fold across her chest as she studies me, lips pressed tight. "And you think Ricky's been tracking us longer than we realized."

"I don't think it. I know it. Which means this move might not be the reset we think it is. If he's ahead of us, we need to rethink everything."

Claire breathes in slowly, but something in her stance shifts. Not visibly. Just enough for me to notice the quiet processing happening behind her eyes. She gives a small nod. "You've got good instincts, Franklin. But let's not overreact. The transfer was arranged with full security protocol. Routes were randomized. Comms are encrypted. No one outside the original three has the coordinates, unless one of us gave them up."

The way she says it, *the precision, the control*, doesn't sit right.

I watch her carefully. "You really believe it was just bad timing?"

"I believe stress makes people see ghosts," she replies, her voice too even.

"And sometimes what looks like a leak is just pressure finding the weakest seam."

I don't answer. Because on paper, she's not wrong. But in my gut, something's off.

She turns and walks away like the conversation is over.

"Stick to the plan," she says without looking back. "We'll

be fine."

But I don't move.

Because fine doesn't mean safe.

And when someone insists nothing slipped, it usually means something did.

We were finally moving. The last bag had been loaded. The safe house once filled with the fragile illusion of peace; stood empty behind us. I was in the second car with Claire driving and Alana silent in the front seat, her arms crossed tight, staring out the window like she was trying to memorize what safety looked like in case she didn't see it again. The lead vehicle was ahead on the route, Clay behind the wheel with one of our senior agents riding shotgun. Everything on paper looked clean. But my instincts were crawling.

I closed my eyes, pressed a hand against my knee, and whispered the only thing that came to mind. "God... please go before us. Cover this car. Cover Alana. If there's danger we can't see; reveal it. Lead us. Protect us. Give me eyes to see."

The second the words left my lips, something shifted.

I'd felt it before; during raids, in rooms thick with spiritual residue. It wasn't fear. It was discernment. And it was loud.

No sound. No cold. Just weight. A heaviness in the air that didn't announce itself but settled over everything, unmistakable and full of warning. My heart slowed, but it pressed harder in my chest. The pulse in my neck pounded loud and fast.

I sat up straighter, scanning the car. Claire looked calm, professional, unshaken. But then I saw Alana. She hadn't moved either, but her shoulders had. Drawn in. Alert.

She felt it too.

That's when I knew.

Something was wrong.

I leaned forward. "Turn left. Now."

Claire's eyes flashed in the mirror. "What? No, we're taking the bypass. The route is already set."

"I don't care. Turn the car."

Alana turned toward me, her eyes wide. "Franklin, what is it?"

"I don't know," I said, voice hard. "But I'm not waiting to find out. Something's wrong."

Claire's grip tightened on the wheel, clearly annoyed. "We've been over this. The route's clean, vetted six ways."

"I don't care how many times it was vetted. Turn. The. Car."

A second passed. Then two. Claire clicked the blinker. "Fine. Rerouting through lower grid. But this better not be,"

"Car behind us," the agent up front cut in. His voice had dropped, serious now. "Been shadowing us since Route 7. Tinted windows. Been matching our speed. Too close."

My blood went cold. "Are they engaging?"

"Not yet."

But it didn't matter. I already knew what was coming.

"Okay," Claire said, snapping into gear. "We're heading back to sector four. Secure checkpoint. Now."

The driver veered right, tires screeching slightly as we peeled onto a narrow connector road. The landscape outside blurred. My eyes were bouncing between the mirrors, angles, shadows, any sign of motion behind us. My whole body was locked into the moment, calculating threats, tracking risk,

Then came the sound.

A roar. A rush.

And impact.

A violent slam from the side. Metal crushing metal. Glass

exploding into the air.

Everything flipped.

The car spun; over once, then again, the sound of Alana's scream swallowed by the chaos. Claire's arm flew across the wheel. My body slammed into the seatbelt as gravity turned sideways.

And all I could think, even in the middle of it all,

*God, please. Let her survive.*

## Alana

All I can remember faint and fractured like something slipping through the cracks of a dream, is Detective Franklin's voice, sharp and strained, shaking the air around us as he shouted from the back seat, telling Claire to turn, to move, to get off the route now. There was something deeper than panic in his tone, something that sounded like knowing, like discernment, like fear wrapped in faith. But now, everything is upside down, literally and inside me. When my eyes flutter open, the world is spinning too fast, tilted at an angle that doesn't make sense. There's this dizzying pull, like gravity is trying to swallow me whole. My body feels weightless and heavy at the same time, as if I'm floating and sinking simultaneously. My head is throbbing with a sharp, unrelenting ache that pulses behind my eyes and wraps around my temples like someone's dragging barbed wire across my skin.

I try to move, but my limbs feel numb, like they've forgotten how to work. When I finally manage to raise one trembling hand, it brushes against the side of my face, *sticky, warm*, and the second I pull it back, blood coats my fingers. A scream builds in my chest, but my mouth won't open. And that's when the chaos comes flooding in, flashes of metal twisting, tires skidding, glass shattering, voices shouting over each other, the pounding rhythm of disaster. Beneath it all, a single, terrifying realization slices through me like a blade. We were hit. We were targeted. This wasn't an accident. This wasn't random.

This was Ricky. He found me. There's no way this was random, not with the precision of that hit. Not with how they found us. And the worst part is, I always knew he would. It doesn't matter how many walls they build, how many aliases they assign, how many safety protocols are in place. People like him always find girls like me. It's like he's a shadow I never asked for but can never shake. No matter how far I run or how hard I try to disappear, he resurfaces, determined to remind me that I'll never be free. I blink through the blur, trying to focus, trying to ground myself, but the air reeks of gunpowder and burning rubber, and the scent clogs my throat like grief I haven't finished choking on. And deep down, I know this is what he meant when he said he'd find me. This is what it looks like when prophecy fulfills itself in smoke and blood and wreckage.

Then I feel arms around me, tight, steady, trembling with adrenaline but strong enough to anchor me in place. I hear Franklin's voice, low and close, fighting through the noise. His chest presses against my back, and his arms shield my head as bullets continue cracking through the air like thunder.

"I got you," he says, each word cutting through the chaos.

"I caught you. I got you. Let's go, we've gotta move now. They have to be running out of ammo soon." And in that moment, I cling to the sound of his voice. To the weight of him. To the way he covers me like it's not just duty, it's personal.

Because it is. Because I see it now. He's not just the one who promised to protect me. He's the one who is.

The shots are still echoing when Franklin shouts again, his voice strained and urgent, calling out for Clay.

"Clay's car didn't get hit! Get her! Get her now! Pull her to the car, we'll meet at the main post. Get her out!"

Hands reach for me, gripping tightly, and even though I know they're trying to save me, my body refuses to move. My arms wrap around Franklin like he's the only thing keeping me tethered to the earth, and when they start pulling me away, the panic splits through me. "Franklin!" I scream, my voice tearing from my throat. "I don't want to leave you, I can't leave you, please, *don't make me*," His hands cradle my face with a gentleness that slices straight through the fear. His eyes lock on mine, steady and clear despite everything burning around us.

"Look at me," he says, firm but tender. "Alana, you need to go. I'm fine. I'm okay. But I need you to be safe. You hear me?" I nod through the tears, committing every line of his face to memory just in case.

"I hear you," I whisper, and then I'm gone.

As they pulled me toward Clay's car, my body moved because theirs forced it to, but my heart stayed exactly where Franklin stood. Even with gunpowder still clinging to the air and the sound of bullets echoing somewhere behind us, all I could hear was his voice, steady, threaded with fear, but still choosing me over everything else burning around us.

The moment before the door slammed shut, I twisted back just enough to see him through the swirl of smoke and flashing lights. He was standing in the chaos like it bowed to him, chest heaving, jaw clenched, eyes locked on mine as if letting me out of his sight was the hardest thing he'd ever done. And for a heartbeat that felt impossibly long, the whole world narrowed to just that, the look he gave me. Not fear. Not duty. Something softer. Something that made my breath catch even through the pain.

His hand lifted, barely, the smallest motion, but it was enough to anchor me. Enough to tell me he wasn't letting me go, not really, not in the ways that mattered. I pressed my trembling palm to the window as Clay's engine jolted forward, and he didn't look away. Not once. Not even when the debris shifted behind him. Not even when someone shouted his name. He held my gaze, solid and unwavering, until distance swallowed him and the glass fogged from my breath.

And in that moment, bruised, bleeding, terrified, I felt something warm break open in my chest. Something I didn't have a name for. Something I wasn't supposed to feel for someone like him.

But I felt it anyway.

Clay's voice cut through the haze, sharp and strained, and I was guided, half stumbling, half lifted, into the backseat of the only car that hadn't been shredded by bullets. The door slammed with a force that shook the frame, and Claire threw herself into the front seat, shouting orders and swearing this wasn't supposed to happen, that there were no signs, but her voice faded beneath the ringing in my ears. Because all I could think about was that I made it out. I escaped. And for the first time in my life, I wasn't running alone.

As the adrenaline drained from my veins and the gunfire fell behind us, my body began to remember what it meant to feel. My fingers ached from how tightly I'd been gripping the door handle. I forced myself to let go, to breathe, to stay present, but it was hard when the weight of what just happened pressed down on my chest. Claire and Clay were arguing in the front seat, voices sharp and rising.

"No, Claire. You don't get to play the righteous card right now," Clay snaps.

"You've been bouncing between offices. You expect me to believe you didn't say anything to anyone?" Claire fires back, her voice raw, defensive, trembling with disbelief.

"I didn't! How dare you accuse me, after everything I've done to keep her safe?"

"You've been slipping," Clay growls.

"Maybe you said too much to the wrong person. Ricky didn't just stumble onto us."

"You think I wanted this?" she shouts, then catches herself. Claire's eyes flash, furious, but also something else. Guilt?

"You think I wanted bullets flying past my head? You think I wanted Franklin out there possibly,"

She stops. Her voice fractures. And the silence that follows is worse than the yelling. It feels old. Heavy. Like something between them has never fully healed. I sit still in the backseat, absorbing every word. Watching every move. Claire's voice trembles. Her hands shake. And the Claire I know doesn't tremble when she's lying. I believe her. But Clay? There's something colder in him. Something harder to read.

She must sense my eyes on her, because Claire twists in her seat, reaching back to brush my arm with trembling fingers.

"Are you okay?" she asks, quieter now, softer. I nod, barely, but the words fall out before I can stop them.

"You said I was safe. You said no one could find me. How did he find me?" My voice cracks, and the fear that had started to thin in my chest creeps back in like smoke slipping under the door. Claire's eyes soften with something close to regret.

"I don't know, honey. I wish I had answers. When we get to the main post, we'll figure it out, I promise. What matters is you're safe. He can't hurt you anymore. Not today." But I don't believe that. Not completely. Because the question still burns through me.

And then another one rises, sharper, more urgent.

"Franklin," I whisper.

"Where's Franklin?" I try to sit up, to look back, to open the door and run to him if I have to, but Claire throws her arm out and presses me into the seat.

"He's okay," she says, firm.

"He stayed to cover us. But he's safe. We've got backup on the way to get him. You're going to see him again."

I close my eyes and try to believe her. Try to hold onto the hope that I'll see his face again. That this, *whatever this is*, doesn't end with another loss.

The moment we pull into the main post, the SUV barely slows before the door's flung open. Agents are everywhere, yelling, moving fast, urgency crackling in the air like static. I'm ushered inside a gray building, cold and sharp-edged, fluorescent light slicing across the floor as I'm led into a small office. Someone hands me a coat, heavy and tactical, and I slip it on just to feel grounded, just to stop my hands from shaking. Outside the door, the chaos surges. Radios blare, boots hit tile like war drums, agents shout and phones ring, but none of it matters, *none of it makes sense*, because I can't find the one thing I need.

Then I hear it.

"Franklin's been hit!"

Time fractures.

"Officer down. I repeat, officer down. We need immediate extraction!"

My body moves before my mind can catch up. I stumble into the hallway, pushing past the people trying to hold me back, shouting over the noise, "No! Not Franklin! Not Franklin!"

And then I'm caught arms wrap around me, steady and unyielding and when I look up, it's Clay. Calm. Collected. Not sarcastic. Not cold. Just calm.

"Alana, you have to stay here," he says.

"You can't help him out there. He knew what he was doing. He's going to be okay. But you need to be safe too."

And somehow, despite everything, I believe him. But as the door shuts and I'm left alone in the sterile silence, all I can do is grip the edge of the table and pray.

That wherever he is, Detective Franklin is still breathing.

151

# 11

# Chapter 11

**Franklin**

We've been under fire for what feels like twenty minutes, though time disintegrates in a firefight, each second stretched into a lifetime when your lungs are burning with smoke, your vision is streaked with dust and blood, and your legs are fueled by nothing but muscle memory and prayer. The street is a war zone, shattered concrete littering the ground like fallen teeth, the acrid sting of gunpowder coating the inside of my mouth, and every breath cuts deeper than the last.

Gunshots erupt like thunder, echoing off buildings, mingling with the screams of men I've trained beside, some calling for help, some already silent. My ribs scream from the earlier hit, a blow that cracked something beneath the vest and drove me to the ground hard enough to leave stars in my vision, but I pushed up through it, forced myself upright because I had to because quitting isn't an option when she's the one they're hunting.

The call for backup was radioed out what feels like an hour

ago, but the seconds have stretched thin, and all I can do is hold the line long enough to keep the worst from happening. Every command over the comms repeats the same cursed rotation Detective Franklin, last man out. If I make it out of this, I'm filing a complaint about always being the last man out.

I crouch behind a blown-out SUV, weapon drawn, blood buzzing in my ears like static, and that's when I hear it: a slow clap, sharp and smug, slicing through the chaos like it owns the silence. And then I see him, Ricky. Standing with that same swagger that makes my stomach turn, his stance loose, deliberate, as if this whole shootout was nothing more than a rerun he's already survived.

His voice floats through the smoke, smooth and cruel, dragging up the memory of every time I've failed to stop him. "You really thought hiding her in a cabin with a Bible and a badge would change anything?" he says.

My hand steadies on the trigger, my eyes locked on his, fury boiling up through cracked ribs and bruised faith. "She's not yours," I say, voice low and solid, "and this doesn't end the way you think it does."

He laughs; a soft, smug sound, not manic, not loud, just assured, like he already knows he's walking away again.

"You think I won't find her?" he whispers as he steps closer, but I cut him off before the filth can fully leave his mouth.

"You won't," I say, the words slicing clean, fueled by the fire I've carried since the day I swore to protect her.

"You're not fate. You're not unstoppable. You're just a coward with a control complex and a God complex, and this time, you're not walking away."

Ricky tilts his head like he's studying me, then lets out a

low, ugly laugh.

"Detective, you really thought this was me trying to take her?" He steps closer, voice dropping into a venomous whisper. "No. This was me showing you that I know exactly where she's gonna be. All the time."

My jaw locks, but I don't look away. "You don't own her. You don't track her. That ends today."

But Ricky's grin shifts—slower, slyer.

"Oh... wait. I get it now." His eyes drag over my face like he's reading every buried thing I haven't said out loud.

"This isn't about a case anymore. This ain't agent and victim."

He clicks his tongue, delighted. "You care about her."

The words hit harder than his fists ever could, but I don't move. I don't give him that satisfaction.

Ricky's grin splits wider. "Look at you. Following her. Protecting her. Bleeding for her. You think I don't see that? You think she don't feel it?" He leans in, breath sour with triumph.

"You're falling for her, Detective."

I take a step forward despite the pain burning up my ribs.

"What I feel has nothing to do with you."

"Oh, it has everything to do with me," he says, tapping his chest.

"Because she was mine first. And I always get what's mine. Life or death—don't matter."

Backup is closing in behind me, boots pounding pavement. Ricky notices, smirks, like this is all a game he's winning.

"Well... looks like this is it for now." He backs up, palms raised like he's surrendering to a joke only he understands.

"Until next time, Detective. Tell her I said hi."

The ride back feels longer than it is, though I know we're pushing the engine to its limits—cutting corners, rolling through intersections, chewing up pavement like the road itself might disappear if we don't outrun it. Streetlights flash by in streaks of white and gold, and the sirens have already faded, leaving behind the heavy silence of survival, the kind that doesn't feel like relief but more like suspended breath. My vest is soaked with blood and sweat, ribs pulsing in an angry rhythm beneath the fabric, and the backseat of this transport feels sterile and wrong, like I don't belong here unless I'm giving orders or fixing something. But right now, I'm just still. I'm just hurting. And the only thing keeping me grounded is the knowledge that she's alive.

I should be speaking. Calling Alana. Coordinating next steps. I should be doing anything but this sitting, staring, swallowing down the feeling that I failed again. But my mind is still back there, stuck on Ricky's voice, the precision of his arrival, the smirk on his face like he already knew we'd be exposed. That means someone talked. That means someone slipped. And no matter how many times I cycle through every variable, every route, every lockdown protocol, it keeps leading me back to the same conclusion that burns like a match pressed to my spine. This breach wasn't accidental. It was internal. And the only people close enough to have known are Claire and Clay.

I lean my head against the window, the coolness biting against the side of my skull, hoping the pressure will slow the spiral of my thoughts. The ache in my chest isn't from cracked ribs, it's helplessness pressing down like a stone. It's the memory of Alana's voice breaking over the comms. It's the look on her face when she thought I was dead. And somewhere in the middle of that wreckage, I feel the prayer before I even hear it, rising up in fragments I didn't prepare, in desperation I can't filter.

"God... I don't know how we made it out of that. But thank You. Thank You for covering us. For covering her."

The words scrape my throat like gravel, thick and raw and real.

"I don't know who to trust right now. I don't even know what move to make next. But You do. You see it all. So show me. Show me who's lying. Show me what I missed. Don't let me trust a traitor. Don't let me walk blind while she's still bleeding."

My jaw locks as I exhale, shoulders shaking just once, not from pain but from fury, controlled, compressed, weaponized. Because if He doesn't show me soon, I'll start tearing this place apart with my own hands. I'll tear through protocol and loyalty until I find the thread that snapped. Until I find the name that nearly got her killed.

The second we pull into headquarters, I'm out of the vehicle and up the stairs without waiting for clearance or protocol. My badge hangs heavy at my side, but right now I'm not a detective, I'm a man chasing truth with blood still drying on his clothes and the fire of betrayal still burning in his lungs. I don't stop at the front desk. I don't slow when I pass the hallway cameras. I storm straight to Claire's office, each step hammering into the floor like judgment.

Clay's behind me, barely keeping pace, and I don't care if the whole building hears me when I slam the office door open and shoulder it shut behind us. Claire looks up from her desk, startled at first, then immediately hardening. I don't give her a chance to speak.

"It was one of you," I say, and the words land like a fist. "Someone gave him access. Someone let Ricky get that close. And I swear to God, I will find out who it was."

Claire pushes to her feet, her face pale but defensive, shoulders squared as if she expected this. "Franklin, slow down,"

"I'm done slowing down," I growl, slamming my hand flat against the desk hard enough to rattle the pens.

"This is the second time. Second time he's been one step ahead. And you want me calm?"

Clay shifts against the wall, arms folded, face unreadable. I snap toward him without warning.

"Was it you?"

His jaw tightens, but his eyes don't flinch.

"I've told you, we've got a leak. It wasn't me."

"How do I know that?" I shoot back.

"How do I know anything anymore?"

Claire's voice slices in, sharp and shaking.

"You're out of line, Detective. I am your superior."

"And I don't care," I say again, louder this time, feeling the heat crawl up my spine. "Rank means nothing if it comes with betrayal. So go ahead, Claire file the complaint. Write it up. But if I find out you're the one who opened that door, I will burn every bridge I've built in this place to make sure you're held accountable. That's a promise."

For a moment, no one speaks. Claire's mouth opens, then closes. Clay's arms drop slightly, his brows furrowed. The tension in the room is suffocating; thick, electric, dangerous.

And I leave it there.

I turn and shove the door open, letting the force echo down the hall as I storm out without looking back.

The hallway is narrow, too quiet, the fluorescent lights

buzzing overhead like a swarm of thoughts I can't outrun. I slow when I reach the observation room something inside me already pulling toward it before I even glance through the glass.

And then I see her.

Alana is sitting in the far corner of the room, shoulders curled forward like she's trying to take up less space, like maybe the danger won't notice her if she shrinks small enough. Her hands twist in her lap, and her eyes scan the room with that haunted kind of focus that only comes from surviving things no one should have to survive. But when her gaze lifts and finds mine through the window, something shifts.

Her face breaks.

She stands before I can even reach the handle, breathless, like she won't believe I'm alive until her arms are around me, pulling herself against my chest as if she's anchoring both of us.

"I heard you got hit," she says quickly, voice catching on every word.

"I heard, you were down and I thought," Her hands are already moving, brushing over my vest, checking for wounds, searching my ribs like she can heal me by finding what's broken.

"I'm okay," I murmur, brushing her hair gently back, letting my hand rest at her jaw longer than I probably should.

"Vest caught it. It hurt, but it didn't go through."

She exhales like she's been holding her breath for hours. I guide her back toward the chair, sit beside her, and for the first time in what feels like a hundred years, the silence feels like peace instead of pressure.

She's still watching me, eyes locked on mine like she's

measuring whether to believe me, whether to hope again and I can see the weight behind her posture, the kind that lives in your bones when you've carried fear for too long. So I lean in, not just physically but emotionally, letting my voice steady her even before I speak.

"I'm not letting anything happen to you," I say, clear and low.

"Not on my watch. Not ever."

She doesn't respond right away. Her expression tightens, like she's torn between gratitude and guilt, like part of her still thinks protection is something she has to earn.

"So while we wait for the next site to be prepped," I continue, "you're not going back to another empty safehouse. You're coming with me."

Her eyebrows rise, disbelief flickering through her exhaustion. "With you?"

"Yeah. You'll stay with me and my dad. Just for a few days. It's secure. He's... good people."

Her voice drops. "I don't want to be a burden."

I move closer, slide the chair forward until I'm directly in front of her, until the air between us is thick with truth I won't let her avoid. "You've never been a burden. Not once. And you won't start now."

She nods slowly, like the words are a balm she doesn't know how to receive.

"Today, when everything went dark... I felt it. You covered me. You didn't just protect me you stood in the line of fire for me. And I realized something."

"What?" I ask, barely above a whisper.

She looks back up, and her voice is reverent.

"I prayed. For you. I didn't even realize I was doing it. But I did. And He answered."

I close my eyes for half a second, letting that truth settle somewhere deep.

"That's the power of prayer," I say, voice tight.

"My Esther."

She gives a shaky laugh. "Your Esther?"

"With a little more sarcasm than the original."

And just like that, she laughs again, real and full and broken open in the best way. And for one holy second, it feels like maybe, *just maybe*, we're both going to make it out of this with our souls still intact.

By the time I pulled into my dad's driveway, the porch light was already on. He stood there waiting, arms crossed like he'd known this moment was coming all along. And when Alana stepped into the house behind me quiet, exhausted, still alive I realized something terrifying and holy all at once; I didn't just want to protect her. I needed her to heal. And I didn't know how to let that matter without losing control.

**Alana**

Franklin and his father have been genuinely kind no conditions, no catch, just steady and disarming. It isn't performative. It isn't rehearsed. It's steady, consistent, and it's been disarming in a way that caught me off guard. I don't think I even realized how tense I'd been until I stepped into this house and felt the walls inside me start to lower. Something about this place let me exhale without permission.

It's strange how the very thing that terrified me nearly to death is what led me here, into a home that feels... different. Not safe in the way people always said I should feel, not in the way that pretends the world outside doesn't exist, but in a way that feels rooted. Grounded. Real. I haven't used the word "good" in a long time, but here; it doesn't choke me. It just feels possible in this quiet, creaking house with its soft lamps and scratchy blankets and mugs that never seem to be empty good doesn't feel fake. It doesn't feel unreachable. It just feels possible.

There's something between me and Detective Franklin now, something undeniable. I can feel it when we pass each other in the hall or when he glances across the room without saying a word. It isn't the kind of closeness you talk about. It's the kind you earn. The kind that forms in the split-second moments between danger and survival, in whispered reassurances and blood-stained silence. Somewhere between him shielding me and saying I wasn't a burden, something cracked open inside me, cracked open with a kind of quiet violence I didn't expect. And now, without meaning to, I find myself softening, slowly, carefully, but unmistakably.

The same day I arrived, Claire kept her word and connected me with a therapist, Christian, but not the kind that weaponizes Scripture or hides behind clichés. She listened. She didn't pressure me to spill everything. She didn't promise healing. Just asked one question: let one person in. Not everyone. Not the crowd. Just someone. And though I didn't say it out loud then, I knew who that someone was.

This morning or maybe it was closer to early afternoon, I woke up from a nap that felt heavier than sleep but lighter than the dreams that usually claw at me. My eyes were still gritty, my chest sore from yesterday's crying, but for once, I didn't wake up panicked. I slipped into the hallway wearing Franklin's socks and a sweatshirt his dad gave me when he noticed me shivering on the porch the night before. I wasn't hungry exactly, just restless. I needed something warm to hold. But part of me knew it wasn't the tea I wanted, it was connection. The kind I'd spent years avoiding but found myself quietly craving since the crash. I didn't want to be invisible anymore. I wanted to be known.

As I stepped closer to the kitchen, I stopped. Not because I heard anything alarming, but because I heard something I wasn't meant to, yet felt pulled to anyway. Voices. Low, steady, thoughtful. Franklin and his dad were sitting at the table, Bibles open, steam rising from their mugs. I heard Franklin's father mention David, asking how someone chosen by God could still end up hunted, broken, begging for mercy. And then I heard Franklin's voice, quiet, tired, honest in a way that made my chest tighten. "Some days, I don't know," he said.

Something about that confession, so simple and raw, made me freeze in place. Because I've asked the same question too many times to count. If God sees everything, if He's all-knowing, all-loving, all-powerful then why did He let it happen? Why did He let Ricky win? Why did He let me lose so much before I even knew what it meant to have anything?

I stood there, motionless, one hand pressed to the wall for balance and the other holding an empty mug I couldn't remember picking up. I could have turned around. Could've backed away without a sound, gone back upstairs and pretended I'd never heard any of it. But something in me the part that's always been braver than I give it credit for, knew this wasn't a moment to avoid. It was one to walk into.

So I stepped forward, careful not to make too much noise. My socked feet barely whispered against the floor as I crossed into the kitchen. They both looked up. Franklin's eyes flicked toward me in surprise, brows lifting slightly, his lips parting like he hadn't expected to see me yet. His dad's face lit up with quiet welcome, and he nodded toward the couch like he'd been waiting for me to come in all along.

"I'm so sorry," I said quickly, my voice barely above a whisper. "I didn't mean to eavesdrop."

Franklin's dad smiled, warm and steady.

"Eavesdropping?" he said, that smile deepening with something like affection.

"No, sweetheart. You came at just the right time."

I let out a breath I hadn't realized I'd been holding. Not quite a laugh. Just relief. I crossed the room and settled on the edge of the couch, tucking one leg beneath me, cradling the mug like it could protect me from the weight in the air. At first, I didn't speak. I just listened. Franklin's dad asked something about David's heart and how trust doesn't always look like strength. Franklin answered quietly, his voice thoughtful. There was no pressure to speak. No urgency to contribute. Just space.

But after a while, something in me needed to say something. Maybe because the door had already been cracked open. Maybe because their honesty made room for mine. I cleared my throat, eyes still focused on the curve of my mug, and spoke carefully.

"What you said earlier... about not always knowing what God sees." I paused. "I think that's something I'm still struggling with too."

Franklin didn't say anything right away, but his jaw shifted, and I saw something flicker in his eyes, a quiet recognition, a shared ache. His father just waited, calm and still, like he

163

knew what was coming and wasn't afraid of it.

I kept going, not rushing, but not hiding either.

"If God is good... if He's really powerful... then why does He let people like Ricky keep breathing? Why didn't He stop it before it got so bad? Why does He protect some people but not others?"

The silence that followed wasn't judgmental. It wasn't stiff. It was sacred. And when I glanced at Franklin, I could see it all over him that same question still lives in him too. That same wound. It doesn't mean he doesn't believe. It just means some faith comes through fire.

I waited, expecting some kind of rebuke or deflection. But none came. Franklin's dad didn't rush to explain away the pain.

He just looked at me with those gentle, weathered eyes and said," I don't have all the answers. But I know God doesn't cause evil. And I know He grieves with us when it happens. Sometimes, the only reason we make it through is because He was there all along; even when we didn't see Him."

He stood slowly, leaning on his walker, and crossed the room to a shelf lined with books. He pulled down a Bible that looked like it had lived a hundred lifetimes its pages worn, its spine faded. He opened it with care, like he was letting it breathe, and read aloud: "The Lord is close to the brokenhearted. He saves those crushed in spirit."

The words didn't land soft. They landed hard. And something in me rebelled. I laughed not loud, not cruel, just tired.

"Then I guess God and I have met a lot," I said, not looking up. "I've been brokenhearted more times than I can count. Especially when Ricky killed my sister."

No one rushed to respond. No one minimized the pain.

Franklin sat still, his hand flexing slightly like he wanted to reach for me but wasn't sure if he should. His dad just nodded, like he'd been expecting that truth to come out all along.

He looked down at the page again and said, "You know where that Psalm came from? David wrote it after pretending to be insane just to survive. He wasn't in a temple. He wasn't sitting on a throne. He was hiding in a cave, humiliated, hunted. This wasn't a praise song from comfort. It was a cry from the wilderness."

Franklin sat up straighter, a quiet click of understanding passing between him and his father.

"Right," he said. "I remember that."

"And David hadn't done anything wrong," his dad continued.

"All he did was say yes to God, and still, he was chased, broken, lost. That season wasn't punishment. It was preparation."

He closed the Bible gently, as if sealing something sacred inside, and looked straight at me.

"Sometimes the call on your life is so heavy, so holy, that the only way to carry it is if you've been strengthened in the shadows first. And the enemy thinks if he can break you there, you'll never make it. But God? God uses even that place to build you."

I couldn't speak. Not yet. But I could feel something moving, low, slow, deep in my chest. A loosening.

Franklin leaned forward, his voice quieter than before, reverent. "Even after David wrote that Psalm, even after all the pain, God still protected him. There were moments when he could've taken revenge moments when Saul was right in front of him. But he waited. He trusted. And God delivered him in the right time."

He paused, then said my name. Soft. Certain.

"Alana... if you whisper to Him, even now, I believe He's already close. Not because you've earned it. Not because it's easy. But because He's still good. And He's still writing your story."

I stared at him. At the way he said it. At the way he looked at me like I wasn't a shattered thing but a sacred one.

Then I turned to his father. The man who had welcomed me, prayed for me, let me question everything without flinching. And I stood, walked slowly to where he sat, and kissed his cheek, soft, deliberate, grateful.

"Thank you," I whispered.

And when I turned back toward Franklin, something in me felt steadier. I wasn't healed. I wasn't whole. But I wasn't hopeless either.

And as I stepped out of that room, I didn't feel like the girl who walked in. I felt like someone who just might make it.

# 12

# Chapter 12

**Franklin**

The house is still wrapped in that eerie kind of quiet that doesn't soothe, it suffocates. It's the kind of silence that whispers something went wrong, that something's still out of place. I move through the hallway, and every creak underfoot sounds like a shout in the dark. The shadows feel heavier this morning, clinging to the walls like smoke, and even though I've walked this route a thousand times, something about it feels foreign, like I've stepped into someone else's life.

I don't need to look at the clock. My body knows it's early, too early for the sun to fully rise, too early for anything to feel normal again. Sleep gave up on me hours ago, not because of restlessness, but because something's been pressing into my chest since the second we realized Ricky wasn't surprised when we showed up.

The coffee maker hums to life as I move through the kitchen. The smell fills the air, sharp and familiar, and I wrap my hands around the mug like it's the only solid thing I've got left to hold onto. I stare out the window, but I'm not looking at the horizon or the sliver of light sneaking in, I'm searching for something behind it, something that might explain how we got blindsided by a man who always seems five steps ahead.

Ricky didn't flinch. He smiled, like he already knew how it would end. That wasn't instinct. That was preparation. Someone told him. Someone gave him access. And that kind of betrayal doesn't come from a distance. It comes from inside.

I take a long sip, letting the heat sting the back of my throat, trying to keep the bitterness from curling into my thoughts.

Then Clay's voice cuts through the memory like a shard of glass.

*"It's Claire. I'm telling you. She's the one who slipped."*

He said it fast—too fast. No hesitation, no stumble, no searching for the right words. Not a theory, not a reach. Just a fact he laid down like he'd been waiting for the moment someone asked. And maybe that's what unsettles me. It was too ready. Too exact.

Claire's never been sloppy. She's precise, steady, composed. I've watched her stay calm in rooms where everyone else was coming apart at the seams. She doesn't crack. She doesn't slip. She doesn't show her tells. And that's the thing about people like her—when someone is that unreadable, you never know what you overlooked until it's already behind you, already turning into something you should've seen.

Or maybe that's what Clay's counting on.

I lean closer to the glass, forehead nearly touching it, and let out a slow breath as the tension coils tighter in my gut.

"Lord…" The word slips out before I can stop it, low and raw.

My voice drops to almost nothing.

"Why was he so sure? What am I not seeing?"

The silence doesn't give me answers, but it shifts something in the room. Not an answer, but a presence. Like maybe clarity isn't a flash of lightning, it's a weight, settling in slow.

I think back to how Claire handled herself. She didn't hesitate. Her orders were too smooth. Her expression never cracked. At the time, I chalked it up to training. But now... now I'm wondering if I've been too close to see clearly.

In the window, I barely recognize myself, drawn, hollow-eyed, unraveling at the edges. I don't even recognize the version of myself staring back.

If Ricky got that close, if someone gave him a map to Alana's location, then this isn't just a tactical failure. This is betrayal.

And if I don't figure out who it was, if I put my trust in the wrong hands again, it won't be my life on the line next time.

It'll be hers.

I close my eyes once more, pressing the mug against my lips like the warmth might keep me steady. Then I whisper again, firmer this time, like a request, a plea, and a warning all rolled into one.

*"Show me who it is, Lord. Show me before it's too late."*

I don't notice him at first. My mind is too full, clouded with prayers that haven't gotten answers, memories that won't settle, and a gnawing tension that coffee can't quiet. But then I hear it, that soft, familiar shuffle against wood. My father's presence is unmistakable, as steady as it is worn. When he speaks, it's with that dry humor he's always used to sidestep the heavier things, like truth sneaks out easier when it's wrapped in a joke.

"Well, at least one of us is up before Miss Jennifer starts barking orders," he says, leaning against the doorframe like he owns the place, eyes warm with that signature half-smile, the kind he usually saves for when he's about to say something I'll pretend not to need. "Gives me a head start before Miss Jennifer comes in here and starts dictating my every move like she runs the house."

I glance back at him, lips tugging into something that might pass for a smile, even after everything.

"You mean the woman who makes sure you don't fall asleep with a lit cigar and actually remembers to refill your meds?"

He waves a hand like I've insulted him.

"That's beside the point. A man needs his silence before the orders start flyin'. I like to sit with God before I sit with anyone else."

That lands heavier than I expect. I nod slowly and gesture to the seat across from me. He eases into it, bones creaking, the kind of silence settling between us that only exists between people who've lived long enough to not need to fill every moment.

"She's not that bad," I say after a beat, looking into my coffee like it holds the answer. "She protects you in her own way."

He hums thoughtfully. "Protection's tricky like that. It always wears a different face, depending on who's giving it." His eyes narrow slightly, not accusatory, just seeing too much. "So what face is it wearing for you this morning?"

I hesitate, words thick in my throat, but something about the way he's looking at me, the quiet patience, the history in his silence, pulls it out before I can stop it. "I don't want to control her," I say quietly.

"That's not what this is. But she's... she's sacred, Dad. Not fragile, sacred. And I don't know how to protect something sacred without building walls. Without making her feel like she's caged again."

His face doesn't move, but something shifts in his expression. He leans forward, resting his arms on the table, voice lower now, like truth always drops a few decibels when it's real. "You protect her by seeing her. Not shielding her. Not rescuing her. You stand beside her while she figures out how to live again. You don't put bars around someone who just broke out of a prison. You become the place she wants to rest."

I blink hard, swallowing down the weight of that, because it hits too close. Too right. "She's changing me," I admit.

"Not because she asks. Just... being near her makes me want to be better. It makes me scared I'll ruin her if I'm not."

He nods slowly. "Afraid of what?"

I glance away, then back, fingers tightening around the mug. "Afraid that if I pretend what I'm feeling isn't real, I'll miss something important. But if I lean into it, if I let myself feel it, then I might already be too far in to come back from it."

"Love isn't the enemy," he says gently, "but if you don't name it, it becomes one."

I stare at him for a long moment, then ask the question I've been circling around since this all started.

"Should I tell her?"

He shrugs, slow and thoughtful, the way he always does when he's about to leave the answer in my hands. "That depends. Do you think she's ready to hear it?"

And just like that, I know. I see the way she flinches when she hears raised voices, how she watches doors like they might close on her. The way she laughs now, timid, like it's something she's still relearning.

"No," I say, voice steady now. "She's not."

171

He nods, satisfied. "Then there's your answer."

Before I can say anything else, three hard knocks hit the front door, quick, clipped, official. His eyes go wide like he's just been caught in the middle of something. "That's her."

I raise a brow. "Jennifer?"

He's already out of his seat, muttering under his breath as he hurries out of the room. "Don't you go rat me out. I need to be 'asleep' before she starts fussin'."

I shake my head as I watch him go, and for the first time in days, I let myself smile without feeling like it might break me open.

By the time I step out onto the porch, the sun is just beginning to push its way over the trees, casting everything in a light so soft it almost doesn't feel real. She's already there, tucked into the far chair, legs drawn up under one of my dad's old army blankets, her hair loose over one shoulder, like she forgot to remember the world is still watching. She doesn't jump when I come out. Just lifts her eyes to mine and gives me a small, knowing smile.

"I figured you might be out here," I say, stepping closer and offering the mug I made the way she likes it, tea with honey, oat milk, just enough warmth to slow her down.

She takes it with both hands, our fingers brushing for a second longer than they need to, and that smile deepens.

"So I'm becoming predictable already?"

"Not predictable," I say, easing into the seat beside her.

"Consistent. There's a difference."

She huffs a quiet laugh, the steam from her mug curling between us.

"Consistent," she echoes. "That's probably the nicest way someone's ever called me a routine."

"Then you've been around the wrong people."

She looks at me then, and there's something in her eyes, soft but wary, like trust is forming in layers she doesn't know how to name yet. We sit in that silence for a while, talking about everything and nothing. She laughs when I tell her how Jennifer rearranged the cabinets again and rolls her eyes at the story about my dad sneaking sugar into his cereal like a criminal.

When she laughs, it lingers. It's not the kind that slips out and disappears. It hangs in the air like it's trying to remember it belongs here.

Eventually, her voice drops.

"It just feels different here," she says, not looking at me. "Not like a new place. Just... soft. Quiet. Like that home I used to imagine when I was little. Steady. Safe."

I don't respond right away, because how do you respond when someone tells you you might be the thing that finally feels like safety to them?

So I don't speak. I just stay beside her and sip my coffee and breathe in this moment like it might be the first real one I've had in weeks.

I'm back inside when the phone buzzes, the screen lighting up with Clay's name. My gut tightens. I answer anyway.

"Hey," I say, keeping my voice even.

"Franklin," he replies, voice smooth, too smooth.

"Just checking in. How's the vest holding up?"

"Still breathing."

"Good. Good." There's a pause, just long enough to register.

"Alana seems to be doing alright. Not everyone adjusts that fast."

Something in his tone makes me stiffen. "What's that

173

supposed to mean?"

He chuckles, but there's nothing warm in it.

"Just saying... she's out there on your porch, sipping tea like it's Sunday morning. Most people don't bounce back like that. Some don't bounce at all."

I grit my teeth, every word coming out measured.

"You don't know the half of what she's lived through. Neither do I. So if she finds a moment of peace, no matter how small, it's not something she needs to earn. She deserves it."

He pauses again. "Sure. Didn't mean anything by it. Just talking."

But I know better. I know him.

I end the call quickly, but the echo of it hangs in the air long after. It wasn't what he said, it was how he said it. The bitterness. The bite.

Something in his voice didn't sound like a teammate checking in.

It wasn't concern.

It was calculation.

And I won't let that slide.

**Alana**

I needed a second out here, before the day got loud, before the kindness felt too heavy to hold, before someone knocked on the door, before Franklin's dad offered me breakfast with that kind smile that always makes me feel like I should accept even when I can't eat. There's something about this porch that holds me still in ways I didn't expect. It's not the weather or the chair or the soft creak of the boards beneath my bare feet.

It's the quiet. The kind that doesn't press or question. The kind that lets you exhale before it asks why you were holding your breath in the first place.

I've been staring at the grass for so long it feels like it's breathing. Out here, everything looks like it was touched with care, the lawn, the chairs facing the yard like someone used to sit and pray, the chipped paint on the railing that tells a story instead of hiding one. This isn't just a safe house. It's a home. And that's what makes it hard.

The last place they put me, sterile walls, blinking lights, not a single window that opened, wasn't dangerous, but it never felt safe either. No furniture that invited you to sit. No books on the shelf that said, *I've been read.* Just empty spaces filled with protocol. We weren't meant to stay there, and everything about it reminded us of that. This place, though... this porch with its softness and stillness... it makes me forget, just for a second, that I'm temporary.

And maybe that's the problem. Because now I know what it feels like to want to stay.

The car ride is quiet, but not the uncomfortable kind. It's the kind of silence that breathes easy, soft road noise, a hum from the vents, a warmth between us that doesn't need to be explained. Franklin's hand rests casually on the wheel, fingers curled just enough to remind me that he's always steady, always aware. The sunlight catches on his wrist, and I watch it for a moment longer than I should. Something about the way he drives makes me feel like I don't have to be alert every second. Like I could close my eyes for once and nothing would fall apart.

I don't know when it stopped feeling strange to sit beside him. Maybe it never did. Maybe I've just been too guarded to notice how easy this became, how being near him doesn't feel like a risk but a relief. He doesn't talk unless there's something worth saying. He doesn't ask questions just to fill space. And every now and then, I catch him glancing at me when he thinks I'm not looking. It's never invasive. Just curious. Careful. Soft.

And I shouldn't read into that. I know better. I know what it means to be protected by someone who's not supposed to get close. I know what happens when feelings grow in the cracks of trauma. But knowing doesn't stop the ache in my chest when he says my name in that quiet, steady way. It doesn't stop my heart from leaning when I see that flicker of something in his eyes.

Still, I keep that hope small. Tucked in the back of my mind. Because even if he does see me, even if he feels something, I know this isn't the kind of story that ends in a house and a porch and a forever. I know better than to trust what comfort feels like too soon.

But I let myself have this moment anyway.

The hallway smells like citrus cleaner and old paper, and my steps slow as we near the office door. My palms start to sweat. Not because I'm afraid of the woman waiting behind that door, but because I'm afraid of what she sees. Dr. Moby has this stillness to her, like a mirror that doesn't lie. She doesn't offer hollow affirmations. She doesn't let me ramble in circles. She just listens until the silence makes me answer honestly.

And that scares me more than being ignored ever did.

I hear my name called and I stand slowly. My legs feel heavier than they should. The receptionist nods politely. "Miss Alana? You're next."

I walk into the room and immediately scan everything out

of habit, the windows, the corners, the space between her and the exit. Dr. Moby is already seated, glasses low on her nose, pen in hand. But she doesn't write right away. She watches me sit. She sees how tightly I pull my jacket around myself.

"You're fidgety today," she says, not unkindly. "What's making you nervous?"

I shrug, eyes fixed on the coffee table. "Everything, I guess."

"Everything is a good place to start." She sets the pen down, folding her hands in her lap like she's preparing to hold something fragile. "Claire mentioned the relocation's coming up."

I nod, my voice small. "It is."

"And how does that feel?"

"Like I'm losing something again," I answer before I can filter it. "Like I finally got a taste of peace and now I have to give it back."

She doesn't flinch. Doesn't smile. Just waits.

Then she speaks, quiet but certain. "Let me ask you something, Eva."

I freeze.

The name hits me from a place buried so deep it feels ancient. My breath stops. My shoulders lock. She has never said that name before—not even when I hesitated on the intake line.

I lift my gaze slowly, expecting an apology, a correction, something. But she doesn't retreat. She holds my eyes with something steady, something knowing.

"I didn't misspeak," she says softly. "I called you Eva because I see you. And that's who you are. Isn't it?"

My voice doesn't come. I nod, barely.

"It was," I whisper. "It still is. I just... haven't heard it in a long time."

177

She tilts her head, studying me the way people study patterns they've been tracking for months.

"You know," she begins gently, "you didn't think I noticed, but I did. When someone calls you Alana, your body reacts before anything else does. Your shoulders tense. Your eyes drop. Sometimes you don't respond until it's said twice. That name feels like something you're wearing, not something you are."

My throat tightens.

"But when you wrote 'Eva' on your paperwork..." Her voice lowers like she's speaking over holy ground. "I saw the difference. Your hand didn't shake. Your breath didn't jump. You were... calm. Completely calm. Like your body remembered before you admitted it."

I blink, stunned she caught that.

"And then," she adds softly, "the moment you realized what you wrote... you panicked. You looked up fast, erased it, replaced it with 'Alana.' Not because it felt right... but because it felt safer. Because that's the name the world has forced you to answer to."

My chest caves around a silent sob.

She leans in—not physically closer, but emotionally, like she's meeting me in the place I've been hiding. "I'm saying this because names matter. They're identity. They're history. They're survival. And yours has been waiting for someone to say it without fear."

My eyes burn. My hands shake.

Her voice goes to a whisper. "So I want you to hear it from yourself. Not as a memory. Not as harm. As truth. Say it."

I inhale slowly, close my eyes, and let it come out—the way it always belonged.

"Eva."

She smiles, warm and patient and proud.

"There she is," she breathes. "That's the sound of you returning to yourself."

Something breaks open—pain, relief, hope—everything spilling together in a way that feels almost sacred.

She doesn't look away. "That tells me something important," Dr. Moby says gently. "You've been trying so hard to survive that you started borrowing pieces of identities that weren't yours to carry."

I blink, confused.

She softens. "Your sister's name... Alana. You didn't cling to it because it fit you. You clung to it because grief made you believe you owed her something. Like if you didn't carry her name, you might be abandoning her."

A single tear slides before I can stop it.

"And that's what trauma does," she continues. "It convinces us that we have to hold the weight of what happened to others and what happened to us at the same time. But Eva... what happened to your sister is not yours to carry. And what happened to you is not hers to fix."

My throat tightens. She lowers her voice even more, almost reverent.

"You can honor her without disappearing. You can miss her without becoming her. You can love her without losing yourself."

A shaky breath escapes me.

She leans in slightly, calm but full of truth. "God does not ask you to carry stories that don't belong to you. He doesn't measure you by tragedy—hers or yours. He sees who you are beneath all the survival. And He sees the woman you're becoming, even if you don't see her yet."

My eyes burn again, but this time I don't turn away.

"And now that you've spoken your real name," she says softly, "I want to give you something for this week."

I nod.

"Once a day—just once—say your name. Eva. Say it in a mirror, whisper it during prayer, write it in a journal. Let your soul remember who she is without fear, without borrowed identities, without grief telling you who you have to be."

Her voice gentles even further. "Your healing is not a betrayal of your sister. It's a return to yourself."

The hallway feels too bright when I step out. My name—*Eva*—still clings to my ribs like something fragile and brave at the same time. Each step feels unsteady, like my body hasn't adjusted to carrying truth instead of fear.

By the time I push open the clinic doors, the air outside feels cooler, quieter, almost different. I wrap my arms around myself, not because I'm cold, but because I feel... exposed. Unlayered. Like someone peeled back everything I've been hiding under.

Franklin's SUV sits exactly where he left it. He's leaned against the driver's side, arms crossed, pretending not to watch the door but absolutely watching the door. His posture is tense—but his eyes soften the second they land on me.

He straightens immediately.

No questions.

No pressure.

Just this deep, steady concern that feels like a hand on my back without actually touching me.

I stop a few feet from him, not trusting my voice, still carrying the weight of my name echoing through me. He studies my face like he's trying to read whether I'm okay—not in the casual, surface-level way people ask, but in the way someone who actually cares tries to measure the aftershock.

"You good?" he asks quietly, like he's afraid to break whatever I'm holding together.

I swallow, nod once. Not a lie... but not the whole truth either.

He doesn't push. He just reaches past me and opens the passenger door with this soft, protective gesture like he's been doing it his whole life.

"Come on," he says gently. "Let's get you home."

And for the first time in a long time, I step forward—feeling seen, feeling shaken, feeling like maybe... just maybe... there's a world where I don't have to hide anymore.

And somewhere between the therapy office and the road home, I feel something stirring. Something soft. Something holy.

"So..." I begin, barely turning toward him. "What made you... actually follow God? Like for real. What made it stick?"

Franklin doesn't rush his answer. He keeps his hands on the wheel, his eyes on the road, but something in his face softens like he was waiting for this moment.

"It started with my dad," he says. "Watching him choose faith when everything in his life was falling apart. He didn't pretend things were okay. He just kept holding on."

I nod, soaking that in.

"That kind of faith... it doesn't always make sense," he adds. "But it makes you want to live differently. To trust that peace doesn't come from ease. It comes from knowing Who walks with you through the fire."

I sit with that. I let it settle deep.

181

"That's beautiful," I say quietly.

He doesn't say anything in response. Just smiles a little. Not for show. Just real.

And after a long pause, I find myself whispering, "I think I'm ready. I want to try."

He breathes in, slow and deep, and then reaches across the console, not to hold, not to grasp, just to let his hand rest near mine.

It's enough.

# 13

# Chapter 13

**Franklin**

I drive toward the new safe house with the address locked in my head like a classified code, not on paper, not in a message, not in some digital trail begging to be exploited. No, this one stays sacred. Only the ones who need to know get told, and even then, it's face-to-face, one time, no repeats. I look them in the eye, I say it once, and I wait until I see that flicker, that click that tells me they've memorized it. That's it. No notes. No records. Nothing that can be twisted or leaked. After what we've already been through, after watching Alana claw her way out of hell just to stand again, I'm not leaving even a crack open for darkness to crawl back through. Not this close to the trial. Not with her name about to ring out in court for the world to hear. I don't want a house. I want a fortress. A war room. Holy ground.

The bottle of oil in my pocket is heavy, not in weight, but in purpose. Jennifer prayed over it this morning, poured it with her hands, sealed it with her faith. Said God fights battles we'll never see and wins wars before we even know we've stepped onto a field. I believe her. I've seen what happens when we don't cover what we care about. So when I step into the house, I don't even think about taking my shoes off. I walk straight through the front door and start moving like I've got fire in my hands.

Room by room, I claim this space. I press my fingers to the wood of the front door, whisper the words like a declaration and a warning all in one, "This door will not open to fear." I hit the windows, the closets, the baseboards, the places people forget that shadows know how to find. I don't rush. I take my time with the silence, speak the name of Jesus like a weapon, declare peace like a man building a wall in enemy territory. I tell the lies to get out. I tell the fear it's not welcome. I plead the blood over her sleep, over her mind, over the trauma that keeps trying to reach for her in the middle of the night.

And when I kneel by the side of what will be her bed, I don't just pray for rest, I ask God to restore what was stolen. I ask Him to pour something back into her bones that even she forgot existed. I touch the pillow and ask for peace. I lay my hand on the mattress and ask for healing in her body, her breath, her memory. I speak against every whisper that's ever told her she wasn't safe, wasn't loved, wasn't chosen. I tell them to leave and not come back.

Something shifts while I'm doing it. Not loud. Not dramatic. But solid. Like a wall just fell in the spirit and something better rose up in its place. I feel the pressure ease. But even then, I don't stop. I go back and check the locks again, not just physical, but spiritual. I stand by the front door and say it out loud: "No manipulation. No demonic residue. No echoes of Ricky's voice. No past ghosts. This house is sealed. This house is covered." I say it until I feel whatever was listening start to back off.

And once it does, I open the curtains and let the light pour in.

Earlier that morning, I kept hearing her voice, that soft one she used when she said Twix used to be her favorite, how she'd let them melt in the wrapper just to stretch the joy a little longer. In that moment, it didn't feel small. It felt like hope. So I picked them up. And I didn't stop there. I remembered the way she said blue made her feel safe, like peace. So I grabbed light blue curtains, soft bedding, a blanket for the edge of the bed. When I tucked the Twix bars in the drawer and hung those curtains, it wasn't protocol. It wasn't protection. It was personal. Just enough to say, I see you. You belong here. You matter

I don't know when this stopped feeling like just another case. Maybe it was the way she held herself through the pain, shoulders up, voice steady even when her hands trembled. Maybe it was the sound of her laugh on mornings when she forgot to be afraid. Maybe it was the way she looked at the world like she still believed there had to be something worth saving in it. I've protected hundreds of people before. Never crossed the line. But with her, it's different. And I'm not just drawn to her pain. I'm drawn to her. To who she's becoming. To the strength she doesn't even realize she carries. I still remember the way she stood in that hallway, hands shaking, voice low, but refusing to flinch. That was the moment I knew. Not just that she'd survive, but that I'd want to be there to see how.

So I sit at the edge of the bed, elbows on my knees, eyes closed against the pull in my chest, and I whisper what I've been too afraid to say. "God... I'm falling for her." I shouldn't be feeling this. Not now. Not like this. But how do I stand this close to something holy and not want to stay?

It catches in my throat, but I don't take it back. I let it settle. Let it burn. Because I need God to hear me, even if I don't fully understand it myself.

*"I know my role. I know the assignment. I'm here to protect her, to walk her into justice, to help her find solid ground again. But something in me wants more than that. I want to be the one who stays when the case is over. I want to be the one who sees her when she laughs for real."*

I pause, hands pressed together, breathing slow. "But if that's not what You've written, if I'm just here to cover her through the fire, then give me the strength to honor that. And the wisdom to step aside when it's time."

The quiet that follows isn't empty. It's filled with peace, like God heard every word and settled it before I even said amen. And I rise from the bed, one hand on the soft blue blanket, knowing something sacred just passed between heaven and earth. Something real.

I stay there a moment longer, just breathing in the quiet. Not because I don't want to move, but because I know once I leave this room, I have to hold the line. I'm not her boyfriend. I'm not her future. I'm her covering. And that has to be enough, for now.

But just before I step out, something in me pauses. Not fear. Not hesitation. Just discernment. Like peace settled here, but it's still fragile. I glance toward the window and murmur, "No shadows. No false comfort. Just truth." And I feel it, the real kind of peace. The kind you don't fake.

I walked through the quiet one more time, just letting myself feel it. The way the light hit the floorboards. The way the air didn't feel thick anymore. It was like the house had exhaled. I thought about how many places she'd been that never felt like hers. Places where safety came with strings. But this? This was different. Or at least, I wanted it to be.

I stood by the kitchen sink for a while, palms pressed to the edge of the counter, just picturing her here. Not because I had a right to, but because hope does that. It imagines. And I let myself imagine it, her making tea, her sleeping without flinching, her walking through the door without scanning the shadows first.

I leave the safehouse with a prayer still hanging in the air, but my thoughts are already shifting. The moment I lock the door, something in me settles, then tightens again. Those boot prints won't leave my mind. Still, I press forward. By the time I pull into my dad's neighborhood, the sun's lower in the sky, casting everything in gold. I kill the engine and sit in the silence for a second, just breathing. Trying to shake off the weight of what I just felt in that house. Trying to prepare for whatever comes next.

I hear laughter before I even reach the gate. And when I step into the yard, I see her, Alana, sitting next to my dad, hair pulled back, shoulders relaxed, her smile soft and real. Jennifer's nearby, hands on her hips, head tilted like she already knows something I haven't admitted out loud. I don't move at first. I just watch. Because she's glowing, not because of anything she's wearing, but because something deeper is coming back to life in her. The weight is peeling back. The light is starting to win.

She catches me watching and squints against the sun. "What are you staring at?" she teases.

"Nothing," I say, grinning as I step forward. "Just glad to see you happy."

But the way she looks at me, like she's not used to someone protecting her joy, not just her pain, it stays with me. We all linger in it for a while. Jennifer pulls her into a hug, whispers something only Alana can hear.

And when Alana turns to me with steady eyes and says, "Alright, I'm ready to go," I nod.

But behind us, my dad and Jennifer exchange that look, the one that makes something twist in my chest.

"You've got a lot on your hands," Jennifer murmurs.

And my dad chuckles, voice low. "Man's been looking at that girl like she's the answer to every prayer he forgot he prayed."

I don't say anything. Just nod. Because I know they're right. And I know this moment is the beginning of something I can't take back.

**Alana**

We hadn't even made it to the new house yet, and already I could tell something in Detective Franklin had shifted, sharp, alert, like he was watching the road for something it hadn't said yet. Not distant, not cold, but sharpened, like his senses were stretched just beyond the car, scanning every side mirror, clocking every set of headlights that got too close, tracking every silence between turns like the road might speak a warning if he listened hard enough. His hands stayed steady on the wheel, calm, precise, but his jaw was tight, like his thoughts were moving faster than the car. He didn't say much, but I could feel the way his focus wrapped around the whole

188

vehicle, like even here, even now, the world wasn't quiet enough to let us breathe.

Because something in that silence felt steady. Covered. Safe. And maybe that's what really shifted, me. Maybe this wasn't about him pulling away. Maybe it was me finally learning to rest in the presence of someone who knows how to stay. I glanced sideways, studying the way the light hit his face, the strength in his stillness.

I hesitated for a beat before asking, "Is Clay coming today too?"

His eyes didn't leave the road. "Clay'll be there tomorrow," he said, voice even. "I wanted us to get there first. Figured it'd be better that way. Just... give you the space to settle in without any tension."

"Tension?" I asked, even though I already knew what he meant.

He finally glanced over, just enough to meet my eyes, and the faintest smile tugged at the corner of his mouth. "I've seen how you two are around each other. Figured your first night should feel like peace, not like you're bracing for a fight."

The way that landed in me was quieter than a thank-you, but heavier than a compliment. I looked down for a moment, my voice soft.

"No one's ever given me that kind of peace before."

He didn't answer, but the smile lingered, and somehow that was enough to steady me again. The ride settled into something warm, like neither of us wanted to break the quiet. And then, without saying a word, he reached over and started flipping through the radio until something familiar floated through the speakers, something I hadn't heard in years but still knew every word to. I blinked at him, surprised, and he

189

just grinned and said, "Don't tell me you don't know this."

I laughed, and before I knew it, we were both singing off-key, windows cracked, wind tugging at the edges of the quiet we'd both been carrying too long. For a second, just one small stretch of road, I wasn't running. I wasn't looking over my shoulder. I wasn't calculating exits or wondering what face Ricky's threat might wear next. I was just laughing.

Just before we turned the corner, something in me braced, like my body already knew the peace was borrowed. When we pulled into the driveway, the air shifted again. It wasn't loud. Just a catch in my breath, a quiet tightening across my chest. But it was enough. Enough to still me. The house didn't look threatening. It didn't feel wrong. It was just... unfamiliar. And sometimes unfamiliar feels dangerous, even when it's not. I reached for the seatbelt with fingers that moved too tight, too slow. And even after I unlatched it, I didn't move. My hand stayed curled near the latch like letting go meant crossing into something I couldn't take back.

He noticed. Of course he did.

His hand lingered near the keys for a second after cutting the engine, like he was still deciding whether to say what he was about to say. The silence stretched, not uncomfortable, but expectant. Careful.

Then he exhaled. Not loud, but deep, like whatever he was holding had to be let out gently.

"I, uh..." He paused, eyes still on the windshield. "I've never done this before with you, and I don't want it to feel weird or pushy or anything like that, but..." He glanced at me, just once, then looked back ahead. "Would it be okay if we prayed before we go in?"

The words landed like something holy. Like a shield being

offered without demand. Like he'd sensed the war still raging inside me and wasn't about to let me walk into it unarmed.

I didn't answer at first. Couldn't. My throat was tight, and my fingers hadn't uncurled from the seatbelt latch. But slowly, I nodded, barely. Then whispered, "Please."

We didn't move.

The engine had gone quiet, but my heart hadn't. It beat loud in my chest, like it wasn't sure whether to brace or soften. The silence between us held weight, thick, steady. Sacred.

And then, just barely above a whisper, he began to pray.

Not loud. Not dramatic. Just firm. Grounded. Like every word was being laid like bricks beneath our feet. My eyes stayed forward at first, but I could feel the shift in the air, like something unseen had entered the car with us.

His voice was warm and close, threading through the quiet like a safety net. He asked for protection. For peace. For God to cover the house, to fill it before we even stepped inside. His hands rested loosely on his lap, but there was strength in them, even still, even calm. I watched the way his fingers twitched slightly as he spoke, like he was holding back emotion or pulling something deeper from within.

My breath caught as I let my gaze flick toward him.

He didn't know I was watching. Or maybe he did, but he didn't stop. His head was bowed just slightly, lips moving slow and deliberate. His jaw clenched as he prayed, not in anger but in conviction. Like he meant every word. Like he was fighting for something.

And then his tone shifted.

He started praying over *me*, not just the house, not just the night, but *me*. Peace into my bones. Calm into the parts of me that still flinched without warning. He asked God to make this place a covering, not a cage. A beginning, not a threat. And then he did the unthinkable.

He started speaking against Ricky's voice.

Called it out. Canceled it. Like he'd heard it himself, like he'd stepped into the echo of every lie I've ever believed and shut it down in the name of someone stronger.

My throat closed. My hands stilled. I couldn't look away now, not with the way he spoke like he'd been standing guard over me long before I ever let him close.

And something inside me cracked wide open.

Because I've been screamed at. Tracked. Touched. Treated like my body was currency. But never, never, has a man spoken to God about me like I was holy ground. Never has someone sat this still beside my silence and called it sacred.

I blinked fast, breath shaking, hands loosening.

Then I nodded. Not because I had it all together. Not because I wasn't still scared. But because something in me had finally been seen.

"Okay..." I whispered, voice barely there.

"I'm ready."

We walked into the house, and my survival instincts kicked in, automatic, uninvited. Even as my spirit tried to settle, my body ran the old script. Scan the corners. Clock the exits. Count the locks.

I tracked every window. Marked every shadow. My hand grazed the wall near the door just to test how fast it might swing open if I had to run. My eyes flicked to the lock placement. My chest tightened as muscle memory whispered every escape route I'd ever mapped.

He didn't say anything at first. Just let me take it in.

But then I felt him pause beside me.

Not watching me like I was fragile. Not crowding me like I was broken. Just *there*.

Then, quietly, just under the breath, he said, "You're safe."

His voice was low and certain, like it didn't need to convince me, just remind me.

My shoulders dropped half an inch. Not because I told them to, but because the room gave me permission. The air was warm. The light came in soft through pale blue curtains, not harsh through cheap blinds. The smell was clean, lavender and linen, and for the first time in what felt like years, I didn't immediately search for the place where everything could go wrong.

He walked with me slowly down the hall, hand at my back, not pushing, not pulling, just steady. Like he was letting me lead without ever making me feel alone.

Then he opened the last door on the left, careful and slow, like he was revealing something sacred.

And when I stepped inside, my breath caught.

The bedding. The color. The way the blue wrapped around the space like sky instead of storm. It wasn't loud or dramatic. But it *felt* intentional.

He remembered.

Soft blue. Not the kind that makes you feel small, but the kind that feels like peace. Like the morning after rain. Like a safe place to land.

There was a single flower in a vase. Simple, intentional, like someone thought about softness on purpose. But what stopped me cold was the Bible on the nightstand. Leather-bound. Worn but elegant. And at the bottom, my name, Alana, etched in soft gold. I didn't even ask. I just looked at him.

"It's yours," he said. "You've been asking questions... I

193

thought maybe it'd be good to have something of your own."

Next to it was a journal.

And something in me bent low under the weight of that kindness. I picked it up, flipping the pages like they might already hold something. My therapist told me to start writing again. Franklin didn't just remember, he made room for it.

"How did you know?" I whispered.

He shrugged, rubbing the back of his neck, suddenly shy in a way that caught me off guard. "I didn't. I just... paid attention."

And I couldn't help it.

I stepped forward without thinking, without planning, just moved. My arms wrapped around him, and for a second I wasn't sure if he'd freeze or flinch or falter. But he didn't. His arms came around me a beat later, and they didn't just hold. They *settled.* One hand pressed firm between my shoulders, the other curved low around my back, grounding me. He didn't sway or shift. He just stood there, holding me like I belonged there. Like I had nothing to prove and nowhere else to run.

His chest rose steady beneath my cheek. I could feel the warmth of him through the fabric of his shirt, the faint brush of breath near my temple. My eyes fluttered shut, and for one suspended moment, I remembered what it was like to feel safe without earning it.

When I finally pulled back, his hands didn't drop right away. They lingered, warm, gentle, present.

Then, soft enough to nearly miss, he said,

"I pay attention when it matters."

I didn't know what to do with that kind of honesty, so I smiled too quickly, made a joke about falling asleep before he finished showing me the rest of the house.

But as I walked ahead of him, I could still feel the echo of his hand between my shoulders. Still feel the weight of the prayer stitched into my skin.

After he left to make dinner, I sat there a while longer. Wrote a few lines in the journal. Nothing deep. Just... gratitude. Small things. The color of the room. The quiet. The way my body didn't feel like it needed to hide.

Then I glanced toward the window and froze.

One of the blinds was tilted just a little too far open. The angle felt... off. Not broken. Not dangerous. Just *wrong enough* that my chest tightened without permission.

I crossed the room slowly, adjusted it, then stood there a second longer than I meant to.

Had it been like that when I came in? Or did I miss it?

Or was I just used to missing things, until it was too late?

I told myself it didn't matter. But it did.

Not because of the window.

But because part of me was still waiting for the peace to break.

Something about the way Franklin looked at me in the car when I asked about Clay. The pause. The shift in his jaw. There's something he's holding. And I'm not sure I want to know what it is.

So I whispered, "God... give me wisdom."

Not just for what's ahead, but for what's true.

And then I heard his voice.

"Dinner's ready!"

When I stepped out, everything had changed.

The living room had been transformed, blankets draped over the couch, soft pillows stacked near the armrest, snacks laid out carefully on the coffee table. Twix. Popcorn. Something

195

fruity. The overhead lights were off, replaced by the warm flicker of a single lamp in the corner. Cozy. Intentional. Like someone had studied comfort and recreated it from scratch.

He stood in the center like it wasn't a big deal. Like this wasn't the kindest thing anyone had done for me in years.

"It's movie night," he said with a grin. "I figured it was time."

I smiled before I could stop myself. Something about the way he said it made the room feel smaller, in the good way. Not like being trapped. Like being held.

I sat down slowly, half-expecting my body to stay tense. But it didn't. My shoulder brushed his. I didn't pull away. He didn't either. We settled there, side by side, as the movie began to play.

Somewhere between the first line of dialogue and the first laugh, something in me let go. I didn't flinch at the volume. Didn't check the door. Didn't study the shadows on the floor like they might reach for me.

He passed me a Twix, unwrapped one himself, and nudged my knee gently. "Told you I pay attention."

I gave him a quiet smile. "Thank you."

He didn't say you're welcome right away. For a moment, he just looked at me, quiet, steady, like he wasn't sure if words would be enough. And then he offered a small smile, one that didn't try too hard, one that felt more like presence than performance, and nodded toward the couch.

We sat down together, shoulders brushing, the space between us growing smaller in ways that didn't feel threatening. The movie started, something light and old and familiar, and even though I barely followed the plot, I found myself letting go, just a little more with each scene, each laugh, each gentle silence.

He passed me a Twix without a word, and I took it, smiling as I peeled the wrapper.

"Trying to win me over with chocolate?" I teased softly.

He gave a half-smile. "If it works, then yeah."

"It's working," I murmured, taking a bite.

He chuckled under his breath, and something warm loosened in my chest.

The longer we sat there, the more my body stopped bracing. I didn't check the locks. Didn't scan the windows. My shoulders softened, my fingers relaxed, my breathing evened out.

Franklin glanced at me out of the corner of his eye. "Hey," he said quietly, "you look... calmer."

"Is that surprising?" I asked.

"A little," he admitted, smirking. "But I like it."

I nudged him lightly. "Don't make it weird."

"What? I'm just saying." He lifted a hand in mock defense. "It's nice seeing you breathe."

The playfulness made something flutter inside me—small, unfamiliar, but gentle.

I shifted, leaning against him. At first, I barely touched his arm, waiting to see if he tensed or pulled back. He didn't. His arm rested behind me, not pulling, not assuming, just there.

"You okay?" he asked, voice low enough it blended with the movie.

"Yeah," I said quietly. "I... I think I am."

He hummed in acknowledgment and let the moment settle.

I let my head rest against his chest, listening to the steady rhythm beneath my ear.

"You're warm," I mumbled, half-sleepy, half-teasing.

He snorted softly. "Gift from God. I keep houses heated."

I laughed quietly. "You're ridiculous."

"And you're tired," he countered.

"Maybe."

"That wasn't a 'maybe.' That was a 'yes,'" he said, tapping my shoulder gently. "Just relax. You don't have to stay awake like it's a job."

"I'm not—"

"You are," he said, smile in his voice. "But it's okay."

His teasing was light, soft, almost playful. And it undid me in the quietest way.

At some point, my eyes slipped closed. The movie blurred. His breathing stayed steady. His warmth stayed near.

When he shifted slightly, I barely registered it—just the soft adjustment of his arm wrapping a little more around me so I didn't slip.

At some point, my eyes drift closed. The movie fades into a warm blur, his breathing steady beneath my cheek. He shifts just slightly, adjusting his arm so I stay tucked against him, and the movement feels instinctive—protective in the quietest way.

I'm not fully asleep, just resting in that soft, hazy place where everything feels far away and gentle. That's when I feel him tilt his head, a slow, careful movement above me. His breath grazes the top of my hair, warm and steady, and before I can register anything else, his lips brush against me in the softest kiss—unhurried, tender, almost like he's afraid to disturb the moment.

The kiss settles into me more like warmth than contact, something my body receives without tension or fear.

He stays there for a breath, just long enough for the moment to steady itself, and then I hear him whisper—low, warm, almost blended into the quiet between us.

"Get some rest, Alana... I got you."

The words move through me like something safe and grounding, smoothing out the last edges of the day. I sink into him without thinking, letting the steady rhythm of his breathing guide mine until everything in me finally settles.

And in that space—held, steady, wrapped in warmth—I drift into sleep with a softness I didn't know I was still capable of feeling.

# 14

# Chapter 14

**Franklin**

I didn't even realize I'd fallen asleep. One minute I was watching her breathe, her body finally relaxing, her lashes fluttering shut like they were surrendering to safety, and the next, I was waking to the faint rustle of morning. Birds chirped somewhere just beyond the porch. Pale light spilled in between the slats of the blinds, casting thin gold lines across the hardwood. It was quiet. Peaceful. But too still.

I checked the time. 5:30 a.m.

For a while, I didn't move. Just watched her. She hadn't shifted much. Her knees were still tucked under that old throw blanket, her cheek pressed softly into the cushion. One hand rested near the edge of where my chest had been. Like she could still feel me there.

I eased out from under her with practiced quiet, moving her gently onto the pile of pillows I'd set near the couch just in case. She didn't stir. I paused, waited. Nothing. Still breathing slow. Still safe. I exhaled and stood, rubbing the back of my neck as I grabbed my boots from the door.

The air outside was crisp, laced with the scent of pine and the faint smoky remains of yesterday's firepit. Dew clung to the grass. I scanned the perimeter, boots crunching lightly over the gravel path that circled the house. No new boot prints. Nothing shifted. No branches broken. But that unease still crawled just beneath my skin.

We were alone last night. I know that. But I also know I fell asleep. Just let myself drift off. With her right beside me. And that's not a luxury I get to have. Not now. Not with Ricky still out there. Not with Claire going radio silent. Not when the case feels like it's coiling tighter by the hour. I made a promise to keep her safe. That doesn't leave room for mistakes.

When I got back inside, the house smelled warm. Safe. I started the kettle, set a few eggs to boil, and pulled out the pan. Something quiet. Something that wouldn't wake her too fast. While breakfast settled into its rhythm, I powered on my laptop and logged into the backup surveillance database, *not* the one Claire manages.

I scanned the logs automatically at first. But then I saw it,

A failed upload attempt.

Claire's system. Two hours after I'd shut things down for the night.

It could've been a glitch. A signal drop. Something benign. But there was no timestamp. No retry loop. Just a gap. A dead patch of nothing. I stared at it, a heaviness tightening across my chest.

That's when my phone buzzed.

**Clay:** *Can't make it today. Got pulled into a last-minute debrief.*
I read it once. Then again. And then a third time, slower.
Muttered it under my breath: "Can't make it today. Got

pulled into a last-minute debrief."

Really? No warning? No call?

Clay knows what today means. He knows I'm alone out here. Either he's avoiding me... or someone's making damn sure he doesn't show up.

My head was a mess. The eggs were boiling, but I barely registered the sound. I stirred them just to have something in my hands, something to focus on while my brain kept spinning circles. The upload failure was bad enough. Clay's last-minute cancellation was worse. And this, this just tipped everything off balance. I went back to the laptop to make sure the footage was saved, encrypted, firewalled on all sides. Double-checked the layers, out of habit more than need. But that's when it appeared, an encrypted message. Not just encrypted, but routed through an internal-only channel that shouldn't even exist outside the task force's closed loop. I clicked it, heart already tight.

**Watch the ones closest to her.**

That was it. No subject line. No sender ID. And when I moved to respond, just to trace it, to get anything back, I saw the tag: **Reply Blocked. Sender Unavailable.**

What the hell.

I leaned back in the chair slowly, eyes scanning the walls like maybe the answers were written there. I ran a hand over my jaw, then locked both fists against the sides of the chair, gripping so tight I could hear the frame creak. Watch the ones closest to her. It rang like a warning bell. But who did it mean? Claire? Clay? Alana herself? No, I couldn't go there. Wouldn't. But it didn't make sense. And the silence in the house suddenly felt louder than it had any right to be.

I stood too fast, needing to move, needing air. The porch

boards groaned under my boots as I stepped outside, and the cool breeze met me like a reminder that the world was still turning, even if mine felt like it had stalled. I paced for a second, then stopped at the edge of the railing, eyes tracing the horizon.

"God," I said softly, staring into the stretch of sky just starting to glow with morning. "I don't know who to trust right now. I'm doing everything I can, but You see what I can't. I need You to protect her... until this whole thing is over. Until Ricky's behind bars and she's safe. And if it's Claire, if she's hiding something, show me. And if it's Clay... don't let me miss it. Please."

It wasn't a polished prayer. I didn't care. It was raw, tired, honest, and it poured out like breath I didn't know I was holding. When I finally sat on the top step, I let the quiet come back, just for a moment. Let the wind brush across my forearms, let the trees sway like they were whispering something older than this case. I closed my eyes and just listened.

The door creaked open behind me.

I didn't jump, exactly, but I sat up straighter, instinct twitching the way it always did when I wasn't sure what was coming next.

"It's just me," she said gently.

Alana stepped out, wrapped in a blanket, bare feet soft against the porch boards. Her hair was a little messy, her voice still coated in sleep. But the smile on her face was clear, and when she saw me sitting there, her eyes lit up with something warm.

"So... where's my tea?" she asked, arching a brow. "You started without me?"

I let out a low laugh, surprised by how easy it came. "Didn't realize there were rules now."

She grinned. "Well, I thought this was our thing. Morning porch. Hot tea. Silence until I'm fully awake."

I shook my head, unable to stop the smile tugging at the corner of my mouth. "Guess I'm still learning the terms of the agreement."

She moved past me, her shoulder brushing mine just enough to make me forget the encrypted message waiting inside. "I'll go check on the stove before you burn down your own safehouse."

"Fair," I said, still smiling as she disappeared back inside.

And that's when it hit me.

I should've been uneasy that Clay wasn't showing up. Should've been focused, tense, watching every angle. And part of me was. But beneath all of that, there was this quieter hum, something I didn't expect. Something that felt dangerously close to contentment.

A part of me was glad it was just the two of us today.

Glad to have one more morning like this. Just her. Just me. Just tea and sunlight and the slow kind of peace that I knew couldn't last, but still wanted to hold onto anyway.

**Alana**

When I opened the door and stepped out, I saw it, the way his posture shifted, shoulders tensing, like his body had been ready for something else. I hadn't meant to startle him, but I could tell I had. It was only for a second, and then he relaxed, but I noticed.

So I slipped back inside.

Made the tea. Two mugs, because even though he hadn't asked, I wanted to do something that might help him feel more grounded. I don't know, maybe it was just an excuse to care for someone again. But I think I also just liked the thought of sharing something warm with him.

When I came back out, the air was cooler than I expected. I handed him a mug and sat beside him on the porch, wrapping my hands around mine, letting the steam roll up over my fingers. We didn't say anything at first. Just sat there quietly like we'd done this a hundred times. Like it was normal. Like we were normal.

And then, out of nowhere, he said, "Let's name three things we're grateful for. Go."

I blinked. "What?"

He grinned and pointed at me. "No stalling. Three things. I'll go first, hot tea, sun that doesn't make me sweat, and this porch that hasn't collapsed under my weight."

I laughed, shaking my head. "Okay, okay. Um... waking up rested, my legs not hurting, and... this view."

He nodded approvingly. "Solid. But you forgot to include your tea."

"I figured that was a shared one," I teased.

We kept going like that for a while, passing the quiet between us with lists of silly, sweet, and sometimes surprising things. At one point he said he was grateful for socks without holes and for my pancakes from yesterday, which made me laugh so hard I nearly dropped my mug.

And somewhere in the middle of all that, I started noticing him more. Not in the tense, on-guard way I used to, but in a quieter way—like my body finally had room to see what my fear kept trying to blur. The morning light caught the warm cocoa brown of his skin, smooth and rich like something the sun liked landing on. His forearms flexed when he shifted the mug in his hand, the muscles there defined beneath the fitted shirt he always wore, like the fabric knew exactly who it belonged to.

When he laughed, everything about him softened—not just his mouth, but his eyes, his shoulders, even the way he breathed. His smile was so bright it almost startled me, teeth clean and white against the deep warmth of his complexion. And his voice... God, the way it dropped when he relaxed, lower and gentler, like he wasn't a detective trying to figure out what I wasn't saying, but a man just existing beside me.

I caught myself watching the curve of his jaw when he turned toward the window, the way the morning light traced the shape of his face, strong and quiet all at once. I noticed the way his shirt pulled slightly across his chest when he reached for the remote, the easy strength in every movement, the steadiness he carried without even trying.

And somewhere in that softness—between the sunlight, his laugh, and the calm hum of the room—I wasn't thinking about who I'd been. Or what had happened to me. Or what waited on the other side of this fragile safety.

For a little while, it wasn't Detective Franklin and the girl they pulled out of the woods.

It was just... us. Two people sharing a morning that felt lighter than anything I'd had in a long time.

I don't know what made me say it. Maybe it was the tea. Or the quiet. Or the way he made it so easy to feel normal again. But I looked over at him, cracked my knuckles nervously, and said, "Can I ask you something?"

He glanced at me with mock suspicion. "Is this going to

ruin my tea?"

I smiled. "Maybe."

"Go for it."

I hesitated, fingers curled around the mug, eyes dropping briefly to his left hand. "You just... seem like one of the good ones. So, what's your story?" I glanced up at him. "No ring. No girlfriend texting you every ten minutes. Why are you single, Detective Franklin?"

He let out a soft scoff, not dismissive, just thoughtful, and looked out toward the trees for a moment before answering. "This life... this job... it's not easy to build something around it. Or inside of it."

His voice was quieter now, steady but honest. "I chose a career that doesn't come with guarantees. The hours, the danger, the mental load. Most people don't sign up for that long term. And I get it. I don't blame them. Especially when I don't exactly go for the easy cases."

He looked over at me meaningfully.

"Like me," I said quietly.

He didn't flinch. Just nodded once. "Yeah. Like you. But not in a bad way. Just... you deserve someone who can be fully present. And I don't know if I ever figured out how to do both. Be all in at work, and all in with someone."

His words hung in the space between us, and I felt my heart fold in on itself a little, not with sadness, but with understanding. I nodded slowly. "And Ricky?"

He inhaled deeply. "I've spent half my career chasing justice for Ricky. Waiting for something to crack open. I guess somewhere along the way, I let everything else go quiet."

I let the silence settle between us, both of us looking out past the trees.

"Ricky's not gonna haunt us forever," he said suddenly, voice firmer. "You're gonna get justice. I believe that. Without a shadow of a doubt."

I looked over at him. "You really mean that?"

His eyes met mine. "I do."

The way he said it, steady, certain, did something to me. I wasn't sure what, but it felt like an anchor in the middle of everything I was still trying to float through.

He stood a moment later and stretched, his movements loose but alert. "I've gotta make a few calls. Check the perimeter again."

I nodded. "Yeah... I should probably get ready for the day."

I went back inside to get ready for the day, still feeling the lightness from the porch. There was something about this morning that felt new, maybe not safe in the way the world defines it, but *still.* Peaceful. Hopeful.

Before I got dressed, I pulled out the journal Franklin had given me and sat on the edge of the bed. My therapist had told me to start writing more on the good days. To anchor the joy. To make it easier to remember when the hard moments came back and tried to lie to me. So I wrote. About the tea. The laughter. The way he looked when he smiled with his whole face.

And somewhere in the quiet, it hit me, Clay still hadn't shown up. I glanced at the time. That was strange. Wasn't he supposed to be here today?

I finished getting ready, tied my hair back, and slipped on one of the softer outfits I'd packed. I was tired of sweatpants and oversized hoodies. Tired of blending into the walls. Today felt different. I didn't want to hide from it.

When I stepped out the door, Franklin was already on the

porch, sitting on the top step like he hadn't moved much from earlier.

I smiled. "Where's Claire? And what happened to Clay? Isn't he a little late?"

He didn't look surprised by the question. Just gave a small shrug. "Said something came up. He won't be here until tomorrow."

A grin pulled at my lips before I could stop it.

He laughed. "Yeah, I figured that'd make you happy."

I sat beside him, nudging his shoulder lightly. "Looks like you know me pretty well, huh? I guess those files really do tell you everything about me."

He shook his head, still smiling. "Nah. That's not it."

"Oh no?" I teased, tilting my head, trying not to let my smile grow too wide. "Then what is it? You've been secretly studying me?"

"Yeah," he said quietly, like it wasn't a joke. "I have."

That caught me off guard.

But he didn't rush to explain himself. He just looked at me, steady and honest. "I watch. I pay attention. Not because it's part of the job... but because I want to understand what matters to you. What makes you feel safe. What makes you laugh."

Something about the way he said it... it didn't feel heavy. It didn't feel like pressure. It felt *seen*.

I looked out at the horizon, the trees swaying gently under the soft sun. "Well... since you're studying me," I said with a smirk, "you should know that I'm not a fan of feeling trapped. And I don't know about you, but I'm getting real tired of staring at the same four walls every day."

He raised an eyebrow. "Safehouse life getting old already?"

"Old, dusty, stale," I said dramatically. "Don't you feel it too?"

He gave a small chuckle. "I mean, yeah... I guess it's starting to feel a little tight in here."

"So let's go outside."

That got his attention. He turned slightly, not alarmed, but cautious, like his brain was already running threat scenarios.

"Outside like... where exactly?"

"Even just a walk around the block," I said. "Nothing crazy. Just... movement. Air. A little bit of freedom."

He didn't respond right away. I could tell he was thinking it through, checking every invisible box in his head.

Then he nodded once, his voice low. "A walk around the block... yeah. Yeah, we can do that."

The hesitation was still there, but the yes came anyway. And that was enough.

We didn't go far. Just down the gravel path, across the edge of the neighborhood, looping past a few quiet homes tucked beneath sunlit trees. But the air felt different out here. Lighter. Like the sky had made room for us. Like the weight I'd been carrying all week had finally loosened its grip.

Franklin walked beside me, close enough that our steps naturally fell into rhythm. He didn't hover, didn't rush, just matched my pace like it was second nature. The scent of fresh-cut grass drifted in the air, soft and earthy. Somewhere in the distance, a dog barked. I smiled without meaning to.

"I miss that," I said. "The noise. The smells. The way a sidewalk feels under your feet when you're not afraid of where it leads."

He looked over. "You miss the city?"

"I miss parts of it," I said. "Mostly my sister. We used to

sneak cereal before our mom woke up on Saturdays. Climb the counters like we were secret agents." I laughed a little. "She always picked the marshmallow kind. I'd trade her halfway through just to make her happy."

"She sounds like a handful."

"She was." My voice softened. "But she was mine."

He gave a small nod. "I bet you miss her."

"I do," I said, blinking back the sudden sting in my eyes. "Every day."

We kept walking, a little quieter now, the kind of quiet that didn't need to be filled. Then, just as we rounded the corner back toward the safehouse, a sharp crack split the air, a dry branch snapping somewhere in the woods behind us.

I flinched.

Before I could think, Franklin stepped in front of me, one arm coming around my back, the other across my shoulder as he pulled me close, eyes scanning the trees.

"It's just a squirrel," he said after a breath, though his voice stayed low, alert.

But he didn't let go right away.

And I didn't move.

We stood there, the tension thick between us, his arm still around me, my hand resting lightly against his chest. I looked up, and he was already looking down at me. For a second, neither of us said anything. The silence stretched, not awkward, not forced. Just... suspended.

Like something could happen.

Like it *almost* did.

But then he blinked, jaw tensing, and stepped back. "We should head in," he said, his voice more grounded now. "We've been out too long."

I nodded, breath catching as I stepped back with him. "Yeah. You're right."

We didn't speak much on the way back. But the air had shifted. And even though the space between us returned, the closeness hadn't entirely left.

When we got inside, I settled onto the couch, curling up in the blanket as he grabbed water from the kitchen.

"We never did finish that movie," I said, watching him from across the room.

He glanced over. "You want to try again?"

I nodded. "I think we need a do-over."

He returned to the couch and sat beside me, close enough that our legs brushed once I shifted to get comfortable. The movie played. The room dimmed.

And somewhere between the laughter and the lull, I leaned into him again, this time without hesitation. His arm came around me like it belonged there.

When sleep came, I didn't fight it.

# 15

# Chapter 15

**Franklin**

I wake to the sound of a floorboard creaking, soft but sharp enough to cut through sleep, and before my eyes even open, I hear Clay's voice behind it. Low. Amused. Threaded with that casual sarcasm he uses when he's about to poke at something personal under the guise of humor.

"Well, well," he says, arms crossed like a man walking in on something he's not sure how to define.

"So this is what we're doing now?" My eyes crack open just in time to see his head tilt toward the couch, where Alana's still curled against me, her breath steady, her body warm and completely at rest.

He doesn't say it cruelly. But it's not kind either. It's calculated, like he's taking mental notes.

"Sleeping on duty?" he asks, one brow raised.

"With the witness?"

I don't give him the dignity of a response. I just shift carefully, doing everything I can not to wake her. Her sleep's too deep, too peaceful to interrupt, and part of me knows that's why I never moved either. I didn't stay still out of carelessness, I stayed because something about her tucked against me felt safer than moving. Like breaking that moment would've done more harm than good.

Clay steps forward and, to my surprise, lifts her gently without saying much else. Her body sags into his arms with a sleepy sigh, her head resting against his shoulder. But his face doesn't shift. No softness. No judgment. Just blank. Like she's an object to be handled, not a woman recovering from war.

"She'll be fine," he murmurs, and I don't know if it's meant for me or for himself, but I watch him carry her down the hallway and disappear behind the guest room door with a silence that feels too smooth to trust.

I stay on the couch a little longer, staring up at the ceiling like it might offer answers if I listen hard enough. Whatever last night was, laughter, rest, closeness, it wasn't nothing. This morning doesn't feel worse. Doesn't feel better. Just... like something's shifting underneath, and I don't know what it's turning into.

Later, after I've showered and dressed, I feel it the second I re-enter the room, the energy's changed. Not loud. Just... tense. Claire's here, standing in front of the monitor with her tablet in one hand and her expression unreadable. She starts her update like always, but her voice is too quick, her tone clipped, the cadence off. She skips over the timeline without stopping, glosses past a key section, then pivots to another slide like she's trying to rush the room past something important.

And Clay notices. I feel it in the way he leans forward, his focus narrowing, his elbows planted on his knees like he's bracing for something to unravel.

"Claire," he says, calm but controlled, "go back."

She hesitates. I catch it, the pause in her hand, the flicker of something in her eyes.

"Back to the surveillance log," he says again.

She taps the screen. The footage returns, seemingly clean. But not to Clay. He steps closer, eyes scanning the data like he already knows what's off before he says it.

"There's a gap," he murmurs.

"Fifty-two minutes. Between 2:14 and 3:06. That footage wasn't missing yesterday. What happened?"

Claire stares at the screen like she's hoping the numbers will rewrite themselves.

"I'll check the back end," she says, but her voice falters in a way I've never heard before.

"Check it," Clay says, firm. "Because if someone accessed this house in that window and we didn't see it, this isn't a glitch. It's tampering."

Before she can even fumble through her system, her phone buzzes, sharp, urgent. She snatches it off the table and walks out without a word. No explanation. No apology. And that's what locks my spine into place. Claire never walks away from an open update. Never takes a call outside the room. Not once since this whole thing started.

The silence she leaves behind is louder than anything.

Clay doesn't move. His eyes stay fixed on the doorway long after she's gone.

I lean in, just a little, voice low. "What's going on with her?"

He doesn't look at me. "Been trying to tell you," he mutters. "Something's off."

And I know he's right.

I don't speak for a beat. Then I say, mostly to myself, "Maybe she's tired. Maybe she's just... off her rhythm."

But even I don't buy it.

Claire doesn't skip steps. Doesn't dodge questions. Doesn't vanish mid-briefing for a call she won't explain. And if this were anyone else, I'd already be pulling surveillance logs, cross-referencing phone records, calling in favors. But this is Claire. Someone Alana trusts. Someone I once believed was solid. So I hesitate.

But I can't afford to.

After the meeting wraps, I step out. Not far, just enough to catch my breath. I reach for my phone, scroll through secured channels, and send a discreet ping to one of my oldest informants, a tech who can trace call logs against internal records without setting off alerts. I don't tell him who I'm watching. Just give him a number and a timestamp. I'll follow it up with metadata requests once I can dig deeper.

I whisper under my breath, "God, help me see what's true. Protect the innocent. And don't let me miss what's right in front of me."

It isn't just about the footage. It's about how it connects. About how Claire's recent calls match the exact windows when things go sideways. I haven't said anything to Alana yet. I can't, not without proof. But if Claire's compromised... if she's involved even a little... this will break her. And it will destroy Alana.

I'm not jumping to conclusions. I'm not chasing ghosts. But something's unraveling in front of me, and I won't pretend I don't see the threads.

Later that night, I follow Claire's car from a distance.

She doesn't know.

She pulls into a strip mall parking lot and steps out, glancing over her shoulder like she's nervous, like someone watching their own back. Then a man steps out of the shadows to meet her. His build's familiar. I recognize the outline before I recognize the face, someone loosely tied to a past raid, someone we couldn't pin down because the records were too clean. But he's not clean. Not even close.

I stay hidden across the lot, engine cut, my hand near my weapon but not drawn. I don't need to move yet. Just need to see. To listen.

Claire doesn't hug him. Doesn't touch him. But her posture changes. She leans in. Speaks quietly. He nods once. Then twice. Whatever they're exchanging, it's fast. Urgent.

And then she freezes.

Her eyes cut across the lot, toward me. Not directly. Just... close enough.

I duck. Too slow.

They both turn at the same time. I can't see their expressions anymore, but I know I've been made.

The man bolts first, cuts left toward the alley. Claire turns to shout something after him, but I don't hear it. I'm already out of the car, moving low, fast, but by the time I hit the corner, they're gone. A door swings shut at the back of a building. I follow, briefly, but I can't risk blowing the whole thing if I'm wrong.

I stand there in the dark, heart pounding, trying to catch my breath as my mind races.

What was she doing?

Why him?

Why now?

I don't have answers yet.

But I will.

Because something's off in this picture, and whether Claire's the traitor or just caught in the setup, I'm going to find out.

Even if it costs me more than I'm ready for.

**Alana**

I woke up rested in a way I hadn't felt in years, like something inside me had finally exhaled after holding its breath too long. The morning light spilled gently across the blanket, casting the room in a soft glow that made everything feel a little more real. I stayed still, letting the memory of last night wash over me, Franklin's laugh, the way safety had crept in without warning. It had been simple, snacks, laughter, a silly movie, but it was everything I didn't know I still needed. There was no pressure. No performance. Just presence. He stayed close without making it heavy. Thoughtful in the kind of way that sneaks up on you and shifts your entire sense of what's possible.

I smiled, thinking of the Twix, the ones I used to save with my sister, letting them melt in the wrapper. A throwaway memory for me. But he remembered.

I didn't remember falling asleep. One minute I was there beside him, and the next I was waking up alone in this soft, quiet room. I sat up, not in panic, just a quiet curiosity. I blinked the sleep from my eyes and let my feet slide to the floor, stretching slowly, but it was the Bible on the nightstand that caught my eye. I'd seen it before, but something was different. A ribbon marked a page. And even before I reached for it, I felt the pull, like it had been waiting for me to open it.

opened it without thinking. The ribbon landed on Esther, and my chest tightened, and the ribbon fell across Esther. I froze. That wasn't coincidence. That was something intentional. Divine, maybe. Or maybe just Franklin. I stared at the name, my eyes moving down the page slowly like the words might already be inside me, just waiting to be remembered.

That's when I saw it, a small folded note tucked carefully between the verses. My breath caught. It wasn't the paper that stopped me. It was what it meant. Someone had placed it there with care. With intention. And when I unfolded it and saw his handwriting, I already knew it was from him.

*This is for you. Hopefully one day, you'll see her the way I see you.*

Just a few words. But they felt like a mirror, showing me a version of myself I hadn't dared to believe was still alive. Franklin saw something in me, something I didn't think was still alive. And somehow, I didn't feel the urge to run from it. I didn't want to reject it or argue with it or fold it back in and hide. I just... held it. Let it settle.

This wasn't just a note. And it wasn't just a story about a brave woman called for such a time as this. It was an invitation to believe that maybe, just maybe, that woman could be me too.

A knock pulled me out of the stillness. My heart skipped, automatic, hopeful, and I sat up straighter without thinking, smoothing my shirt, brushing a hand through my hair even though I knew it was still wild from sleep. "Come in," I said, the words too eager.

But when the door opened, the breath I was holding let out too soon.

It was Claire.

She stepped in like she belonged there, bright smile, familiar warmth, totally unaware she was stepping on the tail end of a daydream I hadn't even admitted to myself. "Good morning, well, afternoon," she said with a laugh. "Sleepyhead."

I blinked, glancing toward the window. "What time is it?"

"Almost noon," she said, setting something down at the desk, casual and easy like always.

"You're kidding," I said, eyes wide.

She grinned. "You needed it. I heard you two had a fun night."

My head snapped toward her.

Her grin widened, full of teasing. "Of course. I'm the boss, remember? He checks in with me. I gave him permission."

I stared at her, unsure if she was serious. She just shrugged like it was the most obvious thing in the world.

"I figured you deserved one night. Just one without Clay and all the tension. You needed to breathe."

And for a second, I let myself believe her.

But even as I laughed, something in her eyes didn't quite match her smile. It was subtle, just a flicker, like her eyes weren't fully connected to the curve of her lips. Maybe it was nothing. Maybe it was just the light. But my body clocked it before my brain did, and I felt the shift in my stomach long before I could name it.

"So he's here?" I asked.

"Oh yeah," she said. "Whole gang's here."

And something in me recoiled, not panic, just pressure. Like I'd been given space to breathe, and now the air was tightening again. I didn't want to see anyone. Not yet. Not while I was still holding the weight of Franklin's note and the ache of what it stirred in me.

"I kind of want to crawl back into bed," I muttered.

Claire stepped closer, slower now. "No one's going to push you. Not unless you're ready. I vetted everyone here. No one gets near you unless I say so."

I nodded, fingers curling around the edge of the blanket. But something in her presence made me hesitate, not because I didn't trust her. Because I did. Or at least, I had. But I couldn't stop the way my brain started tracking things again, her movements, the tone of her voice, the way she crossed her arms a little tighter than usual.

She sat down across from me, posture relaxed but her eyes sharp. "It's been six months, Alana. And I think you're strong enough now to start moving forward. Toward justice, not just for you, but for the girls who won't survive if no one speaks up."

My breath hitched.

I hadn't realized how long it had been. Six months. And yet, I wasn't sure I'd fully arrived.

"Claire," I whispered. "He doesn't know. Not really. Franklin doesn't know the whole story. I haven't told him what really happened."

Her head tilted, gaze narrowing just slightly. "You haven't told him anything about the operations?"

I shook my head, my voice barely above a whisper. "No. I'm not ready."

Claire didn't respond right away. Something flickered across her face — not judgment, not curiosity — more like she was weighing something she'd held for a while. Then she said it.

"Eva."

My entire body froze.

My heart stuttered hard against my ribs.

The name fell between us like someone had opened a door I didn't know she had the key to. I looked up fast, wide-eyed, breath caught in my throat.

"Claire..." I whispered, not even sure what I was asking.

She didn't flinch. Didn't smirk. Didn't act like she caught me in a lie. Her expression softened in a way that made the moment feel heavier, not harsher.

"You look scared," she said quietly. "I figured you might be."

My fingers curled in my lap. "How did you... how did you know?"

She let out a slow breath, like she was choosing every word with care.

"Sweetheart, you didn't think we wouldn't check your real identity? We always run DNA. It's part of every intake, every relocation, every protected case."

Her voice stayed soft, never rising.

"I knew from the very beginning that you were using your sister's name."

My chest tightened. Heat crawled up my neck.

"Why didn't you say anything?"

"Because it wasn't my story to tell," she said simply.

"I could've put it in your file. I could've corrected the paperwork. I could've made it official. But I didn't. Because that name — your sister's name — wasn't something you took lightly. And whatever made you carry it... you deserved to share that on your terms, not mine."

My throat burned. The room suddenly felt too quiet.

She scooted her chair just an inch closer, enough to feel

intentional. "And I wasn't going to expose something sacred just because protocol said I could. When you were ready to reclaim your real name, I wanted it to come from you. Not from a database."

I swallowed hard, heart aching in too many places at once.

She softened even more.

"You don't owe your whole story yet. You don't have to explain what happened or why you felt safer behind her name. But when you're ready to step into the truth of who you are... that's where real freedom starts."

Her voice was gentle. Steady.

And I wanted to believe her — desperately.

But my gut was still tight, holding itself in a way I didn't know how to release just yet.

"We got word about another shipment. Teenagers. Some barely older than you were. This may be our only chance."

The weight of it settled over me like wet concrete.

She continued softly.

"There's a verse. Proverbs. 'Speak up for those who cannot speak for themselves.' I've clung to that through some hard seasons. Maybe it's your time too."

I looked up, surprised. "You're a Christian?"

She smiled. "I've been praying for you since you got here."

That stayed with me long after she stood and gave me a hug. And for a second, as she pulled away, I felt that familiar warmth again. But just as quickly, it shifted.

Her arms were warm, but something about how quickly she let go made me blink. She left with her usual grace. But the moment the door clicked shut, the tension didn't leave with her.

That's when I saw him, Franklin, standing in the hall, eyes

on me, quiet and steady like he'd been there a while.

"What was that about?" he asked.

"Just the case," I answered. A half-truth. One I wasn't ready to unpack.

"She didn't push you?"

"No," I said.

"She was kind. It helped... but I'm still sorting through it."

He stepped closer, eyes searching mine. "If anything ever feels too heavy, you tell me."

The way he said it made something loosen—quiet, warm—in my chest.

"You always this serious?" I asked, trying to sound lighter than the moment felt.

His eyes stayed on mine. "When it counts."

The air shifted, subtle but deep. We weren't stepping closer, but somehow we were closer anyway—like the space between us had quietly decided it didn't want to exist.

His gaze flicked to my mouth before he caught himself. Not long enough to call out. Long enough to feel.

My breath softened.

His hand lifted slightly, hovering near my jaw, not touching—just suspended like he wasn't sure if he should or shouldn't. His jaw tightened, his shoulders drew in a fraction.

"I shouldn't be here," he murmured, low and conflicted. "Not... this close."

My eyebrows lifted. I let my eyes sweep over him—his shoulders, the warm cocoa of his skin catching the hallway light, the way tension settled across his chest. Then I met both of his eyes with a boldness I didn't know I had.

"And why not?"

My voice was soft, but it landed.

"What exactly are you afraid of?"

His breath hitched—barely—but I caught it.

He looked at me like I had just pulled a truth to the surface he'd been trying hard not to face. His throat worked once, a slow swallow, like he was holding words back instead of letting them slip.

"Alana..." he said quietly, warning threaded through my name.

But he didn't step away.

And I didn't look away.

The pull between us tightened, warm and quiet and dangerous in all the ways neither of us would dare name.

His hand twitched once, like he almost reached for me... almost.

Then footsteps echoed faintly down the hall.

He blinked, breaking whatever held us suspended. His breath steadied with effort.

"We should... go," he said, voice rougher than before.

"Yeah," I whispered, though neither of us moved.

We just stood there for a beat too long, our bodies remembering the moment even while our minds pretended to step around it.

Finally, he exhaled and turned toward the hallway, brushing past me with a careful touch—his arm grazing mine, warm enough to feel intentional.

"Come on," he murmured.

And even though neither of us said it out loud, I felt the unspoken words settle between us like a promise neither of us was ready to name.

# 16

## Chapter 16

**Franklin**

The house was quiet in that early morning kind of way, soft light barely touching the edges of the walls, everything still and untouched, like the day hadn't made up its mind yet. I stood by the window, phone pressed to my ear, letting the steady hum of my father's voice ground me.

"You alright?" he asked, sounding like he hadn't had his first cup of coffee yet.

I leaned into the frame, my shoulder brushing cool glass. "Yeah. Just needed to talk."

He didn't rush me. That's the thing about my dad, he knows when silence matters. I hesitated, staring out into the trees, watching the breeze nudge the leaves like it knew something I didn't.

"It's about her," I said finally.

He didn't ask who. He already knew.

"Last night... we almost kissed."

He let that sit for a beat. "Almost?"

"Yeah. We were standing in the hallway. It just... slowed. Everything slowed down. It didn't feel wrong. It felt like something I didn't want to stop."

My dad didn't laugh or make a joke. He didn't try to fill the space like some people do when they don't know what to say. He just breathed on the other end of the line, like he was holding the weight of my words so I didn't have to carry them alone.

"I saw it," he said after a moment. "Back when she came to visit. The way you looked at her. There was this light in you I haven't seen in years."

I swallowed hard, my eyes tracing the edge of the porch outside.

"She's not just a case to you, son. You know that."

That's the thing I'd been trying not to say out loud. Because once it's said, it lives. Once it's said, you have to stop pretending the line you're not crossing isn't already blurred beneath your feet.

"I think I'm scared," I admitted. "Of what comes next. Of what it means if I let it happen."

"Then be honest with her," he said gently. "But don't run from it. Don't be like your Uncle Darryl."

That caught me off guard. "What'd he do?"

"Spent a decade almost kissing the same woman. She moved to Texas, married her high school sweetheart. He still sends her birthday cards."

That pulled a laugh out of me, quiet and real. "Alright. Message received."

"Good," he said. "Now go talk to her. And stop thinking so hard. The answer's not in the overthinking. It's in the looking."

227

After I hung up, I didn't move right away. His words lingered like smoke, curling into places I didn't expect, places I'd kept closed off for too long. I wanted to go to her. I wanted to finish what last night had started. But I also knew if I did it now, it wouldn't be about timing. It'd be about fear. About trying to hold onto something when everything else felt like it was slipping.

So I worked.

I sat at the desk and drowned myself in data, case files, maps, exit points, surveillance logs. It was all noise, all numbers, until I stumbled across the southeast camera feed. It wasn't one of the main angles. It was low-grade, peripheral, meant more for backup than anything useful. But I paused when I saw it.

Movement.

Not obvious. Just a flicker at the edge of the frame. A shadow. Then the corner of a boot disappearing into the bushes.

I rewound. Slowed it down. Frame by frame.

And there it was again.

A shape. Intentional. During the exact window of time we'd flagged earlier, the fifty-two-minute gap in the main footage. We thought it was a glitch. But this? This was different.

Whoever this was hadn't been leaving the scene. They were returning. Not to clean up, but to plant something. That's how the ambush was timed. That's how they knew.

The surveillance had been compromised.

And only a handful of people had access to that feed.

Only one of them had compiled the last packet of data.

Claire.

I didn't want it to be her. I needed it not to be her. But the facts were stacking up, and they weren't lying. I stared at the screen, my stomach tight, my thoughts sharpening like glass. I didn't want to move too fast. I didn't want paranoia to turn me into someone I didn't recognize.

But I needed to know the truth.

I stepped out of the room and made my way through the house slowly, eyes scanning every shadow. I didn't have a destination. Just a pulse in my chest that was leading me somewhere I hadn't decided to go yet. Then I heard her voice.

Soft. Focused. Just outside on the porch.

I paused near the screen door and stayed quiet.

"No... he doesn't know. I still have eyes on her."

I froze.

Every muscle in my body locked into place as my brain tried to outrun what I'd just heard. I didn't move. Didn't speak. I just listened to the silence that followed, trying to make sense of who she was talking to, why she sounded like she wasn't working with us anymore.

I backed away from the porch without letting her see me. I didn't confront. Not yet. I needed more. I needed everything.

So I went to find Clay.

He was in the planning room, crouched over the board like he was already ten moves ahead. When he looked up, he saw it in my face.

"You look like you just found the needle."

I shut the door behind me and nodded once. "Secondary cam picked up movement during the blackout window. Not a glitch. Someone came back."

Clay stood slowly, his jaw tightening. "So we were right."

I didn't say her name. Not yet. I couldn't. Not until I had proof I couldn't argue with.

"We assume the house was compromised," I said. "Inside

job."

Clay nodded.  "I'll sweep the old safehouse.  Look for anything we missed. No one else needs to know yet."

"Keep it between us," I added. "No reports. No updates. Just you and me."

He agreed too fast. Too confidently. And it should've made me feel better, but it didn't. Not because I didn't trust him, but because something in me had shifted. I didn't trust the system anymore. I didn't trust the rules we thought we were playing by.

After he left, I wandered the house again until I found her, Alana.  Sitting by the window, Bible in her lap, tracing the words like they were oxygen.

"I've been reading Esther," she said, not looking up. "Didn't think I was ready, but maybe that's why it hit me so hard."

She looked at me then, her eyes wide and brave in a way that made my chest ache.

"I want to help," she said. "Not just survive. I want to help someone else get out too."

There it was, her courage. Her clarity. And I couldn't stop staring at her, not because she was broken, but because she wasn't. Not anymore.

"I'm proud of you," I said.

And I meant it more than anything I've said in years.

We didn't speak for a long time after that.  Just sat in the stillness, side by side, listening to the rain as it started to fall. It didn't feel like something ending.

It felt like something beginning.

**Alana**

It had been a few days since I told Detective Franklin I wanted to help, and I'd been carrying the weight of that decision ever since, not heavy like regret, but steady like something sacred. Each night I found myself returning to the Book of Esther. First just the chapter Claire marked, then back to the beginning, reading it all the way through. Twice. Somewhere between those pages, Esther stopped being just a name. I saw myself in her. Not because I felt brave or chosen, but because I knew what it meant to be hidden, to stay quiet for survival, and to wonder if silence was the only way to stay safe. When Claire said maybe I was born for such a time as this, she didn't say it like a challenge. She said it like a truth. And for the first time in a long time, I didn't want to run from it.

Now, sitting in the passenger seat as Franklin pulled into the therapy lot, I could feel the nerves crawling through me, tight in my hands, restless in my knees. It wasn't fear of what would be said. It was fear of what might rise to the surface once the words started coming. He didn't speak much on the drive, and I was grateful. The quiet between us wasn't uncomfortable anymore. It felt like space to breathe. When we slowed near the entrance, he reached over and turned the volume down even more.

"You good?" he asked gently, his voice low, almost reverent.

I nodded, then shook my head, then nodded again. "I will be."

He parked where he always did, close enough to watch, far enough to give me space. "I'll be right here," he said, finally turning to meet my eyes. "Same place. Just like always."

There was something in the way he said it that steadied me. He got out first, walked around, and opened my door. Always the gentleman. Always careful not to smother me with

231

protection, even as he refused to let me feel alone. I stepped out, pulled my sweater tighter, and looked at the building. Then at him.

"Thank you," I said.

"For what?"

"For treating me like I'm more than what happened to me."

He didn't answer right away, just looked at me with a calm steadiness I'd come to count on. "You are. Always have been."

I nodded and turned toward the door, whispering a prayer that today would shift something inside of me. Maybe I wasn't Esther. But I was still chosen.

The room was quiet, warm, filled with that gentle stillness that doesn't press or rush, just waits. My therapist sat across from me, her notebook unopened. She never forced anything. She just held space. I breathed deep, let the silence settle, and then spoke.

"I think..." My voice caught, thin in my throat. I tried again. "I think I believed him."

"Believed who?"

"Ricky." I didn't look at her. Just stared at the corner of the room. "He used to say I wasn't strong enough to leave. That I'd be nothing without him. And after a while, I stopped trying to prove him wrong. I let it be true."

The silence that followed felt thick with grace.

"What you're describing," she said after a moment, "isn't just trauma. That's spiritual warfare. The enemy doesn't always shout. Sometimes he whispers, and he uses your own voice to do it."

I looked at her.

"He doesn't have to chain you," she continued. "He just has to convince you to accept the chains already there."

My chest tightened. My eyes burned.

"When those thoughts come, when they say you're weak, used, dirty, I want you to stop and ask: whose voice is this? Because shame sounds like the enemy. Conviction sounds like love. And God doesn't shame. He restores."

I nodded, slowly, but the words were digging deep. Still, I flinched when she asked what stood out to me in Esther.

"That she was scared," I said. "That she didn't feel ready. But she did it anyway."

"And what gave her the strength to do that?"

"She had people praying. She had someone who reminded her who she was."

"Exactly. She didn't walk in bold. She walked in obedient. And that was enough."

She reached into her notebook and slid a card across the table. "These are your reminders. When the lies come, speak truth. You are chosen. You are healed. You are enough."

I stared at the card, the words blurring behind the tears in my eyes.

And then, without meaning to, I whispered, "I've never given my life to Him."

She didn't react with surprise. Only tenderness. So I kept going.

"I don't know how. I've seen people do it, altar calls, prayers, but I was never that girl. I never felt clean enough. But now... now I want Him. I want to belong to someone who won't hurt me. I want to stop surviving and start living. I want to be His. For real. But I don't know where to begin."

She didn't preach. She didn't pressure. She just leaned in with the quiet reverence of someone who knew the weight of what was being said.

"That's where every beginning starts," she said. "With the ache."

And something inside me cracked.

"I've carried so much shame," I said. "I've hated my name. I've hated the mirror. I believed Ricky when he said I was too far gone. I let him shape my identity until I couldn't find myself anymore. I played strong, but I'm tired. I'm so tired."

I couldn't look at her. Couldn't bear the thought of being seen in that raw, wrecked place. But she didn't flinch. She rose from her chair, slow and intentional, and returned not with a clipboard, but a Bible, worn and soft, like it had lived in her hands for years.

She knelt beside me and opened to Romans.

"If you declare with your mouth, 'Jesus is Lord, ' and believe in your heart that God raised Him from the dead, you will be saved."

"That's it?" I whispered.

"That's what He did," she said. "All you have to do now... is receive it."

So I did.

I repeated the words. I confessed. I believed.

And when I said "Jesus is Lord," something broke open in me. I sobbed. Loud. Uncontrolled. Holy. My hands covered my face, but the weight that had lived in my bones for years, shame, fear, despair, began to lift. And she cried with me, whispering truth the whole time.

"You are forgiven. You are new. You are His."

We knelt there, our hands joined, the Bible open between us like an altar. I don't know how long we stayed that way. But when I finally looked up, something was gone. That heaviness, that accusing voice, I couldn't hear it anymore.

And in its place, something holy had come.

I wasn't just surviving. I wasn't owned by the past. I wasn't invisible.

I was His.

When I stepped out of the therapist's office, I expected to feel hollow. But the moment I saw him waiting in the hallway—hands in his pockets, eyes lifting the second the door opened—something inside me eased.

He gave me the smallest smile, soft and steady. "Hey."

My throat tightened. "Hi."

"You okay?" he asked gently.

I nodded, even though the truth was messier. "Yeah. Just... really glad you're here."

His expression warmed, something unreadable flickering in his eyes. Then he opened his arms—nothing dramatic, just an easy offer—and I stepped into them without overthinking it.

He held me for a quiet moment, not tight, not hesitant, just enough for me to breathe. Enough to feel grounded again.

"You ready to go home?" he asked.

I nodded, but the truth was... I didn't even know what home meant anymore. Not after today. Not after everything that broke open in that room. Home wasn't the place I came from or the places I'd been forced to stay. It wasn't a shelter or a safehouse or an address.

The ride home was quiet, not because there was nothing to say, but because something sacred had happened, and I was still living in its afterglow. I held the card from my therapist in my lap like it was something sacred.

Then finally, softly, I said it. "I gave my life to Christ today."

Franklin didn't jerk the wheel. He didn't rush a reply. He

just looked at me with wide eyes and awe.

"You did?"

I nodded. "Yeah. I asked. I meant it. And I believe it."

"Why didn't you tell me first?" he asked, not accusing, just genuinely wondering.

I smiled. "Because for once, I needed a decision that wasn't wrapped around a man. Every other part of my life has been about surviving for someone else. This time, it needed to be just me and God."

He pulled over. Gently. Quietly. Turned toward me with something fierce and kind in his voice.

"I'm not upset," he said. "I'm proud. Because that was between you and Him. And that's how it should've been."

He didn't pull me into a hug immediately. He waited—giving me space, giving me choice.

So when I reached for him, he met me halfway.

His arms wrapped around me slow and strong, not squeezing, not overwhelming—just steady, like he knew the weight of what this moment meant and wanted to hold it with the same care God had offered me.

I sank into him, eyes closed, letting that quiet strength settle everything that had been shaking inside me.

When we finally pulled back, our faces stayed close—closer than either of us intended. His breath brushed mine, warm and gentle, and something unspoken flickered between us that neither of us dared name.

A horn blared behind us.

We both blinked, snapped out of the moment, and he huffed a low laugh.

"Guess this wasn't the best place to stop," he said, shaking his head.

"Maybe not," I whispered. "But it was the right moment."

And the way he looked at me after that made something warm curl in my chest, soft and certain.

# 17

# Chapter 17

**Franklin**

The morning light hadn't fully broken yet. That pale gray stillness stretched across the ceiling like a veil, soft and unbothered, and I sat in it for a moment, unmoving. There was a stillness in the house, not hollow or dead, just... suspended. The kind of silence that let you breathe slow and deep. I stayed there longer than I meant to, letting the quiet settle over me like a second skin before finally pushing the blanket aside and moving toward the window. The chair I used every morning creaked just slightly beneath me, familiar in the way old things are, and I bowed my head to pray, not out of habit, but necessity. I didn't bring a list. I didn't dress it up in theology. Just honesty. God, I need You today. I don't want to move without You. Whatever comes, stay with me.

My phone buzzed. I opened my eyes but didn't lift my head. Just reached for it, thumbed the screen.

Clay: *Swept the house. Sent prints to the lab. If there's anything there that doesn't belong, we'll know soon.*

I responded quickly:

*Me: Keep it between us. Don't mention anything until the report's in. Not to anyone.*

Then I paused. Let the weight of that last line sink in. Not to anyone. Not until I know who I can trust.

I put the phone down, but my mind didn't go back to the case. It went to her. Alana. To last night. The quiet way she had said it, like it cost something to speak it out loud.

*I gave my life to Christ today.*

I had seen her walk through fire and not fold, had watched her fight for breath when the past came back with claws, but last night wasn't fight, it was faith. It wasn't survival, it was surrender. And it undid me. Not because she said the words, but because I saw what it did to her eyes. There was something softer in them now. Not weaker, just steadier. Like something in her had been released.

I thought about my father's words, how he told me I wasn't looking at her like a case file. I hadn't wanted to believe it then. Maybe I didn't know what to do with it. But this morning, in the quiet before the chaos, I couldn't deny it. I saw her everywhere now. In the life I hadn't let myself imagine. A life beyond the task force. Beyond this case. I saw her in peace. In kitchens without locks. In laughter without curfews. I saw her whole. And I saw myself beside her.

It scared me. Not because it was too much, but because it wasn't something I could control. I'd spent years keeping lines clear, hearts guarded. But I wasn't guarding anything now. I wasn't even pretending. And I didn't say it out loud. I didn't need to. The Holy Spirit whispered it so gently I could've missed it.

**You're falling in love with her.**

I didn't deny it. I didn't resist it. I just breathed it in and let it settle.

By the time I made it downstairs, the house had already shifted into motion. Alana was front and center, standing over a spread of folders, maps, and tech like she'd been doing this work for years. Claire and two other agents were listening, following her lead as she pointed at routes, flipped through lists, cross-referenced drop points with shipment logs. She didn't flinch. Didn't stammer. She belonged there. And for a second, I just stood back and watched.

She looked up and saw me. Smiled like she already knew what I was thinking.

"Good morning, sleepyhead," she said, teasing but warm.

"Hope you don't mind, we started without you."

Claire added something about Alana being there before sunrise. That she hadn't moved from that spot. I nodded, said something low about how good the work looked, but I couldn't stop the shift that came over me when Claire spoke. I remembered her call, the tone of it. Cold. Casual. Calculated. I still have eyes on her.

I turned to Claire slowly. Let my voice drop.

"Just remember," I said, locking eyes with her, "you've got eyes on her."

She didn't react right away, but the flicker behind her eyes told me she felt the hit.

"What's that supposed to mean?" she asked.

"You know exactly what I mean."

I walked away before it turned into something louder. But she followed—of course she did. Claire never let anything go without pressing her advantage.

"Detective Franklin," she called sharply, heels striking the floor with purpose. "We are not done with this."

I stopped, jaw tight, turning just enough to face her.

"With all due respect, ma'am," I said, voice low, "yeah, we are."

She stepped in closer, chin lifting. "Watch your tone. I'm your superior."

"And I'm letting you slide because I get it," I shot back. "You're stressed. Stakes are high. But the way you're questioning me—over and over—the line's getting thin."

Her eyes narrowed. "I'm doing my job."

"Are you?" I countered, heat rising in my chest. "Because the only people who knew about that safehouse were me and Command. So how exactly did that slip out of your mouth?"

She didn't answer right away. Her gaze flickered—just a fraction—but enough.

I took a step toward her. Not aggressive. Controlled. Focused.

"You keep grilling me like I'm the one lying," I said. "Like I'm the problem. Alana's been through hell, and instead of protecting her, you're watching her. Watching us."

Her jaw clenched. "Choose your next words carefully."

"Oh, I am," I said. "But maybe you should choose yours too."

For a second, we just stared at each other—two people who'd been on the same side for too long to admit we weren't anymore.

Then she tried to recover, tone sharpening. "If I'm questioning protocol, it's because you're making decisions outside of it."

"And if I'm pushing back," I replied, "it's because you're violating trust."

Her eye twitched. Just a little. Just enough to confirm what I already suspected.

"I'm not your enemy, Franklin," she said tightly.

"Then stop acting like one."

Something cracked in her expression—annoyance, guilt, maybe both.

She straightened her jacket, trying to regain control. "This conversation isn't over."

"Actually," I said, stepping back, "it is."

Her lips pressed into a thin, cold line. She said nothing else. She just turned and walked away, but I saw it—the calculation in her eyes, the anger simmering just beneath.

Trust was gone.

And she knew it.

The rest of the day blurred into quiet momentum. No explosions. No dramatics. Just slow, methodical progress. We linked new drops with old routes, flagged familiar names, started building something that looked like a plan. By the time the sun dipped low, Claire had called it. Told everyone to rest. Catch him tomorrow.

She left. So did the agents.

Clay stayed behind a little longer, said something about calling his wife. Then he was gone too. Just like that, the house emptied out.

As I moved toward the kitchen to rinse a glass, I caught it, just out of the corner of my eye. The front door eased open, slow and quiet, and there she was. Alana. Slipping barefoot into the rain.

I didn't say anything. Didn't call after her.

I just stood there for a moment, watching the faint shape of her silhouette in the gray mist, the way her arms lifted slightly as the rain met her skin. Something about it felt private. Sacred. I didn't need to be part of it. I didn't even need to understand it. I just knew it was something between her and God.

So I turned away. Gave her that space.

I walked down the hallway and opened the linen closet, pulled down one of the softer blankets, and picked out a clean shirt and towel. She'd probably want something warm after being out there. Maybe she hadn't thought that far ahead. Maybe she didn't need to. That's what I could be for her now, the person who thought ahead. Covered the little things. Protected what didn't need to be said out loud.

On my way back down the hallway, something made me pause. It wasn't fear, just a shift in the air, the kind of subtle alertness that rises before you understand why. I slowed near the guest room and glanced toward the side hallway. The lamp in the corner glowed softly, and although I didn't remember turning it on, nothing about the room felt disturbed.

A breeze stirred the curtain near the back window. I stepped closer and saw it wasn't open wide, only cracked just enough for the air to slip through. I locked it gently and scanned the room again, letting my senses settle. Nothing was broken, nothing misplaced, yet that awareness lingered, the instinct to pay attention.

I adjusted the blanket and clean clothes in my arms, ready to take them back toward the main room, when a faint movement outside caught my eye. I stepped toward the front window and the tension eased the moment I understood what I was seeing.

Alana stood outside in the rain, barefoot on the porch, letting the soft mist fall over her like it was washing something heavy from her shoulders. Her posture wasn't distressed; it was open, peaceful, almost reverent. Whatever had drawn her outside wasn't danger—it was release.

The window must've been cracked from when she slipped out.

My chest loosened. She wasn't unsafe. She wasn't being watched. She was simply having a moment she clearly needed, one she wasn't ready to share with anyone. A private pause between her and God, the kind that didn't need witness or interruption.

I stayed just inside the doorway, not stepping out, not calling to her, giving her every bit of that space while still keeping an eye on her in case she lost her footing on the wet boards or the rain chilled her too much. The blanket warmed my hands, and I knew she would want it when she came back in, even if she hadn't thought that far ahead.

So I waited—quiet, steady, present—covering the small things she didn't have to think about tonight. Not hovering. Not intruding. Simply guarding the moment while she found her breath in the rain.

**Alana**

It happened so quickly I didn't realize I'd moved until I was already doing it. One moment I stood near the window, watching the rain slip down the glass in long, delicate lines, and the next I was pulling open the door and stepping barefoot onto the porch, walking straight into the downpour as if something deeper than thought had called me forward. My foot touched the wood and a familiar tension flickered through me, the automatic brace for a creak, a shadow, a hand grabbing me from behind. But nothing came. No voices. No footsteps.

Only the steady hum of rain.

And when the first drops touched my skin, my breath caught somewhere between release and revelation. The water wasn't cold or startling—it felt like an embrace, like Heaven reaching down to wrap around me in a language I didn't have words for yet. I didn't run or flinch; I simply stood with my arms slightly open and my face lifted toward the sky, letting everything fall—each drop, each tear, each part of me that still trembled with fear. The rain began softly, almost gentle in its approach, before gathering into something fuller and steadier, like it understood exactly why I came out here.

As the water soaked through my clothes and traced lines down my arms, I thought about Jesus's words—that anyone who acknowledges Him before men, He will acknowledge before the Father. I thought about all the moments I had hidden when I could've stepped forward, all the times I stayed silent because my story felt too broken, too complicated, too marked by things I didn't want anyone to see. I had lived so long beneath shadows that the idea of being seen by God felt impossible.

But in that moment, I wanted nothing more.

I didn't need a church or a choir or a carefully lit stage. I didn't need ceremony or witnesses. I just needed this—rain on my skin, sky above me, my heart cracked open enough for light to slip through. This wasn't weather. It was holy.

My mind drifted to baptism—not the mechanics, but the meaning. Not the act of going under, but the rising again. Washed. Covered. Made new. Water didn't save. The choice did. The surrender did. The declaration that the old was behind you and something new had begun.

And this... this was my declaration.

My open-air confession. My rooftop moment without a rooftop.

When I opened my mouth, the words trembled out.

"God... I'm Yours. All of me."

My voice cracked, but I kept going, the honesty too heavy to hold back.

"I know I've run. I know I've believed lies. I know I doubted if You still wanted me. But I'm here. I'm standing in front of You. And I want to be clean. I want to be whole. I want to be Yours."

The tears mixed with the rain until I couldn't tell one from the other.

"I'm sorry, God," I cried, the words tearing free like something buried for years had finally clawed its way out of the dark.

"I'm so sorry."

And I meant every word I cried into that rain—not because I thought God was standing above me with disappointment, not because I believed forgiveness was something I had to earn, but because something deep within me had finally broken open in a way I could no longer silence. Everything I'd kept buried—the guilt, the grief, the truth I'd been too afraid to speak—rose to the surface with every shaking breath, every trembling confession, every tear that blended into the downpour around me.

The rain didn't lighten. It softened.

Each drop felt like a hand brushing over my skin, not washing me away, but washing me *clean*.

"It wasn't cold anymore," I whispered, more to God than to the sky. "It feels like You're touching me. Like You're covering me."

Water slid down my arms like strokes of a brush, steady and deliberate, and suddenly a memory cut through the moment with a clarity that made my knees weak.

*"Look outside,"* I had told my sister once. *"It's raining. That means God is painting again."*

She had laughed at me then, playful and confused.

*"You don't even believe in God,"* she'd said.

*"Maybe not,"* I whispered back to her now, voice trembling through the rain, *"but you did. And I wanted to believe in something beautiful with you."*

The ache in my chest cracked deeper.

"God... I'm sorry," I breathed out, voice shaking. "I'm sorry I didn't protect her. I'm sorry I believed the lies he fed me. I'm sorry I carried guilt that wasn't mine and hid from grace You kept trying to hand me."

The rain fell harder, fuller, wrapping around me with a warmth that felt like compassion, not wrath.

"And I'm sorry," I whispered again, "for not believing You could still want me after everything."

Water streamed down my face, and I lifted my hands slowly, palms open, letting the sky cover them.

"Lord... if rain means You're painting," I said, the words trembling out of me like a truth I had been waiting years to speak, "then paint me over. Cover me. Make me new. Wash away the lies he spoke. Wash away the guilt I carried for my sister. Wash away the fear... all of it."

It felt like something inside me loosened—something old, something heavy.

"I don't want to be who he made me," I cried. "I want to be who You see."

The tears and rain blurred until they were one and the

same, indistinguishable, running down my face in a mixture of sorrow and release.

The longer I stood there, the more it felt like the water wasn't stripping me down, but rebuilding me. Not erasing my story, but redeeming it. Not scrubbing away my past, but rinsing off the shame that never belonged to me in the first place.

I breathed in, slow and trembling.

"I'm here," I whispered to the sky, to Him. "All of me. The real me. Not Alana. Not the girl he tried to shape. Not the version of myself I carried out of guilt."

My voice steadied.

"Just me. Yours."

And in that sacred rainfall, the girl who had stayed silent because she believed her voice wasn't worthy finally released everything she had been holding, not fading or disappearing, but being remade—slowly, gently, completely—into someone new.

Right there in the rain, under the brushstrokes of a God who had started painting her life long before she ever knew how to look for Him.

By the time I stepped back toward the house, soaked to my bones and breathing like something holy had just passed through me, I saw him standing in the doorway. Franklin didn't speak. He didn't rush toward me. He simply held a towel in his hands, shoulders broad, posture steady, eyes soft in a way that made my steps slow without trying.

He looked at me like I was something precious returning home.

The moment I crossed the threshold, the warmth of the house met me—and so did he. He stepped in close, lifting the towel with one hand while the other brushed lightly against my wrist, guiding me in with such careful gentleness it sent a tremor down my spine. His touch wasn't commanding; it was reverent, deliberate, like he didn't want to disrupt whatever God had just done in me.

When he settled the towel around my shoulders, I felt my breath slip out in a slow, shaky exhale. His hands moved down the length of the towel, pulling it close across my chest, and the warmth of his fingers seeped through the fabric into my skin. Every time he touched me—my shoulder, the curve of my arm, the place where my neck met my collarbone—something inside me answered, soft and instinctive, like my body had known him much longer than my mind had allowed.

He didn't ask a single question.

He just tended to me.

His fingers gathered the wet strands of my hair, lifting them gently off my back, his knuckles grazing the nape of my neck in a way that made my heartbeat pulse hard and deep. I closed my eyes without meaning to, breathing in slow, uneven waves as he slid the towel beneath the weight of my curls and dried them with unhurried movements. The air between us grew warm, thick, intimate enough that I could feel the heat of his breath near my cheek.

I opened my eyes when he stepped around me, and he was already holding the folded clothes he'd picked out—sweats, a soft hoodie, warm and clean. He didn't say a word. Just held them out like offering, like care, like something quiet and meaningful.

"Thank you," I whispered, my voice barely a breath.

Something flickered across his face—gentleness, longing, restraint all tangled together.

When I lifted my gaze fully to him, the moment shifted. We were standing closer than before. Closer than I'd ever let another man stand. The towel was still wrapped around me, my fingers clutching the clothes he'd prepared, and yet somehow there was a different kind of warmth surrounding me—his.

He stepped forward. Slowly. Purposefully. His hand lifted toward my cheek, brushing the edge of my jaw with the back of his fingers. I felt my breath catch, my lungs filling too slowly, my heart pounding against my ribs like it didn't know what to do with itself.

His eyes dropped to my lips—barely, briefly, but unmistakably.

My own breath trembled. I felt myself lean in without meaning to, drawn by a pull that had been building between us for days, maybe longer. The space between us thinned to almost nothing. I could feel the warmth of his mouth, the soft brush of his breath, the unspoken question lingering in the air.

His thumb glided along the side of my face, slow and deliberate, and my lips parted just slightly as every part of me went still and alive at the same time.

I closed my eyes for just a breath, long enough to let the possibility of him settle into my skin, long enough to feel the warmth of him draw nearer. He leaned in slowly, our foreheads brushing in a soft, electric touch, close enough that a single tilt of his mouth toward mine would have changed everything. And just when the moment tightened into something undeniable, he stopped.

Not abruptly. Not out of fear. His head bowed near mine, his breath warm against my cheek as he whispered, voice low and thick with restraint, "Not like this."

The words weren't rejection—they were protection. A choosing. A holding back for the right moment.

My eyes opened slowly, meeting his in the dim light. Whatever lived in the space between us now wasn't confusion. It wasn't guessing. It was clear, deep, and mutual.

He stepped back just enough to let the tension settle without breaking it.

"Go get warm," he murmured, his voice softer now. "I'll be right here."

And with my heart still racing and my breath still struggling to find its steady rhythm, I turned toward the bathroom, the towel still wrapped around me, the clothes pressed against my chest, knowing that something profound had just shifted between us, something neither of us could deny anymore.

I closed the door gently behind me, skin still tingling where his hands had been. The fabric warmed against my skin, and the simple act of getting dressed felt like a quiet ritual— something marking the shift from who I had been to the person I was choosing to become the simple act of getting dressed felt like a quiet ritual—something marking the shift from who I had been to the person I was choosing to become, someone who no longer hid behind borrowed names or old fears, someone willing to stand in the truth God had just called me into.

When I stepped back into the hallway, my hair still damp and the warmth of Franklin's clothes settling into my skin, the house felt different—gentler, almost reverent, like it understood the change that had taken place. Franklin was sitting on the edge of the couch, elbows resting on his knees, gaze lifting the moment I walked in. He didn't look startled or overly eager; he simply looked present, steady, like he had been there the whole time without needing anything from me.

I crossed the room slowly and eased onto the couch beside him, close enough to feel his warmth but still wrapped in the towel he'd given me. The fabric held the last traces of the rain, and for a moment neither of us spoke. The room felt strangely peaceful—like the storm outside had seeped in and softened everything it touched.

I looked toward the window, watching the rain slide down the glass in slow, shimmering paths. "You didn't say anything," I murmured.

"When I went outside... when I walked out into the rain. You didn't follow me. You didn't... ask."

Franklin turned slightly, his shoulder brushing mine.

"I didn't need to," he said, voice low and steady.

"Whatever that was out there... it wasn't my moment to step into. That was between you and God. I wasn't going to interrupt something holy."

Something in my chest tugged hard at that—his discernment, his restraint, the way he knew when to stand back and when to step close.

My gaze drifted back to the window. The rain had softened to a gentle drizzle, the sky shifting into muted streaks of blue and silver.

"When I was little," I said quietly, "I used to tell my sister that when it rained... it meant God was painting again."

He lifted his brow just a bit, curiosity softening the edges of his expression.

"Painting?" he echoed. "Painting what?"

I let out a slow breath.

"The world. The sky. Our lives. I don't know. I was just

trying to give her something beautiful to hold onto. But tonight..."

My voice thinned, warm and fragile.

"Tonight it felt true. Like He wasn't just painting the storm. He was painting me over too."

For a long moment, Franklin just looked at me. Not in awe, not in disbelief—just deeply present, like he was letting every word settle somewhere he'd keep safe.

"That makes sense," he said, his tone dipped in something gentle.

"You came back looking... renewed."

The way he said it made my breath catch. Not because he romanticized it, but because he said it like he genuinely saw it.

My grip tightened on the towel.

"I don't know how to explain it," I whispered.

"But when I saw you after... everything... something in me just breathed."

He didn't move closer, but the warmth in his voice did.

"I'm glad you came back to me," he said.

"That's all."

He reached for the blanket beside us and pulled it over both of our legs—not as an invitation, but as instinct, as something a man does for the woman he can't help but protect. Our thighs brushed, a warm point of contact that made my heartbeat slow and deepen.

I leaned back just slightly, letting my shoulder rest against his. I could feel the rise and fall of his breathing, solid and unhurried, grounding me in a way I didn't know I needed. Every time he shifted the towel on my shoulders or brushed a curl back from my cheek, something inside me opened—

253

quietly, tenderly—like trust easing into place.

He didn't speak again. Neither did I.

We just sat there, wrapped in warmth and rainlight, the air between us soft with something unspoken but deeply understood.

Whatever this was—this closeness, this carefulness, this connection stitched between silence and breath—it felt like another kind of painting.

Something God was brushing into existence right there between us.

# 18

## Chapter 18

I woke slowly, the kind of waking that happens after a night where sleep never fully settled, and before my eyes were open, the memory of her rose up with a clarity that tightened something deep in my chest. I could see her exactly as she was—standing in the doorway after stepping out of the rain, her dark skin glistening beneath the low hallway light, water tracing down the rich, warm undertones of her cheeks and throat. Her long curls were soaked, spiraling heavy down her back and clinging to her shoulders, and something about the way those wet curls framed her face made the moment feel even closer, even more intimate. The towel felt warm again in my hands as I remembered wrapping it around her, how she let me lift her damp curls to dry the nape of her neck, how she leaned into my touch with a soft trust that caught me off guard. Her eyes had met mine with a steadiness I hadn't expected, and when her forehead brushed mine, the warmth of her skin lingered in a way my body remembered instantly.

I rubbed a hand over my jaw, slow and rough, trying to clear the tension building under my skin, but it didn't move. My body responded before my thoughts did. My chest tightened. My jaw clenched. My fingers curled against the pillow beside me, gripping it like it could anchor me. I wasn't confused about what I felt; I just wasn't ready to say it out loud. The truth was sitting there, unmistakable, almost intrusive. I wanted her—not just to protect her, not just to keep her safe, but in a way I hadn't let myself think about until that moment in the doorway. Something about seeing her step into her healing, seeing her open herself to God with that kind of surrender, had changed how I saw her. I'd always found her beautiful, always felt that pull, but last night made something deepen, settle, sharpen. It was physical, yes, but it was more than that. A man can recognize the difference between desire and connection, and what I felt wasn't simple. It was rooted. Growing. Real.

When I thought about her standing just down the hall, close enough that a few slow steps would bring me to her door, my whole body reacted. My shoulders tightened. My breath came heavier. It took everything in me not to move, not to follow the instinct that told me to go to her, knock softly, and finish the moment we stopped. I could almost see it—the way her eyes would lift, the way her breath would catch, the way her fingers might curl into my shirt again. And if I let myself go there, if I let myself lean into that pull, I knew exactly what would happen. I wanted to kiss her. Not with uncertainty. Not with hesitation. But with the kind of certainty that comes when a man knows exactly what he's feeling. That thought alone made me lean back into the cushions, trying to breathe past the raw honesty of it.

But faith held me in place. Not fear—faith. The part of me that knew timing mattered. The part of me that knew God was doing something in her, something sacred, and the last thing I wanted was to interrupt a season she was stepping into with my own longing. So I sat there for a moment, hands pressed against my thighs, grounding myself while the memory of her stayed vivid and unshakable. Something had shifted last night. Not dramatically. Not loudly. But in a way that couldn't be undone. The space between us felt changed, as if the air had recognized what neither of us had spoken yet. And even though I wasn't ready to say the words, I knew the truth— whatever I felt for her wasn't passing. It wasn't born out of adrenaline or trauma. It was something I couldn't pray away, something that had settled into my chest with a kind of quiet certainty that refused to be ignored.

The house was quiet, the kind of quiet that didn't feel settled, just waiting. Clay was at the coffee table, laptop open, files spread everywhere like he hadn't moved all night. His shoulders were hunched, eyes locked on the screen, fingers tapping restlessly. He didn't even look up. Just pointed toward the empty seat across from him.

"You're gonna wanna sit for this."

I dropped down without a word, my gaze scanning the chaos. He slid a folder across the table toward me, and I opened it, expecting more of the same, scattered chatter, half-coded threats, junk data. But one line jumped out. One sentence. Black ink against cream paper, like it had been waiting for me.

***That Bible-thumping fool don't even see it coming.***

My stomach clenched. My breath hitched, just for a second, but long enough for something old to surface. Ricky's voice, rising from the echo of the shootout, twisted with smugness and mockery.

*"You think that Bible can save you?"*

It hadn't struck me as anything more than noise in the chaos. But now, with that line in front of me, it cut different. This wasn't just an insult. It was specific. Personal. And I knew without a shadow of a doubt, I don't talk about my faith like that. Not with just anyone. I keep it quiet. Between me and God. And for Ricky to come at me that directly... someone fed it to him.

My jaw tightened, pressure building in the back of my teeth. I could feel it, not just suspicion, but something deeper. Something that made the Spirit stir, that made my stomach coil and my pulse slow in that heavy, measured way it always did when something wasn't right. When something needed to be seen.

Clay leaned back a little, grabbing another file, his voice low. "You alright?"

"Yeah," I said too quickly. "Just reading."

He didn't press. Didn't look at me long. Just nodded and went back to work like he hadn't just handed me a live grenade. And maybe he didn't realize what he'd done. Or maybe he did.

I sat there a few minutes longer, acting like I was focused on the folder in front of me. But my thoughts were already slipping sideways.

"I'm gonna run to the store," I said, standing a little too fast.

"We're low on coffee. You want anything?"

"Nah, I'm good."

"Alright. Back soon."

He didn't even look up. And that, more than anything, put me on edge.

The air outside hit sharp. Not freezing, just crisp enough to make me breathe deeper than usual, my hands shoved in my pockets, my steps slower than they needed to be. I wasn't headed anywhere in particular. I just needed space to think. To listen. And that's when it hit me, not a memory, exactly. Just a sentence. A voice from a different night.

Clay's voice.

*"You really say that Psalm 91 thing every day?"*

*We'd been eating fries out of a greasy paper bag in the middle of a stakeout. I'd laughed it off. Told him it wasn't just routine, it was my protection. My covering. And he'd smirked, raised one brow, tossed back something like "Man, you're really out here being a full-blown man of God, huh?"*

Back then, I thought it was harmless. A joke. But now... it felt like a receipt. A breadcrumb. Something small I'd handed him in trust, and he'd pocketed it.

I reached for the cold metal rail near the carts outside the store and leaned on it. My fingers curled around the edge without thinking, knuckles white. My mind spinning. My gut twisting. If Clay had said something to Ricky, even just a throwaway line, that was all it would've taken. One sentence. One smirk. One moment of disloyalty.

But Clay wasn't the only one.

Claire had been acting off, too. Transport shifts without notice. Convenient tech "errors." Her smile always a second too late, her answers always a breath too controlled. I hadn't wanted to see it before. But now, every little thing felt like a thread I hadn't tugged.

I stared out across the parking lot, my body still but my spirit on alert. I didn't have enough proof to confront either of them. But I had enough to stop trusting blindly. Enough to start watching back.

When I returned to the safehouse, the sun had dipped lower.

Shadows cut sharp across the floor. Clay was still on the couch, headphones in, nodding to whatever he was watching like everything was normal. I nodded back. Neutral. Flat. Claire was in the kitchen, hovering over a clipboard with numbers and routes. She glanced up and smiled, but it was tight. Quick. And when I passed her, I saw the way her hand paused over one line before she scratched it out and rewrote it. Fast. Too fast.

Before, I would've let it go.

Not anymore.

I kept walking. Straight to my room. I didn't slam the door, I just let it close behind me with the kind of silence that meant I wasn't ready to talk. Not yet. I leaned against the wood, eyes closed, breath tight.

Trust was a luxury I couldn't afford right now.

And I was starting to realize that the real threat wasn't coming from outside.

It was already in the house.

I opened my eyes and whispered beneath my breath, not loud enough for anyone but Heaven to hear.

"God, give me eyes to see."

**Alana**

There was a lightness in my body I couldn't explain, like the weight I'd been dragging for years had finally lifted and left nothing but breath behind. I stood in front of the mirror, twisting one of my curls around my finger, not to fix it, but just because I could. Just because it felt good to take my time and not rush. For once, I wasn't late. I wasn't hiding. I wasn't trying to survive. I was getting ready for therapy... and

I couldn't wait to get there.

I smiled to myself, the kind of soft, secret smile that blooms when nobody else is watching. I already knew what I was going to say. I'd been practicing the words in my head since I woke up. I wanted to tell her everything, the progress, the peace, the rain. I wanted her to see me the way I finally saw myself: not broken, not used, not haunted. But free. Truly free.

I'd helped with the investigation, and even though it still felt surreal, I couldn't deny what that meant. That I had something to offer. That I wasn't just a victim in need of saving, I was part of the reason someone else might live. That realization had done something to me. It had grounded me and lifted me all at once.

And then came the rain.

I still hadn't found the words to describe it, not completely. I just knew something holy had happened. It wasn't loud. It wasn't dramatic. It was quiet. Private. Sacred. I'd stepped outside into the storm and lifted my face toward the sky with tears in my eyes and a smile I didn't have to fake. And in that moment, as the rain soaked through my clothes and slid down my cheeks like baptismal water, I felt new. Washed. Seen. Loved. It was like God painted something just for me that day, and I said yes to it.

Now, all I could think about was the future. Not with fear or tension, but with wonder. What comes next? Who might I become after the trial? After all of this? What will it feel like to walk down the street and not look over my shoulder? What will it feel like to dream again and not call it foolish?

I pulled my sweater over my head and glanced back at the mirror. My reflection looked steady. Soft. There was still sorrow in my eyes, some memories don't let go just because you do, but the heaviness was no longer sitting on my chest. It had moved. Made room. I could breathe again. And for the first time in a long, long time... I was excited to live.

I was just slipping my shoes on when I heard the knock, soft and quick, like someone trying not to startle me. Claire peeked around the door a second later, eyes bright, her mouth already lifting into a smile.

"I figured you'd be up early," she said, stepping inside with a file tucked under her arm and a kind of glow on her face I hadn't seen in days.

I tilted my head. "You look like you've got something."

"Oh, I do." She held the folder up like a trophy, then dropped it on the edge of the bed before I could even ask. "Intercepted shipment. Ricky won't be getting what he was waiting for."

For a moment, I didn't say anything. My heart just did this little flip, the kind it only does when something shifts for real. I felt it in my chest first, then in my breath, which came out lighter than it went in.

"Are you serious?" I asked, the words slipping out in a whisper.

Claire nodded, eyes shining. "One hundred percent. Franklin's team followed a trail from one of the hacked messages. Everything lined up. It's not the end, but it's a major hit."

I sat down slowly, hands gripping the edge of the mattress to steady the emotion rising in me. This was real. It was happening. We were making progress. We were actually cutting off pieces of what had once swallowed my life whole. I pressed a hand against my chest, not to calm the nerves, but to hold the gratitude.

"I don't know why I feel like crying," I laughed softly,

brushing at my eyes.

"Because you've been carrying the weight of this for too long," Claire said gently, lowering herself beside me. "But you're not alone in it anymore. You're protected. You always have been."

Something in the way she said it made me look at her a little longer, like she was trying to say more than her words were allowed to hold. I nodded, letting the reassurance settle, even if I couldn't explain why a sliver of unease poked through the warmth.

Claire reached into her pocket like she'd almost forgotten something.

"Oh—before I go." She pulled out a small phone, simple and thin, no apps, no color screen, nothing extra.

"This is for you."

I blinked. "For me?"

"Just for emergencies," she said, placing it gently in my hand.

"Not for scrolling, not for talking to the world. This one is strictly for reaching me."

I hesitated, thumb brushing over the corner of the device.

"Only you?"

She nodded, her expression sharpening with something that looked like caution more than concern.

"Yes. Only me. You already have Franklin and the others in the house, but I'm not always on-site. If there's ever a moment you feel uneasy, or something feels off, or you just need a direct line to someone who can move quickly—this is how you reach me."

A small chill crawled across my skin. "Is there something I should be worried about?"

Claire softened immediately, sitting on the edge of the bed like she didn't want the question hanging between us.

"No. I don't want you panicking." Her voice dipped, quiet and sincere.

"This is just caution. Woman to woman, I'd rather you have one more lifeline and not need it than wish you had one when things feel strange."

That eased the tension in my shoulders, but only a little. Her eyes carried something layered—wariness, maybe, or knowledge she wasn't saying out loud—but the warmth in her tone made me lean in anyway.

"This phone is clean," she went on.

"No networks Ricky can tap into. No accounts he'd recognize. No digital trails. He's probably watching every app, every number you used to touch, every old login. But this?"

She tapped the top edge of the device.

"This is invisible. Safe. And it connects only to me."

I swallowed, suddenly aware of how light the phone felt for something meant to carry so much weight.

"Thank you," I whispered, because it was the only thing I could say.

"I want you protected," she said gently. "Truly."

And even though the reassurance settled me for the moment, a small, quiet knot curled under my ribs—because protection and secrets often came packaged in the same tone.

I nodded again, slipping it into my bag, letting the symbolism of it settle. I wasn't being sent out into the world unguarded. They cared. Claire cared. And for a moment, I let myself believe that completely.

She stood, gave my shoulder a soft squeeze, then stepped out of the room, her clipboard already back in hand. I stood there a second longer, letting the joy return, the kind that had been disrupted by nerves, but not erased. I was still free. I was still covered. And I was still going to therapy, not because I was broken, but because I was healing.

I grabbed my bag, gave myself one last look in the mirror, and smiled. This time, I wasn't walking out afraid. I was walking out expectant.

The office was warm in that subtle way, dim lighting, the faint scent of lavender, the quiet hum of something playing low in the corner that I couldn't quite place. I sank into the chair, legs tucked under me, hands folded in my lap, and for a while, I just sat there... smiling. Not because everything was perfect. But because I finally knew that it didn't have to be.

My therapist looked up from her notes and tilted her head slightly, her eyes kind and expectant.

"You look different today."

I laughed, pressing the tips of my fingers to my mouth.

"I feel different."

She set her notebook aside and leaned forward, elbows on her knees like she already knew something beautiful was about to pour out.

"Tell me."

And so I did.

I told her about the rain. The way I walked into it like it was a cathedral, how I lifted my face to the sky and whispered something only God and I could hear. I told her how light I felt afterward, how I'd never known what freedom actually felt like until that moment. Not just being safe, but being unshackled. I told her about helping the team, about the intercepted shipment and the small victories that reminded me I wasn't powerless. That I wasn't broken goods being babysat, I was a woman reclaiming her own story.

She nodded, her expression gentle, but something in her eyes shifted when I mentioned Franklin. She didn't interrupt. She just leaned in slightly, giving me space to keep talking. I didn't tell her about the moment when our foreheads touched, how the air tightened between us like something was about to break open. That memory still felt too sacred to put into words. But I told her the rest—how his presence settled me, how his voice made the knots in my chest loosen, how being near him didn't feel tied to fear or survival. It felt deeper. Familiar. Like recognition.

Dr. Moby folded her hands in her lap, her gaze steady on mine.

"Tell me what that feels like in your body," she murmured, inviting me further in.

I exhaled slowly, tracing the edge of the couch cushion with my thumb.

"It feels... safe," I admitted.

"Not because he's protecting me. Not because I'm grateful. Just... safe in a way I haven't felt in years. My breathing slows. My shoulders drop. I don't brace." I swallowed.

"I don't know what to do with that."

She nodded thoughtfully.

"Safety can be disorienting after trauma," she said, her tone warm but deliberate.

"Sometimes the body interprets consistency as affection, or presence as connection. It's a natural response. When someone shows up for us when we're hurting, it can feel like the heart is choosing something before we consciously do."

I looked down at my hands, fingers twisting in my lap.

"So you think I'm confusing him for—"

"I didn't say that," she interrupted gently, shaking her head.

"I'm saying I want you to be aware of your heart, not afraid of it. There's a difference."

She leaned back slightly, studying me with that quiet, grounding curiosity she always had.

"Do you feel like what you're experiencing is reaction... or recognition?"

My breath caught just a little.

"Recognition," I whispered, surprised by how easily the word came.

"It feels like I've known him longer than I have. Like my spirit responds before my mind does."

Dr. Moby's eyes softened, but she didn't let the moment drift off.

"Then that's worth paying attention to," she said.

"But I still want you to move slowly. Trauma can create strong bonds, even with the right people, and it's important to understand what is yours to carry and what is simply the echo of what you've survived."

Her words settled into me, warm at first, then heavy, and I felt my throat tighten—not in fear, but in honesty.

"I hear you," I said quietly.

"I do. But it doesn't feel like a reflex. It doesn't feel like I'm mistaking him for safety." I lifted my gaze to hers.

"It feels real. And I think... I think God is in it."

Dr. Moby didn't smile, but something peaceful passed over her features. She nodded once, slowly.

"Then honor that," she said softly.

"But don't rush it. Let clarity grow. Let peace lead. And let your healing—not your fear—shape whatever comes next."

Her words settled deep inside me, steady and grounding, I felt like I could hold both truth and caution without losing either.

By the time I stepped out of the building, my heart felt full and light all over again. The sun had started to lower just slightly, casting a soft glow over the pavement, and I pulled the phone from my bag to check the time, only to see Franklin's name appear on the screen.

My smile hadn't even faded yet when I answered the phone.

*Hello, Darling*

My whole body locked. Not in fear, not yet. In disbelief. My breath caught so fast it hurt, like something had punched through my lungs and left a hollow space where sound used to live. My hand froze midair. My feet wouldn't move.

It was him.

*Ricky.*

The moment his voice slid through the speaker, everything inside me clenched at once. My breath stalled, my muscles locked, and for one suspended second, the world around me blurred.

"Well now," Ricky murmured, soft and venomous, "I've been waiting to hear that breath again."

My fingers tightened around my bag. "What do you want?"

"What I always wanted."

A smile shaped itself in his voice.

"You."

My stomach twisted, but I held still.

"You want the truth?" he drawled.

"You really think your little Psalm Boy survived that night in the woods because of God? That's cute, sweetheart. Really cute."

My breath hitched.

"I hit him," he said, casual as weather.

"Dropped him hard enough to feel his bones shake. And I could've ended him right there. One move. One breath. Done."

He paused, savoring it.

"But he wasn't the one I wanted. He never was."

Heat climbed my throat, but I didn't speak. Not yet.

"I spared him," Ricky continued, voice dropping lower, darker.

"Not because he mattered... but because you do. You were always the prize. Always the one worth breaking. I wanted my girl back. I still do."

I clenched my jaw, steadying the tremble in my breath.

"You don't own me," I said quietly.

"Oh, but I do," he whispered, the words curling like smoke.

"I owned every inch of you. That skin... that mouth... that body. You were my top moneymaker. My most expensive product. The one men asked for by name."

A low hum filled the line.

"And you know why? Because you were mine."

My stomach turned, but I stayed still, pressing my back into the wall behind me.

"You were always my favorite," he murmured.

"I miss the way you sounded when you were scared. I miss the fire in your eyes right before you broke. And I miss the way you begged when you finally learned what obedience meant."

My breath quivered, but I lifted my chin.

"You're disgusting."

"And yet here you are," he replied. "Shaking for me again."

I swallowed hard, refusing to give him anything else. He let the silence stretch, then shifted, almost amused.

269

"You walking into that rain last night..." he said quietly.

"Lifting your face like you were something pure now... that was adorable. Really. I almost clapped."

His tone sharpened.

"You think baptism washes you clean? You think it erases what you really are?"

I forced myself to breathe.

"That wasn't a cleansing," he continued.

"That was a spotlight. And you stepped right into it."

His voice dipped lower, sliding toward cruelty.

"You want to talk about being washed?"

A pause—slow, intentional.

"Let's talk about what didn't wash off."

My chest tightened, knowing what was coming before he even said it.

"You remember your sister, right?"

My hand froze midair.

He inhaled softly, savoring the wound.

"I dragged her away from you while you screamed," he whispered.

"You remember that part, don't you? The way her nails scraped across that floor? The way she called your name?"

Another pause.

"You broke before she did. That's the funny part. You were the weak one."

My knees went weak, but I caught myself on the wall, breath shaking.

"You really think God forgave you for that?" he asked.

"You think He washed off the fact that she died because you hesitated? Because you didn't listen? Because you weren't a good girl when I told you what to do?"

Tears burned, but I blinked them back.

"You're a monster," I whispered.

"No," he breathed. "I'm inevitable."

I swallowed the tremble in my chest. "Franklin will—"

"Franklin?" Ricky cut in, laughing low and cold. "Your little Psalm Boy? That man's a crack waiting to split. He won't save you. He can't. He doesn't even know how deep you're marked."

He paused, letting the silence spread like poison.

"And you think that stunt at the warehouse was a win?" His tone sharpened, almost gleeful.

"Sweet girl... that was *me*. I dropped that location on purpose. I wanted to see if you were still alive — and you came running right on cue."

My breath caught. He kept going.

"You really thought your little task force uncovered some-thing? No. You followed the trail I planted. You surfaced exactly where I needed you to. That whole operation?"

A dark chuckle slid through the receiver.

"A leash. And you grabbed it."

My grip tightened around the phone, nails digging into my palm.

"And when I decide to finish what I started," he whispered, voice dropping into something lethal, "your Psalm Boy will learn real fast he's not untouchable."

I swallowed hard, anger rising hot and clean.

"You'll never be the man he is," I said, steady despite the burn in my lungs. "Not even close."

The line went silent—dangerously silent.

When Ricky finally spoke, every trace of charm was gone.

"Oh, sweetheart," he rasped.

"I'm coming for you. And when I get close enough... you won't see me. You'll only feel the dark again."

The call ended, but my body didn't catch up. My hands trembled so violently I had to sit before my knees gave out, breath coming in short, uneven pulls. Ricky's voice clung to me like smoke, every word tightening around my chest until it hurt to breathe.

Then my gaze fell to the phone—*Claire's* phone—and everything inside me went cold. He shouldn't have been able to reach this number, shouldn't have even known it existed. That could only mean one thing: the phone was compromised, and someone close had given him access.

# 19

## Chapter 19

**Franklin**

I had just finished tightening the back panel on the car when I heard it, her voice, sharp and raw, slicing through the air like it had been torn from the depths of her lungs.

"Franklin!"

I didn't hesitate. My head snapped up, instincts already pulling me forward before I could fully register what I was seeing. She was running, barefoot, terrified, stumbling out of the therapy like it was something to flee from rather than a place of protection. Her hair was loose, her face wild with panic, and the moment I locked eyes with her, something in my chest cracked open.

She collided into me hard enough that I staggered a step back, not from the weight of her body but from the weight of what she carried. The phone hit my chest, thrown like it burned her skin to hold it. Her hands trembled uncontrollably, panic rippling up her arms and into her voice.

"It was him," she gasped, the words barely holding together.

"It was Ricky. He used your name, he knew things, Franklin. About the shipment. About you." Her voice broke again.

"I answered because it said your name."

I looked down. My name still glowed across the screen, bold and cruel in its deception. My stomach dropped. A wave of dread rolled through me so fast it left my skin cold.

"You weren't supposed to have a phone," I said, but even as the words left my mouth, I knew the answer.

Her lips parted. No excuses. No defenses. Just truth.

"Claire," she whispered. "Claire gave it to me. She said it was safe. She said it was clean."

And that was when something inside me buckled. Not from surprise, but from confirmation.

I didn't explode. Not yet. The silence that followed wasn't empty. It was suffocating. A slow implosion that started somewhere in the gut and rose until it pressed behind my eyes. I'd suspected something for days, too many missteps, too many coincidences, but I hadn't let myself believe it. Not until now. Not until I saw the look in Alana's eyes, broken trust, raw fear, the kind that doesn't come from theory, but from trauma.

She collapsed right there in the gravel, knees giving out as the weight of it all crushed her. And the sound that came out of her wasn't a scream. It wasn't panic. It was the sound of someone who'd just been yanked back into darkness. The sound of someone who thought they'd escaped and realized too late the cage was still around them.

I dropped to my knees beside her the moment I reached her, hands hovering close but not touching yet, waiting for her to breathe, to focus, to look at me. When her eyes finally lifted, full of terror and disbelief, I eased my hand to her shoulder and pulled her into my chest, steady and firm, the way a man holds something precious. She kept saying he found her, over and over, her words stumbling against her sobs, and I held her tighter, grounding her against the panic.

"Look at me," I said, lifting her chin gently until her eyes met mine. "I'm not letting anything happen to you. Not now. Not ever. We're going to figure this out, and I'm going to find out exactly how he reached that phone. You're safe with me. Do you hear me?"

She nodded, barely, her breath shaking against my shirt, and I gathered her into my arms fully and carried her to the car, shielding her from every sound, every shadow. The whole drive back, she trembled, whispering pieces of fear under her breath, and I kept one hand on her knee, steady and grounding, guiding her back to herself. By the time we pulled up to the safehouse, something hot and fierce had settled in my chest—because hearing my name come out of Ricky's mouth wasn't just a threat. It was a declaration of war. I didn't care who saw. I didn't care who heard. I was done pretending we were safe. We weren't. We never had been.

My eyes scanned the faces in the hallway, Clay, Maddox, two others, and I didn't stop moving.

"Back up," I barked, and the room obeyed before they even processed what they were stepping away from.

I carried her up the stairs in silence. Her head rested against my chest, her sobs muffled, her fingers curled in tight fists against my jacket. I could feel her body trembling. Could feel how small she'd become. But she let me carry her, and I held on like she was the only thing still tethering me to reason.

When we reached her room, I set her gently on the bed.

Brushed the hair from her damp cheeks.

"I need you to stay here," I said, crouching low, meeting her eyes.

"Put your headphones on. Don't listen to anything else. I'll handle it."

She nodded, barely. A breath. A ghost of agreement.

I stepped out, pulled the door nearly shut, and let the rage finally rise.

The moment I stepped back into that war room, the air shifted. Every set of eyes turned to me, and not a single person dared to speak. The temperature dropped as soon as my boots hit the tile. I didn't ask for silence. I didn't need to. My presence said enough.

"Who gave her a phone?" I said, low at first, the kind of voice that makes people freeze even before the words register.

"No, really, someone say it out loud. Who the hell handed her a direct line to Ricky?"

A few agents exchanged glances, the kind people make when they're trying to figure out if they're guilty by association. Ramirez stiffened near the monitors. Simone, the new tech girl, looked like she wanted to disappear into the wall. But it was Clay who leaned back in his chair, arms crossed, mouth tight, not surprised. Not curious. Just still.

I scanned the room again. No one moved. I stepped forward.

"She thought I was calling her," I said, louder now, my voice shaking not from uncertainty but from rage reined in by duty.

"She answered because it said my name. He knew about the drop, the Psalm I pray over her, things no one should know. So either Ricky's sitting in this house, or someone opened a window and invited him in."

That got a reaction, Simone gasped, one of the older agents

cursed under his breath, but not Clay. He shifted his weight in the chair, jaw ticking once, and that was it. No questions. No denial. Just... stillness.

"Start talking," I snapped, my eyes burning into the group. "Who brought her the phone?"

Claire stepped into the doorway right on cue, like she'd been waiting for her line. Her expression was calm, too calm. Arms at her sides. Face unreadable.

"I did," she said.

I turned slowly, letting the silence build behind me like a wave preparing to break. My voice, when it came, was a blade wrapped in velvet.

"You gave her the phone."

"I told her it was clean. Basic. No GPS. No apps. Just in case she needed to reach someone."

"And you didn't think to run that by me?"

I stepped closer.

"You didn't think to question if Ricky had ears on every low-tech network from here to hell?"

"She needed a tether," Claire said, quiet but unwavering.

"She needed to feel like she wasn't in a cage."

I looked at her firmly.

"She needed to feel safe. And now she's shattered."

I saw it in her eyes then, regret. But not guilt. Not the kind I needed.

And behind her, just over her shoulder, I saw Clay shift again. Barely. But I caught it. His arms uncrossed. He glanced at the floor like it had something interesting to say. When he looked back up, his face was blank, perfectly, professionally blank.

"You got something to add, Clay?" I asked, turning toward him slowly.

He blinked once, then shook his head.

"No. I didn't know she had a phone."

"That's funny," I said, stepping closer.

"Because you're the one running logistics. You're the one in and out of every room. You didn't see her with it? Not once?"

"No," he said again, this time with a little more weight, like he was offended I'd even asked.

I held his gaze a second longer than I needed to, just long enough to see the flicker, that micro expression people make when they've just dodged a bullet they weren't supposed to know was fired.

Claire spoke again, her voice sharper now. "Franklin, if you're implying,"

"I'm not implying," I cut in.

"I'm telling you we've got a leak. And it wasn't a lucky guess that led Ricky to her."

The room was suffocating now, thick with tension no one could name but everyone could feel. I looked back at Clay. Still expressionless. Still too still.

"She almost collapsed," I said, softer now, but sharper.

"She couldn't breathe. Couldn't speak. He reached right through her healing and crushed it with one call. And someone in this house opened that door."

Silence again. Not even the hum of the monitors broke it.

Then Clay stood.

"I'll double-check the safehouse systems," he said coolly.

"See if anything's been pinged or mirrored. Maybe there's a breach we missed."

Too smooth. Too prepared. Too detached.

"Yeah," I said, voice flat. "You do that."

As he walked out, I didn't look away. Not until he disappeared down the hall. Then I turned to Claire again, still watching, still unmoved.

"You may have meant well," I said, voice like gravel, "but you gave him a weapon."

Claire's jaw clenched, but she didn't reply. She didn't have to. The damage was already done.

And in the silence that followed, something shifted in me. Not just suspicion, resolve. Someone inside this circle wasn't who they claimed to be. And the closer I got to the truth, the more I realized...

It might not be the one I've been staring at all along.

**Alana**

Everything happened so fast after the call that trying to piece together the order of things felt impossible—the hurried packing, the whispered conversations moving from room to room, the tension so thick it felt like it lived in the air itself. Franklin's hand never left the small of my back, pressing there with a steady desperation, like if he let go for even a second, something might reach in and take me. He kept telling me we were leaving, that his father's home was safer, protected, sacred ground no one—especially Ricky—would dare violate. I nodded, climbed into the passenger seat, and went through the motions, but something fragile in me had already begun to collapse inward, folding like a flame retreating from the air.

The next few days blurred so heavily they barely felt real. I remember doors closing, agents speaking in hushed tones, meals showing up outside my room that I never touched. I remember the weight of blankets and the silence of hallways.

But mostly, I remember the fog—thick, consuming, sitting in my chest like I'd swallowed smoke.

He said he'd find me. And he did.

No matter how many locks they put on the doors, no matter how many plans they built around me, his voice burrowed deep. I heard it in dreams, in the pauses between breaths, in every quiet moment I tried to fill with something other than dread. And beneath it all, I heard something else too— the terrified girl I thought I had buried, the one who froze in doorways and didn't believe escape was meant for her.

I told myself I was safe. I repeated Franklin's words. I stared at the walls of this house built on prayer and protection and tried to anchor myself to truth. But none of it mattered when the darkness inside felt louder than the security around me. I kept thinking how foolish I was to believe I could outrun a man like him. That hope was something I could hold without it being used against me.

The shame settled in my chest like a stone. Heavy. Unmoving. Whispering lies about fault and blame, about how maybe this was the cost of daring to want something better than survival. Franklin tried—God, he tried. He sat with me, spoke Scripture softly over me, kept watch when I couldn't lift my head. He touched my shoulder gently every time he left the room, like he was reminding me I wasn't alone.

But I couldn't look at him anymore.

Not when I felt like a fracture pretending to be healed.

Most days, I couldn't even make myself sit up. I lay there staring at nothing until the room blurred and the pressure in my chest grew so thick breathing felt like wading through mud. My body didn't respond. My mind didn't respond. The girl who'd stepped into the rain so boldly felt a thousand miles away.

That morning wasn't any different. The air felt heavy, my limbs too tired to obey anything but the slow turn from one side to the other. When a soft knock came at my door, I didn't move. Didn't blink. I just turned my face toward the wall and whispered the same words I'd said yesterday, and the day before that.

"I can't do this today."

I expected the knock to fade, the presence to respect the fortress I'd built around myself, but instead the door creaked open, fully, decisively.

That sound shattered something inside me. Someone had decided my permission didn't matter.

Anger rose in my chest, fierce and sharp, faster than the creeping sadness and terror, and I sat up too fast, my voice cutting through the room before I saw who it was.

"I said I wasn't feeling it! Why would you—"

The rest of the sentence collapsed before it ever formed, because the person standing in the doorway wasn't Franklin, or a nurse, or an agent checking in. It was her—my therapist—standing quietly in the threshold like she had walked straight into the heaviness sitting on my chest and refused to let it keep its hold on me. Something in the room shifted the moment I saw her, as if the air softened and the weight that had been pressing down on me finally recognized it wasn't the strongest presence in the room anymore.

"Dr. Moby...?" My voice wavered, caught between disbelief and relief.

She didn't rush toward me or speak in the clipped, clinical tone she used during sessions. She simply stood there, steady and present, her expression warm enough to pull tears into my eyes before I even realized I was crying. Her calm didn't feel practiced or professional. It felt spiritual, almost like the Holy Spirit slipped in behind her and filled the room with a quiet that reached places in me I didn't know how to touch anymore.

"I'm here," she said softly, and something inside me cracked open at the gentleness in her voice.

My throat tightened. I pressed a shaky hand to my mouth as my vision blurred.

"Everything has been so dark," I whispered.

"I didn't... I didn't know how to come up for air."

She nodded once, slow, understanding.

"That's why I came."

That was all it took.

The guard I'd been clinging to—tight and rigid and brittle— broke cleanly. My body moved before my mind caught up. I pushed the blankets aside, stumbled out of bed, and walked straight to her, the way someone walks toward warmth after being cold for too long. She opened her arms just enough for me to step in at my own pace, and the moment I pressed my face against her shoulder, everything I'd been holding in poured out in a rush I couldn't control.

I sobbed, not the sharp, loud kind, but the deep, collapsing kind—the kind that leaves your whole body trembling as the pieces start falling off and somehow landing softly instead of breaking. She held me through every shudder, her hands firm between my shoulder blades, her chin resting lightly on top of my head. She didn't speak. She didn't pry. She didn't try to fix the moment. She simply became a place to fall without fear of breaking on impact.

After a long stretch of silence where the only sound was my

breathing, uneven and tired, she exhaled a tiny laugh into my hair as if dropping a little thread of light into the room.

"Whew," she murmured gently, "you stink."

The laugh that caught in my throat came out tangled with tears, but it was real.

"I know," I muttered against her shoulder, almost embarrassed but grateful for the normalcy.

"It's alright," she said, rubbing my back once.

"It just means you've been surviving. But let's get you into a shower so your body can remember what comfort feels like."

After I washed up, I pulled on the oversized sweater Franklin had left at the foot of the bed, letting the fabric fall over my hands like it was made to hold me instead of just cover me. When I stepped into the living room again, Dr. Moby was sitting calmly in a chair, her posture relaxed, her presence filling the space without overwhelming it. A warm cup of tea sat on the table in front of her, steam curling upward in slow, steady ribbons.

I eased into the chair across from her, still unsure if my limbs were ready to hold the weight of the moment. She didn't force anything. She simply waited until my breath found a calmer rhythm, her gaze steady and grounded.

When she finally spoke, her voice was low and certain.

"Eva," she said gently, "you've faced monsters and escaped them. You've survived being hunted, manipulated, threatened, and abandoned. But the thing haunting you right now isn't Ricky. It's the part of you that still believes you don't deserve peace."

I swallowed hard, the truth of it hitting deeper than any insult Ricky had ever thrown at me.

"You've been praying," she continued.

"You've been fighting. You've been letting yourself hope. But when something tried to break that hope, you retreated because a part of you still believes hope will be used against you. And as long as that fear leads your decisions... Ricky wins without lifting a finger."

I blinked, tears forming again—not from despair, but from the painful honesty of being so deeply understood.

"What if I don't make it?" I whispered. It came out before I could stop it—quiet, raw, the place where my courage thinned.

She leaned in slightly, her expression firm but kind.

"Then you make sure your voice does."

Her words didn't crash over me; they settled deep, like a truth I had always known but never dared to hold.

I breathed in, slow and shaky, but real.

This wasn't about survival anymore.

It was about speaking.

About choosing to live boldly enough that even if fear came, it wouldn't silence me.

And somewhere deep inside, beneath the trembling and the exhaustion, a spark steadied.

I knew what I had to do.

# 20

# Chapter 20

**Franklin**

It was just after six when I finally sank into the chair in the operations room, a mug of untouched coffee cooling beside me. The house felt too quiet, the kind of silence that didn't soothe but pressed against your ribs, reminding you how close the night had come to breaking everything open. I hadn't slept. Every time I closed my eyes, I saw Alana's face, the way she shook in my arms, the way her breath struggled to steady after Ricky's voice cut through her like a blade. I kept telling myself the reason I stayed by her side was vigilance, but the truth was simpler—I just couldn't leave her.

I tried to force my attention onto the monitors, letting the cold blue screens wash over me like a reset. "Come on," I muttered under my breath, scrolling through logs. "Something's gotta give."

I wanted something to focus on. Something that wasn't the memory of her leaning into me like she didn't have the strength to stand on her own. Something that wasn't the ache in my chest when she flinched at the sound of her name.

I clicked deeper into the internal movement logs, letting the data guide my thoughts—until one line stopped me cold.

Clay had logged a routine patrol at **1:14 p.m. Tuesday**, but the corresponding hallway footage was missing. Not corrupted. Not glitched. Completely removed. And the entire west wing camera had gone offline for precisely twenty-eight minutes before returning with a clean slate.

I leaned back slowly, jaw tightening as that detail worked its way under my skin. Clay always clocked in his movements with military precision; he was obsessive about timestamps. But now, the numbers didn't match, and the camera blackout sat in the perfect pocket where no one would notice unless they were digging.

I rubbed my thumb along my jaw, trying not to jump to conclusions, but the unease spread anyway.

Before I could investigate further, Claire stepped into the room—quiet, focused, the way she always was when she thought no one was watching. I caught her reflection in the monitor glass as she approached the server terminal. Her posture was composed, almost rehearsed, and her fingers moved across the keys with practiced ease. The familiarity in her movements wasn't casual; it was confident, like someone who knew exactly which lines of code unlocked which doors.

I didn't interrupt or question her or even shift in my seat; I simply stayed still and watched, letting her movements speak louder than anything I could have asked. She moved with a quiet confidence that didn't belong to someone doing routine work. Every tap of her fingertips, every controlled breath, every deliberate command woven into the terminal told me she wasn't improvising—she knew exactly what she was accessing and exactly how to hide the evidence when she was done.

Her shoulders stayed relaxed as she entered a manual override, scrolling through files with the calm of someone who fully expected the system to obey her. Then the pages disappeared—entire surveillance logs wiped out in a single, precise motion. Not a mistake. Not an accidental deletion. A controlled, intentional erasure.

She stepped back when she finished, smoothing the front of her blazer like she'd just finished a routine task, not compromised an entire wing of our surveillance. She walked out without a word, her heels tapping down the hall in an even, unhurried rhythm.

I let out a slow breath, my thoughts tightening into something sharp and focused.

Whether it was her or Clay—or someone else entirely—I couldn't afford to trust blindly anymore.

A vibration buzzed across the table.

My phone.

I reached for it, expecting a system ping or an update from HQ. Instead, a single message glowed back at me, no name attached, just a smooth, anonymous line carved across the screen:

**It's far from over.**

My grip tightened around the phone as the meaning settled deep in my chest.

"This is about her," I whispered.

And beneath that realization, something colder formed—a promise cutting through the exhaustion, steady and undeniable.

"They're coming for her," I said quietly. "But they'll have

to go through me first."

My jaw tightened as I pocketed my phone, heart racing with the realization that the threat we faced remained dangerously close. With shaking hands, I opened my neglected notebook, flipping past pages of half-formed thoughts and unanswered questions. Without hesitation, I scrawled fiercely into the blankness:

*Why does this betrayal feel like a knife to the back?*

But I didn't know who wielded it. Clay? Claire? Or was it myself, my own failure to see clearly enough, to protect her as completely as she deserved?

I pressed my palms to the cool tabletop, forcing myself to steady my breath, to anchor myself in this moment. This wasn't the time to unravel, not while Alana slept upstairs, not while Ricky still prowled freely in the darkness outside, and certainly not when betrayal threatened to break us from within. I would watch everyone as though they were strangers. Trust had become a luxury I couldn't afford.

It was quiet in the hallway when I brought tea upstairs, the walls humming gently with the tension of our recent storm. The mug was warm in my hand, filled with Alana's favorite blend, steeped longer because somehow, even now, I remembered the small things she preferred. As I knocked softly and eased open her door, I saw her sitting upright, wrapped protectively in a blanket she hadn't reached for in days. Her eyes were tired but open, and that alone felt like mercy.

"I brought you something," I whispered, offering the mug, heart quickening as her fingers brushed mine, lingering for a heartbeat longer than necessary. Silence stretched comfortably between us, gentle and healing, until finally, she spoke.

"You ever think about what kind of life you want after all this?" Her voice was barely above a whisper, eyes fixed thoughtfully on the mug's steaming surface.

I tilted my head thoughtfully, absorbing her vulnerability. "Sometimes."

"I don't think I ever did," she admitted softly, her voice uncertain.

"Not until lately."

I leaned forward gently.

"What would it look like?"

She paused, tentative but determined to give voice to hope.

"A porch. Something quiet, safe. Somewhere I could breathe without checking over my shoulder. Stillness... Maybe that sounds small, but,"

"It doesn't," I assured her, throat thickening with emotion.

"Peace is holy too. You deserve that."

Her breath stilled for a moment after I said it — *peace is holy, and you deserve that.*

When she looked up at me again, something shifted in her eyes. It wasn't fear anymore, and it wasn't hesitation either. It was a bold, quiet kind of want — the kind that comes from realizing someone sees you gently, and you want to step into that light even if it scares you.

She held my gaze like she was anchoring herself to it.

Steady. Unbroken. Intentional.

Not once did she look away.

Slowly, she set the teacup down on the small table beside her bed — deliberate, careful, like she didn't want anything clattering or interrupting the charge in the air. And then she rose from where she sat and walked toward me with a softness that still felt like a pull.

When she stopped in front of me, she reached out with both hands and cupped my face — not tentative this time, but intentional, her palms warm on my cheeks, her thumbs brushing the edge of my jaw like she was memorizing me.

Those eyes of hers held mine so firmly it felt like the world narrowed to the space between us.

Her voice came out quiet, trembling but brave.

"Do you mean that?"

I leaned into her hands, let her feel the truth in the way my body stilled beneath her touch.

"Yes," I whispered, steady and low. "And I'll do anything to make that happen."

Her breath shuddered — not from fear, but from something breaking open inside her — and then she pulled me toward her without waiting for another word.

Our mouths met in a slow, certain kiss that hit deeper than anything I'd prepared for. Her lips were soft and warm, moving against mine like she'd been waiting for this without realizing it. She kissed me with her whole body — her fingers sliding into my hair, her other hand gripping my shoulder, steadying herself as she leaned in harder.

I answered her with equal intention, one hand slipping behind her neck to guide her closer, the other tracing down her side until I felt her waist beneath my palm. She exhaled against my mouth, a small, helpless sound that made my pulse thicken in my throat.

The kiss deepened, grew hungrier without losing its tenderness — her lips parting, her body pressing against mine in a way that told me she wasn't just reaching for comfort. She wanted me. She trusted me. And she was choosing me in a way that felt reverent.

I angled my mouth over hers, drew her in closer, feeling her fingers tug softly at the back of my shirt as if she couldn't stand even an inch of space between us. Her breath hitched when I slid my hand along her jaw and kissed her deeper, slower, letting her feel just how badly I'd been holding back.

I felt her shift beneath my hands, her body leaning into mine with quiet urgency, and for a moment the world narrowed to nothing but the warmth of her mouth and the soft sound she made when I deepened the kiss. Her fingers slid from my shirt to the hem of her top, fumbling with the fabric, tugging it upward in a way that made my chest tighten, not with desire, but with realization.

She wasn't reaching for closeness.

She was reaching for what she thought love required.

The second her hands began to lift her shirt, I broke the kiss—not sharply, not with recoil, but with my forehead still resting against hers, my breath shaking as I gently caught her wrists.

"Hey... no. Alana, wait."

She blinked at me, lips parted, breath uneven from the intensity of the moment. "What do you mean, wait?" she whispered. "Don't you... don't you want me?"

My chest ached at the fear hidden inside her question. I brought her hands down slowly and held them between us, my thumbs brushing the backs of her knuckles.

"You have no idea," I said, voice low, honest. "You have no idea how much I've wanted you, how many nights I've had to force myself to walk away."

Her eyes searched mine, confused, hopeful, hurting.

"Then why stop?"

"Because this?" I said softly, lifting her chin with my knuckle so she'd look at me. "This doesn't honor you. Not like this. Not when you're reaching for me because you think I need your body to stay."

She swallowed hard, breath catching again—not with desire this time, but with something fragile.

I kept my hands on her arms, steadying her, forcing myself to breathe before my mouth betrayed every impulse running through me.

"Alana... listen to me," I said, my voice rough but controlled. "I don't regret kissing you. I've wanted that for longer than you know."

Her lips parted, still swollen from where mine had been, her breath uneven, her hands trembling against my chest.

"But anything past that?" I shook my head slowly, fighting every part of me that wanted to pull her back in. "Not tonight. Not like this. I'm not risking what I feel for you just because my body's begging for you right now."

Something flickered across her face—confusion, hope, fear—blending into one fragile expression. I lifted her chin gently with my fingers, not to lead her anywhere, but to make sure she saw the truth straight in my eyes.

"I want you so badly it hurts," I murmured, "but I'm not losing my mind over you... I'm losing my heart. And I'm not giving in to anything that could cheapen that."

Her breath hitched, soft and startled, her whole body going still.

"Franklin..." she whispered, barely forming the word. "Are you saying you—"

I didn't let her finish.

"I love you," I said plainly, like it wasn't something I'd

struggled with for weeks, like it wasn't something tearing through me at the seams. "I love you, Alana."

She stepped back, not far, just enough to blink up at me like she had to relearn how to breathe.

"You... love me?"

I swallowed once, steady, grounded, certain.

"Yes," I said. "With everything in me."

She flinched—just the faintest pullback.

Her eyes lowered, then lifted again with something haunted behind them.

"You wouldn't... if you really knew who I was," she whispered.

I stepped closer, cupping her cheek again, letting my thumb trace the softness beneath her eye.

"I don't need every detail to know you're worth loving," I said gently.

"I'm here. I'm not going anywhere. We're going to get through this. You're going to get your home. We're going to get justice for your sister. And you're going to have a life that's whole and healed and yours."

She closed her eyes, leaning into my hand like she'd been waiting her whole life for someone to say those words.

And that's where we stayed—close, quiet, steady—holding onto each other without taking anything more than what the moment could hold.

**Alana**

After last night, I didn't know how to walk through the house without feeling like my skin remembered everything before my mind did. Every time I closed my eyes, I felt his hands on

293

my waist, the warmth of his mouth against mine, the quiet way he kissed me like I wasn't broken or borrowed or something he had to be careful with. He kissed me like he wanted me. Not in pieces. Not in pain. But whole.

And I kissed him back like I'd been waiting for someone to show me what tenderness felt like.

But the moment my fingers slipped under the hem of my shirt, reaching for something familiar, something transactional— shame hit me so fast I could barely breathe. Not because he pulled away. But because he did so with gentleness. With conviction. With love I still didn't know how to carry.

He didn't look at me like I ruined anything.

But I woke up feeling like I had.

My body still buzzed from the memory of his lips, but my chest felt tight with guilt—guilt that I almost turned something sacred into something survival-shaped. Guilt that I almost took what he offered and twisted it into what Ricky taught me love was supposed to look like. Guilt that he had to stop me at all.

The sun was soft when I stepped out of the room, the kind of morning light that forgave everything it touched. I wished it could do the same for me.

I wrapped Franklin's sweater tighter around myself, breathing in the faint scent of cedar and something warm I couldn't name. My legs still felt unsteady, not from fear, but from the echo of last night— from the way he said he loved me like it was truth, not obligation.

And I didn't know what to do with any of that.

When I reached the kitchen, Franklin's father stood at the counter pouring steaming tea into a chipped ceramic mug.

The minty scent drifted through the air, grounding me before I could think of anything to say. He looked up when he heard me, his face softening instantly.

"You good, sweetheart?" he asked.

The word didn't sting. It didn't feel like possession or pity. It felt gentle. Safe. Fatherly in a way I hadn't known in far too long.

I slipped into a chair, feeling the wood cool beneath my palms, and tried to steady my breathing. But the truth was already rising, messy and fragile.

"I... tried to offer him something I thought he wanted," I said quietly, my voice trembling. "Something that used to work on people like him."

Franklin's father didn't rush me. Didn't blink harshly. He just waited with that steadiness his son carried too.

"And he told me I didn't have to give myself to be seen," I whispered, my throat tightening.

"And I don't know what to do with that."

He didn't interrupt. He simply set his mug down, pulled out the chair across from me, and sat with his hands folded. His presence was calm, solid, like an anchor in the middle of a storm.

"I know what it looks like to believe you've done too much to deserve someone whole," he said, each word deliberate.

"But love isn't about matching someone's clean. It's about showing up anyway."

I dropped my gaze to my hands.

"I don't have much to bring him," I whispered before I could stop myself.

"He deserves someone who,"

"Knows who she is?" he asked. His eyes held a kindness

that wasn't pity.

"Sounds like that's exactly who he's got."

I looked at him, really saw the kindness there, and felt tears prick my eyes, not shameful tears, but something raw and unguarded. He reached out and lightly touched my knuckles.

"I don't know your whole story, Alana," he said, "but I know God, and I know He doesn't give people like Franklin away to girls who aren't worthy. He sent Franklin to you on purpose. Just like He sent you to him."

I couldn't speak.

Tears gathered in my eyes again, but this time they didn't come from shame or fear. They came from something I hadn't felt in a long, long time.

Freedom.

Not because my story was fixed.

But because someone finally looked at my story and didn't flinch.

Franklin's dad gave my hand one last gentle squeeze before rising from the table.

"I'll leave you to rest," he said softly, nodding once before heading toward the hallway.

Just as he reached the doorway, Clay appeared from the opposite end, walking in like he had been waiting for the right moment. Their shoulders nearly brushed as they passed each other.

Clay let out a low, careless scoff.

"Didn't realize we were running a charity program now," he muttered, just loud enough to land.

Franklin's dad stopped—not fully turning, just pausing.

"Watch yourself," he said quietly, then continued out the back door, letting it close behind him with a soft click.

The house went still again.

I sat at the table, fingers curled around the mug Franklin's dad left behind, the warmth fading against my palms.

Then Clay stepped fully into the kitchen.

He didn't smile. Didn't pretend to be friendly.

He just stood there, blocking the doorway like he had nowhere else to be.

"Didn't mean to interrupt," he said smoothly, though the look in his eyes made my stomach tighten.

I rose slowly. "I was just leaving," I said, voice soft but steady.

He didn't move aside.

His hand closed around my wrist—not bruising, but firm enough to freeze me in place.

Firm enough to remind me I wasn't alone in this room.

Firm enough to make the hairs on my arms stand straight.

His voice dropped, barely audible. "You've fooled a lot of people around here," he said, the edge in his words cutting deep. "But I know who girls like you really are."

That was enough.

I yanked my arm back hard, my heart slamming against my ribs.

"Don't you touch me!"

Burst out of me like a flare, sharp, instinctive, desperate.

Clay's posture shifted the instant I called out. He stepped back with an exaggerated air of innocence, hands lifted, smile tight. Just a misunderstanding, he conveyed.

Franklin appeared in the doorway seconds later, his footsteps thudding against the tile. When his eyes locked on Clay, his jaw clenched, and his arms curled toward readiness, one move away from drawing a weapon.

"What's going on?" he demanded, voice low and electric.

Clay offered that too-slick shrug.

"Nothing major, man. We were just talking."

I stood frozen, the kitchen too hot, too small, everything pulsing around me. Franklin looked at me for one heartbeat and already knew. He didn't need me to explain. After Clay slipped away, his composure tight, Franklin stood beside me long enough to make sure I was breathing. Then he gave a curt nod and left the doorway slightly open, a silent promise of trust: that I was safe, and he believed me.

A few hours later, my therapist arrived. I heard her soft footsteps in the hall, followed by Franklin's low greeting downstairs. When she walked in, the weight in my chest returned, dense and familiar. She offered a small smile, and I held my breath. I needed to know before she spoke.

"You didn't tell anyone, right?" I asked quietly, scanning her face.

She didn't hesitate.

"I didn't tell a soul. It's yours to share, always."

I nodded once, exhaling a breath I didn't realize I'd been holding. We moved to the bed, two chairs arranged like a sanctuary against the white hospital sheets and pulsing florescent lights overhead.

I met her eyes and, with a steady voice I barely recognized, said, "I want to tell him the truth, about who I am. My name."

Tears blurred my vision, but they weren't shameful. They were the tears of something finally breaking open. She reached out, placing her hand over mine.

"Eva," she said softly, as though that single word carried all the weight of my journey.

I repeated it in my mind: Eva. I wasn't hiding from her

anymore.

"I didn't think I'd ever say it out loud," I murmured.

She squeezed my hand gently.

"You're not who you were. But who you were still deserves healing."

After she left, I lingered on that bed longer than usual, my fingers brushing the spot where hers had been. My chest felt lighter, as though each breath had newly carved space for hope.

Franklin knocked lightly on the doorframe before stepping inside, leaning casually against it, respecting boundaries, yet filling the room with his presence.

"She make you cry again?" he asked, a small smile tugging at his lips.

I managed a soft smile in return, though my eyes remained damp.

"Yeah," I admitted. "But the good kind."

He nodded as if that alone told him everything. Then he slid onto the edge of the bed, eyes darkening with concern.

"Heads-up," he said quietly.

"Tomorrow, we have to go back to the precinct. They need you to give a statement, timeline details, anything you remember. It's not a public appearance. Just evidence-building. You won't be alone."

I felt something tighten in my chest, an echo of panic, but I opened my throat.

"I'm ready," I said.

Franklin blinked, surprise flashing across his face before he nodded slowly, as though he understood the full weight of what I'd just declared.

"Okay," he said. "Then we'll go together."

My heartbeat was still racing, but underneath the fear, a steady resolve was rising. I wasn't just going to give a statement. I was going to speak as Eva. And even though I'd barely caught a moment's rest, I knew something irrevocable had shifted inside me: I wasn't afraid to be seen.

# 21

# Chapter 21

**Franklin**

That morning felt good in a way I hadn't let myself feel in a long time. Not just because we were finally making progress with the case, but because Alana had woken up rested. She laughed over breakfast with my dad , real laughter, the kind that came from somewhere deep, not the polite kind people use to fill space. She was starting to look like herself.

My father stood beside me on the porch, coffee in hand, eyes on the trees like always. The morning was cool, the sun still low. I knew that look , he was thinking, waiting to say something he wasn't sure I was ready to hear. That was always his way. Quiet. Then one sentence that cut right to the bone.

"She's a good woman," he said finally.

"Got that quiet strength on her. That don't come from nowhere."

I nodded, because he wasn't wrong. She was strong in ways most people didn't understand. She didn't posture or perform. She just endured. And somehow, after everything, she was still soft. Still kind. Still brave enough to speak the truth, even when it cost her everything.

"She's about to change everything," I murmured. "Once we get all the names and location, it's gonna shift the whole case. It's the beginning of the end, Pops."

He glanced at me and smiled , that patient kind of smile like he already knew something I hadn't caught up to yet. "It's the beginning of something, alright. You just better make sure you're not so caught up chasing justice that you forget to court the girl."

I laughed. "What do you mean 'court'?"

"You know what I mean," he said, sipping his coffee.

"She needs flowers. Walks. Some peace. You don't just fall into love with a woman like that , you build something she can trust. That don't happen by accident."

His words hit deeper than I expected. Because he wasn't just talking about her , he was talking about me.

And when he added, "She's pulling something outta you I ain't never seen before," his voice dropped just enough for me to feel it.

"You always been a good man, Franklin. But you different with her. Better. Softer in ways I didn't think you'd let yourself be."

He was right. Alana had shifted something in me. Not just because I cared about her, but because she made me want to be the kind of man who could carry joy, not just justice. She made me slower to anger. Quicker to pray. She made me want to stay.

"I'm proud of you, son," he said. "For the man you're becoming. Not just the badge. Not just the case. You."

I nodded, jaw tight, throat tighter. I wasn't used to hearing it, not like that — but I felt it. And it settled in my chest like something solid I could finally stand on.

Inside, I heard her footsteps moving down the hall.

Light. Calm. Steady.

She stepped into the doorway, met my eyes for a quiet second, then walked toward me.

She exhaled, lifted her chin just slightly, and said, "I'm ready."

I gave her a small nod, forcing myself to believe it with her. Then I pulled the door open wider and held it as she slipped past me. She squeezed my arm lightly before heading down the steps outside, her eyes searching my face as if to ask if I was really alright.

I followed a step behind, watching her climb into the passenger seat. She closed the door with care, like she didn't want the moment to break too loudly.

I walked around to the driver's side, pulled the door open, and climbed in. I'd barely shut it before the phone buzzed against my hip.

The screen flashed "Crime Unit" in jagged, urgent letters. I glanced over at Alana, already buckled in, her hands folded in her lap. Her eyes were soft but clouded with the weight of everything she'd been through, and I didn't want to shatter this moment. I peeled out of the driveway, trying to maintain calm, even as my pulse spiked.

I swipe to answer. "Yeah, go ahead."

My voice is steady on the outside, but inside my ribs feel like they're pinched tight.

"Franklin," the tech's voice is clipped, like she's holding her breath.

"We just got the fingerprint results back from the safehouse."

I pull onto the street, the tires crunching against gravel.

"Okay. What did you find?"

There's a pause, long enough for static to scratch between us.

Then she says, "The house was clean. Franklin... not just wiped down, sterile. No trace evidence. No fibers. No viable prints. Nothing."

I jerk the wheel toward the center of the road, inhaling too sharply. "Not even mine?" My throat closes up.

"No. Not yours. Not Clay's. Not even hers." Her words drop like stones.

A cold rush spreads from my chest down to my stomach. "That can't be right. We were in that place for weeks."

"We ran triple scans," she says, voice taut. "Even the hallway where you said she fell, there isn't so much as a partial smudge. It's like no one ever touched anything. Like someone wanted to erase the entire time you guys were there."

My vision narrows. The streetlights blur past as if they're speeding backward. All I can feel is the tight coil of dread twisting in my gut. It clicks into place: Clay was the only one who went back to the safehouse after the raid.

I remember handing him the radio and saying, "*Secure it. Dust for prints. Walk every inch.*" I trusted him. Had to, or the plan meant nothing. And he reported back empty-handed, no evidence, no explanation beyond, "*It's a washout from the storm.*" I accepted it without question.

God, how I believed him.

Then it hits me like a punch to the ribs:

**He didn't dust for prints. He erased them.**

Every step I'd taken in this case, he'd been right behind

me, watching. Studying. He asked questions he didn't need answers to. He never looked surprised by what we found because he already knew exactly what would be there.

Because he planted it.

I clamp my free hand over the wheel so hard my knuckles blanch. My breath comes in jagged bursts, but I force myself to stay on the road.

"Thanks," I manage to choke out, then hang up before she can say another word.

The air in the car feels thick, as if it's pressing against my lungs. My eyes flick to Alana's reflection, her face framed by the morning light, lips parted like she wants to ask what's wrong. But I can't meet her gaze. Not yet. I need to swallow back the panic.

I press harder on the gas, aiming straight for the precinct. The road opens into a four-lane stretch, morning traffic just starting to crowd the lights. My phone is still in my hand, Clay's voicemail playing for the third time. Every call went straight there—he wasn't picking up.

My pulse hammered as I eased to a stop at the red light. The world pressed in, unnaturally still, almost watchful. Alana's gaze found me, her brows knit with concern. Then headlights explode in my periphery.

A black sedan screams through the intersection and slams into us, driver's side first. The impact tears the air from my lungs, metal shrieking, glass shattering in a burst of white-hot sparks. My body whips sideways, the seatbelt biting deep into my ribs.

The blast of collision fractures the morning, louder than gunfire. My skull cracks against the headrest, copper flooding my mouth. The world tilts, windows spiderwebbed with cracks, Alana's scream tangled with the sound of twisting steel.

The car jerks to a stop against the curb, steam pouring from the crumpled hood. My ears ring so hard I can barely hear my own breath, but adrenaline spikes enough to shove me back into motion. The passenger door blew wide; a shadow reached in. Alana's buckle snapped free, and she was yanked out into the smoke before I could even blink. The acrid stench of fuel. Heat pressing at my face like the whole street is about to ignite.

I force the door open against the bent frame, stumble out onto asphalt slick with debris. My knees buckle, vision blurred, but movement catches in the corner of my eye.

A figure, slipping away. Low. Fast.

**Ricky.**

He's slipping away, his silhouette a dark slash against the inferno. He moves low, fast, as if the flames are someone chasing him. Every instinct screams to chase, but my body rebels. Pain ignites with each step. Still, I lurch forward, forcing my legs to carry me.

He rounds the corner and I close on him, breath and adrenaline hot. I tackle him into the dirt; he slams down hard, the impact jarring my bruised side. I drive my forearm into his back until his spine folds, roll him, and press the gun to the side of his skull.

He spits a rivulet of blood from between his teeth, a thin line curving along his jaw. Then he smiles, twisted, triumphant. "You're too late," he rasps.

Rage surges through me, hot and blinding. I wrench my gun back, finger tightening on the trigger. The world narrows to nothing but his face, that insolent smirk daring me to pull the trigger.

Then,

**Vengeance is Mine.**

It lands behind my sternum like a hammer. Not a shout. Not a thought. I don't hear it; I feel it, God's voice, steady and final. For a second I want to yank the trigger, to obliterate him and end the noise in my chest. But the voice presses down on the rage and my hands shake as I pull the barrel off his face. I fire low, *a purposeful, controlled shot*, and Ricky screams, raw and animal.

I yank him to his feet and snap cuffs on his wrists. There's no triumph in me, only ice-cold resolve. The smoke thickens, the heat bites harder, and I stagger back, pressing my palm to the ruined brick to steady myself. My ribs scream; every step is a white-hot shard. I don't feel it. I only feel the need to find her.

Then I hear it, a voice, thin and frayed, cutting through the haze. "Franklin! Franklin, help!"

My head snaps up. For a heartbeat the world tilts and slows. Through the smoke I see motion at the edge of the wreckage: a shape dragged past the passenger side of a dented car. A hand clutches hair, another shoulder jerks, and the figure being hauled looks impossibly small against the chaos.

Clay.

He's dragging her, hard, efficient, not panicked, like a man moving a piece off a board. She's twisting, punching, clawing at his arms, but smoke and blood make her movements ragged. She looks up for one second, like she's searching the world for me, and then she screams my name again, a sound that yanks open every part of me.

I lurch forward, lungs burning, but the world collapses into a sudden, heavy shove, someone hits me from the side, hard, sending me down. Pain flares white-hot across my ribs and the air shatters with the sound of falling metal. My vision squeezes to a pinhole and the edges go grey.

Even as I fight to drag myself up, I see Clay's back slip into the smoke, her body dragged behind him. Another figure moves toward them from the shadows, low, deliberate, and something in my chest breaks when I recognize the gait.

Ricky is free again, and he's moving straight for her.

A sound rips out of me, a half-growl, half-prayer—but the hit to my skull blindsides me. The world tilts hard, the floor rushing up, and before I can fight it, everything goes black. Her voice reaches me as I fall, thin and far away: "Franklin..."

**Alana**

My gut had been right all along; it was Clay. The truth slammed into me as his fist tightened in my hair, dragging me across the broken asphalt. My scalp burned, my heels scraped the ground, and my fingers clawed at his wrists, but his grip was iron. Panic knifed through me, sharper than the pain. For weeks something inside me had whispered every time he smiled too easily, every time he stood just a little too close. And still I ignored it. Still I trusted him. And now the mask was gone.

"You think you're smart, huh? I told you what you are. A piece of property. A transaction. That's all you'll ever be." His voice curled low, mocking in my ear as he yanked me upright.

My throat tore with a scream.

"No! You don't get to name me. You don't get to tell me who I am!"

My voice cracked, but I didn't stop. I shoved against his chest, fists pounding even as he caught my wrists and twisted them tight in front of me. Pain flared through my arms, but something hotter burned inside.

He sneered. "Oh yeah, I almost forgot. You went and gave your life to Christ, right?"

His grip wrenched harder, his eyes glittering like glass about to shatter.

My chest heaved, rage choking out fear. I spat in his face, my voice cracking but desperate. "Why? Why betray everything you stood for? Why me? I never did anything to you. Why are you trying to destroy me?"

Clay's jaw tightened. His smirk spread slow and ugly. "Because this, this is me finally cashing in. All those years doing the work, backing Franklin while he got the spotlight, while Claire handed him the cases. Me, always the extra, always the shadow. You think loyalty pays? It doesn't. Money does. Power does. And I'm walking away with both while you..."

His voice dipped, cruel and calm. "...you won't even make it to testify."

His hand cinched tighter around my bound wrists until my fingers went numb. I gasped, thrashing, kicking at his shins, refusing to give him the silence he wanted.

And then I saw it, movement in the haze. Another shape stepping out from the smoke. The gait was deliberate, slow, like a predator circling prey. My stomach dropped as recognition settled in my bones.

Ricky.

Ricky's laugh slid out of the dark, low and sharp. He stepped forward, eyes mean.

"Get out of here before it's too late, he's already seen you."

Clay scoffed, jaw tight. "Just wire the money."

Ricky's smile turned to a sneer. He stepped closer, close enough that the smoke curled between them like a boundary Clay would never cross. "You deaf, Pretty Boy? Run. Or you'll end up like my darling here."

Clay's bravado cracked. His jaw worked, but he said nothing. Then, like the coward he was, he slipped into the smoke. No fight. No loyalty. Just gone.

Then Ricky turned to me. He crouched low, his hand brushing my cheek like a mockery of tenderness.

"Don't you dare touch me," I spat, jerking my face away.

He smiled, slow and ugly. "Don't be dramatic, darling. I made you."

I laughed, short and bitter. "No. God made me."

His eyes hardened. He flicked a glance toward Franklin's crumpled body and jabbed a finger in his direction.

"Oh, right. Just like God made your little Psalm-91 boy. Your protector. Your hero with his prayers. Look at him now."

His voice dropped to a sneer.

"Flat on the ground. Useless. Tell me how that's working out for you."

I swallowed and kept my voice steady. "Franklin is a man you'll never be. He loves me, I know that. You used me."

He snorted, a sound like a knife dragged across stone.

"You really think a man like that would want someone like you?" His smile curled cruel.

"You've been passed around. Used up. Filthy. You're nothing but damaged goods, and men like him don't keep women like you, they toss you when they're done."

He laughed, low and sharp, the kind that used to crawl under

310

my skin. "You forget who found you. Who took you and that pathetic little sister of yours out of that house with your drunk, half-dead mother crying over a bottle? I saved you. I gave you purpose. You think Franklin's any different? He pities you. That's all it is. And when he's done playing hero, he'll walk away"

I leaned into the words instead of shrinking from them.

"No, you're wrong" I said. "And even if the whole world calls me filthy, I know who I belong to and that will never be you, you monster"

His eyes flared at that, pride pierced where no bullet could reach. The words were poison. I forced my jaw up.

"You're just a hungry little boy who needs an audience. You traffic and you buy silence because you can't build a life. You take others because you have nothing of your own. You will never be any type of god you pretend to be."

That cut into him in the way I aimed for, pride meets truth. His amusement curdled into a hard, dangerous silence. He leaned in until his face nearly touched mine.

"You think God's on your side?" he hissed. "Let me tell you about fear."

His fingers found my throat, testing, squeezing, not enough to finish, only to show control. The pressure stole my breath; panic rose hot and white.

"Why are you laughing?" he demanded.

"Because I'm not afraid," I said, calm as a prayer. "You're not taking me , you're sending me home."

His face contorted in hate. Light dimmed at the edges.

Franklin's voice threaded through the haze:

"Alana,"

# 22

# Chapter 22

**Alana**

His fingers are a vice at my throat and the world has narrowed to the scrape of his breath and the pulse pounding behind my ears. I force my eyes open because I need to see him , Franklin , even if it's just the blur of his shape.

"Let her go." Franklin's voice comes from somewhere full and hard, like a hammer. It's closer. I think I'm saved before the thought finishes forming.

Ricky's face twists, angry and thin in the streetlight. He doesn't loosen his grip. He answers me instead of Franklin. "She's mine," he says, low and possessive.

"Been mine a long time." He says the words like proof.

"You don't get to take her."

I try to breathe. The sound I push out is small, a prayer more than a plea: *Lord, just wait , hold me a little longer.* The words are sputtered and sticky, but they're there. I repeat them because repetition is something my body can still do when everything else is failing.

Something in Ricky's expression shifts when he hears it , a crooked smile, a look that says he sees me as smaller now. He leans in close enough that I feel the sweat on his lip.

"Praying?" he sneers.

"You really praying now? How cute."

His fingers tighten, and the world narrows to the ache in my neck.

His arm jerks forward with brutal purpose, and before I can even inhale, the knife is already inside me.

The impact knocks the breath out of my lungs in a single, shattering rush. Heat floods beneath my ribs—sharp, searing, immediate—so real and so sudden it forces a broken sound out of me, more gasp than voice. My body folds instinctively, hands flying to the wound only to meet warmth spilling fast across my fingers.

Pain blooms hard and violent, rippling outward in waves that make my vision flicker.

His arm jerked, and the impact tore the breath out of my lungs, pain blooming hard and sudden. He pressed in close, trapping me where I'd already fallen, his weight pinning me against the cold floor as the world tilted.

His breath ghosts my ear, cold and satisfied, as if he's savoring the way my strength drains beneath his hands.

Franklin hits him then , weight and speed and a raw, animal sound that is not a prayer.

"Get off her," he snarls, and his body slams into Ricky's back. They roll and crash; dirt sprays against my cheek. Everything is impact and grunt and the metallic sting of panic.

Ricky lashes out, spitting through blood in his teeth. "You always thought you were better than me. Hero cop, big savior." He claws at Franklin's face, desperate. "But you're nothing

313

without this girl bleeding in the dirt."

Franklin answers with a blow that is all coiled muscle and years of rage. His voice rips through the fight:

"Shut your mouth." Another strike.

"You're done." His weight pins Ricky down like judgment.

I taste copper and fear. My fingers, slick and trembling, press at the wound that is now a hot wet hole in my side. Blood pools warm under my palm and the pressure of it makes me dizzy. Each breath pulls at the cut, a knife inside the wound with every inhale.

Their voices break through like jagged things. Ricky's voice is a hiss: "You're too late. She's gone." Franklin doesn't sound like Franklin anymore , it's rage unbound: "I've waited years for this. You don't get to win."

They're not arguing philosophy. They're tearing at each other. Franklin hits with a fury that looks like grief made violent; Ricky fights like a cornered animal. Knock, grunt, curse , the rhythm of it is a drum in my skull. The knife skitters away at one point, a sharp clink on the pavement that sounds like a bell. For a second the fight is all hands and teeth and the smell of sweat and blood.

I can see Franklin's face when he leans over them , not the clean cop I met, not the careful man who offers tea and quietness, but something harder, eyes raw and fixed. He pins Ricky, bending his weight into the man like he's trying to crush the air from him. The cuff snaps open then closed; the sound is bright and final in the dark. Ricky thrashes once, twice, his head hitting the pavement with a dull crack. For a second his limbs go slack, and I think maybe , maybe he's down.

I cough. It's a wet, ragged sound that tears something

raw in my throat.  Pain blooms with every breath; it's fire crawling deeper, stealing strength. My vision blinks , close, then distant.  Franklin's voice rushes back to me, a single frantic line.

"Alana! Talk to me. Don't you dare," He doesn't finish. He's on his feet, reaching, and everything else compresses into the simple need of him: come here.

I pull air that feels like gravel and my lips shape the name like a prayer:

"Franklin , please , come here."

He comes like a reckoning, boots skidding, breath raw, a light behind him that makes his edges haloed and huge. For a second , absurd and sharp , the world tilts and something tender and impossible settles over the chaos.  I should be screaming. I should be folding into the pain. Instead there is a thin, impossible calm, like a hand laid across my heart that says it's okay to stop fighting the dark.

Franklin drops to his knees beside me and then he lifts me like I am the most fragile thing on earth. His hands are everywhere , under my ribs, behind my back , and the way he gathers me makes the rest of the world fall away.

"You're hurt," he says, voice breaking, blunt with fear.

"You're hurt, Alana."

I look at him and laugh , a trembling, tiny sound that surprises me because it is half-sorrow, half-relief.

I force the corners of my mouth up and tell him, soft and ridiculous and true, "It's okay. It's okay."

"No... no, no, no," he whispers, and the way he says it isn't panic. It's grief breaking open inside him.

His hands are on me immediately—warm, frantic, trying to hold me together like he could convince my body to stay

315

if he just loved me hard enough. His touch trembles against my skin. His tears fall onto my cheek, and for a moment, the warmth of them feels like the last real thing anchoring me here.

"Alana, please," he says, voice splintering.

"Don't do this. Stay with me. Stay."

I want to answer him clearly, to reach up and take his face in my hands, to tell him I'm okay, or that I'll fight, or at least not leave him like this. But everything inside me is slow and heavy. My body is slipping away from me in small pieces — first my fingertips, then my legs, then the strength in my breath.

Still, I find enough to speak one truth.

My fingers curl weakly into the shoulder of his shirt. It takes everything I have just to hold on.

"You saved me," I manage, voice nothing more than a thin thread.

"You got him... you got him for us."

The words land in him like a breaking. His mouth trembles. His forehead drops to mine, and the quiet sound he makes is agony trying to come out gentle. His breath shakes as he holds me closer, like if he can keep me warm, he can keep me alive.

I cough, and the taste of blood rises fast, metallic and overwhelming. It coats my tongue, fills my mouth, thick enough that I can't swallow. His eyes widen when he sees it. Panic floods him, raw and unfiltered, like he realizes the truth in one cruel, uncontested second.

His hands press harder into my side, desperate, pleading, trying to bargain with a wound that won't listen.

"Don't talk," he begs, voice breaking apart. "Baby, please. Don't talk."

But I have to.

I can feel something inside me dimming, the way light pulls back when the sun slides behind a cloud. I feel the cold creeping up my arms, soft but certain. My breaths grow thinner, shallow slips of air that don't reach deep enough to hold me here.

I fight for one more breath.

One more sentence.

The one that has lived inside me for months, waiting for this moment.

"For... such..."

The blood rises. My chest seizes.

"...a time... like this."

The last word barely escapes. It falls out of me fragile and final.

Franklin's head shakes immediately, violently, like he can undo it, like he can force the ending to reverse if he refuses to accept it.

"No. Don't say that. No, no, no," he whispers, and the sound is devastation turned human.

"Don't say goodbye. Don't leave me. Please don't leave me."

His tears fall onto my cheeks faster now, warm against skin that's beginning to lose its strength. His voice trembles, barely holding together, each word cracking under the weight of everything he's trying not to lose.

My vision softens around the edges. His face wavers in and out, light bending around him like the world is slipping just a little out of focus. I hold onto him as long as I can—his eyes, his breath, the way he says my name like a vow.

I want to stay.

I do.

But my body is so tired, the kind of tired that settles deep, past bone, past breath. And underneath the pain there's a stillness, a quiet rising, a peace wrapping gently around the last pieces of me.

My last thought is him.

The way he held me like I was worth saving. And then, with that peace sitting warm in my chest, everything goes still.

**Franklin**

She was gone.

I don't know how long I held her. Her hand still warm, her lips still trembling against mine like maybe, maybe, she'd take one more breath.

I whispered her name until my throat broke, "Alana... Alana..." like I could drag her back with sound alone.

But nothing came. No breath. No flutter. No miracle.

The woman I loved died in my arms.

Rain soaked us both, cold and endless, but I couldn't feel it. All I felt was her slipping, and me breaking. I pressed my forehead to hers, rocking her like a child, like if I moved enough maybe God would notice.

"I'm so sorry," I whispered against her hair.

"I should've been faster. I should've stopped him. I should've saved you."

Hands touched my shoulders, careful, then firmer. Claire's voice, low, steady but shaking.

"Franklin... we have to go. Please. We can't lose you too."

"Don't." My voice cracked.

"Franklin,"

"No!" I pulled Alana tighter against me.

318

"Don't touch her. Don't touch me!"

The footsteps came anyway. Agents. Strong arms, iron grips. They pried me away.

I fought like a madman, clawing at her clothes, twisting to hold her even as they dragged me backward.

My scream tore through the storm, "Don't take her from me! Please, I'm begging you!"

They unfolded the emergency blanket slowly, the way EMTs do when the outcome is already decided. No rush. No panic. Just quiet, practiced movements. Then they lowered it over her—starting at her feet, smoothing it gently across her body, covering her completely until I couldn't see a single part of her anymore.

When the last corner fell into place, something inside me dropped with it.

I sank into the mud, staring at the empty space where she used to be.

That's when I saw him.

Ricky. Shackled in the back of a black SUV, rain dripping down his smirk. His shoulders shook with laughter, like none of it mattered. Like Alana's life, her death, her faith, was a joke.

Something inside me snapped.

Claire must've seen it in my eyes because she grabbed my arm. "Franklin, don't. Don't go over there."

But I was already moving.

I yanked the SUV door open. Ricky leaned back, blood still crusted at the corner of his mouth, and smirked.

"She's dead," he said flatly, like a punchline. "All your praying, all your little scriptures, wasted. She begged Him, and He never showed."

319

I didn't hear anything else.

Red swallowed my vision. Rage and grief fused until I couldn't tell one from the other. My hands grabbed his shirt, ripped him out of the car, slammed him into the ground.

I hit him once, bone and skin crunching beneath my fist. Then again. And again. My knuckles split, but I didn't stop. The rain mixed with blood until I couldn't tell whose was whose.

"You killed her!" Each word was a roar, a prayer, a curse. "You took her from me!"

Ricky's head lolled, blood spattering the ground, but his grin stayed. He coughed, spitting red, and croaked through broken teeth: "Told you she wasn't worth saving."

Something broke loose in me. My fists blurred, flesh slamming flesh, rage spilling in every strike until I didn't know if I was trying to punish him or resurrect her.

"Franklin, stop!" Claire's voice cracked through the storm, hands clawing at my shoulders. "If you kill him, he wins! Do you hear me?"

Her grip tore me back an inch, but I lunged again, knuckles catching his jaw with one last sickening crack. Ricky slumped, laughing through blood.

Claire wrapped both arms around me, dragging me away, her voice desperate, breaking: "That's enough! Please, enough!"

I collapsed in the mud, chest heaving, blood dripping down my hands. Ricky's laughter rattled in my ears, hollow and cruel.

And all I could think was that Alana was gone. And nothing I did, no prayer, no punch, no rage, could bring her back.

The storm blurred into flashing lights. Hands shoved me

forward, metal doors slammed, and suddenly the rain was gone. I sat hunched in the back of the SUV, shirt clinging with blood and water, my fists still trembling like they hadn't stopped swinging. Every breath rattled like it might split me open.

Across from me, Claire sat rigid. Her hair plastered from the rain, her jaw locked, her hands twisted so tight in her lap her knuckles had gone white. For a long moment, she said nothing. Then her voice cracked, barely more than a whisper.

"I should've stopped him."

My head whipped toward her, blood roaring in my ears.

"You," The word caught, sharp as glass.

"You knew it was him? You knew, and you kept it from me?"

She met my eyes, and for once, there was no protocol, no mask. Just exhaustion and shame.

"I suspected, please Franklin let me explain..."

I leaned forward, fury cracking through the grief that was already tearing me apart. "Don't try to explain it away. Don't tell me about protocol or proof or timing. She's dead. Alana is dead, and you could've stopped it."

The words landed sharp, and I saw them hit her , like I'd taken a knife to the one place she couldn't shield. Her voice broke wide open.

"Don't you think I know that?"

Her hands flew to her face, pressing hard against her eyes like she could hold back everything breaking loose. When she dropped them, her voice was raw.

"She wasn't a case to me, Franklin. Don't you dare think that. I saw her fight her way back. I saw her smile for the first time in months. I saw the light come back into her eyes. And I wanted her to make it as badly as you did."

The SUV was heavy with it , my breathing ragged, her words trembling in the air between us, the sirens outside a distant hum. I pressed my fists against my knees, shaking.

Finally, my voice cracked low. "So what now? She's gone. What are we supposed to do now?"

Claire's head lifted, wet hair falling across her face, eyes burning fierce through the tears. "Clay thinks he can run. He thinks he can vanish with his forged papers and his plans. But he doesn't know what I have on him. And I swear to you, Franklin , I'll find him. I'll bury him for what he did."

I turned toward the window, forehead pressed to the glass, eyes shut tight against the world blurring past. Alana's name rose like fire in my throat, but it wouldn't come out. Not yet.

# 23

# Chapter 23

**Franklin**

The hospital felt wrong for grief. Too bright, too clean, too steady in its rhythms when everything inside me was broken. Machines hummed in the background, monitors beeped in calm defiance, and the sterile smell burned sharp at the back of my throat. I sat hunched on the edge of the bed, stitches pulling with every breath, ribs aching under the bandages, but none of it mattered.

She was gone.

I pressed my palms to my face, trying to smother the thought, but it kept bleeding through, relentless. Every time I blinked, I saw her, the way her body went limp in my arms, the way her voice cracked into prayer, the way the light left her eyes while mine were still begging God to give her one more breath.

The door opened. I didn't look up until I felt the weight of a hand on my shoulder, firm and steady. My father. His voice was low, rough at the edges, colored with the drawl of home.

"Oh, son..."

That was all it took. My throat locked and the tears I'd been holding back broke free. I leaned forward into his chest like I was a child again, like I didn't know how else to carry the weight pressing down on me. His shirt smelled like aftershave and rain, and the sound of his heartbeat thudded steady under my ear. He didn't rush me. Didn't tell me to be strong. He just wrapped me up the way he used to when nightmares chased me out of bed.

"Let it out," he murmured, voice thick. His hand rubbed circles on my back. "Go on, son. Just let it out."

The dam cracked. A sob ripped out of me, raw and ugly. "How could this happen?" I gasped. "It's not fair. She didn't deserve this, Dad. She didn't deserve to die."

"I know," he said, voice breaking right alongside mine. "I know, son."

I pushed back from him, breath breaking, vision burning so hard the room blurred at the edges.

"First it was Vanessa," I said, the name tearing through me like it had been waiting years to cut its way out.

"She trusted me. I was supposed to keep her safe, and I didn't. I failed her."

My voice cracked, deep and raw.

"And now... now it's Alana."

The moment her name left my mouth, something inside me collapsed. I dragged a hand over my face, but it didn't stop the tears.

"Dad, I was meant to protect these girls. That was my job. That was my calling. I was the one they were supposed to be able to count on—and both of them died."

My chest tightened until I could barely breathe.

"Both of them."

My father's eyes softened, but the ache in mine didn't ease.

"But Alana..." My voice gave out for a second. I swallowed, hard, forcing the words through the grief crushing my ribs.

"Alana was different. She wasn't just someone I was assigned to. She wasn't just a victim I wanted to save. Dad, I—" my breath shook, "I loved her."

His hand tightened at the back of my neck, grounding me, but the truth kept pushing forward, unraveling me as it went.

"We were building something," I said quietly, almost afraid of how true it felt.

"She was healing. She was choosing life again. We talked about the future—about her having a home, safety, peace."

My voice thinned.

"And we told each other we loved each other. I meant it. Every word. I was ready to fight for that future with her."

My father's brows pulled together, grief settling in his features.

"Son—"

"I lost her," I whispered, the words shaking loose from the deepest part of me.

"God, Dad... I lost her. And I don't know how to make sense of any of this."

He didn't speak again. He just stayed, hand steady on my neck, holding me like he was afraid if he let go, I might fall apart entirely.

And maybe I would have.

Another voice came softer, from the doorway.

"I'm so sorry, sugar."

Jennifer stepped inside, her cardigan sleeves wrung between her fingers, eyes red and swollen. She moved slow, careful, as if grief itself had made the air heavier. She didn't preach, didn't offer empty words. She just lowered herself into the chair beside me and laid her hand on my back, warm and quiet.

"We loved her too," Jennifer whispered, voice trembling.

"That girl... she was a light. Even when she didn't see it herself."

I pressed my fists into my knees, shaking.

"I prayed, Jennifer. I prayed and I begged Him, and He still let her die. What am I supposed to do with that? How am I supposed to believe in a God who let this happen?"

Her lips quivered, but her voice steadied.

"It's okay to be angry at Him."

My head jerked toward her, startled.

"Good because I am," she said firmly.

"You think He doesn't know already? He wants you to bring it to Him. All of it. The rage, the questions, the pain you can't carry. He doesn't ask you to clean it up first. He asks you to come, just like this. Broken. Bleeding. Honest."

Tears blurred my sight again, spilling before I could stop them. My dad squeezed the back of my neck, grounding me while Jennifer's words pressed into the hollow places.

"You don't have to understand Him right now," she went on softly.

"But don't shut Him out. Even if all you've got is anger, give Him that. He can handle it."

I bowed my head, chest shaking as the room settled into a heavy, aching quiet. My father's arms stayed braced around my shoulders, Jennifer's hand warm and steady against my back, and the grief sitting inside me felt too big for any of us to hold. I tried to breathe, but every inhale felt like it scraped against something broken. For a long moment, no one spoke.

The loss hung between us—sharp, raw, impossible.

Footsteps moved down the hallway—slow, deliberate, almost hesitant. When Claire stepped into the room, the air seemed to shift. The moment my eyes met hers, something inside me locked up. I didn't greet her. Didn't nod. Didn't move. I just stared, jaw clenched tight, every muscle braced under the weight of everything I'd just lost.

My father leaned in slightly, his voice low but firm. "I know you're hurting. And I know you're angry. But don't take it out on her."

His tone left no room for argument.

"Not right now."

I didn't apologize. I didn't soften. But I swallowed the response burning in my chest and forced myself into silence—rigid, tight, and barely held together—because he was right, and because I couldn't trust myself to say anything that wouldn't break open into something worse.

Claire stepped further inside, her hands clasped in front of her like she understood she was walking straight into the center of a wound. She kept her voice measured, not trying for comfort she knew she couldn't offer.

"I came to give you an update." She paused, steadying herself.

"We got Clay."

The words hit hard—heavy, inevitable, and nowhere near enough to blunt the ache still tearing through my ribs. I lifted my head, eyes burning from more than grief.

"He was trying to run. We intercepted him before he crossed county lines."

Her chest rose slowly, like she was bracing for the rest.

"He confessed. It wasn't just the case. It wasn't only a leak.

He said it was personal."

Her eyes flicked to mine, apology and exhaustion woven together.

"He said it was about you."

Something twisted deep in my chest—darker, lower, a new bruise blooming under the one that had never even stopped bleeding.

A sick twist coiled in my chest, deeper than before.

"Me?"

She nodded, her voice unsteady.

"He thought you were going to take something from him. He believed I was stepping down and that you were being lined up to replace me. Said he saw the way I trusted you, the way the team leaned on you. He let jealousy eat him alive until it turned into something worse."

My chest tightened.

"What are you talking about? What promotion?"

Her eyes flicked to the floor, then back to me. She took a shaky breath.

"I hadn't told you yet. But yes, I was preparing to step down. I was reviewing candidates. And you... you were at the top of my list. Clay must've caught wind of it somehow, and instead of proving himself, he decided to burn everything down. He couldn't stand the idea of you getting what he thought he deserved."

The words hit like a weight to the ribs. My father's hand pressed firmer against my back, grounding me, while Jennifer's eyes shimmered with quiet sorrow.

"So Alana's dead because of that?" My voice came rough, sharp.

"Because of his ego?"

Claire's face broke, tears threatening to spill.

"Yes. Because of envy. Because he let darkness swallow him whole."

My fist slammed against the bed, rattling the frame.

"So her blood's on his hands... and all because of pride. Because he couldn't stand to lose."

The words scraped out of me, raw and bitter.

Claire let out a long, shaky breath.

"There's... there's something else I need to tell you."

Her hand slipped into her coat pocket, and when she drew it out, she held a small evidence bag. Inside was a USB drive. She held it like it might break.

My brow furrowed as I took it.

"What's this?"

Her voice softened, almost reverent.

"Before she died... Alana recorded a full statement. Every name. Every contact. The buyers. The distributors. The money trails. Even locations we didn't know existed. We have it all now. Because of her. She got him, Franklin. She did it."

The words hit me like a fist and a balm at the same time. For a second I froze, caught between disbelief and awe. Then a sound tore out of me, half laugh, half sob. My hand came up to cover my face as the tears spilled hot and fast. Because of course she did. Of course she found a way. Even in death, she was still standing. Still fighting.

"She really did it," I whispered, voice trembling. Claire's tears broke loose as she nodded, a fragile smile cutting through. "She never stopped being strong."

I stared at the drive in my palm like it was sacred. "Can I... keep this?"

"You need to," she said gently.

"Because there's something in there for you too. A message. When you hear it... you'll understand."

My throat tightened. I couldn't get the words out, just nodded, clutching it tighter.

Claire hesitated, then her voice cracked with something deeper.

"I'm so sorry, Franklin. This was never the outcome I wanted. I thought,"

She stopped herself, swallowed hard, then pressed on.

"I thought if we could get her safe, if we could just hold the line, she'd live long enough to testify. To breathe. To be free. I hate that it ended here. I hate that her life was cut short. But because of her, women are walking free tonight. Victims we didn't even know about have a chance because she gave us the truth. Chains are broken because she chose to fight. Whole networks are shutting down. She lit a fire none of us can put out now."

Her voice faltered, but she steadied herself, almost whispering.

"Her story isn't ending here. It's echoing. Through every life she touched, through every woman who walks out of the dark because of what she did. She mattered, Franklin. She still matters."

I bowed my head, the weight of her words pressing down until my ribs ached. My fingers curled tighter around the drive, knuckles white.

"Such a time like this," I breathed, the words slipping out before I could stop them.

Jennifer tilted her head gently.

"What did you say, sugar?"

I blinked, forcing the words back down, my jaw tight.

"Nothing," I muttered. "Just... nothing."

But it wasn't nothing. It was the last thing I had left of her. The last secret I wasn't ready to share, because it was mine. Because it was hers.

The room fell quiet again. My dad's hand rested steady on my back. Jennifer's eyes shone with quiet tears. Claire's shoulders slumped under the weight of all she'd carried.

I looked down at the drive, my hands trembling as I reached for my laptop.

I slid the drive into the port, my heart pounding.

And I pressed play.

# 24

# Chapter 24

Alana

**Video Recording (Final Testimony)**

*Recorded May 23, 2023 – 9:16 PM*

"Hello... my name is Eva."

She offers a small smile, nervous but steady, as if she knows the weight of what she's about to say but refuses to let it break her.

"I'm recording this tonight because I want to make sure that, if anything ever happens to me, my voice is still heard. I need to know that no matter what, Ricky doesn't win. That the truth survives, even if I don't."

She leans forward slightly, her eyes sharper now.

"Ricky Monroe has trafficked, abused, manipulated, and destroyed the lives of dozens of women, girls who never had the chance to fight back. I was one of them. For years, I was afraid to speak his name, afraid to exist outside of his reach, afraid to even believe that freedom was possible. But not anymore."

She pauses, breathing in slowly, then reaches for something off-camera, a folded list, thick with names and numbers.

"This file contains every person I ever saw him work with. Buyers. Suppliers. Lawyers. Even two law enforcement contacts I believe were protecting him. I've detailed the dates, locations, the coded language they used. And I'm handing it all over now, because I'm not afraid of him anymore."

She closes the file, and her hand lingers over it like it's something sacred.

"But this part... this part is for you, Detective Franklin."

Her voice softens, trembling just enough to show how much it costs her to say the next words.

"If you're watching this... it means I'm not there anymore. And I need you to hear me when I say, don't be angry with God. Don't be bitter at Him for letting me go. I know you. I know your heart. And I know how much you blame yourself even when you shouldn't."

She wipes a tear from her cheek, then lets out a shaky breath.

"I accepted this a long time ago. Not because I thought death was my only ending. But because once I experienced Jesus... once I really felt His peace... nothing in this world felt as heavy anymore. And I knew if the time came, I could go knowing who I belonged to. I wasn't scared. I'm still not."

She smiles now, small but real, glowing in the quiet kind of joy that can only come from something eternal.

"I wish I had more time. I wish I could've walked into court beside you, stood in the truth, helped set the others free. But even if my body couldn't make it, my voice did. And my spirit... my spirit is with the One who made me new."

Her gaze lifts slightly, like she can already see something beyond the camera.

"And when I meet Him... when I meet our Father face to face... I'm going to give Him the biggest hug and thank Him for sending you. Because He did. You were His hands in my life. The first day I met you, I was shaking in a corner, afraid of every shadow. And you didn't bark orders or demand answers. You knelt down. You reached for me. You touched my shoulder and told me I was safe."

She lets that memory linger, her voice thick now.

"That was the first time I felt peace. And it wasn't just you, it was Him, working through you. That was the day everything started to change. And I want to say thank you. Thank you for showing me a love that didn't ask for anything in return. Thank you for protecting me. Thank you for seeing me."

She pauses. Then lowers her eyes, voice barely above a whisper now.

"And... I love you."

She laughs quietly, wiping another tear.

"I know you said it to me, and I was scared. Maybe by now I've finally said it back. I hope I did. But just in case I didn't... I love you, Franklin. I truly, truly do."

The screen flickers slightly.

She looks up one last time.

"And if I'm gone... please don't let my story end here. Not for me. Not for my sister. Not for the others. Finish it. Finish what we started."

Then she closes her eyes.

And the screen fades to black.

# 25

# Chapter 25

*3 Months Later*

**Franklin**

They put us in one of the small glass rooms on the second floor.

Not an interrogation room, not exactly. Those had hard chairs and one-way mirrors and chains bolted to the table. This room was softer around the edges. A narrow window. Two worn chairs. A table scarred with old pen marks and coffee rings. Someone had set a box of tissues in the center like they already knew we would need them.

The fluorescent lights hummed overhead. The air felt too cold, too clean, like the building was trying to scrub the blood and sirens out of itself. It couldn't. Every time I closed my eyes, I still heard her voice. I still saw the way her body went limp in my arms.

Alana.

Eva.

I laced my fingers together on the table and stared at the stack of files in front of me. Clay's name was printed across the top of the first one, bold and black, like it had been waiting there the whole time and we had just refused to see it.

The door opened behind me. I didn't turn right away. I knew that walk, the measured heels, the calm she put on like a jacket no matter what fire she was standing in. Claire stepped into the room, closed the door with a soft click, and sat across from me.

For a second, neither of us spoke.

She looked different without the command of the operations floor around her. Smaller somehow. Her hair was pulled back, dark circles carved under her eyes like she hadn't slept in days. Maybe she hadn't. Her hands rested flat on the table, but I could see the faint tremor in her fingers.

"You don't have to be here," I said quietly. My voice sounded rough in my own ears.

"Yes, I do." Her eyes met mine, steady but tired. "Internal Affairs asked for a debrief with both of us. They'll be in here in a minute. I wanted a second with you first."

I let out a breath that felt heavier than it should have. "A second for what?"

Her gaze dropped to the manila folder closest to her.

"To tell you I'm sorry," she said.

"Before anyone else puts language around this. Before it becomes reports and timestamps and exhibits. I need you to hear it from me."

Sorry. For a split second my chest tightened, everything in me ready to flare. Sorry for what you missed? Sorry for what you suspected and never said? Sorry for what it cost her?

The questions burned hot, but I swallowed them. This room

wasn't for shouting. The shouting had already happened, out there, in the woods, in the warehouse, in the corridors of the hospital. This room was for something else.

"Okay," I said. "Then say it."

She nodded once, like she'd been expecting that. Her jaw worked for a second before she found the right starting place.

"When the first surveillance gap showed up at the safe-house," she said, "I told myself it was a glitch."

I remembered the footage, the missing window, the way she had stared at the monitor a beat too long before calling for a reset. The way she walked out with her phone buzzing and never explained the call. Every red flag my gut threw up and I kept folding down because I trusted her. Because Alana trusted her.

"I checked the back end," Claire went on.

"It wasn't a glitch. It was manual. Someone had accessed the system and overwritten part of the log. It was subtle, but it was there. File sizes off by a fraction. Shadows that didn't line up. At first I thought... maybe it was an outside breach. Someone tapping us from the perimeter."

"And it wasn't," I said.

She shook her head.

"No. It was internal. The access came from one of our secure nodes."

"Clay." The word tasted like rust.

Her eyes lifted to mine.

"At the time, I didn't know that. I just knew it was someone with clearance. Someone close."

She let out a slow breath.

"I panicked. Not outwardly. I know how I must have looked to you. Too calm. But inside... I was trying to figure out how to pull on the thread without ripping the whole case apart."

"So you stepped out."

"That call," she said, nodding.

"Was to one of the techs I've used off book before. Someone who could trace internal access without triggering alerts in-house. I gave him time stamps, node codes, asked him to keep it quiet. I should have told you. I know that. But I also know how you move when you think someone is in danger. I was afraid if I said 'someone inside touched the footage, ' you would blow the whole thing open in a way that spooked whoever it was. And if it was nothing..."

She didn't finish the sentence. She didn't need to. If it was nothing, we would have shattered trust in this building for no reason. If it was something, silence bought time.

"By the time he confirmed the access trail," she said softly.

"Clay had already been back to the safehouse from his first 'solo sweep.' The prints were gone. The house was clean. Too clean. That's when I knew."

I felt my hand tighten on the edge of the table. I remembered giving the order. Secure it. Dust for prints. Walk every inch. I remembered trusting him because I didn't have the capacity not to.

"How long before you told Internal Affairs?"

I asked.

"Not long enough," she replied.

"But longer than I wish it had been. I tried to get more proof first. More logs. Call records. I thought if I could wrap the whole thing in a neat bow, no one could accuse me of seeing ghosts because I was tired or paranoid."

Her mouth pressed into a line.

"In trying so hard not to jump at shadows, I let a monster

stay in the room longer than he ever should have."

The door opened again before I could answer.

Two IA officers stepped in, both in plain clothes, badges clipped to their belts. Shepherd followed behind them, closing the door. He carried another file box, heavier than the first. He set it down on the table with a low thud and took the chair against the wall, arms crossed, face unreadable.

"Detective Franklin. Director Claire."

The older IA officer nodded to each of us.

"I appreciate you making the time. We won't drag this out longer than necessary, but we want you to hear the preliminary findings before the full report is filed."

I glanced at Claire. Her spine straightened, her hands folding together so tightly her knuckles paled. For a moment, we were not grieving colleagues or friends. We were simply officers in a room with the truth laid out between us.

"Go ahead," I said.

The younger IA officer opened the top folder and slid a few sheets toward us. Call logs. Screenshots. A printed text thread. Even from a distance, I recognized some of the numbers.

"Over the last six months," he began, "Detective Clay maintained contact with an unregistered burner number which we have since connected to one of Ricky's known intermediaries. Those calls spike during three key windows: the night before the first raid, the two-week period when Clay reported he was following a 'warehouse lead out of state,' and the forty-eight hours leading up to the car hit."

The words landed like stones, each one dropping into a pond that had already overflowed.

"That 'warehouse lead'…" The phrase sounded thin now, ridiculous.

"He used that as cover to disappear."

"Correct," the officer said.

"Cell tower pings put him nowhere near the warehouse he reported. Instead, he met twice on the outskirts of the city. Same burner. Same pattern. We also have financial records showing deposits into a shell account tied to him, matching those dates."

Claire's jaw flexed. My stomach turned.

"What about the safehouse?" I asked.

"The missing prints. The surveillance gap."

The older officer flipped to another sheet.

"The access logs from your internal system show that during his solo 'sweep, ' Clay initiated an overwrite on the safehouse cameras. Fifty-two minutes erased and replaced with a static loop. Additionally, the dusting kits checked out for that day were never logged as used. No residue in evidence. Nothing. He didn't process the scene. He wiped it."

I already knew it. I had felt it, like a crack in my ribs that finally broke. Hearing it said out loud still felt like someone pressing a thumb into the bruise.

"And the leak?" My voice dropped lower.

"Alana's location. The move. When did Ricky find out?"

The younger officer tapped the call log in front of us.

"Forty minutes after your team confirmed the transport route internally, Clay placed a ninety-second call to the same burner. That number then contacted a second line we've tied to Ricky's operation. We have geo-data placing that second phone less than a mile from the ambush point an hour before your convoy was hit."

My throat went dry. He hadn't needed maps, insiders on the street, chance. He had needed Clay.

"So Clay told him," I said.

"Time. Route. Exact location."

"Enough of it," the officer replied.

"We'll be able to firm up the language in the report, but for our purposes here... yes. The leak came from inside. From him."

For a moment, the room blurred at the edges. I blinked hard, focusing on the grain in the tabletop, the small white fleck where the veneer had chipped away. The world felt like that now. A surface we had trusted, split open to show rot underneath.

"What about the text?" I asked.

"The one that said it wasn't over."

Claire's eyes flicked toward me; she knew which one I meant. The night it pinged my phone, my chest had gone tight in exactly the same way it was now.

The older officer pulled out a printed screenshot and slid it across the table. I didn't have to read the words. I recognized the layout. The timestamp. The way my own number sat lonely at the top.

"We ran it," he said.

"Traced the origin through the anonymizing app used. It was accessed from Clay's personal device, piggybacking off a public Wi-Fi network three blocks from your apartment two nights after the warehouse operation."

My jaw clenched. "So he sent it."

"At the very least," he said, "it came from his phone. We'll get his statements on intent once the lawyers are done. But we wanted you to know that even the psychological pressure wasn't coming from the outside. It was internal. It was him."

For a second, I couldn't speak. I thought of all the times

Clay had sat across from me, grinning around a paper cup of bad coffee, making jokes about how paranoid I was, how I needed to trust my team. I thought of him clapping me on the shoulder before we walked into the safehouse the first time. I thought of the way he had looked at Alana like she was a mess he didn't want to clean up.

"Did he say why?" I asked. I didn't know which why I meant. Why he turned. Why he doubted her. Why he chose Ricky's money or power over a woman who had already been through hell. Why any of this.

Shepherd shifted against the wall. For the first time since he walked in, he spoke.

"He started talking once the adrenaline wore off," he said. "Not to all of it. Not yet. But enough."

The older IA officer nodded and flipped to another section.

"He said she reminded him of an informant from an old case," he read, eyes scanning the notes.

"Someone he vouched for. She lied, fed him half-truths, got two officers killed when a deal went sideways. He said after that, he decided people like her are always working an angle. Always dangerous. That they wear their trauma like armor to get what they want."

My hand curled into a fist on the table.

"People like her," I repeated, the words sour.

"He also said," Shepherd added quietly, "that he watched the way you looked at her. The way the team shifted around her. He talked about you like you were slipping. Too soft. Too compromised. He said, 'Franklin let her sit in his blind spot, and I wasn't about to let another liar take us all down.'"

There it was. The warped mirror of my own heart, held up by someone who refused to see what I saw.

"He never saw her," I said. It came out more like a confession than a statement.

"Not once."

Claire spoke up.

"He didn't want to," she said.

"It was easier to project the last woman onto this one than admit she was different. That you were different this time."

I swallowed, the back of my throat burning.

"So he punished her for someone else's sins."

"Yes," Shepherd said.

"And he punished you for surviving your last failure when he didn't."

The younger officer cleared his throat, flipping to the final page.

"One more thing," he said.

"Then we'll give you space."

He slid a thin photo across the table. It was a still from a security camera I didn't recognize. A parking structure, dim and grainy. Clay stood half in shadow, phone pressed to his ear, shoulders turned away from the camera. Beside him, just at the edge of frame, another shape leaned against a pillar. Tall. Relaxed. Familiar in a way that made my stomach ice over.

Ricky.

"We pulled this from the garage under the old warehouse," the officer said.

"Dated twelve days before your first move. Audio is useless, but the timing lines up with Clay's first contact with the burner. We believe this was their initial in-person meet."

My fingers brushed the edge of the photo, careful not to smudge it. Two men in the same frame, one we had been

343

hunting for years and one we had trusted with our lives, standing shoulder to shoulder like they belonged there.

"Why are you showing him this now?" Claire asked quietly.

"Because this is the truth he was operating under," the officer replied.

"We wanted you both to see the full extent of it. It wasn't a momentary lapse. It wasn't a one-time leak. It was cultivated."

Silence settled over the room again, thicker than before.

"So what happens next?" I asked.

"Clay is in holding," the older officer said.

"He'll be charged formally once the DA is finished aligning counts with the federal case against Ricky. As for Director Claire..." He glanced at her, his tone gentler.

"Her decisions will be reviewed, but based on the evidence so far, it appears she was actively working to uncover the leak, not shield it. There may be procedural notes. There won't be criminal ones."

Claire let out a breath I hadn't realized she'd been holding. Her shoulders lowered a fraction.

"And you, Detective," he added, turning back to me, are clear of any accusation of negligence. You followed protocol with the information you had. If anything, the record shows you tried to raise concerns when things felt off."

It should have felt like relief. In some distant, professional way, maybe it did. But none of it brought her back. None of it changed the fact that while we were tracing shadows and double-checking our instincts, Alana had walked straight into the center of the storm.

"Thank you," I said, though the words felt thin.

Both officers stood.

"We'll get out of your way," the older one said. "Director Claire, we'll need a signed statement before end of day. Detective, you're free to go home once you've spoken with Shepherd."

They left as quietly as they'd come, the door closing behind them with a soft click. The room felt bigger without them and smaller at the same time.

For a moment, no one spoke.

"I was wrong," Claire said finally. The words were quiet, but they didn't wobble.

"I wasn't wrong about Clay. Not entirely. I saw pieces. Patterns. But I was wrong in how long I waited. In how much weight I tried to carry alone. I kept telling myself I was protecting the integrity of the case. The team. You. Her. The truth is... I was also protecting my own record. My own pride. I didn't want to be the one who raised a false alarm and fractured everything we've built."

She looked up at me, and for the first time since we started working together, I saw something raw and unguarded in her eyes.

"I failed her," she said.

"Not in the way he did. But still. And I am so deeply sorry, Franklin. Not as your commanding officer. As the person you trusted to keep the walls secure while you were in the fight. I let a crack grow in those walls. She walked through it."

I stared at the table a long beat, then at her. I didn't have a clean answer, no easy absolution. Forgiveness was not my department. Not today. That belonged to Someone bigger than me.

But I could see the cost in her face. The weight she would carry from this point forward. I recognized it because I had been carrying my own version since the day Vanessa died.

"We all missed something," I said. It wasn't an excuse. Just the truth.

"The difference is, you're letting it change you. He didn't."

She nodded once, accepting that.

"Internal Affairs will want to put language around this," she said.

"Policy. Training. Safeguards. That's their job. Mine is to make sure we don't lie to ourselves about what happened. I'm going to put every failure in my statement. Every hesitation. Every instinct I overrode. If the board wants my badge after that, they can have it. But they're going to know exactly how it felt in this room."

She stood, gathering the logs and photos into a neat stack, preparing herself for the next meeting.

"What are you going to do?" she asked me, pausing at the door.

For a second, I didn't know. Go home. Sit in the dark. Try not to see her falling. Try not to hear Ricky's voice. Try not to replay all the almosts. The almost rescue. The almost future.

"I'm going to finish what she started," I said. It came out before I could edit it.

"She didn't hand us that file just to get Ricky in a cell. She wanted the others free. She wanted her sister free."

Claire didn't leave right away.

Her hand hovered at the door, her shoulders dropping just slightly, like she was setting down a weight she'd been carrying for too long. When she finally turned back to me, her voice was quieter than I'd ever heard it.

"There's... one more thing," she said.

"And you deserve to hear it from me."

She paused, choosing her words with care.

"I wanted to apologize for not telling you her real name. Eva. I knew it, but it wasn't my story to give. She wanted to tell you herself, and I needed to respect that."

For a moment, neither of us spoke.

Her honesty sat between us, simple, unpolished, real.

I nodded slowly, releasing a breath I hadn't realized I'd been holding.

"It's alright," I said.

"The way it came out... it was right. I'm glad I heard it from her. I'm glad it happened the way it did."

Claire's eyes softened—not relief, exactly, but something close. She dipped her head, turned the knob, and stepped into the hallway.

The door closed gently behind her.

And the silence that followed wasn't heavy anymore.

It was just... quiet.

The kind that lets a man breathe.

The kind that says a chapter—for better or worse—has ended.

# 26

# Chapter 26

**Franklin**

It had been months since the trial ended. Months since Ricky was sentenced to life in prison with no chance of parole. Months since Clay was escorted out of the courtroom in chains, the evidence against him impossible to deny. The justice system, for once, had done what it was supposed to do. But justice didn't undo the loss. It didn't bring her back.

It just made room for the grief to settle.

Not the kind that screams and punches walls, but the quiet kind. The kind that lingers in the stillness of the morning, in the silence right before you fall asleep, in the backseat of a car ride when it starts to rain. That was where I felt her most, those in-between places, where the world kept spinning and I was still learning how to stand.

I hadn't forgiven Clay. Not fully. Not yet. But I was trying. Taking it one breath at a time. One prayer at a time. One step toward surrender without always having the words for it.

And I hadn't stopped missing her. I never would.

But time had softened something sharp in me. I was no longer waking up with rage sitting on my chest. I wasn't chasing ghosts through every room. Now... I was just carrying her. In memory. In mission. In moments I hadn't seen coming.

Today was one of those moments.

Today we opened the doors to something bigger than justice. We opened the doors to healing. To sanctuary. To a place where the broken could come and know they were seen.

Today we launched the God's Painting Foundation.

And as I stood backstage, holding the speech I hadn't even written down, because I didn't need to, I could feel her. Not haunting. Just present. Soft and steady. Like rain.

I stepped out, let the light hit me, and faced the crowd of survivors, advocates, law enforcement, and strangers, people who believed in what she stood for, even if they'd never met her.

Then I took a breath. And I spoke.

*"She used to say that rain meant God was painting again.*

*But I'll be honest with you, when she first said it, she didn't believe it.*

*Not really. Not yet.*

*When I met her, she didn't think God saw her at all. She didn't think anyone did. She was surviving. Hiding. Carrying more than most people could breathe under. And for a long time, she thought silence was safer than surrender.*

*But God... He's not afraid of silence. Or storms. Or shadows. And little by little, He started knocking on the door of her heart. And just before the end, just before the storm that took her, she let Him in. She stepped out into the rain and said, "Let it fall." She lifted her face to the sky, not to curse it, but to be washed by it. And I'll never forget the way she stood there. Like it wasn't rain at all, but mercy. A baptism. A beginning.*

*She didn't die who she used to be. She died who she was becoming. Redeemed. Seen. Free.*

*She reminded me of Esther. A woman who didn't ask for her story, but stepped into it anyway. A woman who risked everything not just to be rescued, but to rescue others. And if you knew Alana, if you knew Eva, you'd know that she would've done anything to make sure no other woman had to suffer what she did. That's why this foundation exists. Not just in her name. But in her purpose. In her heart.*

*There are women walking into this building right now who feel like God can't possibly see them. But He does. He did with her. And He still is, with every storm, every prayer, every act of love that happens under this roof.*

*So if it rains again, and I hope it does, let it remind you:*
*God is still painting.*
*And she,*
*She helped Him color the world with her yes."*

I stepped down from the podium slowly, every word I'd spoken still ringing through my chest like an aftershock. The crowd was rising, clapping in waves, some crying, some whispering prayers I'd never hear. But I didn't hear much at all, not past the thunder of my own heartbeat and the silent ache that always followed her name.

*God's Painting.*

That's what we called it. The foundation. The legacy. The place where survivors would walk in carrying stories they didn't think they'd ever tell, and leave knowing they were seen.

It was hers. All of it.

I lingered near the edge of the stage, not ready to leave yet. Not ready to walk away from the one moment I felt her closest since the night I lost her.

Someone touched my arm gently, just enough to pull me back into the room, back into the hum of applause and the warmth of bodies moving through the lobby of the foundation we had just opened. I turned, expecting a survivor, maybe a volunteer, someone wanting to say thank you.

Her smile was small, almost hesitant, but her eyes... her eyes held something familiar. Not in a way that made me place her face, but in a way that made something deep inside me sit still.

"That was beautiful," she said, her voice soft but full.

"What you said. The name. God's Painting. It... it meant more than you know."

"Thank you," I murmured, studying her, trying to understand why my chest had suddenly gone tight.

She inhaled slowly, almost as if she were gathering courage. Then her gaze flicked up toward the stage, the banner, the lights, and back to me.

"Director Claire told me I would find you here," she said gently.

"She said this was the day I needed to show up."

I blinked, thrown off balance by the ease with which she said Claire's name.

"You know Claire?"

A quiet, knowing laugh left her.

"She found me months ago. And honestly... I don't know how she did it. I didn't think anyone would. I spent years trying not to be seen. Trying to stay alive in the only way I knew how."

Her voice loosened, warm with something grief-shaped.

"But Claire showed up at my door one morning and said, 'I've been looking for you a long time. Your sister would want you to hear what really happened.' And for the first time in years, I let myself believe someone was telling the truth."

My pulse stumbled. This cant be.

She stepped closer, and for a moment, the crowd around us faded until it was just her—this woman carrying the name that had held my world together and then shattered it.

"I'm Alana," she said softly, her voice steadying as she spoke it into the air between us. "The real Alana."

My breath stilled. A slow, stunned exhale pushed out of me as the truth settled with a weight I wasn't ready for. I didn't look away. I couldn't. She looked so much like Eva— same eyes, same gentleness woven with steel—but she carried something different too. A strength that had survived in the dark.

She must've seen the confusion rising behind my eyes, because she nodded once, reassuring, patient.

"Claire told me everything," she said. "She told me why my sister used my name. She told me why Eva believed I died."

My voice came out rougher than I intended. "If you don't mind me asking... how are you here? How are you standing right in front of me?"

She inhaled shakily, the memory pulling her posture inward for a second before she straightened.

"One minute I was being dragged out of my room," she said. "Kicking, screaming, thinking it was over. I could hear Eva fighting for me down the hall. Then a gun pressed to my head and I... I closed my eyes. I thought that was it. I thought my story ended there."

My jaw clenched so hard it ached. I could feel my pulse

pounding, hot and angry, in the side of my neck.

"But the gun jammed," she whispered. "Just... jammed. That split second was all I had. And I ran. I didn't look back. I didn't breathe. I just ran until I couldn't feel my legs."

Her voice trembled, but her spine stayed straight.

"And I guess the men who were supposed to kill me never reported back," she said. "Ricky never knew I got away. I went underground. Stayed hidden. I kept waiting for the right time to find Eva again, but I didn't know how—didn't know if I'd bring danger to her door. That's my regret. I waited too long."

Emotion tightened every word, but she didn't break. It made my chest pull tight with something fierce—respect, grief, maybe both.

"If I'd gone back sooner," she whispered, "maybe she would've known I was alive. Maybe she wouldn't have died thinking she lost me."

"Hey," I said, voice low, steady.

"What happened to your sister wasn't because you ran. You survived something no one should've survived. And you staying alive gave her hope she didn't even know she was holding."

Her lips pressed together, trembling at the edges, but she breathed through it and kept talking.

"She used my name to protect me," she said.

"Claire told me that. She carried it like a shield so Ricky wouldn't go looking. She held my life in her hands even after she thought I was gone."

I swallowed hard. My throat felt thick, my eyes burning in a way I hadn't felt since the night Eva died.

"You loved her," Alana said quietly.

353

"And she knew that. I could hear it in the way you spoke about her. She wasn't alone at the end. She had you."

The words hit me deep. I didn't speak right away. I let the truth settle first, let it steady the ache that had lived in my chest since the moment I held Eva in my arms.

"I loved her," I said, "because of who she was. Because she fought like light fights through storm clouds. And I'm grateful she had you before all of this. I'm grateful she had someone who loved her before I ever stepped into her life."

A soft breath slipped from her, part grief, part release.

"I'm done hiding," she whispered, her voice gaining quiet certainty.

"Eva died protecting my name. I'm going to live in a way that honors hers."

I nodded, my voice low. "She'd want that."

Alana smiled then—small, trembling, but real—and squeezed my hand once before stepping back into the movement of the crowd, a woman stepping out of the shadows for the first time in years, walking toward the life her sister died believing she deserved.

She stepped back, giving me one last look, grief and gratitude wrapped together, before she slipped into the crowd, disappearing into the movement of people walking toward hope.

I stood there as rain began tapping against the windows, soft and steady, the way it always did when God was doing something gentle, something quiet, something new.

And in that moment, I felt her presence not as sorrow, not as ache, but as peace.

*Eva.*

# Epilogue

The house feels different tonight, not heavy, not sorrowful, but full in a way that settles beneath the skin and lingers there. The rain moves softly across the windows, steady and sure, and every step through the hallway feels like walking through the echoes of a promise that finally landed somewhere safe. Alana walks beside me, her eyes moving over each detail as if she's trying to memorize the shape of her sister's dream coming alive piece by piece.

"She talked about home," Alana murmurs, running her fingertips along the wooden trim.

"Not a place. A feeling. I used to think she was just trying to comfort me when we were kids. I didn't know she saw something this real."

"She saw more than people realized," I say softly.

"She carried things she never got to say out loud. That's why I used to call her Esther."

Alana looks up at me, puzzled. "Esther? As in... the Esther from the Bible?"

"Yeah." I let out a slow breath.

"Because Esther wasn't just courageous. She was positioned in a moment she didn't choose, surrounded by danger she didn't deserve, yet she still stood in the gap for people who had no safety of their own. That was Eva. The way she fought... the way she endured... she did everything she could to protect you, and to protect the other girls Ricky hurt. She didn't survive long enough to see all of this take shape, but she planted every seed that grew into it."

Alana's throat tightens as she turns toward the door ahead of us.

Eva's Room.

She hesitates only a second before stepping inside. The soft yellow blanket on the bed glows beneath the warm light, and the framed journal page, the one with Eva Grace Monroe written in her careful script, pulls her into a quiet she doesn't try to escape.

"I miss her," Alana whispers.

"It still doesn't make sense how she carried all of this alone."

"She carried it because she wanted something better for you," I say gently.

"And for the girls who never had anyone to stand for them."

Alana brushes a tear from her cheek.

"Maybe I should… I don't know… read the story. Esther's. If you saw that in Eva, maybe there's something in there that'll help me understand her better. Maybe it'll help me find comfort in all of this."

I nod, letting her words settle in the stillness of the room.

"I think she'd like that," I tell her.

"I think she'd want you to know the strength she never got to name out loud."

She nods slowly, her fingers moving once more across her sister's carved name, the grief in her eyes deep but steady, like she's finally letting herself feel the truth without running from it.

We're halfway down the hall when my phone buzzes, one

soft vibration, the kind you don't think twice about until something in the air shifts. I pull it from my pocket without slowing down, my thumb brushing across the screen as I talk to Alana about the common room and how the first group of girls should be arriving soon.

But then I see the message.

Just two characters.

**PS 91**

I blink at it, my steps faltering before I even realize I stopped walking. The letters sit there plain and harmless, but something about them presses strangely against the edge of my memory. I read it again, quieter this time, like sounding it out might help it make sense.

"P... S... ninety-one?" I murmur, almost to myself.

Alana leans in to see what I'm looking at, her brows drawing together gently.

"You mean... Psalm ninety-one?"

Her voice is soft, even a little curious, but the correction lands with a weight neither of us expects. Psalm. Not P-S. Psalm.

And something in the back of my mind begins to move, slow, like a door opening by itself. I don't understand why yet. I only know that something about the combination feels wrong. Familiar. Off-center.

Before I can grab hold of the memory, before the pieces even start to line up, another vibration rolls through the phone, longer this time, like whoever sent it knew they had my attention.

A second message slides onto the screen beneath the first, the words appearing slowly, almost as if whoever sent them knew the timing mattered more than the delivery. I feel Alana shift beside me, her presence quiet but steady, the house holding its breath around us as I finally read the line.

***You got the real one killed.***

***Now I'm coming for the shadow.***

The sentence settles into me with a weight that doesn't rush, doesn't spike, doesn't shout, it just sinks, steady and undeniable, the kind of truth that rearranges the air without making a sound. My throat tightens before the meaning even fully lands, because I recognize the voice behind it long before I let myself acknowledge it.

Alana watches my expression change, her hand hovering lightly near my arm. "Franklin?" she asks, her voice barely above a whisper.

"What does that mean?"

I keep my gaze on the screen, the edges of the text glowing faintly in the hallway light as the memory fills itself in with a clarity I wish it didn't. It's the same tone he used when he leaned toward Eva that night, mocking the very idea that anyone could protect her.

*"Look at him now, your little Psalm-91 boy."*

The same venom.

The same twisted certainty.

The same man who believed he ended their family for good.

And now he's telling me he got it wrong.

I exhale slowly, the sound almost lost beneath the steady rain tapping against the windows, and even without reading the message again, I know exactly what it means.

Ricky isn't reaching out by mistake.

He isn't confused.

He isn't gone.

He's correcting history.

And he's coming for the girl he thinks survived when she shouldn't have.